Redeeming Choices?

Redeeming Choices?

Simon J. Stephens

Matador
9 Priory Business Park,
Wistow Road, Kibworth Beauchamp,
Leicestershire. LE8 0RX
Tel: 0116 279 2299
Email: books@troubador.co.uk
Web: www.troubador.co.uk/matador
Twitter: @matadorbooks

ISBN 978 1789013 511

British Library Cataloguing in Publication Data.
A catalogue record for this book is available from the British Library.

Printed and bound by CPI Group (UK) Ltd, Croydon, CR0 4YY
Typeset in 11pt Minion Pro by Troubador Publishing Ltd, Leicester, UK

Matador is an imprint of Troubador Publishing Ltd

Prologue

For the purpose of this narrative, call me Steve Barratt. I no longer go by that name, but it seems easier all round to do it this way. You can also call me Kingfisher, if you prefer. Some still use the name of 'The Righteous Corrector', although I find that a bit clunky. I dropped the definitive article from my working persona for the same reason. And because it reminded me too much of The Order, a group I now want to keep firmly in my past.

We're now five years on from when I first revealed myself to the world. In case you missed the beginning, I used to be called Zipoly Hardacre. Zipoly because my parents dug into a bag of tiles whilst playing a popular word game and decided it would be a good name. Hardacre because they had to give me that surname. I lost them fairly young, but I always loved them. Despite the name. As to my activities, well, I got dragged into a situation where I helped correct an injustice, and things just spiralled from there.

To me, five years seems like a good time to clear the decks, consider all that's happened, and empty my head of the activities that those five years have seen me involved in. Circumstances work in my favour and mean that I have the opportunity to work on this volume. Fortunately, I've maintained the habit of keeping records of my work and reviewing them often enough to analyse, critique and store the most pertinent ones in my memory. I can't record it all, and anyway, that's not what any of us want. No, as I look back on the previous half-decade and consider what's happened, I understand both the blessing and the curse of having a store of experience that's more than enough for one man to manage. The rest can remain speculation.

There are things that I am very pleased with. There are so many more that I would have done differently. Looking back over them, with a view to sharing the next instalment of my life, has been cathartic and has helped me to begin the process of purging my mind in preparation for the years I have left. It has also been a very humbling experience. I now know that, despite the occasional foray into vain thoughts about my importance, I remain just one small man in a very big world.

During the period that I cover in this document, I've been able to relax and enjoy many hours of the simple life that is cruising the canals of Britain. I've loved and I've lost. I've given and taken. I've built up and I've broken down, and I've been both gloriously victorious and soundly defeated. I have also played a small part in saving the world. Again. Between the extremes, I've experienced moments of great joy, lots of laughter and too many pints of real ale to remember. There have been periods, of varying length, when I've sunk into the pit of despair, deeper than ever, and others when the crushing power of tragedy in my life has been too much to bear.

On a more positive note, as Kingfisher, I feel that I have become a lot more nuanced in my work and have been able to avoid many of the excessively-violent traits that I exhibited in the past. The punishments have fitted the crime a lot more accurately, which, I guess, is a result of my learning from experience. And I've been helped immensely by a much better support team, with the old crew giving me the guidance I need and being comfortable enough to urge caution when I risk going too far.

For those who missed the first instalment of my adventures, I have added supplementary details that should fill in any blanks. For those who feel they know me from my first volume, I apologise if those explanatory notes feel in any way patronising.

The following relates the long and winding journey that began as I walked away from the churchyard in Weston. It ends on my return there. Along the way, I've found few definitive answers, but then, justice remains a slippery beast. For all that, I do believe that I've found the freedom I've long craved for.

PART ONE:

PART ONE

Chapter One

With a very smooth single malt in my hand and a Mozart piano concerto playing softly in the background, I let the past slip away. It gave me permission to let go and I, in turn, allowed it to depart. It wouldn't be long before I was called to answer for all that I'd done, but nothing that had passed could be changed, so why bother to let the present be infected by questions that I couldn't answer? No, this was the future and there was a lot to look forward to. If I had to carry on doing things that might not, strictly speaking, be legal, then so be it. I wouldn't push it but I knew that things would come to me. Despite my mixed feelings about the work that I had been called to do, there was a strange inevitability about it all. A reluctant servant of justice, it's been easier since leaving ORB (The Order for Restoring Balance), but the waiting always opens the doors to doubt. There's been a lot of waiting. And a lot of doubt. Whilst I've waited, I've had so many opportunities to make the most of life that I can honestly say that I'm looking forward to what the future might bring.

The boat was moored in Weston but I would be moving off the next day. There was just enough time left before the full onset of Winter for me to take her for a short cruise and discover again the delights of the Caldon Canal. My schedule was as loose as ever, although I had decided that the coldest months would be spent in a marina with all the luxury of endless hot showers and full mains electricity. Besides which, Jason King, my mentor and my best friend, had requested that the old gang join him for Christmas at the latest marina-cum-boatyard that he had acquired; one which he hoped would serve as a secondary base for his expanding boating businesses. That made it an invitation I wasn't going to ignore. I looked forward to seeing the others and it would have been tempting to flatter ourselves that King had made the choice to be with us because he valued our company more than the December sunshine of his island in the Pacific. In reality, the plain truth was that there were practical reasons for our getting together. Then there was the simple fact that being in the UK allowed him to indulge his childlike fascination with everything canals. That was something that still had a long way to go until it ran its course and he moved onto another hobby.

I was looking forward to that Christmas. Although still essentially a loner, happy in my own company, there was a bond between those of us who had escaped the clutches of The Order for Restoring Balance which I was reluctant to break quickly. In our own very different ways, we had been released into a new future that was still uncertain but which looked promising for all of us. ORB had hurt us and left some scars which needed time to heal. We all recognised that this was a truth we had to face. Yet, it hadn't broken us.

King had probably suffered the most and had the highest justification for feeling bitter and vengeful, yet, of the troop of us, he was the most together and had allowed the past to be put to rest in order to free up the future. James, my former technician and the victim that I wouldn't allow to be, found life in the outside world something of a challenge at times. He was working on this and gradually making progress as he began to understand the difference between human relations and the less fickle relationships he enjoyed with numbers and abstract scientific theories. Although, he still preferred his own company, Adam, the other technician I had poached from ORB, fed him opportunities to interact with the diverse people that were spread around the various businesses that King had invested in. This had seemed to help.

As to Adam, he was completely at home and thoroughly enjoying life beyond the confines of the Order and, alongside the love of his life, Charlotte. They bridged the gap between the King canal businesses and our work in correcting injustice. Physically, there was very little space between the two as the former technicians had a new laboratory underneath one of the acquired boatyards but there remained a very clear and un-crossable line between our two operations. Tony and Kate were doing a great job in drawing together the public face of the businesses and were able to liaise with Adam for anything that they needed which was, shall we say, a little out of the ordinary. They knew nothing of my Kingfisher role, King's secret funding of my work, of James's background or of his creations. There had been a few uncomfortable moments when the wrong word had been said at the wrong time but we now found ourselves able to keep the invisible boundary in place. Tony and Kate were happy to let some things be left alone, whilst the rest of us kept our mouths shut to protect them. Should it all go wrong, they were blameless, and that's how it had to be.

The other marina, where we were all to get together, was up on the Northern reaches of the Trent and Mersey, just past the Potteries but a little shy of the Cheshire plains. This fitted well with my plan to cruise the Caldon before working my way there in plenty of time to enjoy the festive period. The choice of the boatyard as a place to celebrate Christmas might have seemed unusual. King was much more a luxury hotel and being waited-on sort of person. But that was the point. It was the least likely place that you would expect our respective futures to be determined. And it was in a situation which accorded perfectly with something that King and I remained agreed on, that the best place to hide is out in the open.

It took me a month to get there. That put us in early December and gave me time to settle in to the mooring and reacquaint myself with life in a static location. I could have made the journey in a little over three days had the Caldon not called me. I was so thankful that it had. The long stretches of solitary cruising and the quiet nights moored up under the lightly-frosted trees that kept guard over this beautiful stretch of water seemed to bring me a new peace that was deeper than I'd ever known. The pubs were good old canal pubs and the banter and companionship both genuine and very welcome, but it was in the quiet of the boat's cabin, with the fire gently blazing away, that I found my real solace. I let Fran and the children, now long departed, drift out of my mind, believing that I was letting them go for good, despite that never really being an option. I put aside the doubts about what I had done since their death and kept hold only of those memories that would help me to continue to do the same, but in a better way in the future. I loosed the chains of ORB and let Madame President and all the old faces fade away into the past. I even managed to reconcile myself to never seeing Jean again. The last memory I had of her was on this very canal when our future together had been cut short by an implant in my brain which guaranteed that I have no links with my past. That implant was gone, but so was Jean. In short, by the time I arrived at the boatyard, I had emptied myself as much as possible of all my yesterday's and was ready to see the old year out with a bang, and welcome the incoming one as a period of new opportunities.

It seems that Jason King had the same idea. When he arrived at the yard on December 23rd, bringing with him James, Adam and Charlotte, I could see instantly that he was a man at peace with himself. Of course, he hadn't changed that much that he was willing to forsake the private helicopter for a less ostentatious form of travel, but that too was reassuring. Not only was King a man at peace with himself, he was also a very, very rich man who was at peace with his wealth.

"Steve Barratt!", he ran under the still-moving blades of the helicopter to greet me with a bear hug that took my breath away, "How are you doing, son? You're looking well."

"Jason King.", I replied as he released his hold on me, "It's great to see you too. And, yes, I'm feeling good. You?"

"Never better. Never better."

By this time the rest of the party had embarked from the aircraft and greetings were exchanged all round. The three ex-ORB inhabitants were looking exceptionally healthy and I couldn't help probing them on this.

"We've been cheating a little, man.", Adam laughed as he spoke, "We've just had a week on the island getting tanned up before coming back to dreary old England. You wanna get out there. Man, it's hot, hot, hot!"

"Still manning it up I see.", I replied, "We really must work on that. Still, great to see you guys again. Charlotte, is he still looking after you?"

"Hi Steve.", she gave me a slightly less vigorous hug than King's, "of course he's looking after me. I've told him I'll set the Kingfisher on him if he isn't super nice to me. Hope you don't mind?"

"Not at all."

"Hi Steve.", James stepped haltingly towards me, his shaking hand outstretched.

"James!", I pushed his hand down and hugged him instead, "Good to see you. Still pushing the boundaries of science?"

"Always have and always will.", he muttered, clearly a little uncomfortable with the physical contact, "Although, as always, those boundaries keep moving. Still I've got some really good stuff to show you later."

"Can't wait.", I said, "now, how about we start Christmas a little early?"

And so, we began our week of fun and laughter. The time flew by and King made sure that there was nothing we wanted for. Tony and Kate joined us on Christmas Day but, with their first baby due very soon, they declined the offer to stay over, enjoying a journey home in King's chauffeur-driven Bentley instead. Boxing Day was allocated to James who we put in charge as 'Events Organiser'. Although a little tongue-in-cheek on our part, it proved to be a good decision in the end. Once he'd begun to get over the initial discomfort he felt in the role, he managed to fulfil it in his own unique way. We'd been thinking perhaps of charades or some other equally banal Christmas pastime, but instead we found ourselves paired up for a treasure hunt around the local environs. Had it been devised by any ordinary mortal, this would have involved local landmarks and maybe a few pubs. Having been devised by James however, it took a slightly different and less direct approach. I was paired with Charlotte and King with Adam. We each had a set of ten destinations to find and photograph, none of which had an easy clue to accompany it. The day disappeared and the winning team, Adam and King, proudly waved the two photographs that they had obtained against the solitary one that Charlotte and I proffered. Throughout the whole event James had been secretly filming us at work and, as we, the participants, sat together that evening trying desperately to fathom out what James had wanted us to find, he pieced the footage together into a brilliant parody of a 1930's silent movie.

"Okay, James.", King held his hands up as the image on the screen faded away, "Tell us, what was all this about? Where was the treasure and what on earth were we supposed to have deduced from your clues?"

He laughed louder and more spontaneously than I'd ever known him to, before composing himself and starting his explanation.

"Okay, here goes.", he paused for effect, "you each had different clues. Both were at the same level of difficulty."

"Yeah, the impossible!", I said.

"No, not at all.", he almost seemed offended by my remark, "You see, you made the mistake of thinking too literally. You were thinking in your own, if I might say, limited ways, when you should have been thinking like a James."

"That figures.", Adam muttered, "so come on then man, what does this clue mean, 'Two parts of Dirac make this building special'? We're guessing an anagram, but we looked at every significant building out there and the closest we could get was an electricity substation, with the AC, but we couldn't get the DIR."

"That's so easy.", James really couldn't understand our vague looks. "Dirac's Equation describes an electron in terms of mass and its wave function. Okay, so we've got two parts as mass and wave. The Catholic church in town has a statue at the front of Jesus waving to the crowds. So you see, Mass and a wave. Simple."

7

The rest of the clues were as bizarre and obscure as that. It turned out that even the clues we'd thought we'd solved had produced photographs that bore no relation to what James had intended.

"We give up!", King announced, cracking open a bottle of champagne that was welcomed by all, "But what about the treasure? Where were we supposed to find that?"

"Oh, you found the treasure,", James replied, "both of you did. You want to see it again?"

With that, he set the film of our activities running again, and, amid convulsive laughter from us all he knew that he had given us something worth more than a token gift.

"There,", his face beamed at us, "isn't that a very special sort of treasure?"

We all agreed it was and were still laughing like schoolchildren when we ran it for the fourth time.

Chapter Two

Alongside the sheer, unadulterated fun of that Christmas, there were naturally a few moments of tension. And there were some periods of pensive reflection as we considered, both individually and together, the events that had bound us as one. We mourned those who couldn't share our joy, but we were also able to exorcise a number of the demons that remained from the days when we were a part of a bigger organisation. There were tears and there were apologies. There were regrets and there were considered discussions about what we'd done right and what we'd got wrong. And, for my part, there were moments of true humility as I looked back on what I had done to these people who were now my friends.

Come New Year, we celebrated the passing of 2023 and welcomed in the promise that 2024 held in store for us. We agreed that our partying should end once we'd all recovered from seeing the New Year in, and so it was that on the second of January we said our farewells. Adam, James and Charlotte were picked up from the boatyard in one of King's vintage Rolls Royce's. They stretched the journey out in order to enjoy the ride, but it was all a subterfuge to deposit them only a few hundred yards away at the place where they had their new laboratories. You had to be careful in our line of work. You never knew who might be watching.

Having seen them off, Jason King prepared for his own departure back to the sunnier climes of his former island kingdom, but not before asking me if we could spend a little time together to plan our respective futures in a little more detail. I agreed and he joined me for lunch on my boat, seating himself opposite me at the cosy dinette that I knew to be a world away from the many luxurious restaurants that his lifestyle allowed him to enjoy.

"Steve," he said as we finished off the food and relaxed over a bottle of cognac, "I have to tell you, these past few days have been a real blessing. It's just what I needed."

"I think we all enjoyed ourselves," I replied, "and it seems to have been one of those special times that we'll bank as a great memory, but which we'll never be able to reproduce."

"Exactly. A special time.", he paused before continuing, "And, for me, the best Christmas and New Year that I could have hoped for in the circumstances. I could have run away and splashed out on my usual extravagances, but there's always a comedown from that. It felt right for us all to be together after the madness of last year. Not, despite the baggage we carried over ORB's responsibility for the death of my daughters, but because of it. We were all victims of a bigger show. I can see that now and it's an honour for me to call you and the others my friends."

We slipped out of the dinette and settled into the two captain's chairs that made up the seating arrangements in the boat's saloon. The fire was blazing away nicely and its warmth reflected the feelings that King and I were sharing as we settled down to talk some more.

"With the others gone,", King said, "I think it's right that we discuss our own plans for the short term. In particular, I want to make sure that you're happy. You can put on a show for the rest of them, but you can't fool me. I know that, deep down, you still have a lot of conflict about what you're doing. Agreed?"

I couldn't deny it.

"Good,", he continued, "so, we've got a little time now. First off, I want to tell you where I stand. Hopefully that should give you a better insight into where I'm coming from and a chance for you to think about what you want to ask from me."

He paused to take a long and leisurely draft of his drink, swilling the warm alcohol around his mouth and savouring every nuance of the taste before continuing.

"I'm a very rich man.", he began, "As rich as the papers report me to be and then some. I'm very fortunate to be in a position that only a handful of other people get to experience. I can have whatever I want. Houses, cars, businesses, toys, gold, antiquities. You name it, if it's got a price, then I can pay that price. And, you need to know, that I carry no guilt about my position. From the outside looking in, I know that a lot of people think that it's almost criminal for people like me to pay over a million pounds for a car. When a million seems a lot to someone, of course, I fully understand their thinking. But to me, that sort of a sum is little more than small change. I don't say that to be arrogant, just to help you see it a bit from my side.

And, more importantly, what I get in a million-pound car is just that, a vehicle that is worth a million pounds. You've seen the sort of thing that I'm talking about. You've been driven in the Bentley and it is a masterpiece of engineering as well as a testament to some of the heights of beauty and craftsmanship that mankind can aspire to. The value isn't arbitrary. Every stage of the manufacture of that car costs money because it employs the best of the best in terms of materials and skills. It is, quite literally, the sum of its parts. And, this is perhaps the most important thing, if people like me didn't buy vehicles like that, then the technologies would never be developed and the skills would disappear. I'm not bringing anything new to the table here. I'm just explaining to you that I am very comfortable to be at the top of a system that trickles wealth down through the economy. The system works."

"Which probably has you wondering where this is going," he smiled as he looked at me, "but I'll get to the point soon. What you need to know is that I understand my position in the world and I am comfortable with it. Do I deserve my riches? No, not really. I just happened to be working in the right industry at the right time and it proved to be an extremely profitable endeavour. I never forget that and, perversely, it helps me enjoy my riches even more. I live life to the full and I buy what I want to buy and do what I want to do. But, I know that there are some things that I cannot buy. I cannot buy my morality. Nor can I buy humility. And most of all, I cannot buy peace. Those things need to be earned, worked on and enjoyed and treasured more than anything else in the world. Which is why we are talking now. I want you to try and get to my state of inner-contentment in your situation. It's not the riches that bring these things. Look at how many rich people struggle to be happy. No, it's the inner self that enjoys these outward pleasures. Similarly, in your position, it's not the moral crusade that should bring about fulfilment, it's your attitude to your role in that crusade. I have been blessed with riches, you have been blessed with duty. In both cases, those blessings can very easily and very quickly become a curse."

He stopped talking and looked at me. I'd never seen him like this before or heard him talking so openly and candidly. I can't say that it didn't affect me. This was an emotionally charged conversation and I struggle with emotions. It was all I could do to keep the tears back as I thought of my response.

"You're really something, aren't you?", I told him as I replied cautiously, hiding my feelings as best I could, "Not the person that the press has you out to be at all. I'm honoured that you can be so frank with me. And, I think, I agree with you."

I paused and watched him as he went through to the galley to recharge our glasses.

"Of course, you're right.", I sighed as he handed me the drink, "I really do struggle with what's going on. And, given our very different lifestyles, it's a credit to you that you can see through me. You see, I'm just a little man who is being asked to perform big things. As you said, you were in the right place at the right time, and that defined your future. For me, I was in a certain place at a certain time and that defined mine. You seem to be able to carry your responsibility well, but for me, I still don't know if it's what I want. Or, more importantly, if it's what I can do. I'm just a middle-aged ex-salesman with a second-rate social science degree and an ever-increasing desire to step as far out of the world as possible. Seems like the more I try to do so, the more the world intervenes."

He listened as I spoke and gave me time to compose my thoughts in the silences I left between my words.

"There is a big difference between us though.", I continued, "A gulf that's impossible to span. You see, your wealth is not a crime. People may love or loath you for your Bentley, but you having the money to buy it and choosing to make the purchase is not illegal. I've tried as best as I can to stay on the right side of the law in what I do, but we both know that's not possible. And look at what I've done. I butchered Slater. I killed people, including your own daughters. I've probably broken every law there is and I've done it all in the name of justice. Surely you can understand my conflict?"

"That's why we're talking.", he answered softly, "And that's why we need to talk."

"I can't change the past.", I began again, "and I have to accept the consequences of my actions to date and try to reconcile myself to them. I think on balance, although it's not easy, that I can just about do that. My wrongs have brought about more rights, and the lives I've taken have made this world a safer place. I can live with that. But, it's the future that concerns me. Do I call it quits now and put it all behind me? Or do I accept what I'm doing as some sort of calling and continue to do it to the best of my abilities? Do I think that there is a place for The Order for Restoring Balance? No, I don't think so. Justice, they say, has to be done and seen to be done. ORB doesn't compute with that. I don't want to be a part of a secret order like ORB, that much I know."

I looked at King and saw him nodding even though his eyes were closed.

"Go on.", he whispered, reassuring me that he hadn't dropped off.

"Which all begs the question of what do I want to do? Truth is, the only thing that I can say that I know I want is a simple life, tootling around on my boat and enjoying the most basic pleasures of life. I'm rich in many ways and I'm free from the shackles of work, but I don't get the same pleasure that you get from the things that make up the trappings of wealth. To me, they're just things. I've had enough of stuff to last me a lifetime. No, I guess what I want is validation. I want to feel that I'm living as I'm supposed to be. That's where I'll find my peace."

"Okay,", it took him several minutes to reply, "so I'm right in thinking you need some help. But remember this, I can only give you my take on things and my advice. The decision is ultimately yours."

I nodded my agreement and he continued.

"First off, I think that you have been chosen to perform a work in your life. You have a duty and that duty is to correct injustice. As a victim of justice's failures, your experience equips you and is part of that calling. But, we need to frame that in its context. In your battle against injustice you need to remember that injustice is, and always has been, a part of the human condition. It's as old as the hills and as certain as death and taxes. In essence, if you carry on as The Kingfisher, you are fighting a battle that you can never win. But that doesn't mean that it is a futile enterprise. Think of all those soldiers in the world wars whose deaths seemed so unnecessary. They were a small part of a big thing and victory was won in the end, even though they never saw it. Which I think is where you fit in. As Steve Barratt, you can potter along being nice to people and making small differences every day. We can all do that and indeed, we should all do that. But as Steve Barratt, The Kingfisher, you can do more. You can actively move to correct injustices that go beyond the day to day. And you can do things that can prevent further injustices taking place. That's what I think you are called to do and, whether you agree or not, it's my opinion that the conflict you are experiencing is actually a confirmation of that calling."

"I don't understand.", I said.

"If you were chomping at the bit to don the Kingfisher garb and be out there as some sort of mysterious superhero,", he replied, "then that would concern me more than your being reluctant even to consider carrying on in that role. The word I used earlier is humility. It's the heart of peace and I think you have more of it than you think. Perhaps, for now, you should simply think on what we've talked about and stop trying too hard to be worth something. You can't escape your value as a unique human being. We all have that honour. Let that be enough and let go a little."

"You're saying that I should simply do nothing and see what happens?"

"Yes and no.", he replied, not particularly helpfully, "But probably more yes than no. If that makes sense. You see, the reason I had to talk to you before we parted company is to know how we progress in the future. I have my own vision and yes, it is a little along the lines of a mini-ORB. James and Adam share this vision and we've talked about how we can see this developing. For the most part, I think that our current consensus is to work in the void of cyberspace and use their skills and my money to do our little bit. But I still believe that we need a physical presence beyond the electronic ether, and that the person to be that presence is you."

"Do I need to give you any commitment just now?", I asked.

"Of course not.", he smiled as he replied, "That would defeat the purpose of this conversation. No, you need time to think and you need to consider whether the Kingfisher is where your duty lies. We aren't going to pressure you over this, but we all agree that we want you to be there with us."

"And who directs the show?", I asked, "Who determines when injustice needs rebalancing? That's a key point for me."

"Steve,", he turned to face me full on, "that's the key point for all of us. And the only answer I can give is that nobody can ever tell us, we can only feel it in our hearts. I know that sounds a little wishy-washy and Hollywood-starred but the three of us believe that's how it has to be. We think that if we make ourselves ready, then the call to action will come to each of us."

"I can relate to that.", I sighed, "And I'm sorry I'm being so evasive. I'm prepared to go either way. I just want to make sure I go the right way. You seem to be comfortable with where you are and I understand that you've been through a lot to get to that place. Same with the other guys. So, for the time being, you're happy for me to spend a little bit of time here on the yard, helping out as I can and working for my keep, whilst leaving the other outfit in the wardrobe?"

"More than happy.", he replied.

"Good, then that's what I'll do."

14

He rose to leave and I lifted my brandy-weary body out of the chair to accompany him. But he wasn't quite finished.

"One last thing," he gave me a wry smile, "that I want you to think about. I want to give you a scenario and see what you think. It's a little something that's been playing on my mind and which makes me think about this whole justice versus legality question."

"Go on."

"I follow the business news quite closely," he explained, "and one of the companies I was involved with many years ago, a small retail operation selling furnishings mainly, has just changed ownership and come under the umbrella of a private equity outfit. When I left them, they had about forty stores but that number is now nearer three hundred. Here's the question. The Chief Executive that was responsible for the main growth of the business was replaced a year or so before the latest acquisition. His replacement was a slightly unusual choice as he had been running a much smaller retail business before. He's done a reasonable job since taking over but as part of the acquisition deal is set to pocket several million shares. The store managers are getting an average of about five thousand shares. His salary is commensurate with his position as indeed is that of the store managers. A completely legal situation, but, is it justice?"

I was about to reply but he held up his hand and I knew that this was to be left with me to consider. He led me to the front of the boat, we hugged a farewell and I watched as he clambered onto the jetty and walked towards that same Bentley that we had been discussing before. As he climbed in, he turned and waved goodbye to me, then I listened as the engine purred and that beautiful piece of British engineering slipped smoothly away.

Chapter Three

'The Retail Digest', Issue 114; February 2024

'Family Furnishings to Cut Costs'

Bill O'Connell, the outspoken CEO of the 'Family Furnishings' chain of stores, has announced that the business will be conducting a strategic review of all of its cost centres in a bid to 'substantially increase operating margins'. Family Furnishings was acquired by the private equity house, Refine, two years ago and it is understood that this focus on reducing costs is a response that they have demanded in the light of poor like-for-like sales growth.

Speaking at a press conference, O'Connell, who joined the Board of Family Furnishings in the run-up to the Refine takeover, made it clear that the business remained very strong and that this was merely a routine part of the company's long-term strategy, whereby there needed to be periods where the cost-base was reduced. Proposals on the table include approaching landlords to discuss rental terms, investigating new approaches to the supply chain that better exploit the geographic diversity of their store locations and assessing the benefits package being offered to store management teams. This latter proposal is felt to be the likeliest route taken in the short-term as O'Connell is known to be concerned that Family Furnishing's managers enjoy a considerably better package than those who work for similar retail businesses.

City analysts have viewed this move in contrasting ways. Leading finance house, Chatfield's, believe it to be a timely move that will add shareholder value, however, this is not the view taken by Weisendorf, who have expressed concerns about the effect that these changes may have on continued sales growth.

++++++

I read the reports about Family Furnishings when they dropped into my inbox on a cold and snowy February morning and they did nothing to brighten my mood. It was now a fortnight since I had met with O'Connell and I was still licking my wounds. Since that meeting, not an hour had gone by when I hadn't replayed the events and felt myself cringing at the humiliation that had been heaped on me by that man. I'd tried as best I could to busy myself in menial tasks, taking on the responsibility for all the cleaning duties at a third boat yard acquired by King, and not far from where we'd enjoyed our Christmas. It was a simpler place to be. Earthy and real and with much work still to be done.

Aside from the cleaning, I'd been helping out with the basic tasks that still needed to be attended to, even in this off-season period. I'd jet-washed and blacked several boats, completed some engine oil changes and served diesel to the few passers-by who were braving the Winter chill and cruising the waterways. None of these activities had helped to ease my pain, although I did find myself able to sleep better at nights due to the physical exertions that I was putting my body through. Truth be told, I was working twice as hard as anyone else on the yard and suffering the physical torment of bleeding hands and blistered feet as a martyr. I wanted to punish myself and was succeeding. Still, that punishment brought little relief.

It had been fairly easy to research the situation that King had left me with at our last meeting. His interest in retail had been fairly limited over the years and only Family Furnishings fitted the criteria that he had given me. I studied the business, reviewed the relevant director shareholdings through stock exchange records, and I even visited a few of their more local stores to chat casually with the managers. That King had expected me to recognise the injustice in the award of shares to O'Connell was certain to me. What I wasn't so sure about was the response that he had expected me to take. Was this just an example that he wanted to offer me to underline his point about injustice being a part of life? Or was it a call to action? I read it as the latter and, much to my later regret, began to plan what I would do.

O'Connell was working late in the company's Head Office building when I arrived. This was my first outing as the newly-revived 'Kingfisher' and the first time that I would revert back to the use of the RC tokens as a permanent calling card. It was this token that alerted O'Connell to my presence as I flicked it across to his desk and watched as he saw it land and spin slowly to a halt on the papers that he had been studying. He backed away from the desktop as I completed my entry into the room; an entry that had been affected by simply using the ion-drive boots that were a part of my bespoke outfit, to lift me onto the balcony of his top-floor office suite. Seeing myself reflected in the mirror behind his desk created conflicting feelings within me. The Kingfisher who'd been tied into ORB had caused me a lot of pain and suffering, and yet, the image I saw was also a glimpse into a brighter future.

"What the hell...", he muttered, looking up to see me standing there in my full outfit before being stopped mid-sentence by the sight of the Blue Light that shot out and surrounded him where he sat. It was one of ORB's better gifts to me. I'd used its power to hold numerous people captive in the past and it gave me the upper hand.

"You'd better have a damned good explanation for this.", he shouted, recoiling from the sting of electronic shackles around him as he tried to reach for the phone.

"Please.", I let the suit helmet's synthetic voice echo menacingly across the room, "keep still and let me explain a few ground rules. The Blue Light won't hurt you unless you try to resist it, and I am not here to hurt you. Relax and let me explain the purpose of my visit."

Which, to be fair to him, he let me do without any interruption. When I'd finished, I freed him from his constraints after gaining his assurance that he wouldn't seek to call for any help. He agreed and, free again to move, he rose from his desk and walked slowly to the small bar area beside the washroom. There, he poured himself a large whisky, taking his time to add ice and stir it slowly before returning to his desk.

"So.", he said, picking up the RC disc and turning it over to see his name engraved on the rear, the same as all the discs that I'd used when I'd first started in my new life and still made of the finest sliver of ebony, "the famous 'Righteous Corrector' decides to visit little old me? You've been out of the news recently. Although there are few days that pass when we don't hear something about your activities. I suppose I should say that I am honoured and flattered at the attention. But somehow, I can't seem to feel impressed. Although that flashy blue light thing and the swanky outfit are pretty good."

He paused and looked at me as he turned the disc over in his hands. For my part, I wasn't sure just where this was going, especially since I failed to see the fear in O'Connell that others had shown at my presence.

"Well,", he continued, "you've said your piece and told me what is troubling you. I, for my part, have listened carefully and done you the courtesy of not interrupting."

He stopped again and took a long drink of the whisky, then he took the RC disc and flicked it into a waste bin that sat beside his desk.

"If that's all,", he said, "then I guess I should wish you good day and thank you for sharing your concerns with me. Needless to say, I do not intend following up on your requests, nor, may I say, do I feel that your presence here is a fitting tribute to the fighter for justice that I believed you to be. You may find it easier to use the stairs on the way out. Trust me, I won't alert security."

I stood there for what felt like an eternity, for the first time really unsure as to what to do.

"Is there something else?", O'Connell almost spat the words out, "If not, then I am a very busy man and I have an awful lot to get through this evening."

"You won't do what I have asked you to do?", I tried my best to make my voice calm and assertive.

"No, sorry. Now, goodbye."

"But,", I stood my ground, "you understand the consequences of your choice?"

He pushed back from his chair and stood up to address me, leaning forward across his desk.

"Yes, I understand the threat that you have raised. The so-called consequences that I think are supposed to make me fear you and crumble before you. But, let me tell you, it ain't going to happen."

"Then…", I began before he interrupted me.

"Then nothing!", he was shouting now, "You've got a little bit of dirt that you've dug up on me about my personal life and you're going to share it with my wife. Don't bother, she already knows and she is comfortable

19

with my eccentricities. Who wouldn't be when they get everything else that I give them? So that diffuses that threat. Then, you think that my career will fail because of the slightly dubious business practises that you've uncovered and seem to think are relevant? You need to wake up son, it doesn't work like that. You need to realise that it is those very traits that my bosses sought out in me and that make me worthy of sitting in this office."

He sat back down again and paused as he composed his thoughts, holding his hand up to me dismissively to keep me silent.

"You say you are here," he resumed speaking in a measured tone, "to bring about justice. A noble aim, but, in this instance, extremely misguided. My salary and share options package are legal, as are my private affairs and my professional practice. You may not like them. You may want to stand as a moral judge over me, but who appointed you to that role? The answer is, nobody. And, don't forget the old maxim, when you point the finger, remember there are three others pointing back at you. From what I hear, the Righteous Corrector, or Kingfisher, if you prefer, hasn't exactly been squeaky clean himself over the years. Even tonight, breaking and entering, threatening behaviour. No, if you want to talk about breaking the law, then let's head off down to the local police station and do just that."

"But surely," I answered, "you understand the injustice in your massively disproportionate allocation of shares against those given to employees."

"Of course, I see your point on this," he began to adopt a tone that implied that he felt sorry for me, "I'm not stupid. But that doesn't mean that I agree with it. Those managers were well looked after. They could have been given nothing. And they are amongst the best supported people in the retail trade. Do you really think that justice demands that all be given an equal share? How naïve are you? How many of those managers would we lose if we gave them enough to retire on? How many of them do you think would strive to earn their sales bonuses if we'd already paid off their mortgages for them? How many of them are actually dissatisfied that they have been presented with a decent lump sum that buys them a new car, a new kitchen or a number of exotic foreign holidays? It's how the system works and one day, one of them may well be in my position. Don't you think that there's something wonderful about having an aspiration to rise through the ranks? Yes, I got a massive chunk of stock that I hadn't earned. So what! Live with it."

"But…"

"No buts, live with it. And,", he finished the first whisky and rose to pour himself another, "and don't you dare judge me lacking in my acceptance of those shares. Who are you to say that I don't intend to share that wealth with other deserving causes? Who are you to demand that I follow your socialist redistribution of wealth ideals when I don't actually believe that they work? Who are you to stand there and tell me what to do when I have acted legally in all my business dealings? Seriously, now is the time for you to go. Please, don't take this personally. I've admired some of the things attributed to you, but in this case, you've got it wrong. Don't feel sore about it, but please, learn the lesson."

He sat back down and resumed the work that I had interrupted. I remained standing before him for a little longer but had no choice to withdraw in silence and head back to the balcony.

"Close those doors on your way out,", O'Connell whispered as I left, "they let in a terrible draught."

Which should explain why I now hated myself and regretted ever having thought that my vigilante identity made me into anything special. As far as I knew, nobody else was aware of this mission. But that didn't matter. I was aware and O'Connell was aware. I could do nothing to change the outcome, but O'Connell knew that he could get to me even more by implementing a system that actually threatened to make his store managers worse off. He may have been speaking to the retail press when he announced his cost-cutting drive, but I knew that he was really speaking to me.

Then Jason King turned up.

"Steve!", I heard him calling to me as I swept the snow off the various jetties that struck out from the main boatyard, "Steve, come and have a cup of tea."

I couldn't ignore him, despite the fact that he was the last person that I wanted to see just at that moment. My respect for him remained where it was, undiminished by any of my feelings about his complicity in the O'Connell situation. It was a respect much greater than my own personal shame, and so I put down the snow shovel and joined him in the warm and dry office that we still hadn't got around to refurbishing.

"Mr King, Sir,", I said, "good to see you again so soon."

"Please,", he smiled as he offered me a chair, "I think we can dispense with the formalities and be on first name terms."

"Sorry Jason.", I replied, "I'm just not feeling too good at the moment."

"I know.", he said, "Or should I say that I at least expected you to be a little down. That's why I'm here. Bruised ego? Broken pride? Disappointment and disillusionment?"

"You set me up?", I asked, not really believing it.

"No, of course not.", he bought me a mug of tea as he answered, "Although I may have sown the seeds. Sadly, you set yourself up for your own fall."

"How much do you know?", I asked.

"Enough to bring me here.", he sat down next to me, "But none of the details. You can tell me if you want, or not."

I told him and he listened to every word.

"Which leaves you where?", he asked when he was sure that I'd finished.

"Truth be told.", I answered, "I'm not sure. Just now, I'm questioning everything and trying to understand what I should be doing with my life. On balance, I want to bank what I've got and head away from all this superhero stuff. I don't think I'm the right man for the job and this O'Connell situation only seems to confirm that."

"Of course.", King responded in his usual measured tones, "that's your choice. I won't pressure you either way, but please let me have my say before you decide."

I nodded agreement.

"The thing is.", he began, "that I left you last time with the veiled problem of O'Connell, knowing that you would look into it. I wasn't sure that you would respond. Nor was I sure that it was appropriate for you to do so. That you did feel charged up enough to want to take action is something we need to bank as a credit to Kingfisher. That you acted, is a debit."

"Why a debit?", I asked.

"Because.", he explained, "it was a situation that smacked of injustice but that was wholly legal and not at all appropriate for our aims. Believe me, in the circles that I move in, those sorts of 'injustices', if we must call them that, are run-of-the-mill. It's the age-old story of humanity and it's not one that has an easy solution. There are going to be a lot of similar situations, not just amongst the richest tier but also down in the depths of poverty, where the decision to act or not will cause us some problems. One man can't make those decisions alone. I think you might agree with me?"

I nodded but couldn't bring myself to say anything else.

"So," he continued, "we have a credit for wanting to act and a debit for acting. But, here's the point, that debit is not necessarily for the action, but for you acting alone. If we, yourself, James, Adam, Charlotte and myself had put that one to a vote, I like to think we'd have let it be, or maybe employed subtler tactics. Do you see that? What I'm telling you is that I still believe in who you are but that you need to be a part of a bigger team. A cord of three strands being hard to break etc. Does that help?"

"At the moment," I decided to answer honestly, "nothing helps. But yes, I understand what you're saying. Maybe I've not decided yet."

"Good," he replied, "then my journey wasn't in vain. I hope now that you understand that you have a very clear choice. We're committed to moving forward in a mini-ORB style manner and we would love you to be a part of it. If you don't want that though, we can find someone else to be our outside operative. I know that may seem like kicking you when you're down but humility demands that we all know we are replaceable. I'll leave it with you and be in touch. Meanwhile, keep up the good work on the yard. It's looking better than ever."

"Before you go," I asked, "is the O'Connell thing something that's irretrievable?"

"I'm glad you asked," King smiled, "in fact, that's why I can't stay too long. Seems that Mr O'Connell's reaction was a little too petty for the City to go with and it's backfired on him. I still maintain that we should have left well alone, but, as businessman, I take my opportunities as they come. Here, I'll leave you with this."

He passed me a newspaper as he left, opened to an article that I read with astonishment. O'Connell's cost-cutting proposals had scared more financial institutions than it had reassured and shares in Family Fashions were nose-diving. That is until Jason King had stepped in to buy a controlling interest in the company. I may have been feeling pretty low at that point, but reading that article lifted the gloom for a good few days.

Chapter Four

Doubt can be a very fickle mistress. One day she leads and inspires you to overcome limitations that you'd previously believed to be insurmountable. The next, she tells you that you'll never achieve anything more than you already have. Or even, that you're more likely to achieve even less. She was with me when I left the boatyard to continue my waterway lifestyle, and she remained with me throughout the relatively short journey that I was making to see how James and the team were settling in at the other marina. The boatyard had been my preferred choice to follow our Christmas celebrations, even though the facilities were a little more basic than those at the first of King's marinas. It retained something of an unchanged atmosphere and that appealed to me. It also meant that I'd been pretty much on my own for most of the time there. That said, my boat had enough luxuries to keep me pampered.

The marina I was headed to, where we'd enjoyed the luxury of the converted cottage over Christmas had been purpose built less than a decade ago. That meant it was more luxurious than the boat yard and benefitted from having a number of shops and its own bar, although it was these very attractions that made it a little too busy and popular for my liking. That same popularity had been the reason that King had decided to situate his new laboratories right in the heart of this busy canal hub. We had always agreed that the best place to hide was often in full view and so, under the pretext of drainage works, he'd excavated a substantial area of the surrounding fields and installed new buildings underground. To the rest of the world, James and the rest of the team were simply boaters who stayed in this marina. They were never seen leaving to go to the labs as they each had boats with underwater hatches and their own versions of my pod to transport them the short distance. It was a very high-tech solution to a simple problem but it seemed to be working.

To get to the marina meant my travelling through some of the rougher areas of the canal network. The Potteries, as they were too-sweetly named, were the industrial heartlands that had spawned the birth of the canals, but they now suffered from an urban decay that was not being remedied. Further South, canal-side warehouses were a developer's dream, offering a waterside location and a ready-made building that could easily be converted into apartments. But down South, there was an urgent need for housing. That wasn't the case in the Midlands, despite all the promises that politicians had made about moving investment back into the area. Promises that the vortex of London has prevented them from keeping. No, the buildings that I passed were crumbling away and being allowed to do so as most of them were listed in such a way that they simply couldn't be demolished. This dereliction attracted some unsavoury characters whose presence only sought to underline the neglect that was a part of the dying towns that once housed the workers who made the goods that were loaded onto barges to be shipped around the world. How delicate the Spode and Wedgwood and yet, how earthy their origins!

In short, this was not an area that one wanted to moor up in. Where moorings existed, the towpath was a trail of dog faeces, litter and broken glass, whilst the canal itself presented a thousand propeller-tangling obstacles. Unfortunately, I timed my journey badly and hadn't factored on delays at locks caused by the unexpected proliferation of boats that a little pre-Spring sunshine had created. Boats that were now in safer waters farther ahead.

With the light fading, I pulled into the first semi-reasonable spot that I could find and tied the boat up to rings that looked just about strong enough to hold her. This was the sort of spot that had been created to encourage visitors but which every canal guide advised you to think twice about stopping at. Nevertheless, it all seemed fairly quiet that evening and I had been around enough to know that I could probably deal with any threat. As it transpired, the night passed peacefully and I woke to a strange mixture of glorious sun-drenched fog on one side of the boat and almost apocalyptic desecration on the other.

This was definitely a bacon-butty morning, so I fired up the grill and dangled some bread in front of the fire. It never took too long for the toast to crisp and start to burn, at which point I would let butter melt into it whilst I attended to the bacon. All was going smoothly until I looked out of the side hatch and watched as a pair of mastiffs deposited a mountain of filth right before my eyes, before being called away by their owner. Needless to say, the mountain remained, causing the dream of my breakfast to fade away. I threw the food into the bin, clambered out of the boat and resumed my journey.

The tolerant and understanding part of me should have been allowed to forgive and forget this incident, reminding me that the owner of those two dogs was very likely somebody who had not really been given a chance and to whom the world had done an injustice. After all, anyone who owned dogs couldn't be that bad, could they? But that part of me was noticeably silent that morning and I was barely able to contain my anger that somebody could behave in such a selfish and ignorant way. And who was I that I should make any sort of sacrifice to help them overcome the challenges that society had presented to them? In short, it seemed like Lady Doubt would be close at my side for another day, and she didn't help my mood improve as I fought with vandalised locks and read the most extreme and abusive graffiti as I passed under every bridge.

When the first stone hit the boat, it did so with so much speed that it caught me totally by surprise and I didn't really register it as a threat. When the next handful bounced off the roof and close to my head, I was a little more aware of what was happening. Then the shouting started.

"Oy, give us a go on your boat, mate."

"Yeah, let's have a go or we'll throw a brick at you."

"Here mate, how does your posh boat like this?"

With that last missive, a plank of wood landed square on the roof and I heard the glass in the Houdini-hatch crack.

There were three of them. I couldn't see their faces behind the hoods that they had pulled up over their heads, but I could make out that they were only young. My guess was that they were twelve or thirteen years old at most, obviously skipping school and choosing more interesting ways to occupy their time. I didn't think that reasoning with them would be anything more than a waste of my breath, so I did what most boaters would do in the same situation and pulled out my mobile phone to video them. They didn't like that and I watched as they fled away from the bridge to the safety of cover. The onslaught would continue I knew. This wasn't the first time I'd faced the so-called 'disaffected youth' of our nation, nor would it be the last. Today though, I just wasn't in the mood for it. I'd had enough for one day already and this was the final straw.

The response that I knew they wanted was for me to hit the throttle and get out of there as fast as possible. This was their territory and I was the intruder to their space. But I had other plans. In fact, I chose to face them head on and see what they were really made of. That's why I pulled the boat in, tied her up and then went straight ahead with patching up the damaged glass on the roof. They were close by. Their presence was like a cloud of evil that I could feel and I could sense that they were watching me and planning their next move. By simply pulling up, not bothering to chase them and working on the repair, I was testing them. I was telling them that I wasn't afraid and I knew that they wouldn't like that.

When I finished on the roof, I went back inside and locked the doors. Then I closed all the windows and put the radio on, nice and loud. I figured they were hip-hop type kids, so I made sure that they were blasted with a bit of opera. It wouldn't be long before they came back, but I would be ready.

"Oy, poof!", the tallest of the gang banged hard on the boat's toughened windows, "Turn your queer's music off. This is our manor and we're street."

"Yeah,", one of his buddies shouted, also banging on the glass, "we're the gangster rappers round here and we don't like your gay singing. Shut it up or else."

"Or else what?", I spoke through the helmet in my deepest voice.

They turned as one to look at me. I stood stock still and let them take in my Kingfisher outfit and try to process what was happening. Then I fired the bolts of Blue Light and fixed them to the spot.

"What are you doing?", their leader tried to fight the electric bonds but gave up after the first few shocks, "You can't do this to us. We own this place."

"You own nothing.", I whispered and let the helmet's speaker carry my voice ominously, "In fact, at this point in time, I own you. I could keep you tied up like this for days, weeks if I wanted. So, a little respect please. There's a word you should understand, respect."

They didn't say anything but as they lifted their heads a little I saw the expression on their faces change from false bravado into a strangely moving childlike fear. Good. That was what I wanted.

"What are you doing to that boat?", I asked, waiting long enough in silence for them to offer me their lame replies.

"Nothing,", one of them muttered, "we were just telling him to turn his music down."

"I see.", I replied, "So, banging on his windows and insulting him is the way to do that is it? How about we try a different approach?"

27

I leant beside the window and asked, very politely, if the gentleman would please turn his music down. The sound decreased instantly.

"You'd better stay inside.", I advised the man in the boat, "things could get a little nasty out here."

By the time I turned back to my captives, I was in full avenger mode.

"You see,", I told them, "it doesn't take much does it? A little respect, courtesy and politeness, that's all."

The older of the youths whispered a mumbled, "Sorry.", which the others echoed.

"That's all well and good,", I answered, "but sorry just isn't enough."

"What do you mean?", this time, it was the smallest of the group who addressed me.

"What I mean is, that you will need to pay for your behaviour. And I don't mean by giving that man the money for him to fix the damage you've done. You see, if it was that easy, you'd only do it again. And I can't have that."

"What are you going to do then?", again, it was the smallest boy who spoke.

"Well,", I chose my words carefully and delivered them in a slow and measured tone, "you see, the thing is, that you guys only get away with what you get away with because you make people fear you. Now, fear is a nasty little disease that I hate. In fact, I hate it so much that I don't like to use it. So, instead of me threatening you with anything, trying the fear card, which frankly I don't think is enough, I'm going to take some action. You see, when you make people live in fear, you blight their lives. You make them afraid to go out at night and you stop them doing the things that they have every right to do. Are you with me so far?"

They nodded.

"Good, then that means you're listening. Now, we come to the crux of the matter. How are you going to pay? I think that seeing as you have hurt one person that I know of, the man in the boat, then just one of you is enough to balance things out. So, first off, who is going to volunteer for the punishment?"

"What is the punishment?", one of them asked.

"Oh, that's simple,", I laughed, "I'm going to eliminate one of you."

"You mean kill one of us?", the leader's voice was cracking as he asked, "You can't do that. That's too much. We didn't do much and we won't do it again."

"Wrong on both counts!", I was shouting now, "It's not too much and you did generate a lot of fear and unhappiness for that man. If I let you go, you do the same again and the sum of all the hassle and hurt that you cause begins to add up to a lot. So, I take one of you out and hopefully, that sends a message to the others. Now, come on, I need to know which one of you it is and then we can all go our separate ways."

Strictly speaking, I hadn't been completely honest with them in my saying that I wasn't going to use fear as a weapon, but that was a lie that I could live with. It was certainly working and I watched as the first of the gang lost bladder control and began sobbing as his trousers got wetter and wetter.

"You really are just little children, aren't you?", I mocked them now, "You can't even hold in a bit of wee. It's amazing isn't it, that people are afraid of you. But, the sad fact is, that they are. And they can't be allowed to be for any longer. One of you dies, you tell your mates and hopefully, the message gets out there and the reign of fear stops. See how easy it is. I just need a volunteer."

Needless to say, they remained silent although the sobbing increased as they all succumbed to the moment and their illustrious leader made a mess of his own trousers that was a little more solid than his compatriot's.

"Enough.", I shouted, "I'll take the runt of the litter. You, the little one. You can be the sacrifice. You two can go."

I loosed the Blue Light around the other two, leaving it holding the smallest of them, but neither of them made a move to go. They just stood there looking increasingly more pathetic. Then the leader of the group looked me straight in the eye and said, "No, take me instead.".

It was what I'd wanted to hear. It was their freedom card and I almost rejoiced to hear it but I kept my cool.

"You want me to kill you,", I clarified the deal with him, "and let the others go? Okay, fair enough."

"But,", he said, "can I just say some last words to them. Jimmy, tell mum I'm sorry and tell Tasha I'll miss her. Go on now and don't worry about me, I got you into this and I'm sorry. Go now, run. Go home."

The other two stood staring for a minute or two then turned and ran away. I was left alone with a very upset and terrified teenager. I wasn't going to prolong the agony too long.

"You go as well.", I told him, once I knew the others were a fair distance away, "You made the right choice for once. But please, take on board what

29

I've said. You can live your life terrorising other people or you can choose to do what you did today and make a sacrifice. Believe me, the sacrifice is always worth it. It's not too late for you to sort yourselves out. Now, go, before I change my mind."

Before he left, he wiped his eyes and apologised again beginning to give me some sort of explanation as to why he did what he did, but I simply waved him away.

"That's the past.", I said to him, "It's the future you need to focus on now."

Chapter Five

To this day, whenever I review the footage that my helmet camera beamed back to the boat on the night that I met those youths, I debate whether or not I might have been too harsh. They'd learnt their lesson, of that I was sure, but even so, there had to be an element of bullying about it from my part. At the time, I was so fired up with righteous anger that it's lucky I didn't take more aggressive action. With the coming of The Kingfisher there had been a release of numerous moral inhibitions and false sentimentalities. It was something that was hard to control as it took the emotions out of my activities. Children and animals were all fair game, provided justice was served.

The event was a good turning point for me though. Up until then, I had been battling with doubt and that encounter had introduced me to doubt's very close cousin, fear. And fear was something that I remember still from the limited criminology that I studied as a much younger person. It existed as that most pernicious and subtle force for harm that, so-often, lurked beneath the touch of the law. The power that those three youths believed that they had didn't exist in the damage that they could do, after all, any of us can break things. No, their power was based on fear. They were beneath the law because, for the most part, they didn't actually do what they threatened to do, although I could have had them for very minor criminal damage. The real harm that they exerted was in the fear that they left in their wake and which left the innocent suffering as they worried about what might happen.

So it was, that on that evening I reconciled myself to fear and doubt and accepted that they must be a part of all of our lives but that they should never be allowed to control us. Healthy doubt and healthy fear might stop me being too impetuous, reckless or reactive, whilst it might also help me to empathise with the victims I had pledged to support. Maybe even with those I was acting against. I felt that I'd reached a decision. I was back on board with my role as Kingfisher.

That decision filled me with a new sense of hope and excitement as I completed the short cruise to Jason King's marina where I would take my place in his team as his field operative. I would be my own person and follow my own agenda to a high degree, but would do so in partnership with rest of the ORB refugees. If that meant that I performed only a few low-level actions whilst continuing to cruise and explore the canal network, then so be it. If it meant that I had to plumb the depths of depravity and do some more of those sorts of deeds that I could never be proud of, then so be it. What mattered was that every mission I undertook had to be agreed with all of us. We would have to turn a blind eye to multiple injustices and we would get it wrong as often as we made the right call, but we had an accountability. We had support from each other, and we had the combination of a handful of people's rational considerations and the same people's inexplicable gut-feelings. If we weren't unanimous, then we would move on.

I felt like a weight had been lifted from me as I manoeuvred through the narrow entrance to the marina and pulled the boat into her allocated pier. I would be moored a few boats along from the other team members, ensuring we were near enough to touch base if we wanted to, yet far enough apart that we appeared to be independent of each other. We had an agreement that we would interact with each other only as fellow boaters when in public, leaving our alter-egos to work together in the laboratory complex that was hidden beneath the marina's main buildings. This allowed us the freedom to socialise as friends and be a part of the rapidly growing community around the marina. Unlike our time in ORB, we were now able to separate our work and leisure time, although we remained on twenty-four-hour call.

In the short time that Jason King had been involved in canals and boating, he had begun to make something of an impact on the industry. The marina reflected King's involvement more than any other parts of his marine businesses, promising as it did, a new approach that would bring boater's facilities kicking and screaming into the modern age. 'Boat Space', my original interior design business, was based there and now operated from a series of state-of-the-art buildings that each had a dedicated purpose. In the largest of the units, apprentices and experts alike worked to produce the simple and affordable cruiser that promised to get more and more people out on the cut. The first completed examples of this boat had already been launched and the order-book was fast filling up. The second largest building was used for repairs, maintenance and painting of boats, whilst the third was designated as the place where Boat Space furniture and solar equipment were manufactured. On their own, these units were no different to those you might find in numerous other locations along the canals of the country, however, what made this facility unique was that it was a convenient, one-stop location for anything and everything that boaters required. You booked the work you wanted doing online, then, on the agreed date, you dropped off your boat and either left it to be worked on until the agreed completion date or took up the offer of accommodation in the marina's complex of luxury cabins. Most liveaboard boaters chose the latter option since it was a chance to enjoy a good-value holiday whilst essential maintenance work was completed.

What King had done was to observe the relatively primitive operations that were the hallmark of most marinas and boatyards. In doing this, he had likened them to the kind of family run garages that continued to exist in smaller villages around the country. His vision was for something a little more modern. And that vision was fast becoming a reality. No more were boaters expected to do all the legwork themselves. Instead, when you chose to work with Crystal Clear Marine, you were supported every step along the way. If you were mooring, you had a choice of three levels of luxury, the most basic of which was beyond the best currently on offer elsewhere. If you were passing through and needed refuelling, you simply pulled up at automated pumps, day or night, and paid as you would when you filled up your car. The same was true for sanitary pump-outs, and even for basic needs such as coal and logs. Everything was vended automatically, which made life easier for the boater and for the marina team as well.

Having cracked the challenge of providing the best in maintenance service, Crystal Clear were now working on delivering the best in leisure facilities, which, when completed, would see a new pub built for locals and boaters alike, a small hotel operation, a greater mix of retail outlets and a function and events suite. These facilities were being built when I arrived and had only been delayed a little because they couldn't be started until the underground complex that they masked was finished. King didn't mess around when he decided to act. By Summer, the work would be done and Crystal Clear would be the benchmark for all other marinas to aspire to. And it would be a profitable business too. What had surprised King so much on his first forays into canal boating had been the diversity of characters that inhabited that thin ditch of water. Amongst this community there were the poorest of the poor and the wealthiest of the wealthy, all getting on together. But facilities were less diverse. There were yards and budget moorings dotted around the network and there were various types of luxury marinas that had been built in the past twenty or so years. What there wasn't though, was a single point of convergence where those who could afford to pay could enjoy trouble-free support at the click of a mouse and where those who were less well-off could base themselves and even find work. King was working to create this mixed community and the reaction to date had been positive. Berths were filling up and money was starting to roll in. I looked forward to seeing this place become what King dreamt that it could be, and was confident that his Midas touch would work as well here as it had in his other businesses.

Meanwhile, I had some catching up to do and arranged to meet up with James, Adam and Charlotte in the new laboratory complex the following morning. King was elsewhere in the world but I was able to catch up with him on our secure video network and tell him of my decision to work with him. He was pleased that I had come down on his side and promised that he would monitor our actions carefully and ensure that we never sank into the organisational arrogance that had so damaged ORB. We would meet shortly, he assured me, before thanking me again for my choice and reminding me that humility was the way forward.

I entered the labs via the single terrestrial opening that still remained functioning, dressed as a workman and attracting no suspicion as I keyed my code into the 'out of service' lift that took me down to our new base. James would work on programming my pod later in the day to ensure that in future I could arrive at the labs as they did, via the underwater entrance.

As the lift doors opened, I barely had a chance to take in the sight of this new domain before Adam's voice echoed across to me.

"Kingfisher, man! Welcome to our world."

"Hey Adam," I replied, wrapping my arms around him in a full bear hug, "Thought you might need someone to keep an eye on you. So, you going to show me around, man?"

He laughed at my use of the word that he simply couldn't stop himself using and which we all now accepted to be a part of him as much as his name and his love for Charlotte. We all had our own foibles and habits and it was amazing how quickly you could learn to ignore these when you concentrated on the power of friendship between us.

34

"Kingfisher,", James joined us in the entrance corridor, "or is it Steve?"

"Whichever you prefer,", I replied, "they both apply to me."

I told them briefly of my decision to stop sitting on the fence and to commit to what they were doing.

"That's great, man,", Adam laughed, "because we have got some awesome stuff to show you and we're already getting a backlog of work down here. Come on, we'll show you."

As we walked through the complex, we chatted about recent events and I told them of my new-found passion to act against those who propagate fear. They knew exactly what I was talking about and James, in particular, who had been bullied ruthlessly when he was younger, offered his full support to me in this area.

"I kid you not,", he said, "before ORB got hold of me, there were days when I couldn't even leave my room because of what I was afraid of facing. The stupid thing was, nobody ever actually hurt me, but the threats turned me into jelly. I can still feel that fear to this day and it's not a good feeling."

"Still,", he continued, "it drives me to the work that I'm doing down here and if I needed the pain to spur me on then that's a price worth paying."

With that, he led us into his own workspace and asked us both to sit down while we waited for Charlotte to join us.

"We're like the three musketeers down here,", he smiled as he spoke, "but now that you're here, I suppose we'll need to come up with some sort of quartet theme."

"Not at all,", I replied, "you stay as the three musketeers. You work well together. You need to start thinking of me as a helper. Someone who's around when you need me. As much as I'm convinced we need to decide on actions as a team, I'm also convinced that we need to maintain our own independence as well. We don't want to become a new ORB, do we?"

"No way, man.", Adam waved his arms as he spoke, "You're spot-on with that Kingfisher, we are our own people, working together, yes, but never a passive part of a bigger being."

"My sentiments entirely,", Charlotte joined us and I was immediately struck by how she had blossomed in confidence in such a short time, "Adam and I are getting closer to being one as a couple, but we both have our own strengths and weaknesses. I've never had such a chance to work on my own ideas and this place is really helping me grow up."

35

"Well," I said, "you all seem to be getting it together down here. It's great to see. But, what exactly have you all been working on. I almost dread to ask, but let's go for it anyway."

"Okay," James was first off the mark, "I'll start. I'm concentrating on cyber-justice. You know I'm not good out there in the big old world with all those people, but down here and in cyberspace, I'm a different person. And there's so much that I can do from this location and without having to worry about people stressing me out. So many ways that I can stop the little injustices spiralling into the bigger crimes and so many ways I can defend the helpless who are dragged into the invisible net of computer crime. That's my mission, and when the other guys have updated you, I'll show you some examples."

"Adam and I," Charlotte spoke next, "are working a bit in parallel on equipment, which he can give you more of an insight into. As for me individually, I've really got into studying justice as a concept. I'm working my way through a few distance learning degrees just now, criminology, psychology, sociology and the like. I've never been given the chance to study before but I love it. Hopefully, I can bring a different perspective to things. Maybe help you all make your decisions."

"Brilliant," I told her, "and yes, we definitely need the academic element to stay our impulsiveness. I know that quite a lot of the time it's just rehashing and complicated babbling, but underneath it all there are truths and insights that can help us. Or at least give us a choice of truths to weigh up. So, what about you Adam?"

"Equipment, man.", he said, "Which is why I am so glad that you've decided to stay on board because it's all been made with you in mind. I try it out a bit on myself but I'm quaffing a little too much of the brown stuff these days and it doesn't really fit. Nor am I as good at controlling it as I am at designing it. Man, you want to see some of the holes in the walls I've made. Luckily, Charlotte's being a huge help to me. She stops me going off into the realms of the absurd and her input is unique, man, like she can translate my creations into a language anyone can understand. As James said, we're a trio that just seems to click. It's good."

"So, let's see the details of what you've got.", I said, "And I think we should go with the man behind the treasure hunt first. James?"

Chapter Six

'The Sunderland Evening Herald', 24th March, 2024.

'Police Swoop after E-Mail Confession'

Officers from Sunderland's child protection force executed a lightning raid on the home of local dentist, Charles Graham, earlier today, arresting him and seizing a quantity of computer equipment. It is understood by this paper that Mr Graham, 48, alerted the police himself in an e-mail confession that gave detailed accounts of his online activities, most specifically in grooming teenagers through various chat-rooms.

In a brief statement, the officer leading the enquiry, Detective Inspector Peter Williams, explained how his colleagues had been surprised to receive what amounted to a full and frank confession when they first logged on to their computers this morning.

"As we were able to fully validate the information in this message,", Williams explained, "we felt it appropriate to act immediately and decided to raid Graham's home as soon as we could get a team together and the relevant warrants signed. Whilst we have retrieved a substantial quantity of material from the property, it appears that Graham may have had a change of heart as he now flatly denies contacting us."

Mr Graham is understood to be being held in police custody pending further investigations, although officers remain confident that charges will soon be pressed. Neither his wife nor any of his colleagues from the Farm Hill dental practice were available for comment.

++++++

'Business Online: Breaking City News', 18:30, 24th
March, 2024

'Write-Offs Raise Concerns About Money Pot'

Investors in 'Money Pot', the payday lender, have seen
its share value halve in today's trading as the business
took the unusual decision to write-off twenty percent
of its loan book.

The City was first alerted to this move after anonymous
reports began circulating on the internet, subsequent
to which, a press release from the company confirmed the
move.

Money Pot was one of last year's star performers on
the stock market, following the decision by regulatory
authorities to allow them to charge interest rates that
some consumer rights bodies had said were excessive
and unsustainable. As a lender of last resort to the
poorest people, Money Pot has always maintained that high
interest rates are necessary to compensate for the risk
that loans to this demographic involve. Only last week,
Henry Carver, founder and CEO of Money Pot, outlined
in a speech to potential investors how there remained
a sound business and ethical case for the activities
pursued by his company, explaining that, "We are a
company that meets a need, often in times of hardship,
and we are proud of the work that we do. Our customers
are fully aware of the costs pertaining to our loans and
enter agreements with us with their eyes open."

None of the Board of Money Pot have been available
for comment, however, a number of specialist financial
advisors have raised doubts about Money Pot's ability to
sustain such a significant hit to its loan-book.

38

```
                          ++++++

E-Mail Alert: All Users, Fire Fortress Antivirus
            Software, 24/03/24
```

'DO NOT open any mail referring to J for Justice'

```
Users of Fire Fortress are advised to delete immediately
any e-mails or other communications received that contain
any reference to J for Justice or any similar content.
    We are currently investigating a potentially very
dangerous virus that may be attached to such messages
and will update with more information as and when we
can.
    Thank you for your cooperation,
    The Fire Fortress Team


                          ++++++
```

James pre-empted the reports that were about to hit the press in the presentation he made to us that afternoon. As we watched him set up a flip-chart and sort through his notes, I tried to reconcile this newly confident apparition before me with the shy and socially inadequate James that I had first met. He had always been gifted beyond any comprehension, but his gifts had been hidden until ORB had started to mine them. He wasn't somebody to demand respect, crave attention or shout about his intelligence, but in the secret and underground world of ORB this had never been an issue. They asked him to deliver and he, solidly and quietly, delivered. Freed from the paternal support of the Order, we had naturally worried about how he would adapt to life in the real world. It seemed that he was making good progress.

"I thought I would try and explain my work in a short presentation.", he began, turning over the first page of the flip-chart to reveal a hand-written title of 'J for Justice: Cyber action in a cyber world.'

He looked towards us and took our smiles and nods to be an agreement that we were happy for him to continue.

"Okay", he began, "first of all, a little background. As you all know, I have certain gifts that have allowed me to push the boundaries of physics, mathematics and general science to new dimensions. With ORB, I was close to breaking through on nuclear fusion, which I'm still working on, and I was responsible for some of the breakthroughs that we made in designing and building support equipment for the field team. Adam was always a great help to me and you, Steve, as The Kingfisher, were always encouraging and the keenest to try out my inventions."

"Your work was priceless, James", I allowed myself to interrupt him, "and remains so."

"Thank you.", he continued, "Today, however, I want to present to you a slightly new approach that I want to take as we work together as a new team of, shall I say, justice deliverers? Hence my presentation now on cyber-justice. You all know that I can handle the mysterious world of quantum physics and the beautiful intricacies of mathematical formulae, but I have always been a bit of a geek when it comes to computers as well."

"Never!", Charlotte shouted in mock-surprise, causing us all to break out laughing.

"Okay", James calmed us down, "I know, I can be a bit fanatical, yes. Still, it leads me on to what I want to show you now."

He turned over the first page of the flip-chart to reveal a stick man carrying a bag of tools.

"This is my new weapon against the force of injustice", he smiled as we looked at the drawing, "which I have, naturally and necessarily, dumbed down for today's audience."

This was getting to be a little too much, not only was James making a confident and concise presentation to us, he also seemed to have found a sense of humour.

"A lot of traditional computer work", he continued, "has focused heavily on programming, the more so since the hardware we use is generally working on a generic type of platform that is often improved but never challenged. Remember if you will, computers began as physical entities using valves and switches where the interior workings of the machine and its action were visible to the naked eye. Things have moved on and now we have computers that work at almost the molecular level. But, they still remain physical entities. A lot of people have forgotten this. Now, this stickman represents my new weapon in the war against cyber-crime. Let me explain. Current thinking says that you attack a computer using programmes and viruses that infiltrate the operating system. To counter this, anti-virus software patrols the complex datasets that programmes are created from, and disarms intruders where necessary. My friend here is not a computer programme, he is a physical entity."

"I'm confused, man.", Adam butted in, "What's a stick man got to do with computers?"

"Bear with me.", James replied, turning the page again and revealing a scatter of dots and lines across the whole of the large white page, "you see, this is the same stick man broken down into his smallest components. You can see here his little fingers, some of the parts of his toolkit and this is one of his feet. My theory is that, since computers remain a physical entity, the easiest way to gain entry to them is in a physical way. Now, think of these pieces of stick man as atomic components of the bigger whole. Together they combine to become stick man, but separately they are sub-atomic particles. In short, in order to get a physical attack mechanism into a computer, the answer is to break it down, send it in pieces into the machine, and then reassemble it there."

He flipped the page again and displayed a diagram of two computers connected across a landline.

"The line between these two machines.", he explained, "could be either a power line, a fibre-optic cable or indeed any other type of lead that connects the computer to the outside world. Since that line transmits the physical substance of electricity and data, if you are able to create something smaller than the atomic particles that carry that information and power, you can enter into that computer via the same path. Think of it as being a river that currently carries boats of data, or maybe more appropriately, let's think of it as a canal carrying cargo around. My work is focused on putting my own fleet of boats into that network and by so doing, gaining access to any computer that is hardwired to any cabling."

"But, surely.", I said, "that's only theory. You can't tell us you've managed to do this?"

"Steve.", he sighed, "would I be standing here if I hadn't done it? Yes, the stick man is a reality. I have a number of basic…well, I suppose that I should call them machines that do what the stick man does. They separate into the smallest atomic units that are possible, then, when they are in the machine they reassemble. Of course, their functionality is limited, but I'm working on that. In fact, there's no reason why they should be constrained by any limitations since I can keep building them in a modular way until they become as large as the computer itself. And note, because they are physical entities, not programmes, anti-virus software just ignores them. And more than that, please, don't think me a bit weird if I tell you that this one of the most beautiful things I've ever seen. It's beautiful in its simplicity and its beautiful because it actually uses the defences that have been set up to gain access to the most secure systems. As they carry data back and forward in a bid to keep the user's activity hidden, they bring the components of my micro-machines into the heart of the computer. Not too shabby, eh?"

"Brilliant, man,", Adam gasped, "sub-atomic machines that can go anywhere! Unbelievable."

"I tend to agree with Adam,", I said, "with the emphasis on unbelievable. So, you've actually made them work."

"I'm glad you asked,", James smiled as he replied, "and, with your permission, I hope to demonstrate. But first, I need to abide by our new rules as much as possible and ask that we all agree on the live action I am going to take. All I can say is that I am one hundred percent sure that my actions are justified and they are all reversible if you disagree. Do I have your permission?"

We all nodded assent.

"Thank you.", he answered as he opened up a laptop and connected it to a large monitor, "Now, I am going to make three attacks, all of which should generate a rapid response that we can review in tomorrow night's press. The first is to this gentleman here, Mr Charles Graham, dentist and, I believe, paedophile."

"Sorry,", I interrupted, "on what evidence?"

"Good point, Steve,", he answered, returning to the flip-chart, "and apologies that I missed out a chunk of my presentation."

He turned to the next page which had a face in the centre with lines radiating to multiple boxes that covered the whole sheet.

"Aside from physical evidence,", he explained, "such as ISP's, browser histories etc., we leave huge footprints around the cyber world that are not instantly recognisable. You remember, Steve, when they first tracked you down because everything you did triangulated around the canals? They saw something out of nothing really, a shadow of a pattern. Well, this is pretty much the same principle. You see the person in the diagram, well, he is connected to millions of other points of reference, some of which are linked but most of which exist separately. Think of each of the boxes as a point of personal data, your DVLA record, your bank details, your mobile use, your taxes. What I have done is to create a search tool that mines every aspect of a person's life and throws up anomalies that need investigating."

"And Mr Graham?", I asked.

"Well, in Graham's case, I set up a search programme to monitor activities on social media and chat room sites. It pulls data from each user then correlates it with other sources of information, running silently in the background until it flags up something unusual. And bear in mind, we're not just talking simple data here. I'm talking about every pattern of every activity at any time, which equates to a huge heap of data. Now, what happened here was that a supposedly teenage lad was chatting with a bunch of teenage girls. My programme flagged up that one of the users was operating from a computer and ISP that, although hidden by layers of protection, was also used for multiple other day-to-day activities. I was able to confirm that it was owned and operated by a gentleman who had no children, was single, and who was simultaneously checking e-mails that were coming in from professional sources. Those sources didn't correlate with the profile I was checking. For example, how many young lads discuss the intricacies of dental cavity filling? There was a void in the dataset that alerted my search engines and within that void, the invisible became the visible. The teenage boy was actually Mr Graham. As soon as I had this information I was able to track back on his activities and discover that, not only did he have a penchant for underage girls, but that he also had a cache of illegal pornography on his computers."

"And that's another by-product of this work", he explained to us, "and one which we can really exploit. You see, when we first started sending stuff out into the ether, our interactions weren't really recorded much. With the increase in storage capacity and the rise of the web and cloud based computing, we actively punt everything we do into both the present and the past. Think about the data that exists out there, hidden away to be found. We may think we've deleted records, but because we've passed them on, they lie like dust across the whole cyber landscape. Therefore, like fossil records, we can dig for them, rebuild them and know more about any individual than ever before. And many, like fossils, are footprints of a past that is believed to have been deleted. The invisible becomes visible through the space it left behind. With Graham, the data was there to be found. All I had to do was create the net to catch it in."

"Stunning.", I said, "absolutely stunning. You get to see what isn't there because the void becomes visible when the sum of the parts becomes added together. Amazing."

"Thank you again.", James replied, "Now, to action. In Graham's case, I simply press this button and the dossier of his activities is collated and sent to the e-mail boxes of the local constabulary. There, that's it done."

We watched as the programme flashed up pages of data that gradually resolved into a one-page missive that sent itself across the web and so condemned and disarmed Mr Charles Graham.

"That was fairly traditional stuff.", James said modestly, "but now for a demonstration of my little stick man."

We watched again as he played with the laptop and bought up the website of Money Pot, a payday lending company.

"I hate these people.", he said, "Some of the lads here on the marina have got into a right mess with them and have already paid their loans back multiple times. But you can't get at them in a traditional way. Look, this is the best Trojan software I can create and…"

He pressed a button and after seeming to gain access to the site it instantly froze and kicked him out.

"…there's no way through. But, with a press of this button, I should be able to put our stick man in and get to work."

Engrossed in the demonstration, we were speechless as he attached a small black box to the computer's power supply, then played with a remote control that he held in his hand. Nothing happened for a few minutes and we were wondering if anything would, but James seemed confident.

"Another minute or so.", he said, "and you should see a result. But don't expect anything dramatic."

We waited some more, then the screen changed to display a scrolling list of a thousand or more names and addresses along with financial data, loan amounts and repayments. One by one they were erased.

"That should teach them a lesson.", James laughed, "that's the hardest-pressed twenty percent of their customers free from their debts."

"But,", he interrupted us as we were congratulating him, "I've still got one more trick. I want the world to know that there's a force for good out there and that there's no hiding. So, I'm going into what is reputed to be the most secure ISP on the net, that of Fire Fortress."

Which is exactly what he did. Within minutes, the Fire Fortress screen changed to display the message 'J for Justice', scrolling across the screen. It continued to flash on and off for a few minutes, then James pulled the plug and the website returned to normal.

"Just a shot across their bows.", he said, "And hopefully a message to the world that we mean business. And that concludes my demonstration."

Our applause lasted for longer than James had expected, after which we adjourned to the small, fully-vended canteen to have a break and talk with him some more about his work. We were stunned by what he'd shown us and were impressed by how he had presented it. As we finished our drinks I looked across at Adam who had suddenly gone very quiet and who looked almost miserable.

"You all right, mate?", I asked him.

"Oh, not so bad, man.", he sighed, "I was just thinking about something. James' presentation was amazing, and now, I've got to try and follow it!"

Chapter Seven

I can still remember the sense of excitement that I felt as we reconvened our meeting. It was an excitement that was born of the changes that I'd seen in James and the sense of a greater change that I was feeling in my own heart. It was a feeling of the unlimited potential that the future held, and of the place that I now felt I had amongst this new team of colleagues. Adam's concerns were justified. James hadn't only managed to deliver an interesting and inspiring presentation, but in doing so, he'd also made sure that the revolutionary content of that presentation was matched by the revolution in his own demeanour. We'd had a few questions that we ran by him individually during lunch, but I felt that it was appropriate to give James the chance to summarise his responses to these to the whole group, prior to Adam taking to the stage.

"Steve has asked me," James began as we settled down again, "if I could just recap on some of the questions that you've raised with me and my answers. Firstly, thanks to Charlotte for asking about the resources that I have been using. The answer is that I am still hooked into the ORB computer system and am tapping its power. I hope that this is okay with the rest of you. You see, when we departed from that place, I left behind a note to the computer technicians advising of some safeguards that I'd installed. We needed to be certain that ORB kept its side of the deal. In essence, I have full access to their computers, access that is both anonymous and secure. At the same time as installing that backdoor, I took the liberty of fitting a hard-wired failsafe at the heart of the system which they know about and know to leave well alone. If they go rogue or try and block my access, the system will burn up. I suppose, in time, we will have our own equipment here, but for now, this gives us a volume of computing power that can only help us. Are you all okay with that?"

We nodded our assent and he continued.

"Good, now the other key questions raised were equally pertinent. Adam rightly asked if this work that I was doing was not in fact a category killer and doesn't it make everything else redundant? Well, yes and no. Just now, you could argue that we can get into places electronically that make it unnecessary to have a physical presence out there. But that's not the whole truth. For one thing, everything that I've shown you today could be redundant tomorrow. As soon as the nature of our threat is discovered, it's not unreasonable to suppose that protection can be generated. For another, you should remember that the physical infiltration of systems is only possible where they have a tangible and direct line to the outside world. I can't send something into a computer that isn't hard-wired to the wider grid unless I can physically touch that machine. As to the software that I'm using, well, that requires us all to work together. Yes, I can get software to pretty much search and probe into anything that I want it to, but, I need help to guide me as to where that software looks. In other words, if these new things keep working, I can only maximise their effectiveness with you to support me. Okay so far?"

Again, we all nodded our agreement.

"Which leads,", he concluded, "to the final point that was raised. Steve has asked if the search programmes that I use couldn't be adapted to look for different themes. In the example I showed you, everything was geared to tracking down false and dangerous users of chatrooms. That's quite a specific and targeted approach. Steve's question was whether I could use the same search technology to target the wider sphere of injustice and my answer is, yes, I can. And I think it's a good idea. It means that we can see so much more of what is happening out there in the world and not be dependent on our own awareness. In short, we can have programmes running in the background that search for patterns of injustice and alert us to situations that we might want to intervene in. In fact, it's the heart of where we want to be. Imagine if we could see injustice before it happened? It's a dream, but not impossible. The challenge of course is in defining justice and injustice but we can discuss that later if necessary. For now, I think that I've talked enough. Thanks for your positive response and please remember that this is only a beginning."

He stepped away from the desk that he had used as his podium and walked slowly back to his chair. Adam took this cue to take his place and begin his own update. I could see in his face that he was a bit apprehensive and that some of the confidence and energy that he usually displayed had been drained away. We looked on encouragingly and let him have the floor.

"Thanks James.", he started slowly, "Man, I don't mind admitting that you've caught us all a bit off guard with your stuff. You kept your powder dry on some of that stuff didn't you buddy! So, apologies to you all, but I don't have anything to demonstrate that even touches on what we've already seen. Still, this is my contribution."

He shuffled some papers on the desk, inserted a jump drive into the laptop and waited as his own presentation loaded.

"This won't take too long.", he began, "as I don't have a huge amount of progress to report so far. As an overview, since we set up here, Charlotte and I have talked a lot about what might be achievable. At the same time, James and I have agreed that he will concentrate more on the work you saw before. For my part, I'll continue to pursue the practicalities of some of the tools of our trade. And Steve, I am so glad that you have decided to stay around because most of my work is on Kingfisher stuff. Seriously, man, you had me scared when we thought you were leaving. The kit I'm developing is so you and really, I don't think that we could ever find someone else to be our presence out there."

"Agreed!", Charlotte interrupted, her sentiment echoed by James.

"So.", Adam continued, "here are a few of the projects that I'm tackling just now. Of course, we can talk more and you can ask me to divert onto anything else that you need, but in the meantime, I'll build up the catalogue of tools available and you can choose what, if any, you want. First off, and inspired by one of those all-action movies of yesteryear, there's this."

He changed the page on the screen to reveal an animated clip of my latest suit which separated into three as he clicked the mouse.

"There's only one of you out there.", he said, looking directly at me, "and, truth be told man, I think we are happy with that. I know that our financier friend is keen for us not to become a vigilante army. But, there are times when one of you isn't going to be enough. So, this is the answer. Imagine that you are in that first suit. Now, the other suits are empty, but they move and act as if you are in them. With three suits, you become an army of three even though you are still just the one. It means that you have more presence and it should keep you safer since no one knows which suit you are actually in."

"Nice idea.", I said, trying to recall the source of the movie-allusion he had made, "how far off is it?"

"Oh, not so far man.", he smiled as he spoke, "In fact, it's as close as this."

We turned around as we heard the door behind us open and watched in amazement as two versions of myself as Kingfisher walked in, paused, somersaulted to the front of the room and hovered there on ion-boots.

"Meet the family", Adam laughed, grinning stupidly as the two figures lowered themselves to stand on their feet and gave us a long, slow bow, "I haven't given them names yet, but man, they are a lot easier to work with than you Steve!"

"Not fair!", James shouted out, "You said that they were nowhere near ready."

"Sorry James, old buddy", he answered, "I couldn't wait, could I? Man, I knew you were cooking up something big. To be fair though, they are still a work in progress and I need to work on them some more. Still, not too shabby, eh?"

I was enjoying this day immensely. I wondered what else was in store.

"Of course", Adam continued, "no Kingfisher family would be complete without its pets. So, please will you welcome the new additions to the menagerie."

As he said this, he played with the laptop and, to the theme from a well-known wildlife television show, he instructed his new creations to enter the room. Straightaway, I could see that he had been busy. First into the room was a heron. We all ducked as it flew over our heads before landing next to Adam. This was followed by a swarm of wasps, who were, in turn, followed by a dozen ducks who waddled slowly into the room.

"I know that we have tended to concentrate on flying things", Adam said, "and I think that this is right, given the nature of what we do and the environment. But, I'm working on more underwater creatures as well, which to be honest, man, weren't practical for me to bring here today. These are just a part of the new 'Kingfisher Zoo' that I'm working on. The herons are cool, they just sit there for ages and watch and absorb data like nobody's business. The wasps are carrying the latest microscopic weapons and really do pack a sting."

He waited to let us absorb his work so far. He had a mischievous look on his face, and we knew there would be more to come.

"All very useful, I hope", he continued, "but I do have one new addition to the gang that I am especially proud of. Steve, you need a four-legged buddy if you're gonna be out there on the cut. This is my special gift to you."

We turned towards the door and the most beautiful and perfect dog came bounding into the room. It was the sort of dog that you looked at and immediately smiled. The sort of dog that you had as a child and pulled along behind you, but which was now alive.

"May I present your new canine pal, Gilly.", Adam said, "She's my idea of the perfect pup and she'll keep you company mate. Call her over."

"Gilly.", I called, and watched in amazement as the dog turned and looked at me, then wandered over to where I was seated and jumped into my lap, giving me a lick and a kiss as she did so. I had to admit, she was anatomically perfect and very, very cute.

"Adam,", I said, "she's beautiful, but I can't commit to having a dog. What about when I'm out and about?"

"Oh, you just turn her off.", he replied with a straight face, "Look, like this."

He walked over to where I sat, rubbed the dog's head and then reached around under her collar. She stopped moving instantly.

"You mean, she's animatronic?", I asked

"Of course, man.", Adam switched the dog back on, "Pretty good, isn't she? She's absolutely everything that you could want from a dog but without the commitment. Seriously, she'll keep you company and, let's be honest, man, you need a reason to be sat in those pubs on your own. With her, at least you don't look like some lone weirdo."

We all laughed and then spent a good ten minutes playing with Gilly who ran around the room, sniffed anything and everything that she saw, and who then settled down for a nap at my feet.

"So,", Adam said as he pulled his notes together and closed the laptop, "that's a taste of what I've been up to. Hope it's okay."

As with James, we applauded Adam's work, waking Gilly up in the process. The two suits followed Adam off the stage and took up their station behind us as though they were guarding the doors. It was a bit disconcerting seeing them there. Like being watched by yourself. Still, the dog was enough of a distraction.

"Me next?", Charlotte asked.

"Go for it,", I replied, "the stage is yours."

"Thanks.", she stood up and squeezed Adam's hand as she made her way to the front.

"Well, you'll be pleased to know,", she began, "that I don't really have a great deal to report, so I won't be waffling on for ages. I just want to give you an update on my own progress and secure your agreement to what I plan on doing."

50

As we settled to listen, she sat on the corner of the desk, before continuing.

"I think of myself as contributing in two ways. Firstly, and not for any stupid stereotypical gender reasons, I feel that it is my calling to help you guys with the administrative side of things. Let's be honest, you're all blokes and you're all very good at what you do, but you need a bit of support in keeping the basics in order. James, I know you won't mind me saying, but for all your brilliance in your specialities, you do need someone there to make sure that you have clean clothes, and also, referring to last week's incident, to ensure that you are even wearing clothes."

Adam and James burst out laughing and told me what had happened a few days before when James had been so preoccupied with something he was working on that he had only narrowly avoided arrest.

"And you, Adam," Charlotte continued, "wouldn't be able to make anything if there wasn't somebody keeping your supplies of equipment topped up. Oh, yes, and even making sure that you switch the plug on!"

They told me later that Adam had been just finishing an especially intricate piece of equipment but had destroyed the whole thing during testing. This had happened despite its power pack having been plugged in for several days to charge. Sadly, he'd left the switch off and those power packs hadn't actually charged at all.

"I know that you are a bit more independent, Steve," she continued, "but there are some routine things that I'm sure you will let me help out on. Of course, that doesn't mean that I will be doing much of the actual work myself and I have a team under me who are there to support. I see my role as support and administration for yourselves and the other businesses alike. As I say, this isn't a 'girly' thing. It just plays to my strength and experience. Agreed?"

"I think," I said, "that I can speak for all of us here and say, yes, we agree. You've been a great support to us so far and I know that we can rely on you continuing to help us. If you're happy to do this, then we are very grateful."

"Thanks," she replied, "and trust me, this is no soft option. Considering what you all do, I'm amazed at some of the things you forget. Anyway, that being agreed, the other focus of my short-term plans is to carry on studying all the academic subjects that we need to support our work. I'm working my way through criminology and psychology, just now, but I've really caught the learning bug and think that this is my chance to contribute to our work in delivering justice. The idea you had, Steve, about James creating new search terms, that's a good example. With my increasing knowledge and deeper reading around the subject, I think I can help James frame those search references. Does that make sense?"

"Absolutely," I replied, "and we definitely need your input. I've talked with you enough to know the passion you have for learning in general and for the subjects you're studying, so I'm all for it. I think, over time though, you need to focus on this rather than the admin. You can contribute so much to the intellectual focus of what we do."

"Thanks," she said, "and that's it for me. I'll hand over to you now Steve, as I know you want to say a few words. That is, if we can prise you away from that dog!"

I switched Gilly off and took my place before my friends. I wasn't going to talk for long but I had some things that needed to be said.

"This has been an amazing day for me," I began, "and tonight, the drinks are on me. But before we finish this update session, I need to share some things with you."

I paused while they settled and to compose my own thoughts.

"First off," I told them, "you have each demonstrated today that you are vital to our new way of doing things and that you each make an invaluable contribution. It's an honour for me to work with you."

"Secondly," I continued, "and as importantly, I want to say that I am sorry for all the uncertainty that I have put you through. I could blame this on the long dark night of the soul or on my existential searching for the meaning of life, but the truth is, it boils down to my having been a bit of a selfish prat. I swanned around the ORB headquarters playing the part as some sort of hero, but some of it was how I felt. I've been proud, arrogant, conceited and too self-centred. I know this now and I want to change. Your suits, Adam, are a perfect metaphor for my state; The Kingfisher without Steve Barratt. I can no longer believe that I am special or that I am indispensable. I'm so grateful to have found some sort of purpose but I know I've overstepped the mark. We all have a part to play and whatever we achieve in the future as a group, we will all be able to say that we helped to make it happen. But none of us should ever believe, like I did, that we alone made it happen. Jason told me that the secret was humility. You guys have it in spades. I need help to get there."

I paused to compose myself, feeling my emotions beginning to take over.

"You see,", I continued, "and don't worry, I'm not going to get out a tambourine and go all churchy on you, we are not fighting a new battle. Dig out your Bible if you've got one and the injustices that we are seeing now are merely new manifestations of age-old evils. And that's something we can harness to help us. When I was talking to James about search terms, I was thinking about going back to basics and using the broadest themes that are timeless. Oppression, greed, selfishness, persecution. Yes, they are legislated against but they still continue. The big scheme is bigger than any of us. I hope I'm making sense here?"

As I looked at my friends I saw acceptance on their faces. I was moved by this and concluded what I had to say.

"The thing is, it's as simple as this for me. I just want to work with you and play my small part. I'm open to helping out as and when you guys need me, but I also want to stay that little bit detached from the role of superhero. It panders to my vanity too much. I do want to get to the stage where I no longer have to resort to physical action, delivering a more nuanced rebalancing of justice. And I do believe that, as a group, we should only act when we have total agreement on a course of action. But, I also want to be smaller than I have been. I love you guys and we have been through some mad stuff together, but it's been too much about me. So, in summary, I'm here to help and I believe that I have a purpose in what I do, but I need your help in keeping my feet on the ground. I need you guys to teach me humility."

There was a moment of silence in the room which was broken by a familiar voice coming from the corridor outside.

"Here, here.", Jason King turned and walked into the room, "Couldn't agree more. Now, did I hear right when you said that you were paying for the drinks?"

Chapter Eight

In all honesty, I can't say that I remember much of the night we enjoyed at the nearby pub. I know we had a good time and I know that we all drank more than we should have. This latter fact was testified to me by the pounding headache that was splitting my skull and the foot-long bar tab that I'd paid on our departure. What I do remember though, is the chaos of the following morning. As we'd left the pub, we'd seen the storm clouds rolling above us and felt the bitter chill of an impending night of heavy weather. We'd made it back before the storm broke but the others must all have done as I'd done and clambered into bed to the sound of pelting rain hammering the steel roofs of our homes.

I was woken by a loud banging on the door, which prompted me to throw on a pair of old joggers, slip into some boots and try my best to clamber out of the boat in my delicate state. There were dozens of people wandering around, some of whom I recognised but most of whom were strangers. They were surveying the sight before them of the storm-devastated marina. Despite the size of the pound, it was flooded and all the boats were propping themselves up against the piers at dangerous angles.

"Steve!", I heard Adam call me, "Over here. We need to try and straighten some of these up."

I went over to where he was working on the stern ropes of a boat that looked like it was minutes away from sinking and set to immediately on the bow end. The boat creaked and lurched then righted itself as the ropes slackened. As its bilge drain cleared the water line, the automatic pump switched in and it began discharging the hundreds of litres of water that had been so close to taking her down.

"I've got Charlotte checking all the boats at risk", Adam told me, "and we've got a crew of about a dozen around the place working on those. You stay with me if you want and we'll work this arm of the marina.".

He looked at me and I nodded my agreement.

"You okay, man?", he laughed, "Or suffering a bit from last night? Man, you guys can put it away."

"Thanks, and yes", I replied, "let's just say that I'm a bit the worse for wear, but don't worry, I'll be fine. Let's get cracking on these boats."

It took us another hour of hard labour to clear the danger away from the seventy odd jetties that comprised our part of the complex. Most of the boats were safe but needed retying, although there were a few hairy moments when we thought we were going to lose one or two before we got to them. The piers were creaking against the weight of the vessels and if they hadn't been as solid as they were, there was a good chance that some of them would have followed their occupiers down. Sinking on the canal is unpleasant, but not a disaster, since the water's usually only a foot or so below the base of the boat. Sinking on a marina however, is something altogether different. When you sink in fifteen feet of water, your boat's a long way below the surface.

Fortunately, the end of the storm had bought in a very mild and pleasant morning which meant that we were at least working in some sort of comfort. This was a blessing to us all since we remained in a state of bed-undress and hadn't had time to wrap up in proper clothing. By mid-morning, all the boats were back as they should be and the water in the marina was easing away at its own leisurely pace. None of the buildings had been damaged, although the roof on one of the workshops looked a little shaky. It was when we were surveying that roof that Jason King joined us.

"Morning gents", he said, displaying no sign of any ill-effects from last night's session, "some storm that. Thanks for helping out. Looks like you could do with a breakfast, if you can stomach it. Give us half an hour and the catering team should have a decent spread laid out. All hands to the deck and all that."

"Meanwhile", he continued, "let's go and inspect this place. Looks okay but I want to make sure that there are no leaks."

He led us into the workshop, which was the one that was being used to construct the new-build, everyman's boat that we had designed. It was all intact and there were no signs of any leaks from the roof. Whilst King and Adam went through to the rear of the building to double-check the rest of the place, I stopped and looked at the line of boats laid out before me, all in various stages of build and each one a character in itself.

This boat had been the talk of the waterways press when it was announced late last year. The concept was very simple. For one fixed price, the customer would get a fully equipped, ready to live on, narrowboat, to a standard design but with a choice of various colour schemes. Included in that price were the electric engine and the solar panels needed to power it. Of course, options to pay extra for a premium fit-out were available, but of this first batch I knew that only two would be made at a higher spec. What really fired up the press and those first customers was the short time before order and delivery, roughly only four weeks, and of course the price.

We had the manufacture down to this time period by scrapping the conventions and starting from scratch. The boats were modular and the top was only fitted after all the internal works had been done. Electrics that were fitted into the roof were simply plugged into the main circuits once the super structure had been lowered down and bolted on to the base unit. Since most of the time wasted by other builders was down to their making the shell first and then stumbling about inside to fit it out, our way of working simplified everything. On top of that, the hull was unique in that it was one piece of metal without a single weld in it. I'll be honest and say that we utilised some of our hidden resources to develop this, but the theory was simply. We took a flat piece of steel, worked into it a few secret ingredients, then it was heated to a temperature that made it begin to flex. Once that temperature was reached, a huge press crushed down in to the metal and the hull was formed. Simple, but radical too.

There had been the usual detractors looking to find holes in the design. Yes, the steel was thinner than in most boats, but the way we treated it made it as strong as steel twice as thick and much less susceptible to corrosion. We'd also faced the wrath of a small group of boaters, most of whom were the owners of very expensive and shiny vessels that only ventured out onto the canal network for a few weeks every year. Their argument was that, since our boat was so competitively priced, it would encourage too many new people out onto the canals. Sadly, for them, that had been our plan. The past decade or so had seen the canals of this country turned into little more than a stretch of water that provided a haven for wildlife and a beautiful backdrop for those who walked or cycled the towpath. They were never designed for that. They were built as a means of transport and as a means of transport we wanted them to remain.

Although striving for humility, I looked on the boats before me in that shed with a certain amount of pride. I could allow myself a little glow of satisfaction. There was a lot of good work going on in this place. As I turned to leave, I was reminded again of the other good that had come out of this project.

"Hi Steve.", a voice I recognised called out to me.

"Hey Phil,", I replied, turning to look at someone that I recognised less and less every time I saw him, "how are you doing?"

"I'm good,", he replied, "and these little beasties are coming along nicely, aren't they?"

"They're great,", I replied, "and how are you coping as Supervisor? Looks like you're in control."

"I tell you,", he said, "if I hadn't had this opportunity, I don't know what I'd have been doing. But now that you guys have put your faith in me, I can assure you that I'm going to do better than any of you expected. And not just on the boats either. I want every one of our trainees bought up to scratch and either given a job or moving into a job. If one of them goes back in, then that's a real blow to me."

"Have we lost any yet?", I asked, keen to find out how Philip Rivers, previous inhabitant of a young offender's institute in Worcester before being rescued by The Kingfisher, was working to help us achieve a zero-recidivism rate amongst the numerous ex-offenders we employed.

"Only two.", he seemed disappointed, even though the number was better than any other employer could aspire to, "Truth is, I don't think we should ever have given them the chance. They wanted to do things their way, and drag us down to their level. JK was all for giving them another chance, but I put my foot down. I'd rather lose two now than have their infection cause us to lose more over time."

"King bowed to your decision?", I asked.

"Yes, sir,", he displayed no vanity as he replied, "I laid out the deal on the table, we batted ideas about and he accepted my argument."

"That's right,", the aforementioned JK, or Jason King to the rest of us, joined us, "Philip gave as good as I gave him and he actually got me to change my mind. Not only is that a rare thing, but it's also proved to be a good thing. I keep an eye on this place and the work they are doing and I think we have something of a little diamond in Philip."

"So long as you keep him away from his mobile!", Adam butted in, referring back to the cause of River's initial brush with the law when, as a teenager, he'd been severely sentenced for inappropriate comments sent via his phone.

"Yeah right, Adam,", Rivers took it in good faith, "although the pictures from last night that I've seen tell me that you should keep out of phone view as well."

"Excuse me,", Adam dashed off to check what embarrassment awaited him.

"What pictures?", I asked.

"Oh, sorry, did I say something about pictures?", Rivers smiled, "Maybe I got that wrong."

We left him chuckling to himself and walked back to the suite of offices that King retained in the main marina building.

"So… Jason,", I asked, "what brings you over here. Thought we weren't going to see you for a while."

"Yes,", he replied, "that had been the plan. But plans change. Firstly, and you probably don't know this, but Tony and Kate have asked me to be their boy's Godfather. I don't usually accept those invitations, but I like them so much that I said I would. I'm here for the Christening. And don't feel offended that you haven't been invited. It's a private affair and you know what Tony's like about crowds."

"I don't mind,", I replied, "I'm on their side with that one. It's enough to have to cope with a new baby, never mind laying out a spread for people you barely know. Cute kid though."

"He is, isn't he?", King paused and looked across the water pensively, "And to me, he is like the grandchild that I will never have. The girls would have made great mothers, but that isn't to be. So, I'm going to spoil that boy rotten and make sure that he has every opportunity in life."

"Good on you,", I said as we arrived at the office and walked in to the reception area.

"But that's not the only reason that I'm here,", he said, "I want to get together with the new team later today to run over a few things."

"Work to do?", I asked.

"Yes, I'm afraid so.", he seemed a little frustrated as he replied, "Some things have happened and I need to bounce them off you chaps. I'm afraid it may lead to our first real project together. But I also want to talk about our relationship. You met yesterday, I understand, and you all seem comfortable with things?"

"I think so,", I answered, "we're all on board at least, and there are good things coming out of the team's work."

"Makes sense that we consolidate that then.", he said, "Look, how about we all meet up after lunch, say two o'clock?"

"I'll get the guys together.", I replied, "Down in the labs?"

"No, I don't think so, up here will do fine. Much nicer view."

I left him standing at the window of his office, looking out as the sun shone on the water and reflected off the glass and the brass and the steel of the boats that were now sitting very comfortably on the water again.

Chapter Nine

Gathered around the highly-polished boardroom table that sat to the side of King's office, we waited expectantly to hear what our nominal leader had to say. As an impromptu meeting, and coming off the back of our own catch-up the previous day, the timing of King's visit served to keep us high on the hope we had for the future and eager to hear what he had to say.

"Okay," he began, settling down and looking each of us over before he began, "first of all, thank you for coming. Thank you for helping out with the boats this morning. And, of course, thank you for an enjoyable night last night. I appreciate that you may not be fully recovered yet, but we need to take these opportunities when we can. I'm over here for a specific reason and, truth be told, I'm not sure when I'll be in this neck of the woods again."

He paused to pour and drink a glass of sparkling water, waving the bottle at us and passing it on to Adam who was the first to accept the much-needed offering.

"All I want to do today," he continued, "is to update you on some of the outstanding threads from our past life together that you might be interested in. To talk about what we hope for the future and, of course, to get the necessary input from you all. Needless to say, I'm already up to speed with the stuff that you discussed yesterday, and I have to say that each of you have come through magnificently in your endeavours. James, your work is unbelievable. Yours too, Adam, and you, Steve, seem to be in a better place than when we last met. Not forgetting yourself, Charlotte. I agree, they need someone to look after them and we definitely need you to support Kate in the yard administration. But, over and above all that, I want you to keep your primary focus on your studies. From what I've seen of your work to date, and from the feedback I've had from your tutors, you have a gift for this field. We can get other people in to help with the routine stuff, so please, don't let your studies be interrupted."

"Thank you," Charlotte replied, "that's good of you to say."

King waved his hand to dismiss her thanks before continuing.

"There are shadows that hang over each one us. Despite my various business interests, my financial success and the sheer vibrancy of my own life, there remain shadows. There's the shadow that will always be there from the lives of the loved ones that I've lost. There's the shadow of my identity as my own cousin and the prospect that one day I'll be found out. And there's the shadow of the doubts that even I have at times about what we are doing in our work together. But, I'm not alone in this. You all live under certain shadows. Steve, you have the threat of exposure and prison hanging over you every day, and you also have the shadows of lost loved ones and indeed, a lost love. The rest of you have your own shadows, not least of which are the echoes of the recent past when you lived in the strange isolation of ORB's underground city."

We listened closely as he said all of this, wondering where it was going.

"But shadows need not hold us back", he explained, "and that's why I say that we need to acknowledge them. To deny we are burdened by the weight of past events is to live in some sort of candy-land. No, we need to accept the shadows that haunt us and exploit them as a positive means of moving forward. If there were no shadows, there would be no light behind them. That's what I want us to think about and it's certainly the approach that I intend to take. Today is about moving forward. Moving out of the shadows but never losing sight of them. I hope that makes some sort of sense."

He poured another glass of water and, in so doing, opened up the door for any of us to respond. There were things running through my mind and I almost broke the silence, but then I thought better of it. The other guys seemed to feel it appropriate to respond in the same way.

"Okay then", he resumed, "that's the overview and the end of the psycho-babble part. Now, to practical things. First off, an update on our friends The Order for Restoring Balance. James, I know, is tapping into their systems and, for now, I think that makes sense. They are in touch with me at a very cursory level and they can accept this, although they would like the threat taken off their systems at some point."

"I'm not sure the time is right for that", James said.

"No", King agreed, "I feel the same way. Still, we should have our own systems in time and then maybe we release the hold we have on them. The new Council is working well, as far as I understand, and their operatives continue to do what they have always done. I think they are feeling the loss of their best technicians but they continue to make progress regardless. My understanding is that, sometime in the near future, they intend to move out of their current base and into somewhere less clandestine. They seem to have taken on board the notion that, despite the need for the utmost secrecy, their workers shouldn't have to live and work outside of the wider world. In short, it all looks quite positive."

"You're not intending that we ally with them, are you?", Charlotte asked.

"No, no, of course not,", King was emphatic in his reply, "but I think that we can all benefit by at least recognising each other's existence and respecting the gap between us. Which leads me onto one of the main reasons for our meeting today. I want to talk about the protocols of how we operate. And believe me, this is a difficult one for me to get my head around. You see, we cannot become like ORB, an organised group that has a single focus and a formal leadership board. That didn't work for them in the past, it may work for them in the future, but I don't think it is where we should be. My first question then, is do you agree?"

"For my part,", I said, "I do agree, and I think, for the same reasons. I've already told the guys and yourself that I need to be a step away from what we do. I can't be a part of a controlling system again that directs me into the sort of places I don't want to go to."

"Same goes for us I think,", Adam looked at James and Charlotte as he spoke, "since we're enjoying our freedom here and, to be honest, we seem to have got more done by doing our own thing than by being directed."

"Good,", King said, "so we are all agreed that we remain an affiliation rather than a formal organisation. But that brings with it a challenge over accountability. Here's what I propose. That we do nothing unless it is with the agreement of all of us. That is, every corrective action that we take is a collective decision. The difficulty with this, is that it imposes a certain time restriction on our responses. I believe that even that could turn out be a positive. Nothing we do can be reactive, and everything we do is carefully considered from all angles. Thoughts?"

"Again,", I heard myself saying, "I totally agree with you. One of truths that I've had to accept is that we are not here to eradicate injustice and change the world. So yes, we have to let some issues slip away to ensure that we address only the ones we agree on. Look at the resource we have here. James and Adam are technically unbeatable, Charlotte has an educational and moral grasp of justice beyond any I've seen before and you, Jason, have a leadership style and control of your power that is unique. As for me, I can do a few things in a practical way as Kingfisher. So, you have my support in this."

There was total agreement from the others as well.

"Excellent,", King continued, "so, in practical terms, we identify issues, we discuss them from wherever we each are and then we decide a course of action. Which only leaves us with the issue of how we identify targets. But, James, I think you are the key to this. Your search bots can be our army out there, picking up the injustices that correlate with our vision and feeding us situations to consider. Charlotte, I want you to work with James on this so that, together, you deliver the right tool targeting the right data. Agreed?"

They both nodded agreement.

"So, in summary then,", he concluded, "we are a loose affiliation of like-minded individuals working together to correct issues of injustice that we are alerted to and where we agree on actions to be taken. As Steve said, we know we have the technical resources but I don't believe that there is a similar group with the life experiences that we have and the breadth of knowledge that collectively we possess. I'm pleased you all agree. As to whether we have a name, well, the answer is both yes and no. We are not going to have a name but James, I am more than happy for you to put your 'J for Justice' messages about and Steve, the Righteous Corrector can live again. Other than that, we do our own small bit to help justice prevail."

"And the others?", I asked, referring to the dozen or so additional personnel who had come with us out of ORB.

"Good point,", he answered, "I've spoken to each of them individually and they are happy to be available to vote when necessary, but they prefer to stay in the shadows working on their own things. They're happier now that they have the freedom to discover real life. They couldn't even find that when we all escaped to my island. Our return here to England opened up to them a normality of life that they love. And a freedom they cherish. They'll remain a useful extra resource for when we need more input, but I think the five of us should be enough most of the time. Charlotte and Adam, as a starting point, I want you two to supervise the others if that's okay. Let them have their freedom but direct them as necessary. I'm around if you need any help with this, but I'm comfortable you'll know what to do. You comfortable with that?"

They spoke to each other briefly before Adam answered.

"Yes, Sir, that's fine."

"Ah,", King laughed, "Sir, not man. We are making progress."

Which is how our informal group was formalised, and how we set down the minimum rules that we would operate by. I for one was happy with the vision that King had. I needed help to keep me focused and to stop me believing that I was the worldwide antidote to injustice that I clearly was not. And I needed to be able to get back out there onto the waterways and live my life to the full, enjoying the simplicity of the lifestyle and meeting all those fascinating people that I still hadn't encountered.

"Which now leads me to raise a question or two with you.", King stood up and paced around the room as he spoke, "You see, I think the time is right now for us to begin our operations and, since we are all gathered here, I want to throw something into the hat for us to discuss."

He paused and walked over to the window, seeming to lose himself as he stared out across the water, although we knew him well enough to know that he was merely gathering his thoughts.

"I have a friend,", he began, "and when I say that, it's not a euphemism. I have a very close friend who is facing a manslaughter charge. In short, his wife, also a very good friend, was wasting away with MS and asked him to assist her in committing suicide. He did it and I know that he did it because of how much he loved her. But the law is the law. His actions were illegal and the Crown has a strong case against him. Thoughts so far?"

"Surely that's wrong,", Charlotte said, Adam nodding agreement with her as she spoke, "after all she was going to die anyway and it was her choice to commit suicide. He only assisted her. They can't prosecute him for that."

"Anyone else?", King asked.

"Okay,", I replied, making sure that I took my time to frame my response carefully, "from my side, and you may think me a tad heartless in this, I have to come down on the Crown's side and say that the law must be upheld. Yes, there are moral issues here and yes, there may be a case for the law to be changed over time, through the correct channels, but, he broke the existing law and that's the simple fact."

"An interesting difference of opinion.", King said, "Do you want to add anything James?"

"It's not really my thing, I have to say,", he answered, "but my gut feeling is that I would go with Charlotte on the morality but Steve on the legality. I know that's fence-sitting but I couldn't decide either way."

64

"Hey, that's fine," King replied, "and I probably stand closer to you than either of the others, but here's my next question. Is this something that we should be involved with as a team looking to deliver justice?"

"I vote no," I answered immediately, "It may be unjust but we cannot be above the law."

The other three debated for several minutes, during which time I stood up and made myself a coffee, whilst King flipped on his mobile and checked through e-mails.

"I think that we have decided," Adam spoke for the group, "And we think we have to agree with Steve. We don't agree on his viewpoint, but, we have to respect the law. We need to see what the verdict is and trust that a jury deliver both the right verdict and, more importantly, the right request for sentencing."

"I'm glad you've said that," King replied, "as I agree with you too. We must let the law run its course and trust in the system as best we can. Of course, behind the scenes, I am working with groups that want to change the law on assisted suicide but until that day happens we need to let the law prevail."

"Which," he continued, "brings me on to another topic. What do we think of this one? You have probably read in the papers or heard on the news about the Central Shires National Health Service Trust. Yes?"

We nodded.

"Good. In summary, poor practice at this Trust saw the unnecessary deaths of at least a dozen patients, mainly through infections, but also through lazy practice. Preventable infections and preventable mistakes in treatment, as determined by the board that was convened to investigate and which concluded that the Trust was guilty of gross negligence. The action called for and recently taken was to disband the Trust. In effect, the Trust was guilty of manslaughter and its sentence was death. Now, note my use of the word, manslaughter. Ring any bells?"

He waited whilst his statement settled on us, then continued:

"My friend charged with manslaughter for helping his suffering wife to end her life. An NHS Trust terminated after causing the death of many more people than my friend. Is that justice in action?"

"Surely it is," Adam replied, "since the Trust is now disbanded and replaced by a new one. What else could they do?"

"What else indeed," King spoke cryptically, "since the perpetrator, the Trust, has been terminated. But, an NHS Trust is not an entity in its own right. It is a creation that has its being and does what it does under a leadership team. Who is guilty in this instance, the amorphous body of the Trust, or the team behind the Trust? I contend that it is the team. None of whom have faced prosecution and all of whom continue to operate in senior roles within the NHS. Legal, yes, but just, no."

And that's why we agreed to the course of action that we did. I was released back into the field and King departed to see Tony and Kate's baby christened. The rest of the crew stayed at the marina, James and Charlotte working together to set up some very specific search tools and Adam, to put the finishing touches to his latest creations. Of course, before we went our separate ways, I was presented with my new companion who accompanied me out through Staffordshire and down towards that big old canal that led to London.

Chapter Ten

'The Aberdeen Advertiser', 16th April, 2024

'Grampian NHS Trust Dismisses Two Directors'

The Board of Trustees of the Grampian NHS Trust has confirmed that two of its senior Directors were dismissed earlier this week, but has refused to comment on the details of their departure. Colin Fallow, Financial Director, and Philip Watson, Procurement Director, were last seen by staff yesterday evening as they left the premises of Aberdeen General Hospital carrying several boxes of personal files.

It is understood by this newspaper that they left the country earlier today on a flight to Spain leaving the Trust in some disarray.

The two directors were close colleagues and had joined the Grampian Trust six months ago, having previously worked together for the now disbanded, Central Shires Trust in England. Although both men have courted a certain amount of controversy in their pursuit of cost savings, the last comment made by the Grampian Trust, just two weeks ago, was that they were "...delighted and impressed with the results that our new directors have been able to achieve in a very short time, and we believe that additional savings will be made to further improve resources available for patient care."

Hospital sources have denied that the actions taken by the Board are a response to an increase in the prevalence of antibiotic-resistant viruses within the Trust's units, as reported by this newspaper last week.

Such infections were one of the main reasons that the Central Shires Trust was disbanded, and this situation leaves unanswered, certain concerns about patient safety.

++++++

'Macclesfield Star', 25th April, 2024

'Local Manufacturer Closes Doors'

Workers from 'Power Chemical Solutions' are reeling from the shock of the business's abrupt closure earlier this week. On arriving for work last Tuesday, they were confronted with locked gates and a short note pinned to the front door of the office block advising them that the business had ceased trading, with immediate effect. Police called to the factory affected an entry to the unit, only to find that it had been emptied of any items of value, although the manufacturing equipment remained in place. Due to the hazardous nature of some of the products involved, local environmental health officers have begun the process of making the factory secure and rendering any potentially toxic substances safe.

Since the closure, there has been no word from PCS's Managing Director, Edward Barnes, whose house has been emptied and put on the market, although a neighbour was able to confirm that several vans had arrived late last Monday night and Barnes had been seen supervising the loading of his possessions onto these vehicles.

This factory closure has come out of the blue and is a major blow to the local economy as Power Chemical Solutions was one of the town's expanding businesses. Speculation is rife about the reasons for Barnes's sudden departure, although it is understood that he may have been removed from the lists of NHS approved suppliers. Several months ago, the business struggled to fight back after its products were cited in the failures of the Central Shires Trust, but it seems that this time there will be no recovery.

++++++

Charlotte and James had been able to work quickly on this first stage of our new project. There were ten directors that we had identified who, as a group, had formed the core of the Central Shires NHS Trust. We knew where they all were and what they were now doing. With that information and some of James' smart search software, points of reference were quickly cross-correlated and the link between Fallow and Watson firmly established. Work on pursuing the others would take a little longer, since nothing immediate sprang out of these searches, but these two had been a little lax in covering their tracks. That may have been a function of their being lovers as well as colleagues or it may just have been an indicator of their arrogance after walking away from the Central Shires affair with six-figure payoffs. Either way, they were easy game for James and Charlotte who infiltrated their various business and personal emails and quickly established that they were receiving substantial payments from Power Chemical Supplies in return for their recommending the use of that company's products. It was true that the face-value cost of the product was way below that of the nearest rival, but this masked the fact that, in order for it to be as effective as alternatives, it required additional staff input. Since that cost had been shifted towards the personnel budget, Fallow and Watson could claim huge savings.

Sadly, the additional labour hours were not forthcoming to support the product's use and this had been the cause of increased infections across the two Trusts. Of course, with hospitals being a complex construction of multiple elements revolving around sick people, it was never an easy task to pinpoint any single cause as being uniquely life-threatening. For that reason, and by our calculations, four people had died as a direct result of the incorrect use of Power Chemical Solution's products. In this case, that was an average of two per director at a minimum, which we agreed justified our actions. Fallow and Watson would never work in the NHS again and had been fortunate to escape police prosecution after our report to the Board of Trustees in Aberdeen. We had left it up to the Trust to decide their course of action. Behind the scenes however, we had done our own rebalancing of justice and had emptied out the bank accounts of both directors. When we had been advised that they were in the process of clearing their desks, we had couriers deliver them a couple of plane tickets pinned to a Righteous Correction disc with their names engraved on the rear. An eye for an eye would have been their own infection and death, but we wanted to be a little more sophisticated these days and so, having established that they were motivated by money, we deprived them of their first love.

Since it was important for us to ensure that there could be no repeat of this particular situation, and since justice demanded it, the logical next step was to destroy the source of the problem. Barnes was advised of the termination of his NHS approval by an email that had generated itself after James ran one of his magic viruses through the national procurement database and flagged up PCS as a supplier to avoid. He would just have been reeling from the shock of this when the virus came into his own systems and wiped all of his data, whilst simultaneously rendering his manufacturing equipment worthless. The J for Justice logo preceded a summary message to him, advising that he should make a swift exit. On arriving home that evening, he too would find an RC disc with his own name engraved on the back.

It was always distressing when there was any collateral damage from our work and we felt for the employees of PCS who were innocent victims in this situation. There was no easy solution and, given that PCS products were simply not up to spec, we couldn't allow the business to continue trading. That said, King was able to tap into his network of contacts and we were comfortable that the majority of staff would soon have alternative employment.

I read up on all of this as I cruised slowly towards London. Of the eight remaining members of the Central Shires team, I had been given four to target, none of whom could be reached effectively from a remote position. They were scattered about the country, but in such a way that I could make the necessary interventions if I took a circuitous route towards the capital. This wasn't a short-term project and would need a lot of careful planning if we were to properly confirm guilt and execute the appropriate justice. I was allowing six months, but if it took longer then so be it, after all, I was back where I wanted to be now and loving every minute of being a water gypsy again.

The morning that I'd left the marina had been a proper whisky-cold morning. One of those mornings when the chill is so intense that, despite the fact that you knew it was so very wrong, only a shot of whisky was enough to take the aching cold away. That had been several weeks ago. Since then, I'd retraced my steps through a number of the old haunts and had even passed by the house in Weston that Fran and I had once called home. There was a boat moored at the bottom of the garden and I waved to the fresh-faced couple who were tending our old rose beds as I passed.

"Make the most of it," I wanted to say to them, "and treasure every moment while you can."

Needless to say, I changed this to a simple greeting and continued my cruise down towards Great Haywood and then on towards the Coventry Canal. It was nice to have some sort of a purpose to my journey but it was a lot nicer to be under little time pressure. No longer did I panic at the thought of all that could be going on out there in the world whilst I was idle, since I was merely the smallest part of a very big and complex whole. If I knew specifically that my leisurely pace was putting more lives in danger then I would up the game, but it wasn't like that anymore.

Yes, we would exact a correction on the rest of the guilty parties in the Central Shires affair, but meanwhile we had to trust that we had eliminated the most urgent threat by destroying PCS. The rest of our actions would be considered and timely, and they would be a team effort. It might even be that I picked up a message one day to advise that the others had done the work for me. No more was I the indispensable vanguard. No more did I have to carry the weight of injustice upon my shoulders. The truth of it was that I had placed that weight on myself anyway in vainly fooling myself that I was something that I wasn't. I could live with that. I would do my little bit and enjoy my life as best I could, doing what most satisfied me.

And I was no longer alone in my travels. Thanks to Adam, I now had Gilly to accompany me. Despite the fact that she was no more a genuine dog than were the shoes on my feet, she was proving to be a great companion. Imagine, if you will, the sort of dog that toy manufacturers would construct as the perfect cuddly toy for a child, and you begin to understand what Gilly looked like. She was based on a mix of numerous breeds including Staffordshire Bull Terrier, Otter Hound, Fox Terrier, and several others, and had been chosen from over a thousand proposals that Adam had seen generated on his computer screen. When Gilly had popped up, he'd

71

immediately stopped the programme running and hit the save button. She was everything he would want from a dog and she was also the perfect size for a boat. Not only had Adam given me the most beautiful canine companion, but he had also ensured that her programming made her the most loveable and delightful friend I could have. That intangible quality of dogs is something more than their breeding. It is their unquestioning devotion, loyalty and love that make them more than what they happen to look like. Adam had captured this canine essence perfectly. How? I would never know. Perhaps she was the sum of collected data and the pinnacle of what that defined as perfection. Or somehow, he'd managed to capture and compute the invisible spirit we all saw in creatures that were more than simply another animal.

She was anatomically perfect and fully functioning in all but one area, which was that, whilst she drank water and passed it in public, making her seem like the real thing, she didn't eat and consequently I was spared the need to follow her around with pooh bags. The secret of Gilly's true identity had to be kept at all costs and Adam had figured that this would require at least a modicum of bodily functions to be witnessed. Allowing her to take on fluids meant that she had a natural suppleness and that her nose was wet and her eyes glistened. Refreshing that water made sense and to do so meant a means of losing the old fluids. If I was with somebody, they would think it strange that a dog didn't want to wee to mark its territory or simply relieve itself, however, they would assume that I had dealt with the matter of solids at another time.

Even so, early on in our relationship, I rapidly came to think of Gilly less and less as a machine and more and more as my own pet. She didn't need charging up as she had a heart that maintained its beat through a new generation battery that would last twenty years. She did have an off switch though. As I'd told Adam when he first presented her to me, I couldn't commit to the care that a dog needed, but being able to switch her off meant that I could bypass this concern. Funnily enough, since leaving the marina, I hadn't used that facility at all. She remained with me at all times, bonding with me and learning to see me as her master, and keeping me warm at night as she snuggled under the duvet with me.

When we cruised, she joined me on the deck, leaning over the gunnels and staring intently at whatever we passed by. At locks, she sat on the sofa and watched me through the windows and at pubs, she sat on my knee and watched the world go by, sniffing and licking anybody who passed by and fell in love with her. No longer did I have to take a book with me to the pub. Gilly was now my excuse for a walk and the support that I needed to ensure that I didn't look out of place whilst supping a pint or two. And she was the perfect icebreaker when I met new people. Some had dogs of their own, some didn't. The former ones were amazed at how gently Gilly would play with their pets, even if it was one those nervy dogs that was usually afraid of others. The latter ones either chose to enjoy petting a dog they didn't have time to keep at home, or they ignored her as she slept and we talked. I was smoking a lot less now, so that bond with fellow nicotine addicts had loosened considerably and I couldn't hide behind it as much. Gilly was a much healthier replacement.

Chapter Eleven

I was in a good place by the time I'd reached Huddlesford Junction. The erratic month of April was over and, in its place, was the merry month of May with all her promises of long days and sunny escapes. That feeling of wellbeing was further enhanced when I flashed my Crystal Clear credentials and was allowed to cruise the first five miles of the new Lichfield Canal that had been put into water only in the last month or so. Jason King had been instrumental in making this happen. The team who'd pushed and worked so hard for the past thirty-six years had struggled against so many obstacles that they were beginning to wonder whether they would ever see their dream realised. But then King had begun to get obsessively interested in all things canal related and the situation had changed. It was a no-brainer really. The derelict Lichfield Canal cut right across the existing loop of cruising rings and cried out to be revived. With King's involvement, money was no longer a concern and, more importantly, his connections ensured that this became a priority urban regeneration scheme. From his side, his motives were a mixture of philanthropy and commercial opportunism. He already had the rights to the new marina secured and was busy buying up the pubs that would be within walking distance of this revived waterway.

After winding the boat at the current terminus of the navigable part of the canal, I moored up for the evening and drank in the peace and tranquillity of the surrounding countryside. One day soon, this would be a rare luxury, although it would still be as enjoyable when boats were moving back and forward between here and Hatherton. I wanted to be one of the first to make that journey and had even planned long into the future and reserved a retirement plot for myself in a piece of canal-side woodland. It was currently dank, vandalised and overgrown, but I saw it as I would have it in time, with the boat moored up at the front and a small cabin set amongst the trees.

The following morning, I woke early and continued with the steady research that I was doing on the Central Shires project. Unless I heard differently or discovered additional information, my first point of action was to be somewhere near Oxford which I would pass through on my way to London. I read the catch-up memos from Charlotte with interest and noted any key points that were relevant to me. The team at the marina had agreed that they would avoid the usual slurry of emails detailing every moment of action and copied to everyone who might have a slight interest in the subject. They collated data, assessed its value, agreed the content and, only then, did they hit the send button to update King and myself. They had the targets properly identified now and had thinned out those board members who were culpable from the original ten to a more manageable eight. They explained their reasoning and I confirmed my agreement to this.

Of those eight, two had already been taken out of the picture and their funds directed into a holding account that we had prepared for the victims of the Trust's negligence. I was being asked to look at the former Human Resources Director, a certain Hugo Blain, who was now in a very comfortable position performing the same role in one of the many colleges that made up Oxford University. For now, we were struggling to identify the precise nature of his misdemeanours but were trawling carefully through the records and had established a pattern of work that we felt might lead us somewhere. Meanwhile, I had a life to live and a journey to continue and so, with Gilly beside me on the deck, I set off back towards Huddlesford where I would join the team for a King-funded lunch at the canal-side Plough Inn.

Spirits were high and the atmosphere buzzing as we enjoyed a long and leisurely lunch which inevitably became an into-the-evening drinking session. The original group of volunteers who had begun the vision for reinstating the old canal had dwindled to only a few surviving members, but they had been joined every year by new enthusiasts who were keen to keep that vision alive. Since I was linked with Jason King, there was an element of respect and authority afforded to me which I didn't deserve and which I spent all my time trying to downplay.

"This meal," I told them, electing to make a small speech before the food arrived, "is a thank you from Mr King and I can honestly say that it is my privilege to join you here. I've just cruised the length of canal that is ready so far and I can't wait to make the full journey one day soon. To the original volunteers, I think we all owe a huge debt of gratitude. You battled on to win this waterway back a yard at a time, whilst all around you, billions of pounds were being frittered away on infrastructure projects that could never have the same impact as this short stretch of canal. You exemplify the volunteer spirit that is such a backbone of our country. You carried on in silent dedication and you kept the faith against all the cynical voices that tried to bring you down. Very soon, this waterway will be complete and that is not because Jason King made it happen. It is because you prepared the ground and made it possible for him to help you. Which leads me to my real reason for coming here. Mr King has asked me to communicate to you that every mile of this new waterway will be dedicated and named after that original group of volunteers. On top of that, and since there are more of you than there are miles of canal, he has pledged that every lock will bear one of your names. I know that you are not doing this to be recognised, but your contribution will be celebrated and marked for all the generations to come."

I sat down to a round of applause and tucked into my whitebait starter. This had become my measure of a good pub just lately, although I could bend my own rules if I had to and forego the whitebait for a decent spread of real ales and, of course, the pub being dog-friendly.

"Will we get to meet Mr King soon?", Tom Fielder, the current Works Manager, asked me, "Because I have to say that he intrigues us all."

"Oh,", I replied, "he'll turn up at some point. Just keep looking up and when you see a helicopter, it's likely to be him. He tends to be a bit spontaneous about visits and he doesn't always know when he'll be around. You're right though, he is a man of mystery a lot of the time. I've only known him a short time but he exudes this wonderful feeling of calm and authority, yet does so without any of the arrogance that you might expect. He's no saint, I'll grant you that, but if there were a few more like him then we would all be a lot better off."

"But, enough of that,", I continued, "tell me a little more about progress to date and please, introduce me to the rest of the gang."

Having lit the blue touch-paper, I relaxed and drank in the tales they told me, every one of which was peppered with self-deprecating humour and a fiery passion for what they spoke of.

"Do you remember,", Tom asked the group, "that first week when we moved into the clubhouse and started to dig out the junction? What was the guy's name, the one who had the wooden boat that kept sinking?"

"Oh, Billy Roberts.", replied one of the group, an elderly stick of a man whose beard looked like it had last been trimmed at the turn of the century and whose name I cannot for the life of me recall just now, "We all remember Billy. And his boat of course. I was there when that boat went down for the last time. It had to be held together with nothing but good luck but he wouldn't have any of it. 'She'll be good for another season', he'd say. But on that last occasion, he'd woken up with the hull, or what was left of it, balancing on the bottom of the cut and the first we knew was when we heard him puffing and straining to pump out the bilge with that old hand pump of his. I can see him now, pyjama trousers rolled up and whistling away as he waited for her to re-float."

"That's right", another elderly voice joined the conversation, "it was the middle of Winter and he looked as blue as a Tory. Luckily, the ice helped us slide the thing out into the undergrowth, but he still stood there looking at her and your right, 'She'll be good for another season', was all he could say. Needless to say, she wasn't. Mind you, he got cracking on that old work boat straightaway and had her liveable within a week."

"That's your baby now, isn't it?", he continued, addressing one of the young lads who had been recruited to line the new canal, "How's she fairing?"

"She's good", he replied, "A little bit on the basic side but she does for me. In fact, I think I can safely say, she'll be good for another season!"

And so it went on, the old and the young sharing small victories and humiliating failures and all the time bonding in that way that no amount of forced bonhomie can ever recreate. I was in my element here. They told tales of digging up World War Two weapons and they compared scars. They remembered those who had passed on and they welcomed to the fold all of the newcomers including myself. To the outside world this was one of a million such get-togethers in a million similar locations, but to me it was the vibrant present and a reminder that pleasure was to be found in the small things and in the company of others.

I excused myself and took Gilly into the beer garden for a comfort break, opting to stay out there and puff my way through a few cigarettes before returning to the group. I was getting a bit too old for all those pints and these were guys who couldn't just drink me under the table, they could drink me to my grave.

With Gilly sat on my lap, I looked out over the canal, just catching the stern of my own boat but more interested in seeing what this place would be like in a few years' time. It would be a lot busier and the sound of boats attempting the right-angled turn onto the new canal would break the silence that only the nearby road currently did. But with that activity would come jobs and local regeneration. The canal would be alive again and we would be supplying a lot of the boats that traversed it.

"You alright, lad?", I was snapped back into the present by the voice of Tom Fielder, "You seemed to be miles away."

"Sorry,", I replied, resettling Gilly on my lap and watching her give the visitor a wary stare, "I was just thinking about how this place will change."

"Nothing wrong with that,", he laughed, "as they say in my native Yorkshire, there's nowt so certain as constant change. We're looking forward to it. All the work we've done hasn't been to keep the place all to ourselves. No, we've got to pass it on to the next generation and let it support them. That your boat there?"

I told him it was and, as usual when two boaters meet, we compared notes and bandied insults about shiny brasses and how wrong electric propulsion was. His own boat made mine look like something ready for the scrapyard, but he wasn't snooty about it. When I showed him inside, his opinion changed a little, although I could tell that it all looked a bit too modern for his taste. Then it was time for us to return to the group and continue the celebration of the work to date. Musical instruments were hurriedly gathered off nearby boats and an impromptu concert begun that ranged from traditional boating folk-songs to some very near to the knuckle contributions that managed to rhyme words that I hadn't even heard of. At some point in the early evening, I called it a day and fell into the boat, just about making it to the bed before the heaviness of a drunken sleep took me far away from reality. Not a bad day, all told.

Chapter Twelve

It seems that I always have to face a call to action whilst nursing a hangover. Either that's just bad luck on my part or, more likely, that I wake up with a hangover more often than I should. It was the bleeping from my ex-ORB communications system that dragged me back into the world with such force.

"Yes?", I answered the call with my head in my arms.

"Steve, it's Adam. Need you to help us out if possible. You're out near Coventry just now?"

"Not too far away,", I replied, "you should have me at Huddlesford. Look, can you give me ten minutes to grab a shower and get some coffee? I'll call you back on this line."

I didn't give him time to answer. My head felt like it was ready to explode and I needed caffeine to function at this time in the morning. I left the coffee machine burbling away and let the shower get to work on me. Ten minutes later I was back on the line to Adam.

"Okay,", I said, "now give it to me slowly and remember, my brain still needs to warm up. But, before we start, this is an agreed action, right?"

"Absolutely, man,", he replied, "King's been informed already and Charlotte and James have been working on it for the past few hours. So, here's the deal. It looks like the whole Central Shires Trust thing runs a lot deeper than we first thought. And it leads to some very dark places."

"Go on."

"Right, let me give you the overview first of all. We're checking all the links and the data that we can get our hands on, and James realises that something is missing. In short, even from the incomplete data that we've pulled together so far, the whole that we are constructing looks very different to the official line."

"So, the report's a whitewash?", I asked.

"Exactly man.", he replied, "It's early days yet, but there are too many anomalies between our findings to make any sense when you read the officially published summary. And if we're right on this, I don't need to tell you the implications."

"No, you don't," I replied, "I can see them as clear as crystal even in my foggy state. The problems with the Trust were greater than we could imagine and the cover-up reaches right up to Whitehall and maybe beyond?"

"Spot-on again," Adam concurred, "and man, what it means for us is that we are about to open one serious can of worms. But open it we can, and we must."

"Are we certain of this though?", I asked, "I mean, as you say, we are about to enter some dangerous territory here, what's the detail so far?"

He explained to me how they had reached the conclusions that they had. It had all started with the Chair of the Board of Governance and the chain of events that her life followed just prior to the report's publication. Although an ex-nurse, she was technically a member of the public and performed her role as Chair for a small remuneration plus expenses. It was the tracking of these expenses by one of James' search engines that threw up the first query. Just prior to the enquiry being made public, she had resigned from the Board and received a substantial payment as, what we assumed to be, some sort of settlement. More worryingly though, she was still being sent a five-figure sum every month from a carefully disguised NHS slush fund. Then there were the reported findings. Our knowledge of what Fallow and Watson had been doing was as complete as we believed it to be, but it didn't correlate with the report's findings that '...in finance and procurement, every effort was made to control spending and minimise waste, however, the efficacy of supplies of alternative cleaning materials in particular was taken too much at face value...'.

In other words, the team responsible for the deficiencies of the trust were deemed to be innocent victims, acting to the best of their ability. This was echoed in the report's comments on the HR department and Blain's culpability which they described as '...an honest, if misguided, attempt to utilise finite personnel budgets to deliver the most cost-effective outcomes.'. He gave me a few more examples but I was already convinced.

"So, how do we prove this?", I asked.

"We think you need to go after the Chair.", he replied, "Her name's Margaret Miller and that's the Coventry link. But, you need to move quickly because it seems like our searches are stirring up some activity. Our hope is that it's simply a wariness after the departure of Fallow and Watson, but our suspicion is that the more we are looking into this affair, the more eyes are looking back at us."

"Added to which," he continued, "we have travel documents listed for Miller and her partner, indicating that they intend to leave the country on an extended holiday very soon. That doesn't fit with her profile either. She had extensive debts prior to her pay off, but since that time has only ever holidayed in the UK. In fact, the reason I think she is still in the country now is that she is waiting for a passport. We've hit the system to delay that as much as possible because we can't just see it as a coincidence. If it is man, it's a hell of big one."

"I agree," I said, "she has to be the starting point. What are we thinking, that she threatened to blow the whistle on the whole situation and was paid off?"

"Our thoughts precisely man," Adam replied, "or she was complicit from the start. Either way, now they want her out of the picture in case someone tries to sniff around. Or because they know someone is sniffing around."

"And has James found anything?" I asked.

"That's part of the problem," he answered, "you see, this woman is using computers that go back to the ark and keeping her records on floppy discs. James can't get close enough to the system to find anything out. Besides, we can't be sure that she's got any records there."

"But the records exist?", I responded.

"There must be something," he replied, "or at least we hope there is, because if there isn't, I don't know where we go."

I thought about this for a while, trying to think of alternative routes to access the information we needed. I agreed that if, as the evidence seemed to point to, she was being paid to keep quiet, it made sense that she had an insurance policy of sorts in the form of written records. We had to believe that, because if she didn't we were hitting a brick wall.

"You still there, man?", Adam's voice bought me back to the present.

"Yeah, sorry, just thinking," I said, "We need to act as if the records exist. But I need time to think of how to get hold of them. I presume you want me to visit Ms Miller and I also presume that she is based in Coventry?"

"You got it man," he laughed, "guess that's why you're the man, man. But hang fire where you are because I've got a package on its way to you. It'll be at the clubhouse by ten. Full instructions included. Meanwhile, I'll send you over the data files so far and all the gen on Miller. I've planned a route for you but if it doesn't work then go with your gut on this one. Look, got to go now man, we'll be in touch."

He cut the line before I could say goodbye which, had he been anyone else would have felt like an insult, but I knew him well enough by now to know that it meant that he had bigger and more important fish to fry.

Sure enough, the parcel arrived by ten and I took it back to the boat. In the meantime, I'd sent various requests for data to James and Adam and received answers back, plus a perfectly acceptable route plan that I fully intended to follow. I covered for myself at the clubhouse by telling them that the parcel was an important document that I needed to work on so if they could leave me alone in the boat that would be much appreciated. With the inside of the boat set up to look like this was just what I was doing, I slipped away using the underwater pod that detached from below the boat's waterline and began my latest mission, heading underwater towards Fazeley Junction then up towards Tamworth where I had to leave the water and take an alternative means of transport. That's where Adam's delivery would come into play and, apprehensive as I always was when trying out something new, I was excited as well, and confident that it would work as he said it would. Well, fairly confident anyway.

Margaret Miller lived in a nondescript bungalow in a nondescript suburb of Coventry. In the driveway sat a fairly new car, equally as nondescript. I arrived there quicker than I had expected and in one piece, although I was still trying to calm myself after the hairy experience that Adam's new toy had put me through. The piece of kit that he had sent me was a complicated vest that strapped around the waist of my suit and which I now took off and hid in the small patch of woodland that I'd discovered, about two hundred yards from the boundary of Miller's property. On leaving the water, I had let the pod sink out of sight, then walked the short distance to the railway line that ran through Tamworth and into Coventry. There was a cutting nearby that preceded a bridge and it was here that I had stationed myself. When the scheduled train passed by, I broke cover, pressed the launch button on the vest and braced myself as it threw me towards the passing carriages before slotting me into a coupling space where it activated the magnets that would hold me there. It was all over in a couple of seconds but it felt a lot longer. So much of what I did with the guys required a huge amount of trust, but this situation pushed that trust to the limit.

82

As we neared Coventry, the vest detached itself at the prearranged spot and I was back on the ground just a short walk away from my destination. Adam had definitely come through this time and that vest was something that I could certainly use again, although I'd still prefer to buy a first-class ticket whenever possible.

Waiting under the cover of the trees, I began the next stage of my plan, putting through a call to my target as I painstakingly edged closer to her home. The phone rang several times before she picked it up:

"Hello."

"Margaret, it's Sir Gordon," the voice was a perfect replica of the Central Shires Trust's former CEO and came through my mouthpiece courtesy of files that James had extracted off the web, "are you free to talk?"

"Yes, of course, Sir Gordon," she replied cautiously, "is everything okay? We haven't spoken for a long time."

"I'm afraid we have a problem," I cut to the chase, wanting to panic Miller into action, "and I need you to help us out one last time. I understand that you are going away soon but we need any copies of records that you have. We'll pay, of course, but I can't stress enough that it's in your own interest to provide them. We know you have your own notes on file. Are you able to supply these? Once again, please understand how urgent this is. It seems that the whole Shires report is about to be blown apart."

There was silence on the line as Margaret Miller thought about what to do. This was no easy decision for her and I could tell that she was weighing up her options, not just because of the pause, but because I could also now see her through the eyes of the heron that watched and heard everything that was happening in the bungalow. Not that it would arouse any suspicion, perched as it was with eyes seeming to be focused on the surface of the small pond in her garden.

"We said that it would never come to this," she finally spoke, "and if I go with it, what security am I left with?"

"I know," Sir Gordon replied, "but things change. You can take the chance if you want, but I'm offering you a further lump sum, guaranteed, and I hope that we can bury what we know. You may strike lucky, but I'd advise you to go with my concrete offer. The people who are looking into this are relentless and if I don't free you from what you have, then they will be less generous in the means they use. Seems they cleaned Fallow and Watson out. So, is it a deal?"

"Okay," she agreed more quickly than I expected, possibly afraid of losing all she had stashed away over the years, "I'll do it. Truth is, I want to be free of this whole thing anyway. Same bank account and, one last thing, where's Charlie fishing?"

Now that almost threw me completely off guard, but from somewhere deep inside me, coming through on a memory of late nights lying with Fran and listening to Paul Temple on the radio, I was able to summon up the correct response.

"By the Thames.", I answered in Sir Gordon's voice, "Now, if we are good to go, I'll send someone around in the next half-hour."

"That's fine.", she replied, "I'll get the file together, and good luck with it. Don't let me down on the payment though. I do have other inside information to share if I have to."

As I finished the call, I watched as a fleet of my spiders worked through the locks that held the kitchen door, the heron continuing to monitor Miller as she lifted up a section of carpet in her bedroom and began the process of extracting the disc that contained the files.

Using the floating abilities of the Kingfisher suit, I let it drift silently into the house, reaching up to open a small window as it moved closer to the target. I placed a tiny silver disc on the window-sill before confirming that Miller had retrieved the files we needed and making my appearance known.

"Please don't panic.", I used the softest voice setting in the helmet to reassure Margaret Miller, "I am not going to harm you."

I'd caught her just after she had placed the floppy disc containing the data that I wanted on the sideboard, before settling herself into a flowery armchair. She instinctively grabbed for the disc and managed to snare it before I could take possession.

"I know that you are not from Sir Gordon.", she said, remarkably calmly as she waved the disc at me, "so I am assuming that you are here to steal this?"

"Steal is such a nasty word.", I replied, "but yes, I need to take possession of those files."

"And if I don't give them up?"

"I don't think we will get to that stage.", I replied confidently, "You know that you're not the guilty party in all this and I believe that you will see reason. You can keep the money you already have. We aren't interested in retrieving the money in your case. But, the truth must be

84

allowed to come out. You know that, don't you? Even if only for Jennifer's sake."

"You leave Jennifer out of this.", she stared at me with pure hatred.

"But isn't that what it was all about?", I stayed calm as I let her stare back at herself through the mirrored visor of the helmet, "Jennifer's the reason you chose to blow the whistle. You watched her die in that hospital and you knew that it was only because they had cut corners and allowed her to get infected. Friends from primary school, surely that still means something?"

"And,", I continued, "nobody can blame you for taking the thirty pieces that they offered you. Sure, it stayed the hand of the regulators and left some very unsavoury people to carry on regardless, but I know how all that works. You didn't have a choice, did you?"

I watched as she fingered the piece of antiquated computer hardware and stared off into space.

"No, you're right.", she whispered, "Even if I'd refused the exit route they gave me, they would still have found a way. I wanted to do what's right, but I realised I was fighting bigger forces than I imagined. I had the debts and I was worried about my retirement. They offered the solution and I couldn't resist it. I know it wasn't right but how wrong was it?"

"I'm not here to judge you,", I moved closer to her, "but we need to tell the world what's been happening. Please, the files."

"Oh, take them,", she said, handing me the disc, "they've been nothing but a curse to me."

I thanked her and was just about to pocket the disc when I saw her face change and caught the beginnings of a wicked smile develop on her lips.

"These are the files?", I asked warily.

"Oh, yes, they are the originals, my first testimony,", she paused and began to laugh, "but you will never get to use them."

"Sorry?", I was beginning to worry now.

"Well,", she settled back in the chair and smiled patronisingly at me, "I suppose I should fill in the blanks for you. You see, I'm not as innocent as you may think. I'm not the victim that you seem to have me marked down as. I've been part of the dark side of this for a long time. Yes, I exposed the lesser evils and yes, I did it because I was gutted about Jennifer. But I didn't do it as secretly as you imagine. Sir Gordon and I go back a long way. We have a very special relationship. Getting the information together that I put on that file was my slap in the face to them for hurting my Jennifer, but I couldn't destroy them. I would say to you that you can check further back on the records and you'll see that I've been a part of the whole corrupt thing for many years, but you aren't going to have that chance."

"What do you mean?", I no longer let the helmet's voice soothe her.

"You really are an innocent little darling, aren't you?", she laughed, "Standing there in your superhero outfit and coming to avenge justice, but not really understanding what you are up against. This thing is bigger than me and it's way bigger than you. This goes to the very top and it's been like it since the first days of the NHS. You think I stand alone?"

I watched as she reached into her jumper and slipped out the necklace that she was wearing.

"This is an emergency call button.", she said calmly, "I pressed it when I first saw you and, as you can see, it has stopped flashing now. That means this place is surrounded. You can't get away, not even with whatever tricks that suit has to help you. They'll be mustering now, waiting to come in. If you run for it, they'll gun you down. Better to wait and give in peacefully."

"You're serious?", I asked.

"Oh, deadly so.", she replied, "But don't blame yourself. As I told you, this goes back a long time. We have a minute or two, so let me just explain. This nation's beloved National Health Service is not the philanthropic marvel of the world that it's held up to be. It's a gravy train. And it's the power-monger's perfect tool. Everyone who is anyone has their snout in the trough and it's perfect because the country loves the NHS. Whatever happens with public finance, however hard times become, no politician of any colour would dare to deprive the nation's favourite child of its resources. So, it remains a cash cow to be milked and milked and milked. And the beauty of it is, that those who aren't in the power positions get their succour from being mollycoddled by a system that lets them come and be loved and drugged and reassured as often as they want it."

"That,", she continued, "is what you are fighting against, and that, is what will defeat you. Look, I hope they give you a second chance and all that, but I can't speak for them. Just don't resist when they come and they may go easy on you. I think that's them I hear."

Sure enough, the door hinges creaked and the curtains flew back as the building was stormed. I managed to alert the bat that used the silver disc I'd left to identify the marked window, and which swooped down, snatched the disc from my hand and exited before they were able to stop it. But there was no way that I could battle against the dozens of armed officers who swarmed into the room. The heron could see it all, but it was unarmed. The spiders had a limited bite but not against so many. I had the Blue Light but I could see straightaway that, even if I could deploy it, it wouldn't hold against whatever their own uniforms were made of. In short, this was a challenging situation.

Chapter Thirteen

To this day, I retain the recording that the heron transmitted to me as the mob approached the Kingfisher in that small bungalow. They edged closer, guns drawn and paused.

"Down on the floor!", the person I took to be their leader shouted, but I didn't respond.

"One last chance, down on the floor!", but still no movement.

"Take him!", he shouted.

A dozen bodies grabbed various parts of the suit and wrestled it to the ground. Then the smoke started and they leapt back. After the smoke, came the fire. It wasn't a flickering glow of flame but more like a burst of phosphorescent starlight. The suit melted away before their eyes and they were left staring at the mound of smouldering ash it left behind.

Meanwhile, I had retrieved the vest and my animal companions, along with the disc, and I was already heading back to the railway line on my way home. I could see that they had air support, but the woods hid me and the suit that I was wearing, the one that actually contained the real Kingfisher and which wasn't an empty shell, was able to elude any thermal imaging cameras. They could watch the air and the roads all they liked, but they were never going to track me as I attached myself to a departing train ready to disappear underwater.

Adam had come through with the vest, but his greater contribution had been the dummy suits that he had provided for me. It had been a last-minute decision of mine to go with this approach as my initial feeling was that Miller was just the person that she looked to be. Knowing about Jennifer, we thought there was a genuine motivation for her whistle-blowing, but then I'd stepped back and thought to myself that if that friendship was the reason, why had she pulled back? Those feelings were confirmed when she'd used the code-words with Sir Gordon. That confirmed to me that there was something amiss. Which meant that, as we'd met, I'd been better prepared than they'd expected.

I downloaded the file to the team as soon as I arrived back at the boat, then showered and changed into casual clothes for a quick pint at the pub. When I got back, there was a message for me to call King on his private line.

"Mr King, Sir, how are you?", I asked as he answered.

"Please, Steve, try Jason.", he answered, "And I'm fine, in fact, I'm over the moon with what you've done."

"No problem,", I said, "it was good to be back in action. The files are useful then?"

"Useful?", he laughed, "They are dynamite. And I use that word very carefully. We need to be very cautious from now on. We are up against some big names here."

He explained to me what they had discovered from the data that I'd retrieved and from their further investigations based on this new information. The original allegations weren't all damning. They vindicated another two of the directors of the Trust whom we had earmarked for action. They had apparently taken a fall for the team, which meant that we weren't interested in pursuing them anymore.

"So,", King explained, "we've already taken out Fallow and Watson. We had the Estates Director down for selling off land but now we know he didn't benefit from this. Apart that is from wanting to impress some young lady, and if we started acting every time that happened, we'd be busy to the end of time. He's off the list. As is the Operations Director. He was just punching above his weight and is now in a more junior position which he's better suited to."

"Which leaves us where?", I asked.

"We're left with six remaining of an agreed target of eight.", he replied, "Of which, you are heading towards Hugo Blain, and we trust you with that one, whilst we think we can quickly nail the Surgical Director and the Quality Manager. Are you okay with that?"

"Sounds good."

"Right, so you head off to Oxford and we'll reconvene after that one. Meanwhile, we are putting together the final pieces to work on Sir Gordon last of all. We want that one to be worthy of his position. Try and give it a little thought if you can. Would be interesting to see Kingfisher's take on it."

"Will do.", I told him.

"And finally,", he toned his voice down to a hushed whisper, "you need to be aware that this touches upon some very influential players in very high places. What I've asked the others, and what I'm asking you, is that you trust me to deliver on that side of things. I move in the right circles and I know that we can't change a system that is bigger than we'll ever be. But I will get some justice out of this, I assure you."

I agreed that I was happy to go with everything that he'd outlined and that I would tackle the Blain situation as a priority, although I would do it within the confines of my journeying along the water. I knew the others would act quickly, but Blain was in a place where he was causing little harm, if any, and I wanted to let him stew as he began to realise that things were happening to others who had links to the Central Shires Trust.

++++++

'The Sunday Spotlight, 28th April, 2024

'"You Stuff Them, I'll Stitch Them": Shame of Top Surgeon'

In a Spotlight exclusive, reporter Jean Carter exposes the hidden life of Gustav Hertz, the flamboyant and controversial surgeon, best known for developing the 'quick fix' gastric band operation. Material obtained by this newspaper blows the lid off the secret life of this senior NHS professional, and proves that he has been involved in cynically fattening up as many people as possible, in order to then offer them the life-saving surgery only he can provide.

In e-mails to the head of one of this country's largest fast food retailers, printed in full later in this edition, Hertz discusses multiple ways in which he may be able to provide opportunities for exclusive new outlets within NHS properties. As a substantial shareholder in the company, he makes no bones about his motivation for offering his services, explaining that to him it is '…a win, win, situation…'. The most damaging e-mail seems to have been written late at night when Hertz's guard was down, and describes how the

90

former Surgical Director of the, now disbanded, Central Shires NHS Trust, had successfully vetoed campaigns to improve the quality of the food provided to patients citing cost-savings to justify his standpoint. Later in that same e-mail, he writes, 'People see me as some sort of Messiah figure, able to heal them with my magic touch, and that gives them confidence in me and makes them respect my authority. Whatever you want me to get them to do, I can make them follow like sheep, so get ready to move as soon as possible because I've got a dozen hospitals lined up to let you in. And the beauty of it all is that the fatter they get idling away their time in your joints, the higher the demand for my private and NHS work to fix them up. So, go for it, you stuff them, I'll stitch them, and nobody will be the wiser.'

When presented with our findings, Hertz declined to comment and has warned our parent company of legal action for having obtained source material illegally. To set the record straight early in the game, we can confirm that Ms Carter was supplied with the dossier of evidence via an anonymous source. In line with correct protocol and on the advice of our own legal team, we have chosen to publish this material as it is now in the public domain. The source of the material is believed to be the campaign group who operate under the banner of 'J for Justice' and who seem to be gaining a huge following on the web. Although they are usually very open in revealing their findings, they allowed Ms Carter an exclusive on this story, explaining that they were a great admirer of her past works and their help in correcting the course of justice.

Full story and documents in full, pages 2-5. See also, **Comment***, p.12*

++++++

'Environmental Health Department Baffled by New Rot Case'

Local environmental health officials have admitted that they cannot establish the source of the form of fungal rot that has ravaged the home of local councillor, Peter Hill. Hill, the Quality Manager of Devon Combined Hospitals Trust, first called officials in last week when he arrived home to find that the entire contents of his house had succumbed to a fungus-like mould. Few of his possessions remained untarnished and the building was deemed unsafe as soon as the EHO's arrived on site.

Concerns have been raised that this may be a new form of airborne blight and, for that reason, the photograph below has been released in order that readers might check their own properties. Meanwhile, the mystery grew deeper when Hill took up residence in a vacant property that he was preparing to let out, as the virus seemed to follow him there. After being placed in isolation, exhaustive tests by his colleagues in the hospital trust have found no trace of any unusual bacteria that he might be carrying and he has now been allowed to leave the ward. Latest reports, still to be clarified, point to similar problems happening in the hotel room he moved into on his release from hospital.

++++++

I was loving the work that the team were doing. Not only were they getting the job done but it also seemed that they were enjoying every minute of it and James even seemed to be discovering a mischievous sense of humour that had lain dormant within him for so long.

The Hertz thing was swiftly and beautifully executed. Sadly, it gave credence to Margaret Miller's tainted view of the NHS. This was an area that we would continue to monitor and James had already begun the process of gaining access to the networks of every hospital in the country. We weren't setting out on a mission to destroy this unique and much-loved institution, but it had to be admitted that free healthcare for all was an open invite to the less scrupulous to grab their own share of the pie.

With Hill, there were a number of new dynamics at work that were reassuring. Not only was this a very witty response to the neglect that he had overseen in the Central Shires Trust, but it was also a very sophisticated attack. The virus was a development of the work that Adam and James had done in ORB. Undaunted by the devastating effects of the synthetics virus they'd created for the Order, they'd learnt from past experience and created something that was more effective, yet entirely manageable. It worked by entering whatever item it made contact with and then by disassembling that item at the atomic level. Once its work was done, it eliminated itself leaving no trace behind. All good stuff, but it was the delivery of the virus that impressed me most.

Adam and Charlotte took a day trip to Exeter by train, no doubt enjoying the personal time alone with each other. They were closer than ever now and I looked forward to the day when they would make things official, even though that was the less fashionable option for youngsters these days. On their day out, they had visited Hill's home and delivered the virus personally by dropping a container of it over the house's back wall. Transporting the virus was its only weakness. It had to be placed close enough to the source it was to attack and guided by remote control to within feet of where it was needed. It was smart enough to act from that point, but this had been the only possible means of getting it to the location. That meant that Adam and Charlotte had operated in the field for the first time and done the sort of thing that had been my exclusive province before. That was what impressed me most. I was coming to terms with the realisation that I was not as indispensable as I had once thought, and now I understood that truth even more deeply.

Their field trips would continue for a few weeks as they followed Hill around until they felt that he had learnt his lesson and until he could be advised of why he had had to suffer for his past misdemeanours. His would be short sentence, but he would be under no illusions that there would be further consequences if he didn't change his approach to his professional responsibilities.

Chapter Fourteen

Even as the full boating season kicked in, and the traffic on the canals increased from not too many boats, to a few boats more, there were plenty of times when I cruised in isolation and found myself alone with my thoughts. I am not one of those people who can listen to the radio in the background, although Heaven knows that I used to be. To this day, I retain in my head a plethora of bizarre and useless facts that are the inheritance of my time in sales when I used to drive thousands of miles a year with Radio Four playing to my subconscious. No, the simple pleasure that is enough for me is the background noise of the boat cutting the water and the varied view that changes constantly as I make my progress at three to four miles an hour.

There are distractions of course. Sometimes the ugly world above intrudes as you pass factories and motorways, and, at regular intervals, there are fellow boaters coming at you and numerous towpath users to greet and wave at. As I made slow progress to London, via Oxford, it got a little busier, but the weather was in my favour. That had to be the top distraction that May. It started raining on the first and there wasn't a single dry day for the rest of the month. Now, I don't mind rain. It's only water and without it I wouldn't have the home that I have. But there is rain and there is rain. Proper rain is the stuff that catches up on you and comes flooding down in an hour-long torrent then passes by, leaving behind a residue of water that steams away under the sun that follows it. The rain of that May was a steady drizzle. It was the sort of weather that even when it wasn't properly wet, was still plain dull and depressing.

I felt sorry for the people who'd hired boats at this time and who were now battling to keep to their schedules as even the bright yellow waterproof's that came with the boat were beginning to act like sponges. They'd tie up at night and, after executing a speedy and makeshift mooring, would either hunker down in front of the boat's fire, or make a swift change of clothes and dash to the nearest pub. At locks, they kept their heads down against the steady spray of rain and stalwartly accepted that there was no rushing on the waterways. We were all in this together and there was no point in complaining. Not that many of them did. Despite my sympathy for their plight, they were generally having a great time and the rain was simply adding to the earthiness of their experience. Canals did that to you. They made you accept nature's fickle moods as the option to hide away from it all simply wasn't there.

With all this going on around me and my own reconnecting to the life-away-from-life that I lived on the boat, I was able to put some of the madness of my other life to one side and refresh the spirit that yearned to be at peace in me. My thoughts strayed into anything and everything, from the personal to the profound, and I opened my eyes again to what was happening around me, eschewing newspapers and other media, and only finding out from the team about the mission's progress via their weekly updates. The world out there would survive without me and it didn't need me to blog my opinion or comment on a news story to help it along. Even on the rare occasions that I was in a pub and overheard a conversation discussing either righteous correction or, more likely, the increasingly popular J for Justice movement, I was able to stay distanced. Yes, they were at the heart of me, but their heart was beyond me. I was a part of a bigger thing, but the bigger thing was more important than my part in it. In many ways, it was refreshing to be able to stay silent and try to reach for that place of humility that King so highly recommended.

When I read up about Hertz, my thoughts were primarily on the resolution that had been achieved by the team, but they also strayed to the author of the press articles. I hadn't forgotten Jean any more than I had forgotten Fran and the children. But, like the pain of my bereavement, the pain of my loss of Jean had been managed, controlled, subdued and stored away. That was until it rattled at the locks that held it in and demanded to be heard.

Jean and I had been in love. I now realised that. Our love was a fleeting moment of pleasure that was stopped in its tracked and which we both had to accept could never be resumed. It had been a soft and pleasant love, not the school-child madness of the young. And it had been an all-embracing and comforting love which truly satisfied. When I'd last seen her, the implants that ORB had fitted me with had not only cut our meeting short, but had also, subconsciously, left a bitter feeling about Jean that was only just leaving me. She was the cause of my headache and sickness that day but she wasn't the root cause. Nor was she to blame. I had been the one to want to itch the spot again and she hadn't even known who I was. And there was the rub. I thought about Jean but she thought about Zipoly, the man I used to be. I could hold her now that the implant had been removed, but I could never tell her that Zipoly and I were one and the same. Zipoly died when Steve Barratt was born. My physical appearance was changed beyond all recognition, although they didn't touch my hands. It was one of the sacrifices that I could never reverse. I loved her and yearned to reach out and hold her living body, whilst she simply mourned a corpse.

I won't pretend that thinking about Jean made me a happy soul as I journeyed on. It was a line of thought that needed to be pursued despite how much it hurt me to do so. Now that I was free from the bondage of ORB it might be possible to pick up with Jean again, courting her in my new identity, but I couldn't make that a priority. I had Gilly to love now and that was enough. It was a love that I could control with the flick of a switch but it was a love of sorts. Nobody would condemn a young child for loving and cherishing a ratty and ripped-up old teddy bear, so why should I be condemned for enjoying the emotional comfort of a robotic dog? I was too busy to have a real canine companion. It would have been an act of cruelty for me to be master to a pet that would have to be left alone for long periods and who might very well lose that master at any moment. But with Gilly, and ten out of ten to Adam for understanding this, I had all the benefits that came with being a dog-owner, without the usual ties.

What continued to amaze me about Gilly was the personality that Adam had somehow woven into her structure. She looked beautiful and continued to get many admiring glances, but she had the temperament to match. Now, I know that this was nothing more than the result of some very sophisticated programming that merged the traits of a million scanned pets to generate the ideal, but it was so easy to forget that fact. It was in the eyes as much as anywhere. The eyes give so much away. I use the eyes a lot to read people's characters and they do, as the saying goes, open up a window into the soul. How then could I look into Gilly's eyes and see that beautiful nature and loving spirit that wasn't even there? It was all a bit disconcerting, but it didn't stop me bonding with her as closely as if she had been living flesh and blood.

Every night, we snuggled together under the covers. I know, it would be pathetic enough if she were a real dog. But as my robot friend? Well, I'll leave others to decide. It stopped me feeling lonely and it kept me warm. She seemed to love the companionship and we'd wake together, breakfast together, walk the towpath and cruise together, and end most days at the pub together. I switched her off a few times, mainly due to necessity but occasionally because I remained at heart a tad selfish and preferred to be alone and unencumbered sometimes. Those times became fewer and fewer though and I began to wonder if Adam's creation wasn't something more than she seemed. Yes, the cover was good and made my presence more acceptable in public places, and yes, the companionship was ideal, but the effect that she was having on me made me feel like she was almost a training tool. Steve Barratt, for all his passion and motivation, had numerous personality flaws that needed working on. Was Gilly there to soften this cold heart and silence my selfish streak? Or was I reading a little too much into the whole thing?

Perhaps the most extraordinary and inexplicable trait that Gilly displayed was the way that could interact with other dogs. I walked her off the lead for the most part but, as a responsible dog-owner, whenever we passed another dog on a lead, I'd clip her on. Usually, the other dog was restrained because it was too friendly rather than being aggressive, so, after a brief chat with their owner, we'd let them both off to play together. The rain was something of a constraint on the number of times this happened, but I'd got used to washing her down when we got back to the boat and the best dog owners also seemed to accept that a muddy dog was part of life. In that way, I probably spent more time interacting with the best of people who had the best of dogs.

It was on one of these muddy and wet walks that we met a young couple who were out with their field spaniel, Sierra, and who didn't quite catch her in time to stop her and Gilly meeting. The two dogs bounded out into an open field whilst I caught up with the couple and assured them that it would be all right.

"She can be a bit funny," the male half of the couple explained, "and not everyone likes the way she plays."

"Oh, don't worry about Gilly," I told them, "she can look after herself. They'll be fine."

"Which way are you heading?", his partner asked.

I told them that I was on my way back to the canal at Hartshill as I was moored just up from the Anchor Inn.

"Are you on a boat then?", she asked.

When I told her that I was, the inevitable twenty-questions began and we instinctively started walking together as I explained to them that, no, it wasn't cold in Winter and yes, it was a lovely lifestyle and no, I didn't miss a house, and yes, I had a toilet on board and, luxury of luxuries, even a shower. All the while, the dogs played together with only the occasional bark that was more about winding the other one up than about any sort of anger.

Before we started conversing properly, they introduced themselves as Mandy and John and said that they were thinking of walking down to the canal anyway. We agreed to have a drink together at the pub. It was only as we hit the canal at Grange Road Bridge, that we put the dogs on their leads, happy to see that they were both exhausted although soaking wet and muddy as well.

"They've got a brilliant beer garden," John said, "with loads of space for the dogs to dry out and plenty of umbrellas. We usually wash Sierra off under the taps there and the landlord is fine if we take her in."

"Sounds great," I said, "and sounds like my type of pub. I only arrived here yesterday so haven't had a chance to check the place out yet."

My boat was moored a short way further down the towpath where the trees were sheltering me a little but not enough to spoil the view of the manmade hillside that was now fully back to nature after years of quarrying. This meant that I could bypass the conversation about the boat's details and we could make it straight to the pub where I felt that something awaited me other than the simple pleasure of a decent pint.

I wasn't to be disappointed. Mandy and John opened up to me in the way that so often seems to happen when I meet strangers. Maybe I should have been a priest. I won't always say that it's a blessing but it's certainly a part of me that I am happy to nurture as it opens up so many possibilities to drink in the varied riches of life, whilst also leading me to potential situations where my hidden abilities might be utilised.

The conversation shifted into darker territory when they found out that I was cruising to London, via Oxford.

"Give our regards to the old place," John said mournfully, finishing off his pint and heading to the bar for refills.

"Sorry," I said to Mandy, "seems I've touched a bit of a raw spot."

"Oh, that's not your fault," she replied, "but yes, the mention of Oxford brings back some bitter memories. We used to live there. And we both graduated from there, thinking that the world was now ours to claim and reshape. It didn't quite work out like that."

With John waiting his turn at the bar, she filled me in on the details. They'd finished university just before John's grandmother died. Having chosen to skip a generation with her legacy, she left John a decent amount of money that allowed them to clear their student debts and explore options for setting up on their own.

"I'm not sure if you know Oxford," Mandy asked, "but on the A34 into the city, there used to be an old Traveller's Rest restaurant."

"I know it well," I told her, "I used to rep a while back and it was a nice place to grab breakfast. Not surprised it's disappeared though, it wasn't quite Oxford was it?"

"No," she laughed, "you're right there. It was more fried bread and bacon than croissant and latte, so it's days were always numbered. Anyway, with John's inheritance, we had an idea about the place. We thought it would be an ideal hotel, but a hotel with a difference."

Their vision had been spawned by several years of conversations with the unskilled workers who helped support their college's life and also that of the vibrant city. They found out that, due to the high cost of living in the city centre and the rise in Oxfordshire as a London commuter hub, the staff who were employed in minimum wage jobs were finding it increasingly difficult to secure accommodation.

"We had a young Polish girl," she explained, "who used to clean our halls and then, when she'd finished that job, move onto waitressing for the rest of the day and until the early evening. Anyway, as we started to get to know her, we discovered that she, along with many other migrant workers, and some locals, were having to live in Dickensian conditions. She shared a single room with three people in a large house full of many similar rooms, but still she struggled to scrape the rent together."

"So," she continued, "we got to talking about all this one night and realised that there might be a business opportunity there, creating affordable living spaces for the staff that the city needed to function. That was when we saw the old restaurant and realised that it would be a perfect site. We went through the whole process completely by the book. Plans were drawn up and all the necessary permissions were obtained. The new place would have to be a hotel but we made sure that in all the legal documents there was enough scope to allow for long-term residents so we didn't breach any rules."

"It didn't help us though, did it?", John returned back to the table, "And now look at us."

He picked up the story where Mandy had left off. They'd spent the money on the old property and converted it into a small hotel with fifteen rooms that were simple, clean and had everything a resident would need to live comfortably. They hadn't advertised the place but instead had put the word around amongst the people they wanted to help and, on its opening, the place was fully booked. The location was perfect as there was a bus service into the city that stopped just a couple of hundred yards from the hotel, and, with the prices they charged and with the support of those who lived there, they were able to help the poorest paid to get a start and save up a deposit for their own home, whilst the business also turned a profit.

"It started off well.", John continued, "and I had dreams of similar hotels across the country. Maximum length of stay was always going to be no more than six months but that was enough to help our residents get on their feet. It was a no-brainer to us. And we were helping to staff the city which was always in need of personnel. I know it was only fifteen rooms, but it was start."

"So, what went wrong?", I asked, working my way through the new pint that John had delivered and letting Gilly sit up on my lap.

"The Akita Corporation.", he said, "That's what went wrong."

I'd heard of the Akita Corporation, but couldn't quite make the connection.

"They build golf courses, amongst other things.", John explained, "and our place just happened to be adjacent to their latest planned development. They approached us to buy the place and, to be honest, we were tempted. They dangled a big carrot our way. But we talked ourselves out of the temptation and dug our heels in. If they took this place, then all it would do would be to increase the housing shortage and make the problem worse. So, we hung on."

"And that was our mistake.", Mandy said, "They wouldn't take no for an answer and they still won't. We only moved here a few months ago, when our money finally ran out and my parents offered to put us up.

100

We still own the place, but the legal costs we're facing have pretty much broken us."

As soon as the Akita Corporation had realised that these two could not be bought, they had employed different tactics. An appeal to the Council, asking that the planning permissions be revoked as this was not strictly a hotel, had failed after a year of legal argument. They had been more successful in stopping the bus service however, having tempted the existing contractor with the offer of a direct service into the new golf course. And then, the real problems started. Works on the golf course cut off the water supply to the hotel. Contractors worked late into the night with heavy machinery that even the double-glazed windows of the hotel couldn't silence. And then, the power supply had been severed. The Corporation donated a diesel generator to the hotel by way of compensation for these essential works, but that sat like an eyesore in the small garden area and cost a huge amount to run.

"At that point," John said, "we had to call it quits and close the place. The residents were gutted, but we let them use the car park for caravans so they weren't homeless. As you can imagine, that hasn't gone down very well with the locals, but I understand that they are still holding out there. And now, we can't find a buyer for the place and we may have no option but to cave in and take the blood money from Akita."

"How long can you last?", I asked them.

"Why?", John laughed, "You think you can help us out?"

"John!", Mandy chastised her partner, "Don't be a prat. Steve's been good enough to listen and you need to be less bitter. We've still got each other."

He apologised and told me that they reckoned they could hold out for a month. There was one final appeal against the Corporation that they were mounting in the civil courts but that was their final gambit.

"If it pays off," he said, "we'll be okay. If not, we're back to square one. And it wouldn't surprise me if Akita offer us a lot less as well."

Just then, Mandy's phone rang and she explained that her mother needed her back home. They rose to excuse themselves and we shook hands whilst the dogs said their goodbyes in canine fashion.

"I know it's hard," I told them, "and I can't say that some miracle's going to happen but I hope it does. If not, you two will make it through and, believe me, there is more to life than money. Treasure each other and little Sierra. The rest will come good in the end."

101

I watched as they left the pub and walked off down the towpath, arm in arm. Their story was familiar. I'd heard similar tales so many times and we've all read the same in the papers. Big business plays the game and usually gets its own way by dint of its greater resources. We live in a free country and, where the law is upheld, however controversially, we have to accept that there will be winners and losers. That said, I did get in touch with Adam as soon as I got back on the boat, just to ask him if he could have a look at a few things for me.

Chapter Fifteen

The rain kept me company all the way to Oxford. It poured down as I passed through Nuneaton and Coventry, and it poured down as I arrived at Hawkesbury Junction. Had the rain been softer and my mood more gregarious, I would have stayed longer here and enjoyed the banter of the boaters and the great pubs on offer, but I had places to go and, when the landscape is already greyed out, the last thing you want to do is spend too long beside the M6 which is grey enough in itself.

At Ansty, I tried to take some time out to rest and enjoy the village, but again, the presence of a motorway and the constant background hum of water being hit at eighty miles an hour, detracted from the atmosphere of the place. This proved to be the right choice as it left me time on my hands to drift slowly through to Hungerfield, where the moorings were remote and with fantastic views and from where I could walk with Gilly to the pubs in Brinklow. I remained on something of a schedule but that slipped away and I was only just passing through Braunston when May yielded to June. Still, the rain fell.

I'd done all the sightseeing of Braunston before, and chose to pass through this time, making Banbury my destination after negotiating my way through Napton. It was mid-June by the time I moored up here and I was lucky to find a good mooring spot near to the town, where I planned to treat myself to the luxury of a hotel room for a few days. I needed a bit of a break from the water and I'd seen the best and the worst of things on my journey down. I'd drunk more than I should have done and read a lot less than I wanted to. I'd spent enough time with Gilly and enjoyed her company in a lot of the pubs on the way, but I hadn't walked as much as I should have and I was beginning to feel my fitness fade. All of which I could resolve with a bit of self-pampering.

What I had been able to do was to think. I'd planned my approach to my mission in Oxford and, with the help of the team at the marina, we had laid the foundations for my work in London. Blain was enjoying the end of term break, so I had some breathing space there, and King had authorised us to take our time with Sir Gordon Haywood as he was sowing certain seeds of his own that he promised would be worth waiting for.

But Steve Barratt couldn't ignore his Kingfisher duties. Once I'd checked into my hotel in Banbury and was relaxing in the bath, free from Gilly for a few days, who now lay inert in a cupboard on the boat, I reflected on the little victories I'd won on my journey down.

I couldn't be as impulsive as I used to be, but that probably wasn't a bad thing. Everything I did had to be passed by the others. I knew that we would move away from this over time, as we grew to trust each other more, but was happy to live with it for now. And for all the requests that I made to the others, they were making twice as many to me, as the J for Justice thing took off and it became a public affair. James was thriving. As the J in J for Justice, he rode the internet and became the avatar for the movement, drawing in all the requests for action that he could and firing off solutions where we agreed them. It made my righteous corrections seem a tad trivial by comparison, but this wasn't a competition. Or if it was, I was losing.

Of all the thoughts that had plagued me on my journey down so far, it had been the daily battle with humility and the need to release the chains of my sense of self-importance. As best I could, as the bubbles faded and the water cooled, I believed that I had finally got there. Justice was a force beyond one man and I needed her more than she needed me. ORB was no doubt doing its bit and King was helping the four of us whilst looking to bring on new recruits. I had come close to death several times and would no doubt taste its sting soon enough. When I did, justice would continue to be delivered and I would be a memory.

Because the team were able to tackle the issues they became aware of without my assistance, it had been up to me to keep my eyes open for opportunities on my travels. They came up regularly enough but I limited my actions, preferring to be cautious but finding myself unable to pass by on the other side in certain circumstances.

I'd sent my old friend the owl out to follow the man whose neighbours I'd met in the pub and who, I'd discovered had just built a new carport for his charity-gifted car, despite his officially being so disabled that he could barely walk fifty yards. The footage of his activities had made an interesting film and I had compiled the best parts into a witty short, complete with jaunty background music. His face had been a picture as I entered his house and fixed him to his seat with the Blue Light that had served me so well in the past.

"You have a choice.", I explained, as the closing credits rolled up on the home movie, "You can carry on as you are, living off benefits and being supported in your disability by our nation's most generous systems. Or you can come clean and get back to work. I'd rather you chose the latter. If you do, we can call it a miracle and you won't have to pay anything back. I think that's more than generous."

"And why shouldn't I choose to carry on as I am?", he sneered as he asked me this, "That's one of my choices isn't it?"

"Sorry.", I said, "maybe I wasn't clear enough. You can carry on claiming benefits for your disability, yes, but that means you need the disability."

He watched as I extracted my tools and laid them out in front of him.

"I'm not a doctor.", I explained, "but I think I can do this right. You see, we need to match your disability to your claim if that's the route you want to take. I can't guarantee I'll be totally accurate, but I've been given the rough co-ordinates of the nerves to sever so we'll be pretty close."

He let me get as far as prepping the needle before he capitulated.

"Okay.", he shouted, "I'll do it. I'll go back to work. I've had a good run of it and I suppose it had to end sometime. You won't report me?"

"Not if you do what you say you'll do.", I assured him, "But now that you've made your choice, I need a bit of security. Don't worry, this won't hurt."

I placed my hands on him and he felt a small tickle as the microscopic creature that I placed against his skin burrowed deep into his body.

"That little beasty.", I explained, "will outlast both of us. If you go back on your side of the deal, and believe me, we have access to all the relevant records, this baby will activate and you will become a paraplegic. If you play the game, it stays dormant."

Then there had been the guy selling fake V-Sticks in one of the pubs. With the demise of DVDs and the rise of Internet streaming, V-Sticks had been the industry's solution to storing films and broadcast programmes in a transportable way. As soon as they had been introduced, the criminal gangs had found ways to copy them.

He'd been an easy win. With James' help, I'd introduced a nanobot into the sellers' holdall and this had multiplied itself and infected each of the V-Sticks he carried. I know that this was an attack on the purchasers of these fakes, but that didn't bother me for two reasons. Firstly, as they watched their home computers disintegrate, they would likely choose never to buy such items again. And secondly, I didn't hold out much hope for the vendor being able to come out of hiding for a long time after the damage his products had caused.

This was one of those low-level crimes that seem trivial to many. But crime is crime and, as anyone who has studied the hierarchies knows, this is the lowest tier of a criminal network that peaks at the drug-dealers, the organised gangs and the pimps. Maybe my work would send a little ripple upwards and cause some questions to be asked.

Finally, there had been the case of the booted dog. This one had sickened me and I have to admit I only sought permission for my actions after the event. Sorry, guys.

It had been only a day or so ago, as I waited to negotiate Napton locks. The guy was mid-twenties, stocky and tattooed and I'd watched as he tried to control the dog that trembled at the end of its lead. He'd let it do its business on the towpath and made no attempt to clear up, then he'd had a go at one of the boaters who chastised him for his actions. I'd gone over and picked the dog's mess up whilst the altercation went on and thought that that would be it for my involvement. The other boater wasn't appreciative of my efforts but had fortunately been a few boats ahead of me and was, by now, way out of sight.

As the young lad with the dog returned, I was negotiating the last lock, but that didn't prevent me from seeing him struggling to get the dog to follow him. He hefted a boot at the unfortunate creature and it slowed even more. Then he kicked it again and again until it submitted. Because I was unable to move from the boat, all I could do was shout at him, but that only produced a stream of abuse.

That evening, I met him again. Although tied to taking the boat through the locks, I'd been able to release one of my wonderful kingfisher drones to follow him and now, fully suited up, I crashed into his flat and stood over him as he fell to the floor at the first kick from my boots. The dog watched impassively, choosing not to rise to defend its master. I carried on kicking until I heard the snap of bone.

"Not nice is it?", I whispered as I leant close to him.

Then I'd picked up the dog and used a bolt of electricity to disable its microchip. I then made a couple of phone calls and watched as the dog was driven away in a taxi to a local rescue centre. The wad of cash that I had given to the driver made me confident that he would make the delivery, whilst the envelope taped to the dog's collar contained a nice donation to reward the people at the sanctuary for trusting me in this unusual situation.

All in all, some good results. Nothing compared to the things that the others were doing but enough for me to keep my hand in and keep my desire for justice tamed but accessible. I'd wanted to turn from the crudity of violence but the dog owner wouldn't have understood anything else. I'd check up on him next time I was up this way and if he had another animal I would be sure to take more permanent action. Meanwhile, he wouldn't be in a fit state to replace the other dog for quite some time.

And yet, there was something else about those three actions and a few others that I had to consider very carefully. Kingfisher was a force for correcting injustice. The team I was with now and the team I'd left behind were the same. We believed in the criminal justice system and were there to correct things when that system went awry. Both the vendor of fakes and the benefit cheat were breaking the law. I should have passed my evidence to the authorities and let the system do its bit. The animal abuser should have been reported, although the legal action he would face would be minimal. What I had to come to terms with was that there was more to my role than correcting imbalances. I was now taking the law into my own hands. It was a sea-change.

I assured myself that I was still working for justice and that I was simply offering rapid and alternative solutions to free up the official system to pursue others. I also believed that correcting the imbalances in the system could be interpreted as pre-empting unsuitable sanctions. The benefit cheat might be asked to repay the money, although the chances are that he would paint himself as a victim and claim a recurrence of the injury if forced to do so. The fake seller would face a prison sentence that would benefit him in no way and only help and encourage him to return to other crimes. All of this and more, I tried to understand in my head. The resolution was simple. As Kingfisher, I would focus on righteous corrections and that these might or might not be in place of the correct processes. The team understood this and were happy for me to go my way. I accepted it as a duty. In the big scheme of things, as long as my motivation was right, what did it really matter? I've always been able to convince myself if I have to.

107

Chapter Sixteen

I left Banbury after a week, during which time I had topped up my fitness levels and wallowed in the luxury of hotel life. My next stop was Oxford where I had to finish off the work with Blain and where I had also intended to do some research on the Akita Corporation's activities. Adam had beaten me to it on that one though.

++++++

'Oxford Online', 17th June, 2024

'Golf Course Plans Scuppered by Rare Wildlife'

In a short press release received earlier today, the Akita Corporation has confirmed that it will no longer continue with the development of its latest golfing complex on the outskirts of the city. The reason they cite for this change of plans is the delay that will be incurred now that certain rare species of wildlife have been identified as living on the land that they intended to develop.

Local conservationists were surprised to be called to investigate the possibility of certain species having made this location their home as it had previously been thought to be barren wasteland. Their efforts were rewarded however when they discovered at least six rare and endangered species in the area and they were immediately able to secure a court order stopping any construction and development work whilst these finds were investigated.

The species found include the hazel dormouse, the great

crested newt, grass snakes and the black-backed meadow ant, formally believed to be extinct.

Speaking after hearing this news, the owners of the adjacent Hope Hotel, Mandy and John Cartwright, have offered to make the accommodation available to visiting researchers whilst they conduct their studies. In return for this support, the council will allow the hotel to be extended as a support to the new nature reserve that will be formed. The Akita Corporation has returned ownership of the land to Oxford council at a discounted rate.

++++++

Having seen everything that he could do and having enjoyed the gift of Gilly for a few months now, I had every confidence that Adam would respond to my suggestion in the appropriate way. King was involved behind the scenes, making a few calls to Tokyo, expressing his condolences to the head of the Akita Corporation, whilst simultaneously urging him to get out of this scheme quickly as there were few who could win battles against British conservationists. It would be a good year or two before the studies that were being conducted would reach their conclusion that the animals sighted appear now to have disappeared, but the important work was done. That said, Adam had changed his approach on at least one of the species that he introduced and was hoping that it would be able to replicate itself. Bizarre really, given that they were nothing more than animatronic creations. I looked forward to that twist in the tale.

For my part, I was pleased to have been able to pass this one on, but I now felt a certain sense of urgency about my remaining work in Oxford. I was numerous points behind the rest of the team, and I wanted to score some back. None of us ever mentioned this element of competition in what we were doing, but all of us felt it there in the background. As long as it remained under our control, it would simply be something that encouraged us to reach out of the ordinary. If it began to control us, I for one would be taking a step back.

It was this sense of competition that helped me finalise the approach that I would take with Hugo Blain. His misdemeanours were a smaller part of the Central Shires Trust's problems, but they were also difficult to measure in terms of their impact. Essentially, he had been little more than a presence in the Personnel Department that he headed up. This had meant that the usual screening of applicants, monitoring of progress and regular performance reviews that he signed off on, were very rarely completed. It goes on everywhere. A signature here and who would know any better? But the systems are in place for a reason. Yes, to many, they seem to be overly-cautious, and in truth, they often are. There's a fine line though between over-management and sensible precautions that gets finer each year. When it was about making the big changes, introducing minimum safe working practices, lives were saved. Now that it was about risk-avoidance, the impact was less easy to observe.

In a hospital however, there were justified reasons for asking staff to be that bit more vigilant. Most of them were, not because they were told to be, but simply because their moral compass was set right and they understood their responsibility. The ones who didn't care, were the ones who didn't bother to wash their hands, dispose of waste safely or take the time to double-check prescription medicines handed out by tired doctors. If you had checked the official records for the Central Shires Trust, as we did, you would have been struck by just how great the staff were. Too great in fact. No team, however good, is that perfect. And that was what had led me to establish that there was a gap between the records and the reality and it was a gap that had contributed to lost lives.

Hugo Blain lived in accommodation that was provided for him by the college that now employed him. Access to the facility was limited as it was a college that specialised in scientific research, but the age of the buildings worked in my favour as I used the lightest Kingfisher suit to scale the ancient walls. The heavy security around the place had two major flaws. Firstly, it relied on people rather than complicated alarm systems. This made sense as the academics that milled around the place all year round, were to be seen shuffling about at all hours. The second flaw was that the security guards were all employed and monitored under Blain's budget management system. It's fine to rely on people, but those people just weren't up to scratch although interestingly, they had all passed this year's annual assessment with flying colours.

Once inside the Personnel Department, I was free to explore the paper records and the computer files that would expose Blain's sloth. It didn't take long to find enough evidence. His desk diary detailed performance reviews for the rest of the year, all of which had been completed prior to the event. Files of interview records, matched against those of employees, showed that few references were ever followed up and that even identity checks were not carried out. And his computer yielded numerous memos and e-mails that approved appointments simply on the word of another employee.

With this evidence, it was time to approach Blain. If I'd had firm proof of the effects of his negligence, then I would have been able to match the punishment to the crime, but that was the beauty of Blain's guilt, it was extremely difficult to tie down. Instead, I had to take a personal approach to his case. He was lazy and arrogant, that much I knew. He hadn't always been so, as awards that he had won earlier in his career attested to, but somewhere along the line he had let things slip. He was also a very vain and proud man. Numerous photographs on his office walls showed him meeting and greeting the great and good of the nation, the latest of which showed him in the honorary gowns that came with his position at the university.

I had to wake him up. Mind you, it was three in the morning, so I can't criticise him for that. When he began to come to and understand something of the situation, it was all quite amicable. He was restrained by the grip of the Blue Light, but he asked for a cup of tea and I obliged him, not for one minute falling for his nonchalance as I could see the fear in his eyes. A fear that grew as I placed his cup of tea on the small bedside table and accompanied it with a freshly carved RC disc.

"We'll keep this simple.", I explained, laying out the folders of evidence that I had obtained, "We both know that this paperwork shows your negligence. I don't really care about that in regard to this establishment, but I am tying up the issues with the NHS Trust that you previously worked for."

I paused to check his response and knew that he understood.

"Now,", I continued, "I know that you will tell me that the investigations into that affair have been completed and that you moved on as part of the deal. Officially, you have paid the price. But, is that justice?"

He began to answer but I held up my hand to silence him.

"Sorry, rhetorical question.", I said, "And the answer is, no. You leave there and you come here and you don't change your ways. You're not young and I know you're not poor, so why take up another position like this? Because you love the attention. You love being in an important job. The problem is, you're not very good at it anymore. You seem to see the job as nothing more than a title. And look at the effect. I walk in here because the security team that you employ are currently sitting in their office watching a dirty movie. That might have a serious effect on the work that is being done here. What if vital research is stolen?"

"That wouldn't happen.", he said, "there are too many people around."

"Oh no?", I asked, "Then please explain this."

I held up a prototype of a revolutionary new dental drill head that I had procured from one of the secure areas on campus.

"You see.", I said, "you are incompetent. Not naturally so, but incompetent through laziness. How many people suffered unduly in your hospitals because the staff weren't doing what they should have been doing? We'll never know. But if this minor theft of mine is an example, then you had to have caused at least some harm."

"What do you want from me?", he asked.

"It's not difficult.", I replied, "I just need you to rebalance the scales of justice by paying back the hours that you stole from your previous employers. We can't undo the damage that you've done but there may be a way that you can do some good to offset it. Here's our proposal. There is a vacancy in a local charity, dealing with domestic abuse I believe, and you would be perfect for that role. They need a fully qualified personnel manager but their funds are limited. You will take on that role and, for two years, you will work pro-bono for them, and you will do the sort of exceptional job that you did in your early career. You will also eschew any publicity about your position and take no credit for any achievements that the charity makes."

"And if I don't?", he asked.

"Then we have no alternative but to expose you.", I told him, "And not as what you are. But as what we can make you into. We have the ability to wipe your academic records and expose you as a fraud. We can fabricate evidence of some serious misdemeanours and we can keep going until you are a broken and wretched man, hated by those whose respect you so craved."

"We don't want to go along that route.", I continued, "as it's a little unsophisticated, but hey, you shouldn't have a problem with it as you are more than familiar with fabrication of records, aren't you?"

I left it with him. A week later, I had confirmation that the women's refuge was benefitting from his expertise and that he seemed to be knuckling down and doing a good job. It was early days, but there was some hope in this situation. As to the college, I left out most of the detail but returned the sample I had purloined and urged them to review their security as a priority.

Leaving Oxford, the following day, to complete my slow and steady journey to London, I ticked off the Trust's team in my head and was pleased that this fiddly exercise was almost complete. It had been a nice project for us to work together on and had come together in a reasonable time, but it had also been a bit drawn out. And, dare I say it, not quite as world-changing as some of my previous exploits had been. That changed a little on my first evening out of the city as I relaxed over a very nice claret in a very quiet mooring spot on the outskirts of Abingdon.

++++++

'BBC Radio News', 18.00, 20th June, 2024

'Health Minister Resigns as Cover-Up Exposed'

The Minister for Health, Sir Thomas Richardson, resigned earlier today, prior to the publication of a revised report into the scandal of the Central Shires NHS Trust.

In a brief statement to reporters, Mr Richardson, who has been in this post for the past four years, apologised to the families affected by the failings of the Central Shires Trust and for his own error of judgement in allowing a sanitised version of the review enquiries findings to be published.

"There can be no excuses for my role in this situation,", he explained, "and I take full responsibility for sanctioning what we now know to be an incomplete report."

Before leaving the House to travel home to his Northamptonshire constituency, it is understood that he was questioned for several hours by police, but they have refused to confirm or deny this.

A rising star of the Party, Richardson had been tipped to be a future Prime Minister, although his parliamentary career now appears to be in ruins. With the full publication of the report tomorrow, it is understood that his complicity in what seems to be a cover-up at the highest level, might even cost him his seat and prompt a by-election. Should his Party lose this once safe seat, their majority in the House of Commons will fall below a manageable level and may lead to a coalition deal having to be negotiated.

++++++

Chapter Seventeen

In the aftermath of Richardson's resignation and the release of the full report on the Central Shires Trust, Sir Gordon Haywood, our final target in this mess, resigned his own position as Chief Operating Officer of the country's second-largest private healthcare provider. That was some comfort to us, but the consensus remained on taking further action.

"We're leaving this one to you now," King said as we concluded our conference call, "but we remain here to support you. We're pursuing a few other lines ourselves and this J for Justice thing needs managing a little. You okay with that?"

"That's fine," I told them, "and good luck with the J thing. I'm quite happy that the Righteous Corrector has slipped off the radar, but you're right to be concerned about where the Justice thing is going. I'm reading a bit too much about it and I worry about those who are piggy-backing on the movement."

It wasn't professional jealousy on my part and I fully understood the concerns that King was having. I was confident that he would be able to manage the situation and comfortable that I could finish the work on Haywood alone. As it happened, it didn't quite work out as well as I had planned.

I arrived in London in mid-July, choosing to take up a temporary paid spot on one the waterway's fixed moorings sites where the facilities and convenience more than offset the cost. It was nigh on impossible now to find a mooring spot in the capital. House prices were so exorbitant there that they rendered it financially unfeasible for the young to find any halfway decent housing other than on a boat. The series of events that were to shake the nation in a few years' time would turn the tide on this situation as the city became less habitable, but nobody could truly have predicted that in the Summer of '24.

Sir Gordon Haywood was a mysterious character. He was a man who appeared to have been plagued with a certain amount of bad luck in his various roles in both the public and private sector. As CEO of the Central

Shires Trust, he had overseen an organisation that was unfortunate enough to have suffered the unnecessary deaths of a fair number of patients due to infection, lack of adequate care, cancelled surgical appointments and a number of other unforeseen difficulties. In the role that he had just vacated with Health Force, he had presided over a period of declining share prices where speculative investments had led to a higher than expected debt to earnings ratio. Prior to his involvement in the health sector, he had been unfortunate enough to Chair the final meeting of the Board of a mobile communications retailer when it collapsed owing millions. His knighthood was inferred when he had presided over the last remaining independent car manufacturer in the UK. He received it three days prior to that company's demise.

Anyone seeking to find a more tangible reason than bad luck would fail in their search. Sir Gordon seemed just to be a very unlucky man. Not that his personal situation reflected this. He was one of those class of Englishmen who are born into a certainty of life that keeps them above the day to day of the nation. Private schooling and family contacts helped, but it was his self-confidence and affable character that kept him afloat. Anyone who claims that we live in a true meritocracy is living in candy-land, but that's not to say that I believe this country suffers under the yoke of a ruling class. Our leaders may not be the most talented in a lot of situations, but they rise to the top on the labours of those who they manage to activate in a very special way. Personality and self-belief make the difference. And, to be fair, it seems to work better than any other system that we can envisage. So it was that Sir Gordon always managed to find a new position, never fatally tainted by lack of success and always confident enough to blame his misfortune.

I struggled to find anything to bring Sir Gordon to book with. I even began to feel myself sympathising with his problematic career path and doubting whether he was the malevolent force that we had him down as, or was instead simply a bumbling fool. My only option was to engineer a situation to test him. He was culpable for the failings of the Trust and the deaths that had ensued, but what we needed to determine was whether he was an active driver of those failings or a passive instrument in their occurrence. You could imprison someone for throwing a rock at a car and causing it to crash, you had less luck seeking justice when an unfortunate bounce of a trailer flung a rock into the highway that was later picked up by a lorry's tyre and catapulted through a car window.

This wasn't going to be an easy one to get right. I pondered over it for days as I sat in the warm sunshine on the deck of the boat and looked out over the heaving skyline that loomed above Paddington Basin. I was fairly safe here. It was booked under my current assumed name and the boat was secured, as were my comings and goings due to the extensive CCTV network that I was a part of. King was in the process of acquiring a property for me around Kensington way, having already found a rare patch of canal-side dereliction, protected by its listed status, from where I could disembark the pod. Distance didn't matter so much in London. This was a city where a mile could comfortably carry a million bodies along.

Once the property was booked, I made several trips from the Basin, under the waters of the canal and into the dank tunnel that hid the pod and allowed me to emerge into a side street dressed respectably and coming home to my place in town. It was August now and the city was teeming with tourists. The short walk that I had to make was an unpleasant rush through the bustle and the madness of that bizarre country-within-a-country that was the capital. I never got used to it, but I had my proper home to come back to and that remained a haven of peace even within the walls of this fortress of vanity.

My first contact with Sir Gordon occurred on the 15th August. It's a date that I remember well as the planning to get me that meeting was a complex and laborious process. This was the date that Haywood's semi-reclusive friend, Nick Willis, was due to meet with Haywood as they did every few years by way of catching up on each other's worlds. They had been at university together, had watched their families play and grow up together but had then drifted apart as Willis struggled more and more with a form of agoraphobia that kept his public appearances to a minimum. All of this information had come to me via James who, let's be honest, could work up the full biography of any UK citizen within a couple of hours. Adam meanwhile provided me with the means to carry out my plan. He supplied the hours of footage of Willis at his home, and he supplied me with the voice synthesizer and facial prosthetics that would change me into that man. He also introduced the soft virus into Willis's home that rendered him bedbound and helpless under Charlotte's care.

Our first meeting took place in the refined surroundings of the club that was preferred by both Haywood and Willis and which went under the unofficial title of 'The Herringbone'. Officially it was The London Court of

Master Haberdashers and Slave-Traders, although this name was rarely used nowadays, for obvious reasons. The Herringbone had been settled on in the nineteen-twenties as a safer and more manageable option, taking its title from the suits then so much in fashion with its patrons. This was a different world for me and one that I would never be comfortable with. For that reason, I affected a relapse of a bout of bronchitis that I had known Willis to have suffered a few months back and which helped me hide behind the sniffles and the coughs.

"Nick", Sir Gordon had arrived at the club before me and now rose from a sumptuous leather armchair to greet me, "how on earth are you? I must say, you look a bit rough."

"Gordo", I replied, slipping perfectly into character and trusting the artificial parts of me to hold up, "so good to see you, old chap, and yes, I feel rather poorly I'm afraid. Difficult enough to make these meetings as it is but even worse with the chest playing up as well. Still, never mind, I believe we have the bottom half of a single malt left to complete?"

"You remembered!", he laughed, calling over the porter, "Jenkins, last year's deposit if you please."

They settled down and waited as the porter returned with a half bottle of whisky that had been opened exactly one year ago to the day. He poured them each a generous measure.

"Well, now", Sir Gordon said, "what news from your neck of the woods?"

I played the part with skill and got away with the few lapses of memory that I attributed to my illness as I detailed the limited activities of the previous year, finishing off with an update on the grand-children and the schoolmates that I knew were no longer with us.

"And yourself", I concluded, "I understand that you've had something of a run of bad luck just recently. Saw you in the paper last month if I'm not mistaken."

"Too true", he replied, "too true. Got stung with that NHS Trust thing. I knew I should have followed your advice and left well alone. Still, I didn't leave empty handed and Binty placed me straightaway with another firm. They dropped me like a hot coal. Not surprised there. Didn't leave them empty handed either though."

He burst out laughing and I joined him as best I could until the coughing stopped us both.

"Looking for something new now", he said, "Quite fancy another health thing, people always sick and all that. You hear of anything, I'd appreciate it."

"You know," I replied, "that's one of the reasons I didn't let this damn illness prevent our getting together."

"Sounds intriguing", Haywood drew closer to me, signalling the porter to top up the glasses.

"It's a bit hush hush.", I whispered, leaning in conspiratorially towards my new best and oldest friend, "Before I say any more, are you open to something that may be a little…erm, I hesitate to say, illegal, but it might challenge your ethics."

"Oh, Nick, you do amuse me.", Haywood choked on his whisky as he chuckled away, "Remember our old motto, all for one and all for one! My legality and my morality are me. So, what's the gen?"

Having explained everything to him, we parted earlier than would have been normal, due to my illness, but arranged to meet the following week. I made it back to Paddington in less than an hour and was relieved to slide back into the boat and straight into the shower to wash off both the mental presence and the physical marks of Nick Willis.

The plan continued to move forward smoothly. We met three times in the fortnight after our first meeting and I was fully geared up for our final session as September drew in and the city quietened down a bit. We arranged to meet at my London pad, now carefully assigned in the name of Nick Willis although via multiple hidden corporation's and trusts. Haywood would trust his old friend, but only so far. We knew this when the first calls came into Willis' home and Charlotte had to field them via her own voice synth. It worked fine, but we were getting a little nervous. All the other checks that Haywood conducted were responded to electronically by James who returned back to Sir Gordon all the answers he needed and who set up the necessary smokescreen behind the proposed project.

It was straightforward enough. There was a huge demand for donor organs and there were plenty of people willing to sell a piece of themselves to clear their debts. Of course, this great act of personal sacrifice remained illegal, but that was the point. The centrepiece of the scheme was a small private hospital whose website mirrored everything that would be expected of a clinic that offered 'discrete and effective treatment for addictive behaviours'. It passed inspections and was highly praised by celebrities and politicians alike. The fact that it didn't exist was a minor detail and not relevant to Sir Gordon who had spoken with the staff there and who regularly checked out the website that only he would ever see.

I already had plenty of footage of Sir Gordon discussing how the clinic could best utilise the available resources and what procedures he would introduce to mask the true operation. What I didn't have was his signature on the document that would incorporate his name into the scheme and send him off to prison. Any notion of entrapment would be dismissed as Nick Willis would appear after his short illness and confirm that he had had no contact with Haywood for over a year.

Sir Gordon was worryingly late for the meeting. I paced up and down the small living room in the flat and worried that it was all about to fall down around me. This was a complicated plan that had numerous holes in it, but it was coming together. I put these worries aside when the doorbell rang at nine o'clock and I saw Haywood at the front door via the CCTV. I buzzed him in.

"Gordo,", I said, "welcome to my small pad. Trouble getting here?"

"You could say that,", he replied distractedly, "something came up last minute."

"But, I'm here now.", he seemed to shake off his uncertainty, drawing his frame up to its full height, "Shall we commence with proceedings."

It took me a full fifteen minutes to go through all the paperwork with Sir Gordon. It had been drawn up by one of King's trusted lawyers and was a totally legal front for what was a nastily illegal operation. The pages had numerous sections and sub-sections that already had Willis's signature in place, as well as the signatures of certain other high-profile backers who again, Haywood had studied carefully on the web.

"Before you sign these,", I said, "you need to be totally sure of what you are buying into. This paperwork is the cover. The guys behind this don't suffer fools gladly but they look after their own. Now's the time to back out if you want. This is organ harvesting. A win-win for the donor and the recipient but not totally legit here in the UK. You need time to think?"

He scanned through the papers and looked ready to sign. I watched as he reached into his jacket for a pen only to jump back as he drew out a nine-millimetre pistol and aimed it straight at my head.

120

"Just one problem, Nick.", he snarled as he spoke, "A minor detail. You see, you are not Nick."

"What are you talking about.", I tried to laugh it off, "you know me well enough Gordo, we've been friends for years."

"Oh, I've been friends with Nick for many years.", he said, "very good friends. Friends and lovers in fact. You didn't know that did you? That's what made me suspicious. You didn't make a single move on me and, believe me, that's not like Nick at all."

"But I've not been well…", I tried to answer.

"Shut up!", he shouted, "And sit quietly over there. The game's over and so will your life be in about five minutes. I don't know who you think you are, but you're playing with the big boys now and you don't seem to be able to keep up."

He walked to the front door and opened it. I couldn't believe what I saw. I stood up and it was like I was looking in a mirror.

"This.", Sir Gordon said, "is Nick Willis."

Just then I heard a buzzing in my ear and with a slight breath opened up the line to receive the communication.

"Steve, it's Charlotte, they've got the real Nick. I'm sorry. Get out."

"Bit late I'm afraid.", I whispered back, "you okay?"

"She's fine.", Willis answered for her, "We do have certain standards you know and believe me, if we felt she was anything more than your paid nurse we'd have terminated her. The drugs we used on her are military grade. If she was lying, she deserved to go free."

"No, you're right.", I lied, "she was just somebody we picked to nurse you. I presume we got the dosages wrong."

"It doesn't matter now though, does it?", Haywood ushered me back to the settee, "Your scheme seems to have failed. Not sure what it was you were after though, you want to enlighten me before you depart?"

"Justice.", I told him, flicking the RC disc so it landed at his feet, "justice for the people who died on your watch and justice for all the others who you have hurt or put out of their jobs."

"Oh, dear boy.", he laughed as he fingered the disc that he had picked up, "this is just so quaint. You're the Righteous Corrector? How very lovely. A bit disappointing though, given the nature of this situation. You should have been a bit less subtle about it. We certainly aren't going to prolong things here, trying to make some clever point. In fact, our only question is which one of us terminates you. Nick?"

121

"No can do.", he answered, "This flat's been set up in my name. We can prove that that was all a scam but better if we waited until I was back on my sick bed. It'll have to be you. And I suggest we delay it no longer."

"Certainly,", Haywood replied, "and it will be my pleasure. Any last words, hero, or any last-minute surprises?"

"Aside,", I replied, "from the satisfaction of your life sentence when all the material we are now recording is broadcast, no. My last words aren't for you. They are to the team that I love and they are simply to thank them and tell them to carry on doing what they do best."

I watched as he pointed the gun towards me and stood as calmly as I could as his finger eased back on the trigger. The first shot rang out and I felt myself thrown backwards, feeling the impact as my head hit the wall and realising I hadn't been fatally wounded. I opened my eyes, ignoring the pain and watched as Haywood drew closer to me, the gun pointed at my head. I waited for the shot that I knew would finish me off. The last I remember, is the smile on Sir Gordon's face as he let that shot loose.

PART TWO:

PART TWO

Chapter Eighteen

I woke up in what I first assumed to be a hospital. I was attached to the usual monitors and everything that I saw around me confirmed this impression. My shoulder felt like it was on fire and I couldn't stop myself crying out in pain as I tried to lift myself up. The door to the room opened and a matronly figure in a starched uniform came in.

"You're back with us then?", she said as she moved towards me, "Try not to move too much. I imagine it hurts like hell doesn't it?"

I confirmed that it did and, as she shook out some painkillers from a bottle beside the bed, I took the opportunity to take a closer look. On first impressions, she could have been a ward sister, but then I noticed the jeans under her tunic, the front of which sported an unfamiliar logo.

"Where am I?", I asked as I finally managed to sit upright.

"You're in Mr King's country house.", she replied, "They flew you in a couple of nights ago and asked me to take care of you. You missed the worst of it yesterday when the surgeon dropped by and fixed up the biggest chunk of the damage. It should be easier from now."

"And you are?", I asked.

"Oh, so rude of me.", she chuckled, displaying a softer character beneath the harsh exterior, "I'm Mrs Quinn. Mary to my friends. I work for Mr King. Have done since before his little ones were born."

"You're a nurse?", I asked.

"Amongst other things.", she replied, for the first time revealing the slightest hint of a Dublin accent, "at least, that's what they employed me for first off. Since then, well, I pretty much get involved in everything. Keep the place running whilst Mr King does what he does. This part of the property is fairly new though, only installed a couple of years back when Mrs King was battling the Big C."

She went on to explain that Jason King had made numerous changes to this country house since buying it when his first business went stellar. Since then, she was never surprised by the next project, although she did wonder why the place needed to retain its own clinic.

125

"'Mary', he said to me,", she explained, "'we've been together long enough now to trust each other. Let me just say that there are some darker parts of my life that need a bit of extra support'. Well, I've seen some things in this place, I can tell you, so I wasn't surprised. He asked me if I might want to retire instead, but the look I gave him soon shut him up. I told him that I would be with him until I draw my last breath and that I was long past doubting what he did with his life. Mind you, I hope the hit that you got was worth it."

"It was,", I replied, "although I'd have preferred it not to have happened."

"Well, you were lucky.", she told me, "Or at least I think you were. A couple of inches lower down and you would have been gone. Mind you, it wasn't a tidy wound. They tell me that the bullet chose a complicated route through you, which sort of mangled up your shoulder and collar bone. That's why the surgeon flew in. I never ceased to be amazed at the people Mr King can call on, but that man was incredible. He invited me to watch as he rebuilt the bones and muscle that looked to me like a scrag-end of beef. You've got all sorts in there now. Plastic and gold mostly. I joked with the surgeon that you were like the six-million-dollar man, being called Steve and all. He didn't get it. Boy, did that make me feel my age!"

"But enough of that,", she fussed over the wires and tubes that projected from various parts of my body, "you need to rest. You should be up and about tomorrow and then you can start enjoying the nicer side of this place. Believe me, if you can think of it, we've probably got it here.".

I closed my eyes and drifted off as she left the room. Still unsure about how I had avoided that last bullet and the death it carried with it.

The answer to that conundrum came the following day when Adam appeared and showed me footage of my 'last moments'. It took me a while to understand where the images were coming from as they were low down and taken at an unusual angle. When I twigged to what they were showing me, I couldn't help but laugh.

"Gilly?", I asked Adam.

"Watch the footage.", he replied by way of answer.

I watched from Adam's perspective as Gilly ran up to my prone and bleeding body and began to lick my face. I'd sat up, although I don't remember having done that and the film showed me wincing at the shot of pain that ran through my left-hand side. It also showed the smile on my face

126

as I saw my canine friend standing over me with her best stupid smile in full flow. Then it showed me drifting back into unconsciousness.

Adam's camera panned around and I was able to see what had happened to Haywood and Willis. They were still in the same place that I'd last seen them but not quite how I had left them. They had been bisected at the waist. Their legs remained in place but their torsos had slipped down behind them. I wasn't sure what to make of it all.

"You get it, Steve?", Adam asked as he came and sat beside me.

"I think so,", I replied, "but first off, is Charlotte okay?"

"She's fine man,", Adam laughed, "although a bit self-critical just now at having let Willis detach his drip. It could have been a lot worse and man, I'm so pleased that Gilly turned up."

"And what happened after I blacked out?", I asked.

"All went very smoothly,", he replied, "we got you away and out here then we sent a clean-up team to sort the flat out. We are sorry about the mess up. It shouldn't have happened"

"Don't worry, buddy.", I said, "And make sure Charlotte doesn't beat herself up too much about it. We're all of us fallible. I should have understood the relationship between Haywood and Willis better. That's my bad. But, I think you have some explaining to do about my furry friend."

"Oh, yeah,", he laughed sheepishly, "I didn't tell you everything about her did I. Sorry."

I was beginning to feel a bit feint by now, but still needed answers.

"So, what's the score with Gilly then?", I asked.

"Well,", he explained, "when I put her together it wasn't just as a companion to you. I also built in a little bit of the protector too. She's not heavily armed, but she has enough firepower to do the job. Of course, she doesn't make very considered decisions, although, in this case, I'm sure you're quite glad of that. She cut them in two with her lasers. I know it's a bit corny. They fire out of her eyes. Quite impressive when you see it."

"That explains a lot,", I said, "but it doesn't explain how she got there and what prompted her to come."

"No, it doesn't, does it?", Adam was choosing his words carefully, "The how, well, that's straightforward man. She can swim and run faster than we ever could, so getting to you wasn't an issue. But…"

I waited as he paused and scratched his head before continuing.

"The problem that I've got, is that I don't know *why* she came. Sure, she responds to commands and distress calls, but in this case, man, how did she know you were in danger? Beats me."

"She's something special, isn't she?", I remembered saying, before drifting back off to sleep again.

++++++

'The Sunday Spotlight', 15th September, 2024

'Exclusive: Final Shame of Disgraced Health Chief'

The reputation of Sir Gordon Haywood, erstwhile senior NHS chief, takes a final and fatal blow today, as we reveal, in an exclusive by star reporter Jean Carter, how he planned to set up a clinic to harvest human organs.

Named and shamed as the CEO behind the Central Shires Trust scandal, Haywood was forced to resign from the healthcare provider Health Force on the back of the resignation of the Health Minister, Sir Thomas Richardson, back in June. In papers that we publish today, we can reveal that since that time, Sir Gordon had been making plans to start up a clinic where needy donors could sell their organs for transplant. The scheme, which appears to have been developed with long-term friend, Nick Willis, was very close to being put into action when it appears that the police might have caught wind of the project.

Haywood and Willis fled the country a week or so back, leaving behind the incriminating documents. Airline records along with CCTV images captured at several airports, seem to indicate that the two have fled to the safe haven of Ecuador, and to since have disappeared.

Members of Haywood's family are not said to be concerned about Sir Gordon's welfare, as they have had contact with him since he left the country. However,

128

they have admitted that they are still in shock after having discovered this darker side to his personality.

Police sources have confirmed that the documents that we hold are genuine and that they carry the signatures of the two men involved, although they have admitted that the other names on the papers have not yielded any positive identifications so far.

Full story, pages 2 and 3.

++++++

The newspaper lay open on my bed as I forced myself back onto my feet after too long in recovery. It was satisfying to see the end of this particular mission but I still would have preferred that it had ended in a less dramatic and murderous way. I wasn't racked with guilt. We hadn't set out to kill either Haywood or Willis. They were the ones who had chosen to commit murder, at which point all bets were off. It was untidy, even if it gave us the opportunity to make Haywood's shame a public affair.

Behind the scenes, James had been working with King and they had orchestrated the passage of two lookalikes from London to Ecuador, always in First Class and always visible enough to the cameras they passed. It was highly unlikely that the police would take this much further and, having been able to speak to the families through our faultless synthetic voice system, Charlotte had reassured them and advised them to carry on with their own lives for the present. The two actors had been picked up and integrated into the crew of one of King's fleet of cargo ships as it passed by the port a week or so later.

Mrs Quinn had continued to feed me information about the house which, with hindsight, I now realise was her way of encouraging me to get off my backside and explore the surroundings that she described with such admiration. She wasn't around when I finally made it to the door, so I opened it and followed my instincts.

Beyond the hospital room door, I had half-expected to see a long corridor with more beds laid out, but was instead presented with a very small lobby. Two steps across this saw me standing in front of a velvet, studded door, beside which was a switch panel. I put two and two together and pressed the button marked 'Call', shuffling into the lift as the doors opened and choosing the obvious 'G' selection.

As the doors opened again onto the ground floor, I found myself at the rear of a marble-floored entrance hallway, scattered with bundles of assorted party equipment. I moved closer to have a look, thinking how nice it was that they were planning to welcome me back in this way. That vain thought disappeared as I remembered that it was King's birthday next week.

"Steve, my boy," Mrs Quinn's voice echoed around the hall, "good to see you up and about at last. Now, come over here and let me introduce you to the rest of the gang."

I followed her into a beautifully decorated reception room and was rapidly paraded past the staff who stopped work to greet me.

"This is my husband, Declan," Mrs Quinn explained, pointing to a grey-haired bull of a man, who was clearly carrying his years well.

I shook hands with him and felt the warmth and the power of huge hands that had become rough and calloused over the years.

"Good to meet you, lad," his voice carried a thicker accent than his wife's, "and sure, it's grand to see you back on your feet. Here now, this is my son Patrick."

I turned to the younger version of the father and could see the likeness straightaway. What they shared in physical features however, they certainly didn't share in their tone of manner of speech.

"Very nice to meet you.", he shook my hand, "And an honour indeed. Mr King has told us something about you and I hope that we can be friends."

I was too shocked to make much of a reply, as I tried to equate the very refined accent with what I knew of his parents.

"Patrick's the brains of the family," Mrs Quinn explained, "and Mr King has seen him through his schooling since we first started working here. I think there was a hope of young Patrick becoming a closer part of the family, but, well, I suppose you know about his daughters."

I nodded that I did, choosing not to pursue what remained a painful subject to me.

"But then again," she continued, "that was Jason King the First if you like. We made the transition very smoothly when his 'cousin' took over. I know you know what I mean."

"Yes," I replied with a wink, remembering the night when Jason King had been 'terminated' at my hand under the instructions of ORB, and the cover-up that was necessary when his being still alive presented certain problems, "I am aware of that. His cousin is so like him though. But anyway, who else do we have here?"

"Oh, how rude of me.", Mrs Quinn chuckled away, "This is Janie and Genie. Easy to confuse but you'll get used to it, I suppose you could say that they are my deputies but they seem to be more of a help to Declan at times. They've been with us about a year now. Mr King met them through one of his projects."

"And these two young lads,", she continued, "are Paul and Ralph. They are supposed to be training as groundsmen under Declan, but Paul seems to spend more time in the kitchen and Ralph displayed some serious skills in helping to nurse you better. I'll need to speak to Mr King when he gets here. See if we can't rearrange duties a little."

"Is that everyone?", I asked.

"It is, it is.", Declan sighed, "We're a small team and the house seems to get bigger every year, but we get the work done. Mind you, when we have these special events, it can get a bit stressful."

"Oh, ignore him.", Mrs Quinn laughed, "He wouldn't have it any other way. But, as you can see we are a bit busy now, so if you don't want to lend a hand, and I don't think that would be wise today, then you go off and explore. If you find it, your bedroom is C12. You should have everything you need in there. If you don't find it, then use this. Can't be doing with all this technology but Mr King insists we carry them."

She pressed a small handset into the palm of my hand and showed me the button to press to call her. I wasn't too concerned about getting lost, but I took it anyway. After all, how big could the place be and wasn't I, Kingfisher?

Just under an hour later, I gave up and pressed the button. Declan answered and I explained where I was. It took him ten minutes to guide me from that location, but eventually I found myself in front of a door marked C12, which opened as I pressed my palm against the lock. I thanked Declan and hung up, hearing him laughing like a trooper as he said goodbye.

I knew that this was one of King's little jokes the moment that I entered the room and saw a detailed fold-out map of the premises placed right in the middle of the bed. Okay, I could live with that, Jason. The rest of the room was indicative of his endless thoughtfulness and generosity. I opened cupboards and wardrobes and found everything that I could possibly need. There was a well-stocked fridge in the small kitchenette, and an equally well-stocked drinks cabinet in the lounge. I made a ham sandwich, popped a couple of painkillers and, ignoring the missive on the label, treated myself to a very nice bourbon.

While I ate, I let the enormous whirlpool bath in the exquisitely furnished bathroom fill to the brim, then I indulged in a long and pampering soak that soothed my shoulder immeasurably. As I lay there, I let the past chapters of my life file themselves in my head, compiling the data, setting aside the lessons to be learnt and considering alternatives to the route we had taken. By the time I climbed back out of the water, the past was neatly stored away and I was ready to embrace the future.

Chapter Nineteen

The guest of honour at King's birthday party was somebody he would never have expected to be at liberty to join in the festivities. The court case had been concluded with a little help from some of the influential friends of the main man, and the sentencing had happened only hours before.

Jonathon Watts had been found guilty by a jury of his peers of aiding and assisting in the suicide of his wife Norma. They had no choice but to find him guilty, since he had never sought to plead his innocence. As he'd stood there in the dock awaiting sentencing, the judge had eyed him up for a long period, before summarising the legal position. After this, he had made one closing comment and asked Watts very simply, "Would you do it again?"

Without any hesitation, Watts confirmed that he would.

That was enough to convince the judge and he handed down the sentence that would shake the nation for weeks to come. Four year's imprisonment suspended for an indefinite period. The jury applauded the sentence, but quickly resumed their seats when the judge scowled mischievously at them.

Free to go, Watts had hot-footed it to King's house and walked through the door just as the first chorus of Happy Birthday had been completed. Nobody blamed King for the tears that he shed. And the best of it was that it had all been done in a totally legal way. Well, almost. We'd set up monitoring systems in the jury room, so we had known that Watts would be, quite rightly, found guilty. We also knew that the jury would ask for the judge to be compassionate in sentencing. Where we'd bent the rules, just a little, was in our approach to the judge's mother. Whatever you say about men, they almost invariably have to listen to their mothers, so we'd made a discrete approach and found her to be a shrewd old dear who was happy to put a word in her son's ear for us.

When King had recovered from the shock of seeing Watts, and after all the other guests had arrived and begun to settle down to enjoy themselves, he tapped his glass with a fork and called for silence. Making a speaking platform of the steps halfway up the grand staircase, he addressed the party.

"Friends", he began, "this is a remarkable day and I cannot express the joy in my heart that you are all here to celebrate another of my birthdays. Friends old and new, young and old, and of course, those recently freed from the shackles of the judiciary, I welcome you all."

He paused to consider his next words carefully, scanning the room to make sure that there were no unwelcome guests.

"Of course", he smiled as he resumed, "this is the first time that I, as the cousin of the original Jason King, stand before you."

He raised his fingers to indicate inverted commas as he mentioned the word cousin. The truth was that everybody knew that Jason King the first and second were one and the same person, but it was an unwritten code that we respected his presence as his own relative. All very confusing, but necessary after the reported death of the original Jason King. A necessary ruse in my bid to tackle the growing problem of the Order for Restoring Balance a few years back.

"I feel", he continued, wryly chuckling away, "that I have known you as long as you knew my dear, departed relative. Long may we continue to be friends."

The guests applauded and cheered him as he raised his glass for a toast.

"Before I finish my little speech though", he raised his hand for silence, "I must perform another duty that has been requested of me. We have a guest with us tonight who I feel that I know very well, even though we have only met on a couple of occasions. You too, I am sure, will feel that you know this lady in the same way. I refer to Ms Jean Carter, the rising star of the journalistic scoop. Please Ms Carter, come and join me."

I watched with wonder as Jean slipped through the crowd and walked calmly up the stairs to stand by King. She was wearing a shimmering pink ball-gown, cut to accentuate her figure perfectly and set off with just a smattering of plain silver jewellery. As soon as I caught sight of her I realised that I had never stopped loving her and my heart was torn between the joy of being in her presence again and the agony of never being able to reveal my identity to her.

"It is my honour and pleasure", King began as Jean joined him, "to announce that Ms Carter here has just been awarded the 'Journalist of Journalists' Award by the National Association of the Written Media. And

I have the pleasure of presenting her with that impressive trophy tonight, along with an equally impressive cheque to recognise her contribution. In particular, the Association has highlighted her recent work in exposing NHS scandals as being the driving factor behind their choosing her."

He paused to let the applause die down.

"Jean," he continued, looking directly at her, "you have done a great service to all of us and you truly deserve this award. Congratulations."

The room broke out into applause and cheers again, whilst Jean was presented with her trophy and cheque. The ceremony was recorded by the single official photographer at the event and would be front page news tomorrow, as her employers sought to emphasise the quality of their team. For now, I swelled with joy to see Jean there and to know that she had battled to earn this award and that it was truly a recognition of her support for all that we had been doing before and her discretion in handling the sensitive data we fed her.

Once these brief formalities were over, the party got into full swing as King hosted another amazing night. Everywhere I went in that house, guests mingled and played games, lost fake money at the casino or went for a spin on the dodgems that had been installed in the grounds. The highest and the richest in the land were there, as were some of the lowest and the poorest in the form of apprentices from King's various businesses. This was a night for equality though and people knew that, in King's presence, the usual social conventions were suspended. You met and talked to people as fellow humans, or you left. A point that was emphasised by the sight of two extremely famous footballers who were escorted from the premises only minutes after making their, 'do you know who I am?' comments.

Watching King in his home environment and away from the usual dynamics of his business activities, my admiration for him grew to new heights. He was that rarest of creatures, a multi-billionaire who lived and breathed humility. By his own admission, he was no saint. But to be able to carry the burden of wealth in the way that he did put many revered people to shame. Here was a man who had everything and could have anything that his heart desired. Yet, here also was a man who never failed to appreciate the blessings of his life. And, here too was a man who deserved more than anybody to claim that he had made it on his own, but who got his greatest pleasure from seeing others succeed. And here too was a man who had every right to rage at the injustice of his murdered daughters and his wife's death to cancer, but who chose instead to give, even in his grief. I had grown to love Jason King and I looked to him as the role-model of what I wanted to be. Without the money, of course. That sort of wealth would finish me off in a week.

Jean caught up with me about halfway through the evening. I had slipped out onto one of the balconies and was puffing away at a discretely rolled cigarette.

"Well, if it isn't headache boy.", she laughed as she approached me.

"Sorry?", my lame response escaped me before I had a chance to stop it as I turned to the voice I recognised instantly.

"You don't remember?", she asked, "The Caldon Canal, a couple of years back. We met at the pub and you ran away with a headache?"

I remembered it all too well. That had been the day that I had had to put Jean firmly away in the box of the past and never look back. Now, it was different. The implant that ORB had put into my head designed to stop me ever digging up past acquaintances, had been removed and I was free to get close to Jean again.

"Yes.", I replied cautiously, "I remember. So sorry about that. Something I really can't explain."

"Don't worry.", she held out her hand to shake mine, "Jean Carter, as you probably know, given Jason's little presentation."

"Steve Barratt.", I replied, almost unable to speak as I felt our hands touch, "and congratulations. I know your work well. You started the Righteous Correction thing, if I'm not mistaken?"

"Sort of.", she looked away as she spoke, "along with some others. Well, one guy in particular."

"Zipoly Hardacre?", I asked.

"I suppose it's common knowledge.", she replied, "but still not official, so let's just say you are not far off the mark."

We settled down to chat on one of the benches that had been placed on the balcony to overlook the sweeping expanse of the grounds. A waiter bought us fresh drinks and, as the evening turned into night, we carried on talking. King slipped out onto the balcony and joined us briefly, a glint in his eye as he saw how well we were getting on.

"We really should join the rest of the party.", Jean apologised to King, "this is very rude of us."

136

"Not at all.", he said, "You two spend as long as you like out here. I'm glad you've met each other. Steve is an interesting chap and I think the two of you look good together."

Having said that, he gave me a mischievous wink and left us alone.

"You don't mind me asking,", I said tentatively, "but is there a, how shall I put it, a significant other in your life?"

"No,", she sighed, "not since Zipoly. It's never felt right."

I knew that this was my moment. Not since losing Fran and hooking up with Jean in my past life had I felt any stirrings of passion, but now they were back with a vengeance. Love is more than skin deep and I was looking at the woman that I couldn't stop loving. My question was, was she looking beyond the skin and seeing something else in me?

"I know that this may seem presumptuous,", I tried to stop myself from mumbling, "and I must apologise if it all comes out wrong, but do you think that maybe, we could meet again? Perhaps spend a little time in private?"

As I spoke I looked deep into her eyes and urged the soul inside of me, the soul of Zipoly that loved this woman so much, to fight its way past the eyes that she would never recognise. Then I remembered James' words from so many years ago and I reached out my hand to hold hers gently in my own. They didn't change the hands when they changed me. Maybe she would remember.

"Oh, Steve,", she gasped, as she felt my fingers entwine around hers, "I thought you'd never ask. Since I saw you at that pub, I felt something stir in me. Being here now, it reminds me of all that I've lost and all that I've missed. Yes. We can meet again."

Then we kissed. Not the fumbling, cautious kiss of the young, but a deep and all-embracing kiss that joined us together as one. I held her close to me and she pushed closer still to feel me against her. Nothing could describe my joy at that moment, but it was a joy that was tinged with fear. I drew away from her.

"Jean,", I said, "I know that this sounds crazy, but I think that I might love you. Forget the whys and wherefores of it and trust me when I say that. But, I don't want to hurt you. You need to know that I am not all that I appear to be. If you turn away now, then that's fine. It'll hurt me, but I can live with that. I just can't bear to see you hurt again. My life is bound in a lot of shadows and darkness and I can't really open up about a lot of it to you. I shouldn't even be thinking about us being together, but I can't help it."

I stood up and walked to the edge of the balcony, fumbling to roll another cigarette and then fumbling to light the tapered effort that I produced. I felt her presence behind me before she touched me. She reached around took my hand, lifting the cigarette to her own lips and taking a long draw on it.

"Everything has its dangers," she whispered as she blew the smoke across my face, "but what would life be like if we lived in isolation and afraid of everything?"

"No," she turned me to face her and put her mouth against my ear, "I'm not afraid of you or what you might be or do to me. I'll never say this again and we'll never mention it again, but I just have to tell you that it's so good to find you again. Whoever you are."

Chapter Twenty

Let's fast-forward now to my own birthday in that year of rediscovered love. Jean and I had grown closer together and, although we lived our separate lives and pursued our own diverse paths, our greatest joy remained in being together. We snatched time together in our respective homes and we were seen together as a couple on the social circuit. We were both cautious, but the feelings that we had for each other were a force that we couldn't contain. Lust played her part in our dates and we learnt to give each other pleasure in ways that would make an adult movie star blush. But love was the longer lasting feeling and our nights of union, comforting each other with slow and sensual lovemaking were the ones we most enjoyed.

I was often out of contact or in places that I couldn't share with Jean and yet, she understood this without a hint of jealousy or curiosity. How I had become what I now was, remained a mystery to her and yet, despite her journalistic instincts, she never probed into the past. And I, for my part, made sure that she had the freedom to do her own thing. Of course, I knew that she knew more than she ever let onto. We were happy to leave that bond of the unspoken between us. We were happy too, because the love that we felt for each other was a today love that existed in its own time and space and which didn't need any falsities about the past or foolish dreams about the future to exist.

"I've booked us a holiday for your birthday," Jean told me as we lay together on a lazy midweek morning, "and I don't care whether you like the idea or not because it's something that we need to do and it's something that I've never done."

She was referring to hiring a narrowboat for a fortnight.

"We are going to do one of the cruising rings and take a little detour down memory lane as well," she explained, "and we are going to be proper tourists, running aground, dropping mooring pins into the cut and stumbling into pubs, soaked to the skin."

I couldn't argue, nor did I want to. I lived on the canals but this would be something new to me. In fact, despite the fact that we could have travelled anywhere in the world and booked the most luxurious of hotel suites, it was this sort of thing from Jean that proved we were on the same wavelength. We weren't even going to use one of King's boats. This was to be a break away from it all with just us and a well-travelled hunk of steel, puttering around the waterways.

Prior to our leaving, I'd cruised my own boat slowly back from London and, as the new team, we had reviewed progress so far and analysed what we'd done with the Central Shires Trust. King had been sunning himself in the tropics but had joined us over a media link. The general feeling was that it had been worthwhile and that we had learnt a lot along the way. James had managed to complete the task of installing monitors into every NHS computer that he could access which meant that any anomalies were flagged up to us straightaway. We decided to ignore the many minor transgressions that we discovered, since to follow them all up would have taken an army. However, the search terms that we were using had already flagged up instances of bribery, mismanagement and, worst of all, more instances of the excessive use of both highly-expensive drugs and unnecessary surgical procedures.

This was to become James' new project, working with Charlotte to define the parameters, but seeking always to look at instances where the bottomless pit of NHS funding was being exploited to spend money that needn't be spent. It was a moral and political tightrope. Every penny spent could be justified in one way or the other. Our goal was to look at the justice of that spending. Bizarre anomalies reared their head all the time: the poorest patients were forced to take the bus or walk to clinics, whilst the wealthy car-owners who lived in the suburbs qualified for free taxis due to the distance they were away from the hospital; seriously injured victims were left to wait for hours in over-crowded accident and emergency departments, whilst 'Gender Definition' units were being built and staffed with abundant qualified teams.

Fortunately, once we as a team had discussed the limitations of our work, we were able to tweak the search robots to minimise the injustices that they flagged up.

Adam, meanwhile, was happy to work on his new inventions, adding as many as were suitable to the fleet of boats that the team were building, whilst at the same time, ensuring that we weren't using our knowledge unfairly. To flood the market with his innovations in one go would have been to have seriously impacted the existing boat-builders. Whilst I was away, I left my own boat with him, trusting him to refurbish and tweak her as necessary as it was a few years since she had been out of the water. I didn't leave him with a list of work that needed doing. Truth be told, I couldn't think of anything else that I might need. The excitement was in waiting to get the boat back and discover, on my return, the extras that he had installed.

I left Gilly with him as well. Although Jean and I were getting closer to each other each day, Gilly would have been a little too much for her to comprehend at this stage. I'd miss her. I know that sounds stupid, but she was more than just another of my animatronic support team. She was my pet, my companion and my friend. How much learning and adaptation Adam had built into her, I couldn't really tell, but it never ceased to amaze me when I saw that true dog-loyalty in her eyes. The plan was that she would be tested, improved and then switched off until my return. I didn't believe this for one second and knew that she would be a familiar sight as she trotted around the workshops and offices of the marina.

At the end of our review meeting, King asked to speak to me alone for a few minutes. We talked about Jean and he encouraged me in pursuing that relationship, even over and above the work I was doing as Kingfisher.

"You're in a period of choice," he told me, "and I need you to know that the decisions that you make, whatever they are, are alright with me. Jean will always be a part of our group, albeit as a participant who remains unaware of much of the bigger picture. You too will always have a place in the group, but that doesn't have to be on the front-line. Take your time and enjoy yourself."

I'd thanked him and finished the conversation feeling a lot better about things. My life was starting to fill up again and this was leaving me unsure about certain things. For one thing, at first, it had just been me and I'd been happy with that. I'd found a place in my isolation, my anonymity and simple life. Then ORB had happened, then the new team, then Gilly and now Jean. I'd packed my life with work before and it was fine if you remained in control of it. Now, I was feeling the weight of it a little and wondered if anything needed to be dropped. Although that then led to the inevitable question of what. Mind you, it wasn't as if I was that busy, and I still had a lifestyle that

141

would be the envy of many. Apart, of course, from the morally dubious and increasingly dangerous covert work that I did.

We picked the boat up on the anniversary of the death of Fran and the children. I didn't mention this to Jean for obvious reasons. This was the future. My family was in the past now. They were gone, never forgotten, but not a force to take away the life that I had in front of me. This wasn't a cold-hearted, mean-spirited way of thinking. It's the way that I would hope that Fran would have coped with my death. And the only way that I believed death could be neutralised in its power. Yes, it can hurt us and stir us and shake us and nearly break us, but it should never be allowed to bind us. For that reason, I was comfortable making love to Jean on that first night of the holiday.

The boat that Jean had hired was everything that a hire-boat should be; solid and reliable, comfortable but not luxurious, and coming complete with everything that you needed and nothing of the stuff that you thought you wanted. Even to me, a liveaboard boater, the hire-boat felt like something out of another world. Which is what makes this uniquely English holiday option so very special. Not only do the canals take you into a world-under-a-world, existing only minutes away from the familiar madness above it, but the format of the standard hire-boat takes you into a world away from all the mod cons and into one of functional minimalism. You have to take on water every couple of days meaning that every drop becomes precious and taps are never allowed to run and run. You have to find room for everything you'll need for the week in a space that's not much bigger than a prison cell, because the option to store all that extra stuff you thought you needed just isn't there. And you have to contend with a chugging and smoky engine, controlled by rough and ready manual levers because boat-builders still insist on keeping refinements to the minimum and believe that diesel remained the authentic choice for the waterways. Oh, yes, and you have to remember that all the gas you have to cook with is in that tank in the front, all the waste you deposit on board is going to sit in a tank underneath you for a week, and all the sockets and plugs and electrical equipment that you are so used to, will very quickly drain those four batteries in the stern.

And that's only the practical aspect of spending time on a hired boat. The biggest transition is the mental one. Forget the person that you were when you pulled the fancy car into the marina car park. Now, you are only the person that you are when all the trimmings are stripped away. Your identity is in yourself only. The boat belongs to someone else, the canals are a mysterious new territory, and every social convention that sways and swerves you in the world above is set aside. You are free to wear the worst pair of shorts that you can find, despite your milk-bottle white legs and the fact that it's way past the height of summer. You are free to don the daftest hat imaginable, even one with 'Captain' stitched into the peak. And yes, you are free to pour that first gin and tonic with your breakfast, despite the seven pm. rule that you set yourself at home.

What surprised me most, was how much of this transition of the self I also experienced as we headed off to do the Four Counties Ring. It was all new to Jean and, if I'm honest, I think it was a few days before she understood the limitations of the facilities on board. But to me, this was my way of life. Except that it wasn't. My own boat was my home on the water and I had become accustomed to travelling around in her. She was also extremely well-equipped. This was a holiday home, stripped of any aspects of my own identity and a different type of boat altogether. I too slipped into the holiday-boater mode and, after the first day's cruise, could feel myself relaxing more than I had for a long time, knowing that we were isolated, but never alone, and out of the mad, mad world for a period, even though we were cruising through its belly. I was so pleased that Jean had decided on this holiday for us. It was what we both needed.

We had the boat for a fortnight. The plan was to do the Four Counties Ring but take a detour down the Caldon Canal as we passed through the Potteries on the return leg. Jean had it all planned. I, on the other hand, was happy to let the journey sort itself out. I knew that there were expected times for certain parts of the journey but I had always doubled these because you never knew what was around the corner. At first, I humoured Jean and we stuck rigorously to her timetable. On day three, as we approached Audlem and the huge lock-flight there, I decided to wind her up by checking the spot that she had meticulously marked on the map for us to moor at, and then by using a tape measure to ensure that we were precisely at that point. She looked at me uncertainly as I looked back and forward from book to mooring space, adjusting the pegs as I went. My face was as dead-pan as I could make it but I couldn't keep it going.

"You seem to have measured the boat a little short, dear," I said, "as this space we are now in doesn't correlate exactly to the dimensions that you have supplied. I can check on the GPS if you want?"

"I'm sorry", she sulked, "I did my best."

I almost felt a twinge of guilt, but laughter won out.

"Hang on", she said, finally getting it, "you're taking the mickey, aren't you?"

"Not at all", I carried on laughing as I tied off the last rope and just before the bucket of canal water came towards me.

It was like that for the rest of the journey. We both knew the dangers of the diseases in the water that we were flinging about, but it still didn't stop us from catching each other at every opportunity. The best of it was watching the posh boat owners who thought our antics so very yobbish and childish, and typical of hire-boaters. Childish, I could admit to, but a yob? And as to my status on the waterways, well, they weren't to know that my other boat was worth more than their own with an added zero or two on the price-tag.

Chapter Twenty-One

Somebody had knocked a retaining pin out of one of the locks at the Audlem flight. That was the point at which Jean's plan went to pot and she accepted that we could get by if we just went with the whole journey on 'canal time'. From that moment on, she relaxed and began to understand what the canals were all about. She lived in the city, packed full of people, and yet, she rarely spoke to anyone. Here on the Shroppie, dressed in clothes that she would never dare to be photographed in, she couldn't stop chatting to strangers. And they were all happy to join in the conversation.

We were stuck about half-way down the flight, tied up in a space that would normally be prohibited, but without any choice in the matter. We congregated with a few other families and single boaters, just above the pub, and discussed what had happened and how long it would be. Jean was amongst the worriers who panicked about being stranded here for days. That was until the rest of us voted to adjourn to the aforementioned hostelry and let the official guys fix the lock in their own time. We won out and the worriers stopped worrying once the first pints were in.

The numerous topics of conversation that afternoon and evening were varied and interesting. Amongst the stranded were several groups of foreign visitors, Scandinavian, American and Dutch, who surprised us with their agreement over just how English they found this holiday to be. The rest of us, English to a man and woman, were forced to realise that they were seeing what we never saw despite it being right in front of our eyes. And it was always Englishness, even though we did try and correct them by reminding them there were canals in pretty much every country in the world.

"The way I see it,", one of the Americans first introduced the subject, "is that you English are summed up by this canal life. Take this lock closure for a starter. Now, back home, we'd already be getting together and thinking about how best to start a class action for the lost days of our holiday. But you guys, well, you're just, 'let's go down to the pub'. It's like you accept the cracks in things and just work around them."

"No help from you guys though.", a stocky, elderly member of the English group piped up, "We've been plagued by your litigious passions from across the Atlantic. These days all you get on the television or on your phone is some legal firm trying to tell you that you've been hard done to and that you're entitled to compensation. No offence, but it's an infection. And even when they do let them act for them, I guarantee to the man that underneath all the bluff and bluster, there remains a sense of guilt, even with those whose claim is justified."

"Yeah,", the American conceded, "we do have that to answer for. But let me give you another example. We were stuck at some other locks back there, just as soon as we'd picked our boat up. Where was that place, honey?"

"It was just past Stone,", his wife struggled to remember, "just as you head towards that big city. What was it called, Etruria?"

Her pronunciation was terrible, but nobody corrected her. Whatever arguments that we might use to defend our nation, some of the place-names and how they were pronounced were indefensible.

"Yeah, that's right,", her husband continued, "and we were queued up behind about ten boats. I asked the guy on the first boat up how long he reckoned we'd be there and he just looked at the line of us, added up some numbers in his head and told us about ninety minutes. And he was right. But not a single Brit batted an eyelid at that and we all just plodded through one by one."

"We do have a reputation for that,", I decided to join the conversation, "and as much as we complain, we still put up with it."

"I find,", the soft voice of one of the Scandinavian crew members entered the conversation, "that this country is one of many contradictions. Not that I say that as an insult. It is just how I am finding it."

"You don't know quite how right you are,", Jean replied, "and it's certainly something that I see a lot of. I work on newspapers, and some of the reports that I have to put together make me wonder what I'm doing. Don't forget that we are a nation of people who take a lot of their information from the press. Which may be the root of the contradictions you mention. Popularity sells papers and if my editor gets wind of a shift in opinion, we ride that. And along for the ride come the population. Take this whole immigration thing for example. One minute, we are proud to be a country that welcomes in strangers and there's a feeling of goodwill about that. The next minute, we're calling for the drawbridges to be raised and demanding an end to the

146

inflows. A few years back we had the whole Europe scaremongering thing, which you know all about, and I'm certain that it will come back again when somebody decides that there is some journalistic gain in it."

"And of course,", another of the Scandinavians intervened, "you never seem to remember that you are a nation of immigrants from the beginning. You still have our Viking blood in your veins, as well as a good mix of French and, of course, a German royal family. That's why we see you as a contrary nation."

"And,", the American gent added, "I don't get how you rant and rave about immigrants coming in and changing your national culture, when you bend over backwards to help them keep their cultural differences when they get here. Boy, how many mosques and temples and multiple language signs have we passed since arriving here! We'd never put up with that in the US. We're a nation of incomers but we have an identity of sorts that we seek to protect. We make them pledge an allegiance to the country and we don't let the drum of diversity bang louder than the drum of patriotism."

"I've got one for you.", a local who had been sitting at the bar joined us, "Hope you don't mind me listening in?"

"Hey, no problem.", the American lawyer answered for us all, "You go ahead."

"Okay,", the local man pulled a chair into our group and squeezed his pint onto the table, "so I heard Etruria mentioned before and I'm guessing you're doing the Four Counties. Now, did you meet 'Rod the Lock'?"

"Yes, yes!", the Dutchman seemed overjoyed to hear that name, "Look, I even have his card. He helped us with the locks and offered to come all the way out here on his bike and see us through these. Hey, what a character."

"You're right.", the local replied, "A real character. Been doing it for years and now he will even take washing in, although actually his Mum does that for him, and he'll move boats as well. Now, I'm not always politically correct in my language but it would be fair to say that Rod's a little unfortunate. I don't know what his story is but I think he's a bit simple. Or to be more politically correct, autistic."

He paused to take a long drink of beer.

"When you talked about contradictions,", he resumed his contribution, "I thought of Rod. You see, to operate locks for other people, even as a volunteer, you have to be approved and trained by the authorities. But Rod is allowed to do it in his unofficial capacity. Perfect example of us having too-rigid rules and then letting somebody work outside them because he's a little... well... special. That's one contradiction. But, my main point is this. Did you see the homeless lad at the small lock in Great Haywood?"

"Yes, we saw him,", I said, "he's done the lock for me in the past. I gave him some tobacco, but he didn't ask for anything."

"Okay,", the local continued, "well somebody wrote to the boating press about him, saying that he should be moved away and not allowed to help. You see my point? He's special in his own way. Not disadvantaged by nature but by circumstances. I can tell you, he was abused by his step-dad and has been in and out of prison. He does the locks to keep himself busy and off the drink. But the public reaction is different. We love Rod and let him do his bit, but the other lad is chased off. Contradictions again."

"Or plain prejudice.", Jean said.

"Maybe,", the local agreed, "but a good example of what you're talking about. Very, very English and very, very contrary."

With that, he finished his pint and bid us farewell. I knew the two people he referred to and he had a good point.

And so, it went on. I sat back and listened as everything and anything was thrown into the pot. I drifted off into my own world and let their thoughts and words conjure up a picture in my mind of this country that was so much a part of me. There are some things that will be forever England, but nothing could be more English than my lifestyle and the canals on which I pursued it. This network of hand-cut ditches spawned an industrial revolution that spanned the globe. And yet, the technology was delivered in such a uniquely English way that no other nation on Earth could have done it in the same way. They were functional waterways, diverted and directed by brilliant engineers, the first wave of multi-national industrialists and by the ruling classes. They did the job and everyone was happy with that. That's why they symbolise so much of what we are as a nation in our contradictions. We revolutionised transport but Heaven help us if we chose to bring it all up to modern standards with a new revolution.

Nowhere is England more English than on the canals. Yes, they meander through scenic fields and man-made landscapes that exist in no other countries and yes, they are English because they are predominantly found within the boundaries of the nation. But Englishness is more than a legal classification. What makes us unique are the very contradictions that were

148

being bandied about all around me in the conversation at the pub that night. We are a nation that has jumped firmly onto the train of sexual equality, but we wouldn't dream of letting Woman's Hour disappear off the air. We are a nation that has a cuisine which could only ever be described as plain and functional, and yet, we love a decent curry.

All the practicalities of my life on the waterways were there to sustain my being forever English; The Archers continued to run in the background, the churches and farms along the cut were the same as they had always been and the weather was a daily topic of conversation. No wonder we were so contradictory when we could never tell what the weather would be doing from one day to the next. I saw it all on the cut. The English passion for the rule of law and our pleasure in bending those rules or supporting those who bent them. The waterways authorities were the preservers of the rules but it was fine to overstay on a mooring as this was the single individual making a heroic stand against the faceless conglomerate. We are a nation of individuals who are known for their shyness and reticence with strangers and yet, on the canal, it was normal to strike up an instant friendship with a passing boater and to do so wearing the worst combination of sandals, shorts and waterproofs. A world leader in fashion, we dress like scarecrows at times and everybody has their own viewpoint, but so much of it smacks of deference to the press. Yes, there were many things that to me would be forever England, but each of them was reflective of our contradictory nature.

"On a positive note though," I felt myself drawn back onto the conversation as the wife of the American gentleman made her contribution, "you do seem to be a consistent and fair people when it comes to justice."

I was naturally keen to hear more of this.

"You see," she continued, "you are the nation that is the mother of justice and democracy. The English way of doing things seems to be about right. You respect your laws and you do so with tolerance. Yeah, sure there are contradictions in some of this, but generally, we feel safe over here. What I don't get though, is this stuff we read about with this new breed of vigilantes and, what is it, Righteous Correction and that other one, J for Justice?"

"You said it!", the youngest of the Scandinavians interrupted, "Man, we have our mythological heroes at home and our own avengers in Thor and others, and I know that you Yanks have more superheroes than the world will ever need, but this Righteous Corrector person seems to us outsiders

149

to be nothing special. Like, he or she could be any one of us here. Is there a place for that sort of stuff in England?"

"Here, here," that was the Dutchman intervening, "we think the same over in Holland. We're sort of getting a bit excited about the idea of a vigilante but man, we can't picture what these guys look like. They seem to be a group of people who want to play at justice, finding little things to take out a personal vendetta. And we can't imagine what an English superhero looks like. Maybe a bowler hat and tweed suit? Does that make sense?"

Jean and I agreed that it did. Nevertheless, I tried to defend the movement.

"What you have to remember," I said, "is that sometimes the law gets it wrong. Yes, we are pretty good in general at delivering justice, but there's a difference between justice and law. I think."

"Go on, I need to hear this.", the American laughed as he turned to me, "Oh and hey, I let the other comment go, but don't you forget that I'm a lawyer."

"Well, from what we know about these people," I framed my words carefully, "they look at situations where either the law has failed to deliver a balance of justice or situations where the legal framework is different from the justice of morality. A businessman legally avoids paying tax, thus depriving the nation of his fair share. It's even enshrined in law that tax avoidance is okay but tax evasion is not. That leaves a void in justice. Or, at the other extreme, a young kid is banged up for years because they got themselves addicted to heroin. Rather than treat their addiction, we write them off and put them in with the other outcasts. Legally faultless, but morally?"

"Okay, I get it with the drugs," the Dutch guy said, "but shouldn't you simply work to change the law. Why do you need a vigilante?"

The worst of it was, I couldn't give him an answer. Everything that they had pointed to about our rule of law and our justice system fought to silence the crusader for justice that I believed I was destined to be. It was something of a turning point for me. I'd been sucked in so deep into the RC and J for Justice movements that I had forgotten that they were not the root of justice in the nation but were simply a, possibly unnecessary, addendum to a system that generally worked. It was a painful revelation, but a liberating one.

"Okay," I conceded, "maybe you are right. Remember, these people aren't like Superman or Batman or the Norse gods. They seem to be a small group of individuals who want to make a difference, but yes, I can see that it's a fine line between delivering justice and creating new injustices by taking the law into your own hands. And what they do provide, is something of a voice for the marginalised and those who feel they have been treated unjustly. J for Justice in particular. It's a sounding board for the most part. A chance for everyone to think about justice and injustice."

"Like we say back home," the American's wife said, "about things being as American as apple pie, I guess that these people are as English as fish and chips. I say that we toast these very English superheroes and wish them luck in all they do."

I would never have believed that I would be in that position, but toast them we did. Jean winked as we downed the last of our pints in this gesture before excusing ourselves and returning back to the boat. That evening, I found it hard to settle. Much of my identity was in question, but that was nothing compared to the revelation that perhaps Jean and I could enjoy a life together without all the other trimmings that caused me so much conflict. Maybe it was time for me to move on and abandon Kingfisher. Hadn't I done enough already?

Jean continued to settle in to life afloat and, after a few days, we were enjoying a generally stress-free journey cruising around the Four Counties at a slightly more rapid pace than we would have liked. This was accentuated by Jean's demand that we leave time to drift off down the Caldon on the return leg.

"You know," she said to me as we set off down the Middlewich Branch of the Shroppie, "I think I get it now. This life is just one long pub crawl isn't it?"

"You may be right," I laughed, "But you're not complaining, are you?"

"I love it," she said, "it's like being in a foreign country on home territory. Reminds me a little about the time I spent in Gibraltar. England with sunshine. I'd never think of wandering into a pub I didn't know but here it just seems the natural thing to do. And you meet so many different people. It makes me question so much of what I perceive people to be. It's good. But how on Earth do you manage to stay so fit and trim with all that beer?"

"Oh," I told her, "I keep myself active in my spare time. I do a bit of running, help out in manual jobs when the opportunity arises. And push myself in a few other things."

"Of course," I smiled at her, "you and I have been burning off a few calories lately. I'm not sure what's wearing me out more, you or the rigours of navigating."

And it was true. We weren't fawning all over each other like teenagers but we were falling deeper and deeper in love and celebrating that feeling in the most intimate ways. We were away from everything else and happy to be together. So happy in fact that, by the time we had arrived at Consall Forge and were sat together in the pub where I had bailed out years before, I did something that I never thought I would be capable of doing. I asked Jean to marry me, and she accepted.

Prior to that night, we'd experienced another little incident that was part of the fun of our holiday but which affected my decision to seek a lifetime with Jean in a number of ways. We'd been working our way down the Trent and Mersey and were pushing on to Wheelock to catch up on our schedule. It was unseasonably warm and I had a perverse desire to see how Jean would react to a bit of night cruising. She didn't like it. Not surprising really, as I wasn't a great fan either, but it gave us the chance to get back on track and have a bit of a laugh as we moored, recalling her panic at the journey.

"Don't ever make me do that again.", she said as we tied the boat up.

"Bit of fun wasn't it?", I laughed.

At which point she just pointed to a nearby café and told me to get the boat sorted whilst she started on a well-earned full breakfast. That breakfast was followed by a midday nap, which was followed by the inevitable night out around the nearby pubs and the consumption of too much alcohol.

Where we'd moored, there were a few boats next to us and we stumbled back to ours just before midnight, trying to be as quiet as we could, but failing every time we fell into a fit of giggles. Not that our silence would have made much difference, as we were in for a slightly disturbed night. We were wrapped up well as we sat out on the deck of the boat to enjoy a last drop of whisky and a few cigarettes before bedding down for the night. Then the commotion began.

"You're a dirty little man.", the harsh Geordie accent echoed along the towpath from the open window of the boat next door, "Now you just wipe that up and make sure you do it properly."

We heard a mumbled voice apologising and started laughing uncontrollably. Then the first of the plates was thrown and we shut up pretty quickly.

"I said do it properly, you pig.", the cackling voice accompanied the smashing of plates and a few grunts and groans, "Look at the mess you've made. My mother was right. You are a filthy little man, aren't you? I said, aren't you?"

152

We were torn between laughter and fear. Yes, we knew that we should have been very English about it all and scurried away to bed but it was a strangely addictive conversation. We hushed each other as we waited for the rest of the drama. It soon stopped being remotely funny.

"Get here.", the female voice demanded, "Now, apologise."

Another smash and then the unmistakeable cry of a man in pain.

"Oh, you wimpy little man.", the voice taunted, "I should punish you properly. You make me come out on a boat and all you can do is make a mess and leave your stinking, dirty underwear on the floor. You're pathetic, that's what you are."

We looked at each other as we heard more bangs and clatters, each one accompanied by a plaintive cry from the person we assumed to be the Geordie woman's husband.

"Oh, and don't even think about doing that.", she continued to scream at him, "because you've made enough mess already. You can go out there, like a dog. Yes, that's what you are. You are a dirty little dog. Now, get out."

As we heard the key turn in the lock, we slipped back inside and peered out through the curtains. The moon was full and there was enough light for us to see the stooped figure of a man exit the boat and slip into the bushes. On his return, we could make out the blood on his face and we watched as the pain of aching muscles caused him to grimace as he opened the door.

The following morning, we started off at the same time as this couple. We greeted each other in the usual way and I asked if everything was okay as we'd heard a couple of noises that seemed to come from their boat.

"It's all fine.", he smiled at us, "I just dropped a few plates doing the washing up. Nothing to worry about."

We let them go before us and we held each other closely as we sat in the morning sun. At that point, I realised just how much I loved Jean and just how lucky I was to have a partner who accepted me as I was and who would never seek to hurt me. We weren't perfect, but we had more in our favour than a lot of couples and that helped me decide on what to do.

The marriage proposal was the main fruit of that night, however, I also broke all my own rules and switched on my phone to send a brief message to James. I'd witnessed something that might be worth investigating.

Chapter Twenty-Two

'London Evening Post', 15th November, 2024

'Gamers Facing Meltdown Demand Answers'

Members of the 'Strike Force' gaming community are up in arms at their loss of service following what has been described as an unprovoked attack by the 'J for Justice' movement.

At exactly 12 noon today at least 40% of Strike Force accounts were rendered inaccessible at the same time as the affected account holders received messages advising them that they had been caught using their accounts to share copyrighted data.

Strike Force began life as another variant of an online, simulated world, however, its popularity has increased in recent years as users have seen it expand into a wider community that computer experts have likened to a world within a world. Part of that expansion has allowed users to create secure zones in their accounts where they can meet with other users and swap data files in the privacy of their own domain.

It appears that the attacks on accounts by the self-styled, 'J for Justice' movement are an attempt by them to stop the illegal swapping of copyrighted data, particularly film and television content. But there are concerns that this action may backfire on the movement who have previously received a great deal of public support.

"What right has some unaccountable group got to tell us what to do?", asked Harry Frobisher, a senior

Strike Force player whom we interviewed today, "They may not like some of the things that happen in our world, and I confess that yes, some illegal data trades do go on, but who appointed them as judge, jury and executioner?"

In their message to users, the J for Justice group explained that their actions were 'unpleasant but necessary' as they sought to make a point about material being swapped as being nothing more than common theft. 'We ask that you refrain from stealing in the future, or we will be forced to take further action. Theft is theft and we are not working on behalf of the film industry or any other interested parties. Our concern is that if one crime becomes acceptable then this can lead to further transgressions.'

Only account holders using systems that were hardwired to the internet seem to have been affected, although the team at Orbit Software, who run the virtual world, believe that accounts were targeted based on the amount of data being exchanged by that user.

Tomorrow, we aim to run a special feature on the legitimacy of the action taken by J for Justice and would ask any readers with a point to make to contribute via our website.

++++++

'The Huddersfield Guardian', 26th November, 2024

'First Male Refuge to Open in City'

Following a substantial anonymous donation, a team of activists have opened a new centre for victims of domestic violence. One with a difference. The Sea Change Centre opened earlier today on King Street with a stated aim to ensure that male victims of domestic violence have their own refuge and place of safety.

It is estimated that a large proportion of domestic violence goes unreported every year, primarily because many of the victims are male and are therefore reluctant to be exposed as being weak.

Grant Cheshire, the interim Director of the centre admitted that things had moved extremely quickly after they were asked to put the centre together by an anonymous benefactor. Although a local initiative, referrals have been coming thick and fast from all over the country as a specially designed web forum begins to expose the depth of this rarely discussed problem.

Special Report, pages 5-6, 'A Sea Change in Responses to Domestic Abuse?'

++++++

'Preston Tonight', 31st November, 2024

'Naked Councillor Steps Down'

Controversial local councillor, Lewis Thomas, has resigned with immediate effect from both his public position and from his role as 'Preston Property Tsar'.

His resignation follows an incident last week when he was arrested and charged with indecent exposure, having been seen running up and down the city's high street, naked but for a jester's hat. Video footage of the hapless councillor's antics has been a hit on the web as he was captured on CCTV before being stopped by local police and taken into custody.

Although Thomas, 45, has agreed to undergo psychological testing prior to his first court appearance, he appears to be unapologetic about his behaviour and will only say on record that 'I am the Emperor and that was my best outfit'

It has been speculated that this comment refers to his role in some recent property exchanges conducted

156

by the council where purchasers of redundant housing stock have found out that these properties are not the bargains they had been led to believe they were.

Since accepting Thomas's resignation, the leader of the city council, Mary Goldsmith, has advised that full refunds will be offered to any buyers of those properties who feel they were misled.

++++++

Our holiday was long over and Jean was on an extended assignment in South America. I was heading up North for the Winter, hoping that the solitude and the rigours of a proper canal journey would be enough to help me forget her absence. There were also some things that I'd been asked to look into which required me to be on the Leeds Liverpool Canal.

We hadn't kept up to speed with what the team were doing whilst we were on holiday, although I had chuckled a couple of times at news articles that had the imprint of either ORB or J for Justice all over them. In November, we'd met to catch up and I had put my boat back into the water, thanking Adam for not changing her too much, but knowing that she would reveal her secrets to me over time. And I'd got Gilly back by now. She was activated pretty much all the time and I marvelled at the programming that had her crying and jumping around as she saw me after a month away.

The team gave me a summary of what they'd been up to. James was particularly proud of his work with the men's refuge and thanked me for tipping him off. I was happy with his work on this and felt that it adequately began the debate about some of the potential and very real injustices of masculinity. Adam and Charlotte had been responsible for the naked councillor incident, having heard rumours from a visitor to the marina which they were able to confirm in a secret visit to Thomas' home.

All three of them had pooled their resources to bring about the development of the Injustice Anticipation Programme, or IAP, that was feeding them data about situations that were developing and enabling them to stop the injustice before it occurred. It had been this programme that had targeted the users of Strike Force.

The IAP worked in a fairly straightforward way. Charlotte led the way and was able to spearhead the development of this system because her

157

particular approach to the study of criminology was about looking at the root cause of transgression. She was drinking in all the available theory that she could in criminology, sociology, psychology and all the related sciences and was working to use these to track what exactly had been the deciding factor in the transition of a normal, law-abiding citizen into a moral deviant or criminal. What was particularly challenging for all of us in this, was that Charlotte insisted on refusing to separate crime and justice. We had to call King in on the discussion. His input had been invaluable and helped us reach a decision about our future.

"I like what Charlotte is saying,", he told us after listening to her presentation, "and I think we should go with her proposal. We've separated crime and justice for too long. Steve, I know your views on this and that's fine, you keep on with the correcting injustices. Oh, and congratulations on your engagement. The rest of you seem happy enough to include crime along with moral corrections and adjustments to compensate for official failures. I can go with that. Just remember, the legal system first. That has to be a condition."

This freed up the guys at the marina to work on projects that prevented crimes as well as on those that simply corrected injustices. For my own part, I kept my activities distanced from this aspect, but they were never destined to stay that way forever. As King had said, it was a step too far for me, but I also understood that if we were in a position to intervene prior to a crime being committed then that had a justice element to it. He wasn't to know I'd already reached a state of equilibrium in my own mind and was less averse to crime-stopping than he believed me to be.

On the back of this agreement, James punched in the data and the search programme was live. It picked up activities that were the pre-cursors to crime and allowed for an intervention from the centre that might prevent the crime being committed. Hence, in the Strike Force situation, alerts had been generated that had stopped the perpetrators in their tracks before the harm had been done. What the press reports were not aware of was that all of the targeted users were making preparations to slide off the visible radar and join the file-swapping element. This was a shot across their bows and hopefully a timely warning. Those already using the system for this activity had also been blocked and that element of their account disabled. But this was my concern, that we were acting on crimes that had not yet been committed or acting to punish offenders in our own way. I trusted the team to deliver a system that was fool-proof, but I was also reminded of the errors we'd made in the past with ORB. Errors that had taken innocent lives with the use of a faulty, artificial virus. Lives that belonged to young people who were close to our leader's heart.

Jason King contacted me a week after that first discussion and helped me reconcile the activity of the team and my own position.

"You're still your own man, Steve.", he told me, "The others are moving in a slightly new direction and, believe me, I share a lot of your concerns. God forbid we do what the Order did. You can keep your distance from it, no problem, just trust me that I am monitoring it more closely than the team may think."

I thanked him for taking the time to speak to me directly on this.

"Oh, that's not the only reason I'm calling.", he said, "In fact, we have a little Winter project for you if you're up for it. The others are aware of it and happy that we are right in pursuing it. We wanted you to settle back in first before I ran it by you."

I listened as he explained what he wanted me to look into. It was one of those missions that wasn't particularly time critical and which required some thought to tackle. It was perfect for me and just what I needed to round off the year and take some time to work on a real Kingfisher project. Once I'd agreed, the team put the files together for me and waved me off from the marina as I made the journey back up the Shroppie again, heading for a city that I still hadn't visited despite the distances I'd racked up in my travels.

Chapter Twenty-Three

Liverpool was not the city I expected it to be. I came the long way around, up through Chester and then into the docks on the Mersey. Adam had assured me that the boat could handle this and she didn't let me down. The pilot led me into the docks after a smooth passage across the river, commenting on what a pleasure it had been to escort my boat through. He knew it had an electric engine, which seemed to impress him, much to my surprise, but what he didn't know was that she now had extendable fins below the waterline that turned her into something of a mini-catamaran. Add to this the new coating of extremely low-friction hull paint that had been applied and you can understand why she cut through the water almost as if it wasn't there.

Mine was the last crossing before the closedown for the Christmas period. My mooring had been reserved in the docks for a few weeks, but it had taken me longer to get here than I had expected. I'd like to say that this was because I'd been diverted on route to perform my duty as Kingfisher, but the truth of it was that I drifted quickly back onto canal-time and made the most of the journey. Without Jean, I was back to my solitary existence and thought that I ought to enjoy the bachelor life a little, prior to our getting together for the rest of our lives. I had no regrets about asking Jean to marry me. Quite the opposite. I couldn't wait for us to be together all the time, but that only added to the pleasure that I found in being on my own for a period, away from other people and alone with my own thoughts.

Gilly was good company. She forced me to get out and about and to walk the Winter-crisp towpaths, although I never forgot that I could switch her off whenever I wanted to. Those times were few. When I did take a break from her it was usually for a practical reason like not being able to take a dog into a launderette, although sometimes it was for the purely selfish reason of wanting to be in my own space.

During this cruise, I watched the last remnants of autumn fade away and, as the nights drew in, I settled in front of the fire and worked my way through all those books that were mounting up and demanding my attention. I was still trying to tackle Shakespeare, but that was something you couldn't rush. His was a rich, exquisite food that you ate in small portions. Between courses, I'd cleanse my pallet on some Ogden Nash, or tuck into the fast food of a decent, mainstream thriller. The boat and all that came with it was a constant reminder of the other string to my life and yet, even with so many reminders so close by, I could easily disappear into a parallel world of fiction and switch off from that part of me.

There had been a few situations that I could have taken action on along the way. Not major breaches of justice, but instead, annoying little situations that I was made aware of, usually by talking to people in the pubs I worked my way through. Since that holiday with Jean, my thinking had mellowed quite a lot, partly because we were to start a new life together and partly because of that multi-national conversation that we had been a part of in Audlem. If you looked for unfairness and injustice, then you were sure to find examples all around. And yet, for the most part, this country was a pretty decent place to live in, peopled by a mixed and diverse race of individuals who lived good lives. I'd spent too long in the shadows, forced to look at the exceptions to the rule. Now I was getting a fuller picture and was truly understanding that people were people the world over and that injustice was part of life, but not quite as big a part as I'd made it out to be.

That said, I was forced to intervene once. It was in Chester. I'd planned on staying just one night there but those plans went to pot as soon as I started working my way through this city. There was a show that I wanted to see, and there were a lot of pubs to visit, particularly pubs that served proper ale and which had an offering that you couldn't really do justice to in one visit. All told, I think I was there for a week. And it was on my third night there that I met with George and Georgina. Once we'd got the predictable questions and jokes out of the way about their names, and I'd told them they weren't the first pair of George's I'd met, we drifted into the usual talk about anything and everything that came up. I wasn't probing for any information to act on. In fact, I was probably, subconsciously, trying to avoid that sort of thing. Nonetheless, it was Georgina who threw the grenade in.

"Of course, it's going to be a lean Christmas this year.", she said, "What with having to look for a new job."

I asked her for more information.

161

"Oh, it's nothing really.", she explained, "it's just that I'm being encouraged to move on from my current role. Change of management, face doesn't fit, you know how it is."

I pressed her for more details.

"I'm UK Sales Manager for a cosmetics firm.", she told me, "And I was hoping to get the role of Sales Director. I got through all the interviews, was shortlisted down to two and then had to watch as one of the Managing Director's boys was given the position. Once that happened, I knew I was on borrowed time, although they were nice enough to write to me to tell me that I was first reserve if things didn't work out with the new guy."

She continued to explain how, within weeks of this new appointment, she had been approached by the HR Manager in a 'without prejudice' conversation and had been offered a decent settlement agreement if she would leave quietly.

"The money's good.", she said, "but it's not about that. I've put so much into that job and I just know that I was right for the next step up. I'm not so daft as to think I am the perfect person for the role, but I do know that I should have been given the chance. The new guy, well, his background isn't even in sales. I'm just worried about how long it will take me to start over again. My identity, my confidence, so much of me is wrapped up in that company."

She gave me more details and, by the time we parted later that evening, I knew that she had suffered an injustice. This was the sort of low-level injustice that happened every day to ordinary people and which broke no laws, officially, but which could have such a dramatic impact on people's lives. It was rarely a clear-cut situation, although in this case, I thought it was. At least it was worth investigating.

The following evening, I went back to the same pub. For one thing, I had only worked my way across half of the beers on offer and, for another, I hoped to see some familiar faces. I wasn't to be disappointed.

"Steve.", I heard Georgina call across to me.

"Oh, hi.", I took my pint to their table, "You're looking chipper."

"We're celebrating.", George smiled as he answered me, "Georgina got the promotion.".

"Fantastic.", I said, "but how did that come about?"

"Well.", Georgina explained, "it seems like the new boy had a bit of a history that he hadn't disclosed. They found out this morning and called me up. Looks like the MD has some explaining to do as well."

162

We sat talking about the situation for a good while as they gave me the full details. Of course, it was all old news to me, but I didn't let on.

What had happened had begun with my being unable to sleep on my return to the boat the prior night, thinking about their situation. I now take this inability to drop off as a sign that I need to look into things. I'd had to wake James up at 2 a.m., which didn't go down too well, and then I'd had to set off early in the morning. If the information that James had supplied wasn't bulletproof then I'd have left it, but he came up with the goods within an hour and had sent them through to me. He'd also woken up the others and it was Adam who rang me in the middle of the night to confirm the documents had been sent.

"Look man," he said, "if you need to go there, take the bike."

"Yeah, sure!", I replied, "You want me to peddle up the M53 motorway?"

"Seriously man," he was adamant, "take the bike. It's all kosher and you'll love it."

When we'd finished talking and we'd all agreed that I was okay to proceed, I had to think about how to make the journey to Birkenhead. Adam rarely let me down, so I checked out the bike anyway. I couldn't believe what I saw as I watched it rise up from the bow of the boat. This wasn't the old electric bike that had served me so well. This was something else. In fact, it was a fully-fledged motorbike, full sized, if a little slim, and as it emerged, a number plate dropped down over the rear wheel, blank at first, but then taking on a legitimate registration.

The Kingfisher outfit had always had a helmet. That meant I would be street-legal. What else could I do but hop onto the vehicle and let it take me to my destination.

It had been years since I'd ridden a motorbike, and I'd never ridden one quite like this, but it was so easy to get back into it and I was soon speeding to where I needed to be at well over a hundred miles an hour. Traffic was thin and I was fairly certain I would evade any police who were around, however, if they did clock me on a speed camera, the guys at the centre had assured me that the plate recorded would have had every trace of its existence removed. Try and justify that one, Steve Barratt!

I arrived at the house at six in the morning. It wasn't long before my target was in his car and behind the wheel and I was following him to his destination. I thought he would take the bait of the e-mail that James sent, but chose to follow him to make sure. After a ten-minute journey, he pulled into the drive of another house and I watched as he approached the door.

"Jim.", he greeted the man who opened the door.

"Peter?", the man asked, "What are you doing here?"

"You wanted me to drop by?", my target was clearly confused, "You sent me an e-mail."

"Sorry mate,", Jim replied, "not from me. Come in anyway, we need to discuss some stuff that's happening."

They entered the house and I watched as they moved through into the kitchen. I hadn't bought any of my friends with me on this journey but for what I needed to do, the window-sticker that I applied to the kitchen window would do. It was almost invisible, and yet, it was able to focus sound and visual images from whatever it was looking at into my helmet's monitors.

"I've had Bill on the phone already this morning.", I could hear Jim saying, "Seems they have something on you. It's not what I think it is, is it?"

"You mean Bill as in HR Bill?", a very confused Pete replied, "Because, seriously, I don't know what's happening here."

"Look,", Jim was losing patience with his friend, "I got you into this role and you assured me that the other stuff at Grayling Technologies was cleared up. Seems you were a bit optimistic. Our guys have been tipped off about the 'borrowing' incidents and about some of the, shall I say, unconventional interviews that you conducted with various ladies."

Pete, my target, was speechless.

"I stuck my neck out for you,", Jim continued, his voice getting angrier, "and I had a lot of opposition. Please tell me you haven't shafted me here."

"I don't know how they got that information.", Pete mumbled as he spoke, "But what do you want me to do?"

When I heard what they planned, I decided that my role in this was ended and I slipped away and boarded my bike just as the window sticker melted and ran clear over the windowsill.

That was why I knew that Georgina would get the job she deserved and that MD Jim would have a few questions to answer. As for Pete, I didn't really care too much about him as the stuff that James had dug up on him was more than enough to satisfy me that he wasn't right for the role. It transpired that the two were old school friends and golfing colleagues and that Pete's appointment was more to do with this than any ability he might have. It went on all the time, and it will go on all the time, I'm sure. It's not just the old-boy's network either, it's about friends of friends, it's about secret societies and it's about placing unsuitable but safe people around shaky leaders. I couldn't change it all but I felt very good about intervening in this little situation. It would be a happier Christmas for the two Georges now.

As I moored up among the old tobacco warehouses and hooked the boat to the power supply, the Chester thing seemed so far away. Every week was a new adventure for me and I still had my project here to finalise. Then of course, there was my Christmas Day to enjoy. Jean was stuck in South America. We had tried to work out how we could get together but decided in the end that it wasn't going to happen. I'm not a great one for celebrating dates anyway. Last year had been brilliant but it had been more about the companionship than about the festival. This year, I would be happy simply to book into a local hotel, have a blow-out of a Christmas dinner, get steaming drunk and wallow in a decent bath. Which is exactly what I did.

I enjoyed that hotel so much that I stayed into the New Year as well. It wasn't cheap, but then, I wasn't poor. The selling point to me was the height of the suite that I was given and the fact that it had a balcony. On the boat, I was away from people enough, due to my being under the big world above. In that hotel, I was away from the hurly burly because I was so high up, but I was also able to enjoy a stunning view over the celebrations without having to prance around singing Auld Lang Sine. The balcony meant that I could smoke to my heart's content as well. Altogether, a rare few days of enjoying the luxuries of the outside world and a great opportunity for me to discover this new city of Liverpool that I barely recognised from the days I travelled here to sell sanitary equipment. You could never change the weather, nor would the Mersey ever be a particularly dramatic river, but putting those things aside, this city I was now in was a vibrant, cosmopolitan and very upwardly mobile, modern European metropolis.

The city's growth was spreading outwards too. That was the real reason that I was in the area. I was going to visit Bootle. Once a place that I would be reluctant to park my car in, but now, a town that even I would struggle to buy property in. The boom had come about for several reasons. Fracking was big business in the area, but the main core of the activity was around the recently gentrified parts of the coastline. Logic dictated that new properties exploit the old and tired parts of the coast, the docks that were no longer carrying a great deal of cargo and the Victorian beaches that had long disappeared under years of detritus.

The big change had come with the campaign to rename the town. It kept the same spelling, but since Bootle was impossible to say without it sounding like the last place on earth that you would want to stay, the marketing men started pushing for it to be pronounced Boolay. They couldn't quite get people to buy in to the addition of an accent to the last e, but even so, that simple change of pronunciation had been more than enough to begin the revival. This was the new 'Northern Riviera' and Bootle (Boolay) was at its heart.

Chapter Twenty-Four

All that remained of the Bootle that I knew was the meandering Leeds Liverpool Canal that was now clean, tidy and provided with plenty of moorings. The new moorings were adjacent to what was once one of the most notorious shopping centres in the world. It must be over forty years now since that tragic day when the worst of human evil was played out in that location. Still, our race had redeemed itself with the justice delivered to the perpetrators. They were imprisoned but given the second-chance that ten-year-olds deserve. One of them, if you could believe what was written in the press, was now a productive member of society under a new name, the other had thrown it away and was back in the prison system. That was the best justice we could hope for.

In its new incarnation, the shopping mall spanned the moorings and these were easy to access, under full CCTV protection and had the complete range of facilities. Part of the regeneration of the area had been the call to get boats back onto the canal and this had been the result. That January, I had them all to myself. Not particularly unusual, due to the season, but also reflective of the time-lag that blackspots on the waterways system suffered from. In a few years' time these moorings would be full.

I wasn't moored there for comfort though. This was the spot that was nearest to my intended destination, which was a ten-minute walk away. Having arrived in the late afternoon, I put off my visit until the following day, choosing instead to do a bit of shopping, enjoy a very nice chain-restaurant meal and then have a leisurely stroll about the town. I'd had clients here in the past, when government offices had been dotted around the area in a desperate bid to bring employment to the area. On those visits, I always wondered how much of my car would be left when I returned to it. Now though, the place felt safe. In fact, I felt a little underdressed as I walked around in my boater's scruffs. The tower block that adjoined the shopping mall was now clad in glass and way out of my league financially, whilst only a handful of government departments remained housed in

167

the newly refurbished office blocks that had thrived as they fed private enterprise.

It was to one of these blocks that I walked the following morning. In my time it had been Balliol House, grey and ugly but in need of a substantial amount of new porcelain and therefore the source of a decent commission to me. Now, the grey was gone and surfaces that weren't glass were either painted in bold colours or clad in polished stone. I was in jeans and a casual shirt, trying to look like one of the many workers who milled about on the tree-lined avenues that linked this network of offices. Grabbing a coffee from a mobile stand, I sat and looked at the building, contemplating my best course of action.

The man I was looking for had his headquarters in this building. They occupied a whole floor somewhere in the upper reaches. His name was Sir Stewart Landry. He was a familiar face to most, both as a successful businessman and as an A-List celebrity who attended the functions that the fashion papers loved to cover. King had asked me to look into his activities. In a brief conversation he outlined his concerns. Landry had met him in some resort or other and, unaware perhaps of who he was talking to, had mouthed off about the secret of his success. He thrived on the anonymity of the limited company. His modus operandi consisted of buying into failing businesses at ridiculously low rates and, if they worked, taking the profits and the credit. If they didn't, and this was his trick, he would let the administrators take control, write off the company's debts and then swoop to cherry-pick the leftovers. It was a familiar story, premised, in King's view, on a broken system. He wanted to make an example of one of its worst practitioners.

"And not for vengeful reasons, Steve.", he'd assured me, "It's to try and put an end to the harm that's caused to countless individuals who only ever lose out at the transition of a company. Countless small suppliers go bust because of this practice and then people like Landry come in as supposed white-knights to take over. Individuals lose their jobs, can only get basic redundancy payments and then find that their pensions are diminished. Okay, so the government backs the pension schemes but not one hundred percent and always at the expense of other tax payers. And Landry and his ilk get away with it because it's always the company that is the problem, not the people who run the company."

"Anyway,", he'd concluded, "have a sniff around and see what you find. You have our authority to act if you feel it necessary, but if you do, be a bit smart about it and let's get a powerful message out there."

168

Which explains why I was sitting on that bench on a frosty January morning staring at an office block in Bootle. There were enough outdoor heaters dotted around to make the place a good meeting spot for locals and office staff alike. This also attracted a few brave souls willing to risk being evicted if they could just get a chance of begging a few coins. One of these beggars was sitting as close to Balliol House as he could without breaching their boundaries. A few people dropped coins in the cup he proffered, but most just walked on by: the homeless remained invisible even now, if you chose to make them so, that is.

I spotted Landry heading towards the entrance just a moment before hearing the raucous cry of the beggar as he passed.

"I know you.", he screamed, "I know who you are."

Landry sidestepped the outstretched hand that threatened to trip him then hurried into the building. I decided to follow and get a feel for the man. I too had to pass the beggar, but my passage wasn't as smooth.

"I know you.", he screamed at me, "I know who you are."

"Very good.", I whispered, dropping a few coins in his cup.

"No.", he screamed again, "I know you. I really do. I know who you are. I know what you are. I know."

As I tried to walk away he was that bit too quick for me and grabbed at my ankles. He pawed with both hands at my trouser legs and seemed to be trying either to pull himself up or pull me down.

"Enough.", I shouted at him, "Let go. You don't know me. I don't know you."

With that, I pulled away, but as I looked down at his face I had to wonder even to myself whether we did in fact know each other.

I followed Landry into the building, joining the public queue to edge through the security scanners. I had a hastily made appointment with a team of financial advisers that I had set up a few days earlier and that was to be my route into the building to get a feel for the layout. As I approached the scanners, I took out the keys and coins that I knew would set off the buzzers, thinking that that would be enough. It wasn't. The moment that I entered the scanning zone, every emergency light that they contained flashed up an alert, whilst sirens and bleepers filled the hallway with an ear-piercing din.

"Step back from the scanner.", one of the uniformed guards shouted, as every one of his colleagues moved towards me.

"Step back now and raise your hands in the air.", he said raising what looked like a cattle-prod just in case.

"Hold on.", I protested, "this has got to be a mistake. Come on, I'm not carrying anything."

"Sir.", a more senior guard shouted to me, "you need to listen very carefully. We need you to lie down on the floor."

"Come on.", I thought this was a joke.

"Now!", he screamed, "Do it now or we will be forced to neutralise you."

I didn't like the sound of that, so I decided to comply. As I started to lie down, the guards circled me with their cattle-prods to hand, and that was when I realised what was going on. As they put all their attention on me, and as every other member of the public had run out of the reception area, I could just catch a glimpse of the beggar from outside slipping under a barrier and making an impossible leap up towards the edge of the atrium. That was when I remembered where I knew him from. He was no beggar. He was Charlie Burrows, AKA 'The Indigent'. ORB were ahead of me here and whatever he had tagged me with was powerful enough to have me detained and give him an entry to the block.

"Look up there...", I tried to say, but by that point I was being tightly restrained by at least half a dozen guards.

They searched me for twenty minutes whilst the building went into lockdown. As a private company they were allowed to do this. It had been like that since the reforms of the early twenties, when regular police officers were under so much strain that it made sense to let private matters be dealt with privately.

When they were satisfied that I was clean, their supervisor sat me down in his office and tried to apologise.

"Look, I'm sorry.", he said, "You lit up every light on those scanners and that means you were a potential risk for guns, explosives, drugs and numerous other things. I don't know how that happened, but we're quite satisfied that you're clean. We'll have the machines checked as soon as possible."

"You don't get it, do you?", I said, "That was a distraction. I tried to tell you but you were too busy trying to bust me. Now, listen carefully. I was tagged in some way to make that happen, right, and the reason I was tagged was so that somebody could get into this building. Check your cameras, check with your team. Someone is in here."

170

"Yes, sir,", he replied wearily, "the beggar from outside. We heard you first time."

"Okay,", I tried to reason with them, "let's take a different tack. I think that Sir Stewart Landry was the target. He went in before me. You saw him go in. Now see if you can get him on the phone. He's the one you need to worry about."

They left me in the locked office whilst they made enquiries. After ten minutes, one of them came in with a cup of coffee and a sandwich for me and explained they'd be through with me in a few minutes. Another ten minutes went by, then the door opened again, but this time it was a regular policeman who stood there.

"We need to speak, Mr Barratt.", he said, "But not here. I need you to come with me to the station. Mr Landry appears to have gone missing and you seem to know something about it. I hope you don't mind but we will need to cuff you first."

I was speechless. They cuffed me, read me my rights, then bundled me into a van for the short ride down to the police station. That Sir Stewart was missing was no great surprise to me. That I was to spend the night in prison, I must confess, was not something I could have predicted. Still, I wasn't going to let ORB get to me too much. They'd won this round but I wasn't out for the count yet. I didn't like being beaten and certainly not by them.

Chapter Twenty-Five

I left Marsh Lane police station the following morning and trudged back to the boat along icy pavements. They'd treated me fairly but I'd had to think on my feet as they questioned me into the early hours. Nobody could understand why I had set all the alarms off. I knew that when Burrows had grabbed my ankle he had attached some sort of device to me, but they weren't accepting that. I can understand why. There was no trace of anything that might point to this. How ORB had done that, I wasn't entirely sure. Their theory then was that I was setting up a distraction to allow the kidnapper in. It didn't even seem to help that it had been my own tip-off that sent them searching for Landry.

"Look," I tried to explain, "I saw that guy enter the building. I tried to point it out but they wouldn't have any of it."

"And you just happened to think of Sir Stewart Landry?", the interviewing officer asked wryly.

"Yes," I said, "after all, I'd seen him enter the building just before me. I put two and two together and helped you guys to get four, now look at me, being held here on suspicion of I don't know what."

And so it had carried on. They gave up around two in the morning and let me go to my cell to sleep. I managed to catch a couple of hours but was woken early for a final round of questions before being given a cursory breakfast. Then they simply released me.

Back at the boat I huffed and fumed through the morning. My mood wasn't helped by the roars of laughter that came from the team as I briefed them on the situation. I didn't find it funny. I was gunning for The Indigent and I was going to make him pay. I don't like revenge. I don't like vendettas. But this was different. There was a righteous correction that needed delivering and I was going to make it happen. I just wasn't sure how.

By lunchtime I was a bit calmer. I decided to take Gilly for a walk and harnessed her up in preparation. The police were monitoring me, that much I knew, but what more innocent activity could I be involved in than taking the hound for a stroll? Naturally, I would want to walk past the spot where yesterday's excitement had kicked off, so that's just what I did.

There were a few more people hanging around the offices that morning. Not a lot had been reported in the press but that hadn't stopped the rumour-mill. This gave me a bit of a problem as I needed to get as close to the front of the building as I could. At least I thought I did. Then Gilly started to pull me. I tried to pull against her but she was focusing on something about twenty feet to the left of the bench where I'd been sitting the day before.

"Come on Gilly.", I whispered to her, "That's only me you can smell. I was here yesterday."

Still, she persisted in dragging me nearer. Then I saw what she was looking at. It was a small piece of torn card that I recognised as a part of the paper cup the fake beggar I was pursuing had been waving around. I realised then what she wanted.

"Litter bugs.", I muttered to myself as I picked the piece of card up and walked towards a bin.

Needless to say, the card never made it into the bin. Instead, I let Gilly grab it in her mouth and lay it down at her feet as she sniffed it. After a minute or two she looked at me and I knew that she had picked up a scent.

"Show me.", I said to her as I let her guide me away from the office and further into the town.

The Order for Restoring Balance and I go back a long time. They had been my mentors, my instructors and my support network. They had encouraged me and given me the freedom to develop into what I now was. It had all gone wrong and we had parted company, but their thought processes were still my own and their methods were engrained in my heart. Because of that, I had a hunch that I hoped would pay off.

The Indigent and his captive could be anywhere. They may not even be together, and it might even pan out that Landry reappeared for business as usual. The police, for all their suspicions, hadn't even received a ransom note or any similar communication. But I knew ORB and I knew how they operated. I'd had plenty of time to reflect on our crossing paths again and reconciled myself to the fact that it was inevitable. Our systems and their systems were working to highlight instances of injustice and for the two separate search routes to meet at one person was always going to happen. I knew that King was still in touch with them in the loosest possible way, monitoring their work and ensuring that they avoided the excesses of the past. Even so, I think he would be surprised that we were targeting the same person.

Gilly kept up a steady pace as she followed the scent that she'd picked up from the piece of discarded coffee cup. According to Adam, she not only had the scenting capabilities of a normal dog but was also able to process DNA to aid her in her tracking. I'd long since stopped doubting Adam in his claims and yet, I never ceased to be amazed as I watched his workmanship in action. Fortunately, the weather was on our side. It was a cold afternoon, but there were no hints of rain and the sky was bright overhead. We must have walked for a good hour, Gilly staying focused with her head down and me simply following wherever she led us. We walked through the bustling centre of the town, onto the main road that led away from Liverpool, eventually picking up some side-streets as we entered one of the less gentrified suburbs.

Gilly paused, sniffed the air, then proceeded down a short road that was a copybook image of the terraced, artisan dwellings that were the natural fabric of this region. She slowed as we passed by one of these houses and gave the slightest nod towards the gate. I looked the building over quickly and read the sign in the window: 'Bed & Breakfast – Vacancies'. Then Gilly turned on her heel and led me away before anyone could see us.

That evening, after much soul-searching, I switched Gilly off. She had her uses and I would even begin to say that I was beginning to love her a little, but for what I had to do, she would have been more hindrance than help. Whenever I pressed that switch on her, I had to look away, even though I knew that the plaintive look in her eye was nothing more than the pre-programmed response of a multitude of electronic circuits. With that job done, I prepared everything that I needed and suited up in the light, waterproof Kingfisher outfit that Adam had recently upgraded.

"Oh yeah, man,", he'd told me, "apart from the updates on that suit, and I mean updates man, just watch out for the boots. And I also took the liberty of cleaning them all. Man, I know it's not something you can take to the laundry but come on, you really need to find some way to freshen them up after you've used them."

I had to concede that it was true. In a house, so many of the practicalities of life would be that much easier. Not that they were filthy. It was just that I was back on the cigarettes now, more than I should have been, so that nuance of odour a fresher nose would sniff out was often lost on me. And they weren't exactly suited to being washed at a launderette.

174

I used the pod to take me nearer to my destination, exiting it at bridge number seven where a healthy collection of dumped detritus made a perfect hiding place for it. I floated a little back the way, then, after checking that the coast was clear I let the boots lift me out of the water and onto the street above the towpath. This was an area that had yet to be incorporated in the new town plans and therefore had very few cameras monitoring what was happening. It was almost as if the heavy surveillance further into the redeveloped zones had been a means of pushing the less desirable out into these suburbs. Or maybe I was overthinking the whole thing. Either way, it worked in my favour and allowed me to move unseen towards the boarding house where I slid over the back gate and floated gently up to the roof.

I sat in a gully between two slated eaves and prepared what I had to do. The first thing on the agenda was confirming that both Gilly and my hunch were right. She had sniffed them out to this location and it fitted well with my understanding of the way ORB operated. They liked to hide in full view and part of this approach, one that we emulated, was to take up residence in the least likely spots, often on top of the scene they were involved in. I chose a mouse to help me out in this. They weren't uncommon in the area and they were able to bend and flex into the most unexpected positions. I watched its progress on the monitor in my helmet as it manoeuvred down through the loft, into the corridors and then up and past every bedroom door. It was programmed to pick up the DNA that I had downloaded from Gilly earlier in the afternoon. And it found it in the last bedroom it approached.

I called the mouse back to me and identified the window that I needed. Carefully, heeding Adam's warning about the boots that had already caught me out a few times that night, now that he had supercharged them, I lowered myself down until I was resting against the wall with the window to my right. Reaching out towards the frame, I let a spider slide onto the woodwork, watching as it scurried around seeking an entry point before disappearing from sight. Once that was away, I released one of my new toys and hoped that it did what I was told it would do. Disguised as a snail, it moved incredibly quickly as it tracked around the perimeter of the glass. Having completed the full circuit, it moved to the centre of the window, emitted the faintest jet of gas from the top of its shell, then began to fall away, taking the window with it.

This was the point at which I had to trust in the friends that helped me in my role. As the glass was removed I slipped into the room and saw what I needed to see. Recognising the suit that I'd seen him in the day before, I knew that it was Landry who had his back to me and who was slumped forward in his chair, out for the count thanks to the injection the spider had delivered. Opposite him, the sight was less reassuring. Burrows was still conscious and was staring in my direction. As soon as I saw him I fired out a bolt of Blue Light that encircled him and pinned him to the spot, stopping him in his tracks as he tried to rise to confront me.

"Kingfisher.", he sighed, "I might have known."

"The Indigent.", I replied, "Nice to see you again. And well done for yesterday, you had me there."

"Well, don't say I didn't try and warn you.", he laughed, "I did tell you that I knew you."

"But,", he continued, "that doesn't necessarily work in your favour. Because, knowing you, I can anticipate you. We're not as naïve as you think we might be. You might have got Landry with it, but that little insect of yours would never be able to carry enough sedative to knock me out. ORB still tweak our biology a little. Oh, and this stuff is so yesterday…"

As he said this, he shuffled in his chair and I watched as the cords of Blue Light that bound him, slowly unravelled and fell away.

"You can't really blame us.", he said as he rose and walked towards me, "After all, that stuff was an ORB invention. You should realise that we have all moved on and finding a neutraliser for your little electric rope wasn't too hard."

"You might want to stay seated.", I looked him straight in the eye as I spoke, shaking down my arms as if to loosen them, "As you say, we have all moved on."

Before he had a chance to react I lifted my hands and let out a stream of Green Light that instantly wrapped its tendrils around him and rendered him rebound.

"Okay,", he said, "I'll let you have that one. Do I have to stand here now? Or can we be a bit more civilised about things?"

The Green Light was stronger but more malleable than the Blue Light had been. James had developed it as an improvement on Adam's design and they had told me that I could alternate between the two with a shake of my wrists. The Blue used less power so was the preferred option until they'd sorted the Green out properly. I loosened the grip of the current circling my opponent and let him settle himself in the single armchair that was tucked in a corner of the room.

"Landry will be out for an hour or so,", I told him, "which should give us long enough to agree terms."

"Sorry,", he told me, "no negotiating. That's one of the new rules. We have missions, we deliver on those parameters. No deviation, no embellishments."

"Okay.", I replied, "Give me a moment to think."

I looked around the room and saw that Landry had slumped on top of a computer tablet as he'd slipped into unconsciousness. I moved him to the side and picked up the tablet.

"Let's see now,", I whispered as I looked at the multitude of open files on the computer, "looks to me like we are having Mr Landry impoverished and yes, transfers of his funds are moving out to compensate some of his victims. Am I close?"

"Whatever we're doing, Steve,", he almost sneered as he answered me, "is whatever we are doing. My mission. My duty."

"Be like that, Charlie.", I replied nonchalantly, flicking open the communication switch in my helmet and connecting to James.

"Hi buddy,", I said, "can you take a look at a hard drive for me please? I'll hook you in now."

I placed a small glass bead on the screen of the computer and watched as James accessed it remotely and started working his way around the hard drive. I could hear him mumbling to himself as he worked, picking up a few of the things that he was saying, but generally not comprehending much. After a few minutes his tone changed.

"Steve", he whispered, "I think I've made a boo-boo. You may want to step back."

As I did so, the tablet began to smoke and then melt away until it was an amorphous blob on the desktop, not quite smouldering but certainly emitting a foul smell.

"I should have realised.", James chastised himself and explained to me, "This is ORB we're dealing with, right?".

"It is,", I told him, "and sorry, I should have warned you. Our paths have crossed a little unexpectedly."

"Well, you ain't getting anything more from that computer.", James sighed, "So stupid of me. I wrote that destruction programme myself."

We disconnected and Burrows and I sat silently for a few minutes.

"I suppose.", I broke the silence, "that I should let you contact your guys. See what they want to do."

"It's an option.", he shrugged.

"But.", I continued, "we do have a bit of a history and just now, I seem to have the upper hand. Of course, I understand that your support team will be joining us soon."

"Okay Steve.", he leant as far forward as the Green Light would allow him, "why don't we lay our cards on the table and be less hostile in this? You know my position, you've been there. I know it's hard for you to accept but you can trust me. We can call it honours evens so far, but I would like to know what the Kingfisher's response would be. How about it?"

I released him from the electronic shackles and we reached out and shook each other's hands.

"It's not enough.", I told him, "What you plan for Landry isn't enough. Sure, his victims get some sort of redress and he suffers financial meltdown but it doesn't stop him doing it again. That's how I came into all of this vigilante stuff. Years back, the driver that killed my family would have kept on causing harm if I hadn't prevented him from driving. I hated myself at the time, but my only option was to cut out his eyes. Anything else, he'd have been given an adapted vehicle. Same here. Landry will do it again."

"So, what's your proposal?", he asked, "I presume that you were casing Landry with an intention. And by the way, yes, you are right my team will be here shortly. We have a few minutes though and I'm curious to know, what's Steve Barratt's plan? You're still a legend at the centre and I guess I maybe owe you for helping us get ORB back on track."

I detailed my plans to him.

The following day, in a small village in the Yorkshire Dales, an unidentified man was found wandering aimlessly along the High Street. He appeared to be extremely drunk and was taken to the small police station there and kept overnight to sober up. When his condition remained the same and showed no sign of change, the local psychiatric hospital was contacted and asked to take the man in.

There he remained for several months. He could make no coherent explanation of what was happening, despite his having a full understanding of the situation in his own mind. Every word he tried to speak came out as garbled nonsense and every time he tried to use his hands or his feet to write what was in his heart, they simply would not obey. His face and

178

his fingerprints were copied and circulated to any organisation that had an interest in missing persons, but these drew a blank. He was in essence a nobody. He was a mystery individual who nobody could identify. In fact, he was as nameless and faceless as the limited companies he had once controlled.

The Indigent had backed me up on my plans and ORB had, reluctantly I feel, agreed to my proposal. The money was moved, of course. But once that had been done, Landry was reborn as the man that the Yorkshire Health Service now referred to as Jonathon Dorrell, a fairly lame variant of the American John Doe, but chosen because it was the Chief Executive's idea.

We knew all of this because we could see through Landry's eyes. The army of tiny viruses that we had injected into his brain had rallied in a spot in the centre of his frontal lobe and were feeding us data, whilst at the same time interfering with his muscles to distort his face, recolour his hair, stop his speech and give him the motor control of an advanced Parkinson's case. Whenever they were scanned from outside, they separated and became invisible, although each continued its action autonomously. They would test his DNA at some point. At least, we hoped they would. That would identify him as Landry. That is, if they were still considering Landry to be a missing person after the anonymous sightings and rumours that were circulating. These seemed to point to his having fled the country after embezzling funds.

Either way, we had agreed that this would be a one-year sentence. We weren't evil after all. Then it would be up to Landry. He could choose a more honest career path or he could try and get back to his old ways. We hoped he'd learnt his lesson, but you never could tell with people like him. We laid it all out for him, prior to our intervention, advising him that this was only temporary but explaining that temporary could be quite a long time if he chose not to act differently. It was up to him.

Chapter Twenty-Six

Jean came back to the UK in early March, 2025. I met her at the airport and spent a couple of days with her in London. We caught up on everything that had been going on and quickly settled back into the deepening love that had continued to grow even when we were apart. We were old enough to be out of the whole possessiveness thing, but we felt ourselves knocking years off our days in some of the ways that we acted. Love has its own momentum and neither of us were bound by the dreamy convictions and delusions so prevalent in youthful, first-love days.

We walked the capital, took in the sights and the shows, and we spent long, lazy days together, doing nothing but loving each other and loving being with each other. I'd left the boat up North, just beyond Skipton, and had hired a car to bring me to the big smoke. There was something liberating about being with Jean in her flat, where I had all the luxuries that came with a modern apartment but had them without the mass of encumbrances that came with actually owning one of these places.

We remained undecided about what our marital situation would look like. I was reluctant to be dragged back onto land full time, whilst Jean was wary of moving onto a boat. We didn't stress or fret about it. It would all become clear as we neared our nuptials. And, if it didn't, we'd try one, then the other, or we might even consider a third way. We were one of those lucky couples who had everything that they wanted in each other, but were supported by having a financial situation that gave them everything that they needed.

"South America gave me a lot of time to think.", Jean settled into my arms and let me play with her hair as we relaxed in her flat, "It was longer than I thought it would be, and I covered areas that were never on the original agenda. You know that I'm going to have to hide away for a few weeks to put it all together, but after that, I'm not sure what I want to do."

I didn't interrupt or try to add to the conversation as I let her think about what she was saying.

"You see,", she continued, "this assignment seems to me to be an end in some way. I want to put it to bed and move on. While I was out there, and one of the reasons for it taking so long, the paper kept sending me rookies to work with. I'd like to say that they were hard work to be with, but the truth of it is, they were damned good at what they did. I may have had the experience and the contacts that were guiding us through the project, but they had that youthful passion of ambition and dreams. They looked to the future with wide-eyed wonder and believed that they could reach the heights that I've scaled, and then some. And, I have to admit, I believe that some of them will."

"Go on.", I whispered, when the next pause seemed to stretch forever.

"I don't have that passion for the business anymore, Steve.", she seemed relieved to have said it, "And without that passion, I don't think I can carry on in journalism. I've had a great career and I've been very fortunate to get the plaudits and the awards. But it's not enough. Now that we are together, I want to take a step back. I feel like I've paid my dues and now, all I really want to do is to spend my time with you. That's not too soppy is it?"

"Jean,", I laughed, "soppy is not a word that can be attributed to either of us. No, I get what you're saying. I was the same when I first came out of the world of work and chose to settle on the boat. Then Boat Space came along, and Jason King, and that gave me enough to fire me up again. Things come along, even when you think you're escaping it all. You go for it."

"It was a film that I watched that made my mind up for me,", she said, "and, for the life of me, I can't remember what it was called. It was awful actually, but there was a scene in it where this couple who'd been married for years were settling into retirement. Something struck me about it as being so, I don't know, so real. They were ordinary people, had lived ordinary lives and would die without anyone noticing the loss. But still, they seemed to have it all in each other. Maybe I'm getting old, but that's all I want now. You and me, living, loving, laughing together and then fading away."

"Sounds morbid.", I turned her head to me and kissed her gently, "But actually, I can see where you're coming from. Maybe it is an age thing. I know that you loved the limelight and attention of being a top-notch reporter and I've had my moments with Boat Space when we're launching something radical. And yet, just being together like this is more satisfying. Let the younger generation take over, that's fine by me. Let them enjoy the moments we've enjoyed. What we have now is what we both want just now.

181

Whatever anyone says, there are very few lives that make a massive impact on the world, but, by the same token, we all do our little bit every day."

"When we were on the boat," she said, "I began to get a sense of that. It's a different world there, or at least, it seems to be. You don't have any of this manic chasing to get your name in lights and, like you say, it's a world where little human interactions make up a whole that just works."

"But," she continued, "it's also damn cold at times and the showers leave a lot to be desired."

"Which puts us back at square one," I replied, "with the choice between boat or flat."

"How about," she lowered her voice into a very pleasant and sensual purr, "a little country cottage for half of the year and the boat for the rest? With lots of extra holidays and adventures dotted in there as necessary. Sound like a plan?"

"You didn't really say, 'a little country cottage', did you?", I laughed, "Jean, my dear, you may be a few years older than me but you're not that old. But yes, I'm happy to go with that for now. It'll come right, whatever we end up doing. And, as for us being together and easing back on the work front, I'm all for it. You can have a crack at that novel you always wanted to write, whilst I can get properly into the role and spend my time tinkering with the boat."

"Tinkering?", she laughed and punched my arm, "Now who's the old fogey? Are you sure that you don't want to do some pottering as well?"

It wasn't the sort of conversation that changed the world. I remember it though because it was the night that I knew for sure that I was making the right choice in marrying Jean. I could admit to her that I was in the same situation with Boat Space, in that I was able to leave it to the new generation and know that they would take it to the next step. What I couldn't share with her were my mixed feelings about the other job that I had. Being Kingfisher gave me a sense of purpose, and yet, I was increasingly worried that that sense of purpose was about me rather than the delivery of justice. The new generation of James, Adam, Charlotte and the others were more than capable of doing more than I could ever do. They didn't need me as much as I needed them to need me. This was the bitter-sweet revelation that I was battling with. I think it was the same conflict that Jean was working through. Now that I'm older still, I realise that it's the universal conflict we all experience at some point in our lives.

The evening had finished with a game of Scrabble. It was a slightly inebriated game that descended into farce towards the end as we decided to call it a draw. We might have sat and watched a film together instead, or we might just have sat with our noses in two completely different books. We might even have taken ourselves out for a stroll in the nearby park. The detail didn't really matter. What mattered was that we were together and that being together was enough for us. Maybe Jean had a point. Now might indeed be the time for us to step back and simply enjoy each other. She seemed more than happy to do so and, for my part, reluctant as I am to admit it, I shared her feelings, and I missed her more and more when she wasn't around.

Chapter Twenty-Seven

Whilst Jean was finishing up the assignment that had taken her away from me for so long, I returned back to the boat and cruised her down towards the Midlands. The 2025 International Boat Show was promising to be 'the biggest and best yet', as it always did and Crystal Clear had taken a decent sized stand at the exhibition. Because we were now a relatively big player on the boating scene, I was offered a mooring at Gas Street, putting me right at the heart of the event.

I was there to help out. Tony and Kate had been given free rein to organise our part in the event and, despite having the burden of a particularly energetic one-year-old, they had done us proud. Not only that, but the guys in the boatyard had delivered some great work. It was a strange feeling for me to wander around the exhibit just before the show opened and see what Boat Space had become. It was no longer a single guy making innovative furniture for narrowboats. Now it was a fully-fledged boat-builder, hire company, training provider and design centre, and a part of the Crystal Clear Marine Group. How well they had done in the short time that they had been going was testified to most powerfully by the ranks of training certificates, diplomas and yes, even a degree, that were the centrepiece of the exhibit. I almost shed a tear when I read the degree award. It was a BSc., awarded to a young trainee who had stunned everyone at the yard as he discovered a savant-like ability to comprehend engineering principles. His lack of formal qualifications forced him to crunch through an Open University degree which he'd nailed with a first in record time. The recipient's name was Philip Rivers. The secret of his success had been that Kate had recognised his dyslexia as soon as he arrived at the yard and had worked with him to shake the scales from his eyes.

But it wasn't the awards that caught the public's imagination that year. Boat Space was showcasing a second-generation of their electric engine, and had coupled this with batteries and a solar array that meant they could offer a guarantee to those who used the system that there would be zero running costs. The purists were still clinging on to diesel, as were most of the hire companies, but it was only a matter of time before they would have to concede defeat. Now that electric cars were becoming the norm, there had been a shift in public opinion something like the move away from smoking. Users of fossil fuels were penalised by the tax system and were finding it increasingly difficult to justify their position. As a returning smoker, I felt a little for them, but even still, couldn't really argue their case.

My role in the exhibition was to demonstrate the new boat support systems that had been developed by James and Philip, who seemed to be getting on very well together. I sometimes watched them in their interactions and it was amazing to see the combination of their intense respect for each other, coupled with a competitive jealousy when one of them made a breakthrough. This time, they had approached the problem of boat blacking. I was demonstrating two systems. One of them was a compact and portable boat lift that could be used to raise a boat out of the water, wherever it was moored, thus negating the need to take the boat to a slipway. It was a simple idea but even I struggled to explain how it worked exactly. The operator would take the equipment along the towpath, drop it into the water under the boat to be lifted and then the system would balance the load and use hydraulics to lift the vessel up. Having been raised, it could be blacked from the towpath, the system spinning the boat around when one side had been done. For those who didn't like this idea, their second invention was for use by boatyards. It was an all-in-one machine that could black a boat in two hours. Again, it was simple idea. A vertical unit, not dissimilar to the scrubbers on a car wash, was positioned alongside the boat. It read the profile of the boat and then began a circuit around the vessel, jet-washing and scraping the hull with its leading edge then drying it and applying blacking from its rear. One circuit was enough to finish the boat. In addition to this, and my small contribution to the affair, the unit was fitted with ultrasonic sensors that scanned the boat as it went around and produced a comprehensive hull survey report as a bonus.

King's input into these two items had been as dramatic. The boat lifting kit formed the core of a franchise operation that I knew would soon be taken up nationally, whilst the blacking machine was only available for lease. Had we been a publicly listed company, by the end of that show, our share price would have doubled. As it was, we left the event knowing that our own privately held shares in the business were making us all quite wealthy.

As the exhibition drew to a close, Jason King flew in to give a short presentation and to announce to the nation that Crystal Clear would be trebling the number of apprentice engineers in the business. This was a shrewd move and a timely one. Young offenders were fast disappearing from the diminishing number of institutions still operating. Of course, there were still the feisty, the disadvantaged and the just plain nasty young kids around, but they were now given a lot more support in being helped back on track. Philip Rivers knew something of the reasoning behind this, as did I. Things had begun to change with the new institution that had been built when our paths crossed in the recent past. Neither of us made any claims to have been a part of the change though, we were just happy to see it happen.

With his usual flamboyance, King finished his speeches by announcing an end of show party that Crystal Clear were throwing in the adjoining exhibition centre. Never have displays that took so long to create and install been dismantled in such a quick time as exhibitors rushed to clear the decks and get to that party. I was one of them and I am reliably informed that I had a good time at the event but, truth be told, I remember very little of it. There are some odd images in my head of an impromptu singalong that I may have started and of some highly embarrassing dance moves, but other than that, I only remember the feeling as I woke up the following morning.

King stayed around for a few days and called us together to discuss our work beyond our public image. Since we'd last met, he'd been in touch with ORB a few times and they had agreed a set of protocols that allowed our two separate organisations to operate as independently as before, but which allowed for a new level of mutual support where necessary. Alongside this, they'd instigated certain cross-checks to ensure that we didn't meet again unexpectedly.

"They've come a long way.", he told us, "And I mean that both figuratively and literally. They've changed the way they operate and I can assure you that we can be confident that the excesses of the past are over. On top of that, they've abandoned the underground centre and pretty much everybody who works with them lives in the real world. They still retain some live-in associates, but only where that is the individual's choice. They're in the heart of London now, right there in full view of everyone, but you'd never know they were there. I promised not to tell you guys any more than that."

He'd collated a dossier for us to read through at the meeting, outlining a brief summary of the work we'd achieved so far. It was a 'read it until you're finished with it' document, of which no trace now exists, but I remember how brilliantly it was put together. I could do the sums. Adam, Charlotte, James and the newest recruits won hands down in the number of interventions that they had successfully delivered. They also won the imagination award for not only identifying target areas but also the way that they delivered justice. My own contribution was tiny in comparison, but King had created the document in such a way that we all looked to be contributing equally. I was thankful to him for that. It was so typical of him. And the last thing I needed just now was something that told me the truth that I already knew deep down, that I was fading into the background as these bright new lights were taking up the torch of justice.

"Anything to add, Steve?", King asked as the meeting was drawing to a close.

"I'm good", I told everyone, "although I do think that this is the time for me to congratulate you all for the work you are doing. It's humbling for me. I feel like a proud parent at times when I read all this stuff. I hope that doesn't sound patronising. You have made your way on your own, let none of you ever doubt that, but I still feel I've played a part. All I can say is, keep up the great work, and don't forget your old Papa out there. I can still take the fight to the baddies when you need me to."

"Steve", James, surprisingly, was the first to respond, "you will always be our inspiration. Without you, ORB would be what it was and we would still be hidden underground. I know this isn't the place for daft sentimentality, but I also know what it's like to feel isolated. Please, don't ever feel you're not the lynch-pin of what we're doing. Without you, even doing less of the dirty work than you used to, we'd be nothing. Is that right?"

He looked across to Adam and Charlotte.

"Man, I couldn't have put it better", Adam said, "Don't leave us Steve. We need you."

"Same goes for me.", Charlotte had tears in her eyes as she spoke, "You're more to us than Kingfisher. You and Jason are the family we never really had. We may see less and less of each other as we grow apart, but your place, Steve, will always be in our hearts."

There was an uncomfortable silence which King did nothing to break. He simply looked at me and arched his eyes. He knew me better than I knew myself and that look meant a lot to me.

"I'm not going anywhere", I laughed, "but you do seem to forget that I am getting married. Kingfisher may have to stay in the closet a little more than before. I'm only glad that I can do that and not worry that you guys aren't filling in for him."

"Which reminds me.", King said, "I need to have a quick word with you Steve, about the wedding. The rest of you okay to break for lunch? Head down to the restaurant and tell them you're with me. They'll look after you."

The others filed out of the room and King and I moved towards the small bar area at the side of the meeting room.

"Still whisky?", he asked.

I accepted the offering.

"So, you and Jean, everything set?"

I told him where we were at. The date was set for October and everything was going to plan. I also mentioned that we still hadn't decided about where to live.

"I might be able to help you there.", he said, "In fact, that's why I wanted to catch up with you. Thing is, I've just bought a spread over Norfolk way. Farming enterprise as its main concern and a lot of land that we're allowed to develop for manufacturing. That's why I snapped it up. Now, part of the purchase is a beautiful cottage just on the edge of the plot and half a mile from the nearest town. I'd like to give that to you as a wedding present."

"You don't have to.", I protested, "You've done more than enough for us as it is."

"Nonsense,", he snorted, "do you want it or not?"

"Okay,", I laughed, knowing that he knew my protest was half-hearted, "yes, we'd love to take it off your hands. Thank you. My only proviso is that Jean has to agree as well."

"Dear boy,", this time he was laughing, "she already has agreed. You don't think I'd dare do anything without asking her first. Here, take the keys. The address is on the tag there. Think it looks alright inside but if it needs any work, catch up with my guys on the main site and they'll sort you out."

I took the keys from him and thanked him again.

"One last thing,", he said, "about you and Jean. Whatever you may be thinking about the other parts of your life, forget them. I see you two together and I see a very special love that you need to put first, above all other things. Listen to me, Steve, you can let the other stuff go if you have to. You've done more than enough. Nurture the love that the two of you have and let it blossom. And that's an order!"

We clinked glasses and downed the whiskies, then we adjourned to join the others for lunch.

Chapter Twenty-Eight

'Aberystwyth Observer', 20th June, 2025

'Teachers Reinstated as Education Board Makes U-Turn'

Two primary school teachers who were suspended in early May for refusing to comply with an instruction from the Welsh Education Board, have been reinstated after an unexpected reversal of policy by the same Board.

Julie and Harvey Peters, who teach at St. Mary's primary in Aberystwyth, hit the headlines last month when they ignored the ban on three-legged races imposed by the Education Board. Parents and teachers were in unanimous agreement with the teacher's decision and the annual town race went ahead without incident. As the responsible parties for Health and Safety overseeing the event, Mr and Mrs Peters were shocked to return back to school only to be suspended pending disciplinary action.

Whilst support groups have campaigned vigorously for their reinstatement, it was a surprise to all when the four members of the board of governance announced that they had had a change of heart and would no longer impose rigid controls over school safety. In a brief statement, their Chair, Helen Wills, explained that 'We feel that parents should exercise their own judgement in assessing the risk to children of playground games and sports day activities.'

The Board apologised for any distress that may have been caused to the two teachers and has thanked them for their understanding in this matter. Local Head-teachers, contacted by this paper, have all expressed delight at this unexpected change of direction and feel that it is the right decision to allow parents and teachers to decide certain aspects of governance at a local level.

++++++

'Macclesfield Sentinel', 6th July, 2025.

'Flood Barriers to be Installed by Hooper Homes'

The long-running dispute between Hooper Homes and owners of properties that they built in Parker's Field, seems to have been resolved with the company agreeing to build a 'comprehensive and impenetrable' flood barrier around the development.

Hooper Homes have been locked in a bitter battle with those who purchased houses on this site and have always argued that the risks of flooding were minimal and that the new estate was a positive contribution to the local housing stock. Residents appealed to the High Court for Hooper Homes to take action, after insurance companies assessed the new-build properties as uninsurable. They lost their case last week, which makes it surprising that Hooper Homes have now chosen to act.

In a press release, the owner of the house-builder, John Hooper, explained that, '…whilst the High Court decision vindicates our stance, we do sympathise with those who bought these properties and have decided to complete the flood defence works as a gesture of goodwill.'

Residents of the estate are, naturally, delighted at the news and extremely pleased that a new children's play area will be incorporated as part of the works, making the money they invested in taking legal action seem worth every penny.

++++++

190

'The Leek Weekly Advertiser', 14th July, 2025

'Local Church to Host Month Long Revival Campaign'

Father James Gardner, vicar of St. Peter and St. Paul's church, the iconic building at the centre of our High Street, has announced a month-long series of events to encourage locals back into the church.

There had been some speculation recently that the church might close, due to dwindling numbers in the congregation, but these seem to have now been well and truly scotched.

"Our church,", Rev. Gardner explained, "is too precious to be allowed to just disappear. We want to place it back in the heart of the community again and I sincerely apologise that we have not been as helpful to the town in the past as we might have been. With a new parent and toddler group, an open-door café and a team of counsellors on hand every day of the week, we believe that we can offer support to those in need, whilst explaining in simple terms, what the Christian message is."

The revival month will begin at 7 p.m. on Sunday night with a special service where the famous comedian Sammy Sanders will make an appearance to speak about how his own life was turned around after he found faith. Tickets are on a first-come, first-served basis, free from the church offices.

++++++

As that last meeting with King and the team was drawing to a close, they presented me with a gift that was worth much more to me than even the present of the cottage. They unanimously agreed that I would be allowed to do my own thing again and not have to get authorisation from them for anything and everything that I did. They weren't cutting me loose, nor were we going our separate ways. They simply recognised that the shift in

191

the type of work we were doing gave me an opportunity to do what my heart felt needed to be done, whilst they tackled the challenges that their search engines threw up. I would still be able to call on them for support and they, in turn, could ask for my help. But now, they would monitor each other and I would be trusted to do what I did. It was encouraging and I saw the positives in it. We were a family, but we were heading our own separate ways. I could live with that. In fact, I was quite fired up by the prospect.

The big test came when June finished her project and we agreed to spend a couple of months on my boat, tootling around the canals and generally enjoying ourselves. This would be a first taste of the life we had planned and I needed to see how far I could pursue my other goals when being so closely observed. Marriage would potentially clip my wings but, I figured, you can clip the Kingfisher's feathers but you can't stop him flying.

It wasn't easy. We met the teachers at the far side of the huge aqueduct that we crossed after cruising along the Llangollen Canal. I love that aqueduct. More so now, after seeing Jean's face as she tried once to peer over the side. One look was more than enough for her and she cowered in the main cabin with all the windows shut as I plodded slowly along, thoroughly enjoying the breath-taking view.

"Are we nearly over?", she kept asking, not believing me when I told her we were clear.

When we were eventually over, she dashed off the boat and sat on the nearest bench, no doubt plotting a suitable revenge for me. I tied the boat up and joined her, unable to stop myself chuckling and trying not to get myself into more trouble.

"I did the same to her.", the man on the next bench said to us, pointing to his wife, "So don't worry."

"I think that our response was by far the most sensible.", his wife quickly intervened.

"Agreed.", Jean said firmly, "If people were supposed to go across valleys like that, we would have wings. Or at least do it on bridges that had some sort of side."

They were on a day boat, enjoying the Summer weather and trying out something that they had always wanted to do but never got around to, or had the time to. We chatted, as you do, and then we walked the short distance together to the nearest pub. Over a pint, they explained their situation. They had taken a stand against the ridiculous rules that were being imposed on them and the ban on the three-legged race was the final straw.

"For over a century," Julie Peters explained, "the town of Aberystwyth has run its three-legged race. This year, they banned the kids. It's a step too far. First it was having to wear safety glasses for conkers, then an end to British Bulldog, and then no to snowball fights. Kids need to be free to take risks."

We all agreed that the situation was crazy and Jean and I expressed our shock at how they had been treated by the Board. They were confident of reinstatement eventually, but it still hurt them to have to pass by the school that they loved and not be able to enter it.

For my part, I initially put this meeting down to another canal-side encounter to be filed under the 'interesting people you meet' part of my brain. When we set off back the next day, I replayed this in my head and felt that old righteous anger beginning to stir again. I wanted to act to help them, but with Jean at my side, how could I do it?

We talked that evening and I told Jean one of my little 'secrets'.

"Sometimes," I said, "I like to be alone. The best place for me, I find, is the towpath in the early hours. I know you're not policing me, but I just thought I'd share this little foible with you in case you wake up and I'm not there."

"I'll look forward to it," she laughed, "It'll give me more of the bed to myself. Don't worry, Steve, our love has to be premised on trust. I know there are parts of you I'll never fathom. Doesn't mean I don't love the bit I know."

"But," I pushed the conversation further, "I may end up away for a little longer, maybe the whole day. Is that okay?"

"Steve," she held my hand and rubbed it in the curious way that she was apt to when being especially affectionate with me, "we're not kids. You come and go as you need. Just, don't expect me to drive this thing. I've got loads to do on my own anyway, so don't worry. I've told you, I trust you and I want the person you are. Don't change too much on my account."

"I'm fine with your not driving the boat," I said, "In fact, I'd prefer to know where I lived on my return. Mind you, you're going to have to have a go at moving it some time."

I thanked her again for her understanding and planned my actions as we navigated back towards England.

From Jean's perspective, if she knew anything at all, I had taken myself on one of my early-hours walks that had stretched into a day away. What I'd actually done is taken myself along the canal in the pod to an agreed meeting point back in Llangollen. James had done the legwork for me, using the old technique we had of copying voices and arranging with interested parties to meet for an urgent discussion. The four members of the Welsh Education Department's Board of Governance, had all had to shift their diaries around, but they managed this in the face of the implied threats that James's communications alluded to.

I was waiting for them in the function room of the pub that we'd frequented with Mr and Mrs Peters. It was easy to book, paid for over the phone by card, and the hostess was very hospitable to these visiting dignitaries. She showed them into the room where they all settled down, looking at each other expectantly and clearly wondering who was going to speak first. I wrapped them in Blue Light. It was a little more comfortable than the green one. Then I introduced myself.

"Thank you for coming.", I moved to the head of the table, "And apologies for the surprise and the subterfuge. For those of you who don't know me, my calling card."

I flicked four of the RC discs onto the desk, each carved with their individual names.

"We're here to play a game.", I told them, "It's called 'Save Yourself'."

One of them began to protest but I simply waved my hand and an extra shot of Blue Light silenced them.

"First of all though.", I smiled as I retrieved the large parcel that had been delivered to the meeting room earlier, "we need to think about our safety. Now, don't struggle or you might get hurt."

I wrapped each of them in bubble-wrap. They looked like that guy who used to advertise tyres. Then I explained the rules.

"It's a very simple game.", I explained, "You are my captives and you need to try and escape. Not too difficult I hope? If you escape, you can call the police, try and capture me, whatever. So, let's start."

I released the Blue Light and sat back to watch.

The group consisted of three women and one man. I had thought that the first to move would be the male, but he was beaten to it by the youngest of the females. She reached for the scissors that I had left on the table and was about to cut her way out of the bubble wrap when I intervened.

"Whoops, silly me.", I laughed, "You can't use those, they are potentially dangerous. Sharp edge you see, could have someone's eye out with those."

I retrieved the scissors and let them carry on. It was hugely enjoyable. They eventually got themselves free by helping each other, but I had to stop them ringing for help as they didn't have a hands-free earpiece and I knew how dangerous mobiles could be when placed straight to the ear. Nor could they scream for help. I had to stop them doing this with tape as it might injure the hearing of the others. And so it went on. I wouldn't let them climb out of the window because they didn't have appropriate footwear, and I refused to let them through the door as the space beyond was a busy public environment and they didn't have high-vis jackets. It took them an hour to get my point.

"Why are you doing this?", one of them asked.

"Good question.", I replied, "you see, I don't have children but I hate to see young people being mollycoddled and straightjacketed by fools like you who want to steal away the joy in the danger of childhood. How are kids going to grow up to survive out there if we turn them into fearful and needy imbeciles? I want a reversal of your decisions."

"But you said you don't have children.", the man protested, "how then can you dare to tell us what to do?"

"I didn't say that I'd never had children.", I hissed in his ear, "and please, don't think this is just about me. The teachers and the parents want freedom to make the choices for their children. That's the issue."

I told them that that was the game over and that I really didn't have any choice but to award them for participating. I told them that I hoped that they would do better in the task I'd asked them to go forward with. When I read the press reports, I thought they at least deserved a bronze.

Jean said nothing when she woke up as I climbed into bed that night. I think I'd got away with it. And now I knew that I could still operate even when we were together so much.

The other interventions happened as we cruised back along the familiar routes that we had travelled before. The Hooper Homes situation was something that Charlotte asked me to get involved in. Hooper had built the properties on cheap land that he knew would flood. I trusted the team to feed me the right information but wasn't sure why they had asked me to get involved.

"It's a weird one.", Charlotte explained, "It seems that Mr Hooper is very distrustful of computers, mobiles and the like. We just can't hack into him to act. You okay to help out?"

I slipped away one night and reached Hooper's house by using the motorbike. Adam had sent the necessary gear, which I found in the place where he'd promised it would be. Then all I'd had to do was arrange my army of flying friends to fit the new skin around the house. They sealed it on with rays of heat, after which I turned the hose on and watched as it filled up. When the water was a few feet deep on the ground floor, I woke Hooper. I left the RC disc on his bedside table and accompanied him to the upstairs landing.

"This is a warning shot.", I told him, "Do the right thing, or next time, I don't wake you."

Leaving the building, the birds that were helping me pecked holes in the skin and then tore it away. I disposed of it in a skip and returned to the boat.

With the Vicar, it had been quicker and less aggressive.

We met the young couple on the towpath near Leek, whilst journeying again along the Caldon. They were annoyed and frustrated at the lack of energy in their church and I had taken myself for a walk to the Vicarage to speak to him and see what their problem was.

He welcomed me in reluctantly as I explained that I was homeless and needing some pastoral care. I sat there for an hour or so, spinning a story but watching in disbelief as he offered me no help and, in fact, fell asleep at one point.

That night, the Angel visited him. He woke to see a shining white vision (a new adaptation of my suit), and hear the celestial choirs (speakers floating in the four corners of the room).

I never claimed to be anything other than what I am. I simply gave him the opportunity to question what he was doing and decide to get back on track with what he was paid to do or take the quieter option and retire.

How much of his story he shared with his flock, I couldn't tell you. My visit seemed to do the trick though.

Chapter Twenty-Nine

We extended the holiday into August. I was fine with that as I had the opportunity to play my part in delivering justice as necessary, but was preferring the time with Jean. The continuation of the journey was something that Jean planned and, at first, I was a bit unsure about the route that she was proposing. It was all very familiar territory to us and didn't take us that far from home turf. That was until she explained her thinking.

We were still on the Caldon when she told me. It was after we'd winded at Froghall and moored up near to the pub that we both knew so well. Since the weather was being kind, we'd headed to the pub and had sat for a few hours in the very seats where we had met a few years ago. This time, I was a lot more comfortable. Jean was pensive. Perhaps she was worried about me running off with another headache. There remained things that were unsaid between us, but so much of the time, we didn't have to say anything. It was enough to have found each other and be free to share these moments. The food was good too. The beer, even better.

It was a more confident and relieved Jean that returned to the boat with me. Her choice of venue had been for a reason and that reason had been to cement her conviction that the past was yesterday and that the future was ours. And she had it well planned.

"I think that I'm almost there with something of a plan for the future," she told me as we returned to the boat and tidied everything up ready for an early departure the following morning, "and that's why I want us to go back to places we've already seen. You see, I want to carry on writing. I think it's in my blood and I could never give it up. But rather than working as a journalist, putting other people's ideas into a readable format, I want to create something a bit different. Maybe the novel will come at some point, but I'm thinking of something else to start with."

"Go on," I told her, topping up the gin and tonics that were helping us with our packing.

"Okay", she replied, "so how does this sound? At the moment, when you set off on a narrowboat journey, you plan your route using either a standard guide book or map, or maybe even one of the apps that are out there. What I want to do is create something that complements those guides by giving readers a slightly off-beat but more detailed and up-to-date picture of the places that those guides don't mention."

"Sounds interesting", I said.

"But it's not unique.", she continued, "I'm not claiming that. You only have to look at the number of boater's blogs out there and most of what I will be writing about has already been said. The beauty is though, that it will keep my creative juices going and may add to the experience of people using the canals. We don't need to make money off it, so I'll probably just charge the print cost, or offer it free to download."

"And the extra stuff is what?", I asked her.

"Oh, you know", she replied, "pubs that are within a fair walking distance, interesting historical landmarks that maybe forgotten, the local industries that still survive and also the big players whose names span the globe but who may be based in the most unusual places near to the canals. And, I want to put in dog walks. That's why I need to tell you about the other side of the plan."

"There's more?", I laughed as I sipped my drink.

"Potentially", she said, "a load more. So, we are out and about and wherever we are I take the dog that we still don't have yet, but which we will need to get after we're married, and I just wander off exploring the area and giving a 'dog's eye' view of the area as well as my own. Which is why we need to be thinking about a good five years for us to cover the whole network."

"Five years!"

"Yes, five years.", she turned and gave me a proper stare, "And don't laugh at my plans. Look, we have all the time in the world. Why rush? I've started to put together the plan and, in order for us to do it properly, five year makes sense. I'm calling my plan our Grand Tour. But, and this is something that you need to register, we only cruise for eight months in any year."

"Ah, now that makes things clearer.", I said, "You don't want to be on the boat all year? I'm not surprised, it was only a matter of time before that subject came up."

"It's not going to be a problem is it?", she drew closer to me as she spoke, "Please Steve, tell me you're okay with it."

I wondered whether I shouldn't string this one out a bit. This was a moment for me to rack up a few bonus points if I'd wanted to. I decided not to exploit the situation this time. The truth was, I was in complete agreement with her.

"Jean,", I held her closely, "you know that my life has been spent on board a boat for the past too many years. I still love it, but I'm not precious about it. You prefer bricks and mortar, whereas I prefer the water. With you in my life, things are bound to change. I'm more than happy with that, and if necessary, we can stretch to six months each. It's the being together that matters to me."

"You do realise,", she smiled as lifted her face to me, "that you are beginning to change into a very soppy person. I think, given time, we may even find you have a heart somewhere."

"Don't push it.", I replied.

The following morning it rained. We set off nevertheless after I had explained to Jean that if we were to be as meticulous in our cruising plan as she had laid out, then we had to take the rough with the smooth. She was happy to agree with this. Mind you, she was nice and dry inside whilst I was at the tiller. That said, I never had a problem with the rain. The right waterproofs kept most of it out, although there was a perverse pleasure in finishing a very wet day's cruise and peeling off damp clothes in the warmth and shelter of a warm cabin. The weather also ensured that there were fewer boats out and about and causing delays at locks.

The extension to the journey we were undertaking was into and around the Birmingham Canal Navigations, specifically taking in the Wyrley and Essington Canal and then heading back towards the Coventry. That was the plan anyway. What was nice about being on my own boat was that we weren't under too many pressures to keep to the schedule. That was why Jean's five-year plan made sense to me. In fact, with everything that I knew could potentially distract us, I was thinking the first pass could take twice as long. But as Jean had said, we had all the time in the world and this was now our time to enjoy each other and discover new things. We'd earned our money and we'd paid our dues. We wouldn't be idle, but we were certainly going to make the most of the freedom that we had.

Having cruised slowly through the heart of the vibrant, newly gentrified, Potteries, and taken a little longer than we might have to make it through Stone and Great Haywood, it was the end of August before we hit the Staffs and Worcester Canal. Weston was a tough one for me. With Jean on board, the passage through the land of my old life broke the heart that so many said that I didn't have. It broke my heart to think of the children who had never had the chance to experience the joys and the challenges of a full life. They would have been teenagers by now. And it broke my heart to realise the gift that I had been given in the future that lay ahead. Jean could sense my discomfort, but left me alone on deck to my own thoughts. She knew that I had a past and that some of that past came back to haunt me at times. She also knew the specifics of the past that was now troubling me as she had been the one to visit me after Slater had wiped my family out. We had an unwritten pact between us though, and that was that we let the past be the past between us and that our time together was to be focused on the now and the tomorrow.

I would have liked to have dropped into the Saracen's Head again, so different now from the throwback to the seventies that it had been, or maybe taken a walk up to the Hall. Both of those places held a lot of memories for me. But I couldn't do it in the end. I had to move on and let the past go. And so, without any major incident we found ourselves outside The Cross Keys in Penkridge, anticipating the best chips on the cut and ready to start phase two of this particular journey. It was there that we made the final preparations for the wedding. I was taking the regular backseat role in all this that any self-respecting groom was expected to take. Jean was arranging the rest but without the usual stress and worry of a first-time bride. We'd agreed early on that it would be a very simple affair. We wanted it to be in a church and were fortunate that the parish priest of the town where our cottage was located was open to our request. Jason King had built up a certain influence in the area already and the contribution that he had made to the church's renovation fund worked in our favour. Not that the priest was to be bought. Both Jean and I had had to meet with him and explain why we wanted a church wedding. We wouldn't lie to him. Nor would we disrespect his office. We simply laid out our own feelings and he was happy that we be wed there.

"If I was only allowed to marry couples who lived and breathed the Gospels," he'd said, "then I'd rarely wed anyone at all. It's enough for me that you both tell me that there is something inside you that can't not believe in a Higher Power. I still struggle myself with explaining it all. I don't think we need worry about any bolts of lightning hitting us if we go ahead, but, when you do move into the village, it'd be nice to see you here some time."

With the church booked and the few guests that we had asked to attend having confirmed their presence, there wasn't a lot else to do. We both wanted a simple ceremony centred on what we were doing in becoming a united couple, rather than on how we did that. Family for both of us was not an issue. Steve Barratt had nobody and Jean had only a few distant relatives who rarely communicated with her. My family, if any, was with the marina team. Jean's had been the newspapers that she wrote for and the transitory comrades who would not figure in her future. It was nice having a blank slate like this. It meant that we could start again and make new friends as a couple.

Setting off from Penkridge and mooring for the night just past Autherley Junction, we prepared ourselves to hit the thirteen locks at Wolverhampton first thing the following morning. Of all the parts of this journey that I was dreading, those locks had to be the worst. Not that I have any problem with lock flights. No, that wasn't the issue. The issue was Jean and I working the flight together in standard narrowboat mode, with me driving and her doing the locks. This was a potentially explosive situation. And she would have the windlass if we came to blows.

As it was, apart from her walking away at around the sixth lock and telling me that I could do them on my own if I thought I could do it better, we managed okay. I used the opportunity to work on my patience muscle and genuinely felt that, by the end of the day, it had grown just that little bit stronger. Jean was less enamoured of the process and insisted that we pull in and moor at lunchtime with a view to not carrying on anymore that day. Her decision was partly a genuine exhaustion and unwillingness to continue when we didn't need to, and partly a reflection of what she was planning with her book.

"You see," she told me as we moored up in the middle of a retail park, "this is the sort of thing that will go in my book. Who'd have thought it, we disappear through the City of Wolverhampton and hardly see any sign of city life, then we turn onto this canal and within seconds we are moored next to a chain pub and slap-bang in a retail park. You couldn't make it up, could you?"

"Not great for your dog walks though!", I replied only to feel the rap of the windlass that up to that moment I had avoided.

201

"Shops will do me.", she said, grabbing her handbag and walking off, "I'll see you in an hour or so. Meanwhile, book us into the pub for dinner."

As the only boat moored here and probably one of only a handful that ever did moor here, we received a bit of attention as we sat on the deck in the evening. Not only had we enjoyed a very nice meal at the pub, but we had also been able to take in a film at the cinema. We chose not to do the ten-pin bowling this time. Jean was writing notes about the day and our current location. She was already onto her fifth page.

"You know, Steve?", she said as she finished writing and put the pad down, "There is so much that I can write about. I can't wait until we get started. I'll do as much as I can on this run but only as a trial. You can tell me what you think then, and I'll refine it all ready for our first adventure after we've sorted the cottage out."

"You're only missing one thing.", I said to her, "The people. You should try and find a way to incorporate that in your work. Maybe as a parallel work, 'Characters of the Cut' or something like that."

"Do you think so?", she asked.

"I know so.", I replied, "And by the end of this holiday you will agree. The places and the sights and history are all amazing, but believe me, it's the people that make this lifestyle special. We had some of it last time, think of that afternoon in Audlem, but this time, I think you'll need a couple of extra notebooks."

My prediction proved to be accurate.

Chapter Thirty

Sample chapter: 'Characters of the Cut' by Jean Carter.

"To many, the attraction of the waterways of England is their solitude and isolation. They are, and will forever remain, a vein that pulses with yesterday's pace of life when things moved more slowly and where natural beauty was enough to satisfy the eye. And yet, the canals of England are a living space, populated by a multitude of individuals as diverse as can be found anywhere in the world. Perhaps it is because life on the water encourages interaction between humans who, in the world above, might pass each other without even a transitory nod, or perhaps it is because the waterways have become the last bastion of open community in a nation where the mainstream is so divisive.

This is a book about the characters of the cut. They are all real people. Their names may have been changed where they have requested that I do so, but otherwise, they are presented as found. Let us begin with the first set of these people, all of whom we met during a two-week cruise in August 2025.

Carl and/or Carly:

Pelsall is a small town in the West Midlands which retains something of a village feel to it, despite its proximity to the major conurbations of Cannock and Walsall and the thriving motorway network nearby. Work continues on the Lichfield and Hatherton Canals restoration which will, one day soon, open up this town to many more boats. Meanwhile, the Wyrley and Essington Canal that meanders without locks into the lush, green heart of Pelsall, remains a haven of peace for those boaters who make it there.

Our boat struggled to get close to the bank as we pulled in to moor next to the single boat that was already tied up there. As my fiancée battled to draw the boat to the bank, we were joined by a bear of man who, without our asking, took the centre-rope off me and drew the boat in. We felt the bottom scrape a little, but were not inclined to argue with someone quite so solid.

"There you go.", his voice was a deep baritone, "It's a nightmare here. They never seem to dredge it. Anyway, nice to see another boat, I'm Carl."

It didn't take us long to shed our initial prejudice based on our fear-fuelled first impressions. I grabbed some beers from the boat and we were soon chatting away like old friends. Carl was, by his own admission, outstaying his time on these moorings and was planning to be there another month.

"Like I say to the waterways people when they come and chase me.", he told us, "If it ever gets so full here that nobody can moor up, then I'll be happy to move on. Meanwhile, they should be glad that somebody's here, keeping this waterway alive."

He went on to explain that he was a builder and was working on the renovation of a historic house in the town. After that, the conversation went in numerous directions, before the beers were all gone and we agreed to take a break and meet later that evening at the pub.

We arrived at the canal-side hostelry a little before the agreed time. Half an hour later, there was no sign of Carl and we wondered whether we shouldn't go and check on him. Then the doors of the pub opened and a stunning blond walked in. She was no elfin sprite but she carried her plus-size frame beautifully and you could see that she was having an immediate impact on the drinkers at the bar. Turning to us, she waved and mouthed a hello, before ordering a glass of Chardonnay that she bought to our table.

"I saw you already had drinks.", she said as she sat down, "Didn't think we should start on the whole, you owe me one, I owe you one thing. Hope that's okay."

My fiancée was speechless. I struggled to reply but managed to get something out of my mouth.

"No, that's fine Carl.", I think was my attempt.

"Carly tonight.", she turned to me with a wink, "Carl couldn't make it. Now, where did we get to."

As if it was the most natural thing in the world, we resumed the conversation that we were having earlier in the afternoon. Not that it was difficult. Carly was as affable and charming as Carl and had lived a life that wasn't reflected by his current situation.

"When I was married", she said, "I was a high-flyer in finance. Cars, houses, money and anything I wanted. But I wasn't happy with it. We separated, I took very little with me. Bought the boat and started working odd jobs when I could. The building thing came about and I found out I had an aptitude for it, so that's what I do now."

It was difficult enough for us to reconcile the beauty before us with the man who had pulled the boat in, but more so to imagine that man in a business suit in the City. His boat was not a pretty sight from the outside, although he did have a certain refinement to him that had come through on occasion. As Carly, that refinement was more noticeable. She walked the walk and carried herself with great style.

"So, that's why I was a bit late.", she told us, having explained that she'd broken a heel as she clambered off the boat, "I know I should wear more practical footwear on the towpath, but I simply could not have matched any of my other shoes with this outfit."

After several hours, a very pleasant meal and quite a lot of alcohol, Carl was long forgotten and we were thoroughly enjoying our time with Carly. She probably had just one glass too many and we had to help her back to the boat at closing time, but that too was worth it because I was privileged enough to be invited on board. A more palatial boat I cannot imagine. It was meticulously clean, full of beautiful objects and lit in such a way that it seemed to glow with a subtle sheen.

As we returned to our own boat, I waited for the anticipated comments from my fiancée, as he no doubt waited for what I had to say. In truth, neither of us said a thing. Carl had been great to chat with and Carly a bundle of fun. Who were we to judge? After all, we'd met two new friends for the price of one.

Jack 'Jump in the Canal':

There was something of a delay as we approached the Perry Barr Locks, which meant that we would have to moor up at the top end of the flight until a minor repair was carried out. There were a number of us there, and a mix of boats that included hired cruisers, some very shiny marina-based boats and a number of boats that were evidently lived on all year around.

Since the weather remained in our favour and since we were all in this together, it seemed only natural that we fired up a couple of barbecues and contributed what food that we could and a little wine as well. Although this vignette is centred on Jack, before I proceed with him, let me also share the gist of what comprised our mixed and diverse group hanging around the sizzling meat.

The two hire boats were crewed by six medical students on one and two elderly couples on another. They were travelling the same route over the same two-week period and had met regularly. At one point in their respective journeys, Bill, the 'Captain' of the senior citizen's crew, had spent several hours fixing the other boat's tiller after they had popped it out of its housing following an overenthusiastic attempt to free their grounded boat. This favour from Bill had been repaid when his wife, Marjorie, needed urgent medical attention as she suffered what she was convinced was a heart attack.

"It was actually only a touch of heartburn.", the student told me later, "But what can you do? She thinks we're miracle workers now, but it was only about calming her down. Still, it's all good experience as they say."

Of the other boats that were there with us, only one crew kept their own company. They were the team who could be identified by the matching polo shirts they wore, lovingly embroidered with their boat's name. Our increasingly drunken antics weren't their cup of tea, but we respected that. Sort of. They became the butt of a few cruel jokes later in the evening and one of the students decided that putting the smallest smear of burger fat on their newly polished paintwork would be a 'witty jape'. Other than that, we left them alone. Amongst the other marina boats, the crews were generally older couples where the men talked about the good old days of diesel and the women talked about more interesting subjects.

Then there were the liveaboards who included Jack and his wife Carol. It was halfway through the barbecue and the sun was beginning to set on our party, when a bird appeared to fly out of a tree and hit the boat behind ours. A few eyes were turned on the scene but it was Carol who went to investigate and who saw the bird flapping in distress in the water.

"Jack.", she shouted to her husband, "you'll have to do something. Jump in the canal."

We expected a voice of protest or at least an alternative solution but, without batting an eyelid, Jack placed his wine glass on the table, took his phone out of the pocket of his shorts and stepped along the gunnels of our boat and into the water. Everyone had now turned to see what was happening as Jack walked carefully towards the bird, picked it up in the palm of his hand and placed it on the towpath. He climbed out and we examined the bird which had not simply fallen but which had been attacked by another bird and was *mortally wounded. It died within minutes of its rescue. Jack bagged it in a dog pooh bag and threw it into the undergrowth.*

What happened then is a perfect example of such a uniquely canal-only moment. Jack returned to the group he had been with and they picked up the conversation from where they had left off. Carol meanwhile, was busy checking that there was enough salad.

Angela and Frank:

We met Angela and Frank on the return leg of our journey as we cruised up the Coventry Canal towards Fradley Junction. We were moored somewhere near Tamworth with a curious view of the beautiful canal scenery on one side and a bustling retail park below us on the other. I'd sent my fiancée to get supplies from the supermarket and by the time he had returned was already into a second game of rummy with the couple that had moored next to us.

Frank had been a lawyer. A very successful one at that. Angela was a primary teacher. They explained to me how they had come to live a different life and both the high and the low points that they'd experienced in making the change. Since Angela still worked, picking up supply work or taking fixed contracts at schools in the Staffordshire area, the change had been less dramatic for her. She was happy to downsize the living space and more than settled with the minimalist lifestyle they were enjoying. Although the decision to make the change had been primarily his, Frank had had a less trouble-free transition.

"You know what the toughest part is.", he said to me, "It's the role reversal that we've gone through. When we were in the house, I was the breadwinner. Always had been and it felt right. Not that Angela's job isn't important. She's good at what she does and makes a difference to those kids. But it was my working all hours and my salary that gave us everything that we wanted."

"Yeah,", Angela interrupted, "including a nervous breakdown."

"Okay,", Frank agreed, "so it wasn't all plain sailing. And yes, I was either going through a breakdown or about to experience one when I decided that enough was enough and we made the move onto a boat."

He explained that because of a previous marriage, they weren't well off and that he had had to get some part time work to pay the bills, but that had only been a few hours a week in general.

"No,", he said, "the hardest part was getting to the point where I was happy to be the one who did all the washing, the cooking and the cleaning. It seems daft, I know, but it's taken me three years to reach that point. We both work hard enough but, at first, I was letting Angela do the stuff that she did when we were in the house as well as her work. Then I started to get bored and found myself tidying up, even vacuuming. But I used to curse Angie for that because it felt like I was being feminised."

"And you weren't very good at it.", his wife intervened, "I used to have to come back from work and redo what he'd done."

Over time there had grown up a tension between them which was threatening their marriage. Then Frank had met somebody who listened to his story and told him how lucky he was to have broken the cycle of gender-defined roles.

"That made me think that maybe my life wasn't that bad.", he concluded, "And it made me realise how deeply held our traditional views on male and female roles are, even now in twenty twenty-five. It's mad isn't it?"

They were a lovely couple and seemed to be as happy together as any I'd known. And yet, it had been a difficult journey for them as they moved into reversed roles. There was no logic to Frank's concerns as he worked just as hard as Angela and they both enjoyed their respective roles. And yet, I began to sympathise a little with Frank and others like him who were often forced into having to deny a gendered role that had been written in their core form early years. We accepted it easily with women. It was a tougher transition, I now realised, for a man.

Steve:

Steve is an enigma. His boat is one of the first all-electric vessels and is fitted with all mod-cons inside. And yet Steve won't watch television nor will he leave the radio blaring in the background, preferring instead to sit in silence or read a book.

Steve is an innovator. He is part of a boating operation that stuns the waterways world every year with new and radical inventions. It was Steve who invented the solar-parabola that you see on numerous boats today. It was the solution to bringing solar onto any boat without the need for it to take up too much space or impinge on the aesthetic of the vessel. You see this invention everywhere now, but Steve would credit its invention to his team.

208

Steve sometimes appears to be cold and heartless, distant from the world, but you look at him at the end of a decent movie and he'll be sniffling with the rest of us. Steve seems to be a troubled character at times, in conflict with himself, but also at peace.

When did I meet Steve?

Oh, I meet him every day. He's my fiancée and a real character of the cut.

END

******

"Apart from that last one," I said to Jean after reading the pages she presented me with at the end of our holiday, "I love it. You really seem to have something there. Combine it with the travel guide and you've nailed it."

"Thanks," she said, "it was you that gave me the idea and after what we've just enjoyed over that past few weeks I just had to put something down on paper. It's only a sample, but it's also a nice reminder to me of the people we've met and the people that we're going to meet."

I was pleased that Jean had had such an enjoyable time. It was important to me that she didn't just cruise the waterways to please me but that it was her own pleasure too. Similarly, I knew that she wanted me to enjoy the cottage and I had to admit to her that I was quite looking forward to getting stuck into it.

That led onto a slightly awkward conversation about my skills, which I had to frame in such a way that she was confident that I could do all the basic works that I claimed I could, but without reference to the training that her old friend Zipoly had experienced.

"Let's get the wedding over first," I said, "and then we can move into the place and decide what we need to get done. We'll have a bash at the things we think we can handle then if it's all too much we'll call Mr King's team in."

"Why does 'have a bash' not inspire too much confidence in me?", Jean laughed, "But yes, let's get married first. The rest will come together."

The following night we parted company for a few weeks. Jean had plans of her own, not least to do with the wedding and getting the cottage furnished, whilst I had to take the boat to the marina where it would spend the Winter. We stayed in a very nice hotel suite and splurged on the luxuries that we like to enjoy from time to time. As we drifted to sleep on the four-poster, we lay in each other's arms and felt closer than ever. The wedding would cement the deal, but at that moment we both knew that we had become one.

Chapter Thirty-One

By September, I was feeling increasingly comfortable with the life that I was enjoying. These were the last days of my solitary life and I made the most of the freedom that solitude gave me. J for Justice was gaining momentum and my lack of activity as the Righteous Corrector was barely commented upon as the press looked to this new justice movement instead. In the past, Jean had been instrumental in promoting my activities. No longer in the position to do so as her career shifted, all of us agreed that J for Justice was the way forward. It was a movement that generated its own publicity. Everybody knew somebody who had been touched in some way by the activities of James, Adam and Charlotte, which led to the internet being alive with testimonies of justice delivered. They managed to remain anonymous however, and, despite the rumours and speculations that were as prolific as the examples of their work, the world was no closer to identifying them.

I did my best to keep fit, running every morning and then cycling a few miles every evening. My days of youth were well past me now and I had to make the conscious effort to burn off the beer and neutralise the cigarettes I abused my body with. In the past, it had been easy to eat, drink and be merry then offset the effects with a few days of abstinence. Now, not only was the abstinence that little bit harder to embrace, but my body also took longer to recover. My motivation was Jean, although I hadn't written off Kingfisher. If she was the incentive, then my alter-ego would benefit as a result.

There were times when I waited for the call from the centre. My mind could so easily play tricks on me and turn their respect for my solitude into rejection. Truth be told, they didn't need me. That was how it had to be. Times were changing and, so long as James was able to use the atomic to enter the physical world then my input was, at most, advisory. I still had the scars to remind me of what I had been and I had my journals to remind me that I had made a difference in some way. I was coming up to the ten-year anniversary of the events that sparked it all. And, around the time of that anniversary, I was marrying Jean and starting again. Those ten years had been eventful. More eventful than I cared to think about. And they had changed me both physically and mentally. I would never lead a conventional life, if such a life existed, but that was fine with me. I'd moved from salesman to widower to engineer to craftsman and then to vigilante. In the next ten years, who knew what might happen?

Thinking about the past led me to discover a new interest. It had been a good few years since I had done anything creative and Jean's idea of what she wanted to do in our time together, led me to think about how I could work with her. She was the writer but there might be scope for me to add to her books by providing illustrations. I'd done the carved boat panels in the past so it seemed a logical step to exchange the woodworking tools for paintbrushes. That kept me occupied for a while.

By the time that the wedding came around, I had a few fairly decent sketches to show to Jean and we were both in agreement that the books we were to put together would be joint efforts. What I was producing could never be described as fine art but it was effective enough to illustrate what Jean would write. If somebody wanted a perfect image of a place, there were numerous photographs available to search through. My aim was to capture something of the spirit of the canals in my work. Needless to say, my early efforts were fairly poor, but I was time-rich and believed that I could make them passable with a little more practise.

"We'll be like bohemian hippies.", Jean chuckled as we discussed our life on the cut, "You with your pipe and an easel, and with paint spattered all over your smock, and me, scribbling notes into a journal with my hair growing longer and greyer every day."

"We should paint flowers on the boat.", I replied, "Go the whole hog and light some incense as well."

"And we can play up to people as they pass.", Jean laughed, "Pretend that we are children of Mother Earth, finding our spiritual centre in each other and in being one with the world. Then, when they're gone, we can fire up the home cinema system and watch the latest Hollywood blockbuster!"

You could only get away with that on the waterways. We'd met people who did just that. They were out in the world doing regular, professional jobs during the week, then at weekends, they would don wigs of New-Age braids and trade their suits for knitted rags. And why not? Everyone was playing a part, one way or the other, so fair play to them. And, on the canals, you were expected to be just a tad eccentric. Those who passed by on the

212

towpath may have been out cycling, walking or looking at the wildlife, but you knew that, at the same time, they were thrilled to look at the specimens from the human zoo who lived on the boats.

We were having this conversation the night before the wedding. My boat was in the marina and the cottage was habitable, although we'd chosen not to live there until we were officially joined together. Jean's flat in London was on the market and she had buyers queueing up to get hold of it once she'd moved out. For the week preceding the wedding, we stayed in a very nice country house hotel. We certainly had no qualms about all the wedding myths about not seeing each other before the big day. We knew how much work the cottage was in need of, so all thoughts about old wives' tales were set aside in favour of a bit of time spent in luxury. The only concession we made to tradition was that Jean kept the dress a surprise and that we would arrive at the church separately.

"Don't let me down.", she said as I left the hotel on the big day, "I've not hassled you at all about this wedding, but I do expect you to make a bit of an effort. Tell me you're getting changed?"

I thought about winding her up but one glance at the stare she was giving me made me think again.

"It's fine,", I reassured her, "I'll be presentable. I can do it if I have to. And for this occasion, I'd wear a tutu if that was what you wanted."

Of course, it's easier for a bloke. A trip to a decent shop and within an hour I had a very nice and very expensive new suit along with all the matching trimmings. I hadn't worn a suit for a long time and I certainly didn't carry one on the boat. Not one that I could wear to a wedding anyway. But for Jean and for our wedding, it was worth it.

As I stood at the altar on that October morning, with Tony beside me and my few friends lined up on the pews behind me, I felt better than I had in a long time. This was the future and it was beginning now. It got even better when Jean entered the church. The organ started up, I heard the rustle of people turning in their seats and I knew that she had arrived. I resisted the urge to turn but could hear the whispers of our guests as they admired the dress. As she moved next to me, I turned to her and was stunned by how beautiful she looked. Despite the nonchalant show, she had put everything into this day and I could barely hold back the tears when I realised the lengths she had gone to for me.

"Hi.", she whispered as we turned back to face the altar.

The ceremony over, we commandeered the local pub and celebrated our union. Jean had invited a few of her work colleagues and a couple of distant relations, but it could never have been described as a big affair. I only had the team from the marina on my side, but even they were now shared friends with Jean. James and Adam had scrubbed up surprisingly well and were barely recognisable, both surprisingly at ease in such a conventional space. Charlotte had been Jean's Maid of Honour, and looked stunning. So stunning, I think Adam began to realise that he needed to take their relationship a little more seriously. You could see it in their eyes. It wouldn't be long before another wedding was in the offing.

We didn't want the usual speeches but allowed Jason King a word or two since he was acting as Father of the Bride. Our family affairs were something that we rarely touched on but I knew that Jean's own parents were either no longer with us or were no longer a part of her life. As for me, I had the only family I wanted in Jean and the marina team.

"Ladies and gentlemen," King rose and called for order, "it is my pleasure to welcome you here today as we celebrate Jean and Steve's marriage."

The guests applauded.

"I'll keep this speech short.", he smiled as he spoke, "Partly because you don't want to hear me waffling on, but mainly because, and this I am afraid is the truth, I will find it difficult to hold back my emotions if I say too much."

He paused and we were all surprised to see that he genuinely was struggling to hold back the tears.

"Steve and Jean are both wonderful people.", he continued, "As a couple, they are equally as wonderful. We first became acquainted when we worked together and, believe me, although you hear a lot of plaudits bandied around about Jason King, I can tell you that I am nothing without good people working for me. Steve and Jean both worked brilliantly and helped me in ways that I can never express. Then our working relationship morphed into friendship and again, I can tell you as someone who spends time with Presidents, Prime Ministers and Royalty, I am never happier than when I am with this couple. Thank you both for being who you are. A toast to you and to a long happy marriage."

We all raised our glasses and watched as King sat back down, dabbing the corner of his eye with a napkin.

After the wedding came the new house. I say new house but it was actually a very old and fairly run-down cottage. King had offered to renovate it for us, but we both preferred the challenge of doing the work ourselves. For my part, I looked forward to surprising Jean with the woodworking skills that she didn't know that I had, whilst her own motivation was that this would become our home, restored by our hands and in a way that reflected our own personalities.

Chapter Thirty-Two

'The Eastern Echo', 4th November, 2025

'Telecoms Company Admits Service Failure'

In a surprise move, Norfolk Telecom has abandoned the multi-million-pound, computerised customer helpline system that it launched less than one month ago. The system, hailed at the time by the company as a 'revolution in automated service', has been the source of numerous complaints from the company's customers but, until recently, Norfolk Telecom put any problems down to teething issues.

Their change of heart may be related to a campaign supported by the J for Justice movement who are believed to have intervened and encouraged Norfolk Telecom to reconsider the use of this system. Company spokesperson, Annette Walters, denied that undue influence was placed on the Board to make this change, stating 'insurmountable technical challenges and a desire to make the customer journey more navigable', as their reasons for reverting back to the use of a local call-centre.

At the time of the introduction of the new system, company Chief Executive, Anders Smit, was applauded by shareholders for the move which would create savings of five million pounds or more over a three-year cycle. With profits at the company already exceeding several hundred million pounds per annum, Smit was swift to defend the company's strategy by stating that making savings was a permanent part of the healthy growth of any private business.

See also Editorial page 12, 'J for Justice: The People's Movement?'

++++++

'Norwich Tonight', 28th November, 2025

'Local Restaurants Agree Better Working Practices'

The Association of Norwich Restaurateurs has agreed to trial a more generous system of staff support over the coming Christmas and New Year period. In a motion proposed by two prominent members, the practice of staff being required to cover main holiday periods at the minimum, legal level of compensation, was argued to be unfair to those who wished to offset financial gains for the benefits of sharing quality time with their families.

This move appears to be a response to the increasingly tense relationship that restaurants have had with their teams, particularly over the last decade or so when eating at home over Christmas has been replaced by eating out.

Various unions have been seeking a similar outcome for quite a while, but nationally, the situation remains the same. What has prompted this local move is unsure, however it has been welcomed by all in the trade and one member of staff interviewed for this paper was ecstatic about the prospect of being able to enjoy Christmas with her family.

As the law stands, employers can request their staff to cover these periods as part of their normal working hours, with additional payments only being required if specified in that employee's contract. Whilst this is reflective of practice in the service sector, the main concern that the local Association wanted to avoid was the feeling that any staff felt that their job might be at risk if they were to request time off.

++++++

Moving back to bricks and mortar was more of a challenge to me than I first thought it would be. On top of that, I was reminded again of all the additional expenses and commitments that came with the supposed benefit of being in a house. The money wasn't an issue to us. It was the stress that got to me. Why couldn't things be simple? You would have thought that it would be a simple process to have a telephone line installed and, when we first placed the order via the internet, the company promised that it would be straightforward enough. When the engineer failed to arrive on the day stated, I tried to call. That was when it all started to go crazy.

The long and short of it is that I spent a week or more being moved around various automated systems, only once managing to reach a real human who in turn seemed so surprised that I had made it that far that they put the phone down. That was when I asked James to help me out. It was a simple enough for him to seek opinions via the J for Justice portal and, within a few hours of my request, the guys at the marina were convinced that there was a case for action.

I explained to James what my plan was. He was happy to go ahead with it and did what he had to do that night. The following morning, the Board of Norfolk Telecom began to feel what it was like to be one of their customers. Every call that they tried to make was intercepted and dropped into an automated system that sucked them deeper and deeper in. Every call that they received was intercepted in a similar way. I was sent a transcript of the call that stirred Anders Smit into action and which ended his company's use of their wonderful new system:

Smit: Hello, Anders Smit.
Voice: Hello Mr Smith, we have an urgent call waiting to come through to you. Would you like to receive it?
Smit: Who is this?
Voice: Sorry, Mr Smith, I didn't understand your request. Did you ask me if I was okay? Yes, thank you Mr Smith, I am very well. How are you?
Smit: Look, the name is Smit, not Smith, please put the call through.
Voice: Your custom is important to us. Please say what it is that you would like me to do?
Smit: Please, put the call through.

218

Voice: Did you say that you could fall for me? Mr Smith, I really don't know what to say. Perhaps we should finish this call first. What would you like me to do?

Smit: Connect me!

Voice: Did you say reject me? Oh dear Mr Smith, I am sorry.

Smit: Connect me! And it's Mr Smit not Smith.

Voice: Please hold the line. [Music for three minutes]

Voice: Thank you for holding, how may I help you?

The restaurant thing had been a bit different. Jean and I had been in the cottage a month and decided to treat ourselves to a night out in the big city. Or at least, the biggest city that was nearby. We had a superb meal in a restaurant and were casually chatting to the waitress about her work and how she enjoyed it, when it became clear to us that one of the less visible aspects of the hospitality trade was the pressure staff were under to work unsociable hours.

In short, I couldn't shake the feeling of injustice that it left me with and, a day or so later, I used various chatrooms to get a better picture. I discovered enough to want to act. That was when I came across the Norwich Association and decided that maybe a local action might become a national movement. Even if it didn't, at least the local teams would be able to enjoy the Christmas break if they wanted to.

Stripped of my equipment and having to work with Jean close by, I tapped Jason King for a little help. He was more than happy to support me and able to supply the means by which we could act. His agent approached the two most influential restaurant owners who would be opening on Christmas Day and advised that he was representing a large business that had just purchased a very nice old property equidistant from their two locations.

"We'll be open for Christmas,", he told them, "and offering a free Christmas Dinner to anyone who books. And we'll also refund deposits placed with other suppliers."

"You can't do this.", one of them had protested.

"I think you will find that we can.", the agent replied.

He then continued to tell them that the owner of the business was passionate about employee rights and wanted to see a revolution in the service sector where waiting staff and retail employees were seen and treated as the asset they were.

"Of course.", the agent told them, "if we felt that the staff in Norwich were sufficiently well looked after, then maybe we might choose to set up in an alternative location."

And that had been enough to bring about the change. King retained the property however and was already making plans to turn it into a hotel.

"Glad you got me involved with this Steve.", he said to me, "I think this hotel business looks like a bit of fun. You'll have to come and check the place out when we open."

Whilst all this was going on in the background, the cottage was being transformed. It had all begun with the plans that Jean had secretly been putting together on visits to the property before our wedding.

"Come with me.", she'd said as we tidied away the breakfast dishes on our first morning as a married couple, "I want to show you my vision."

I followed her as she led me through the semi-derelict rooms. At each one, she produced a sketch of how she wanted it to look. The kitchen would be kept pretty much the same as it currently was, although it would be deep-cleaned and all the exposed beams polished and sanded. The stone floor would remain, as would the original stove, however, a central workspace would house all the appliances that we needed even though it would look like a simple wooden unit.

Each of the bedrooms would be themed. Ours would be a classic four-poster bridal suite because, as Jean explained, this whole place is about our marriage. The guest rooms would be as different to each other as possible. This was because we had such a diverse mix of friends and acquaintances that we needed to cater for visitors ranging from Jason King to some of those I most liked from the canals. There would be a modern suite, a narrowboat themed suite, a cottage suite and an austerity suite. There would also be a nursery.

"Don't worry.", she laughed, "I'm not changing my mind. It's just that some guests may have children."

"You sure?", I asked her.

"Yes.", she paused, "Well, I think so. I know we can't have children ourselves, or at least I don't want to take the risk. But maybe, in the future we might want to think about fostering or adoption. Just a thought."

She moved me quickly back down the stairs and into the rest of the cottage, over-enthusiastically trying to take my mind off what she had said. If the truth be told, I was open to the idea. More so now that we weren't tied to our chaotic pasts. It might be nice to share our lives with another and give them a chance in life.

"Now.", she said, "as we moved towards the back door, "this is where the real vision lies."

She opened the creaking door and we both looked out over the couple of acres of overgrown wilderness that were the cottage's back garden.

"Let me walk you through.", she said, picking up a long hoe, "starting with the arbour that welcomes all to our country garden and which takes us on a path through orchards, herb beds and on into the wilderness retreat."

We hacked our way through the undergrowth with the hoe and she showed me what her plans were. I could see it in my mind's eye but it was a long way off. The collection of old outhouses attracted me the most, as I would never profess to be a gardener, and Jean caught this in me.

"Yes.", she smiled, "you can do what you like with the buildings. I always had you down as a shed man anyway. I thought you could have one as a workshop, one we'll keep the tools in and then one of the others can become a summer-house."

"Even though we're on the boat in the Summer?", I asked.

"Don't be so selfish.", she slapped my hand, "When we're not here it can a holiday place for those in need. That's your type of thing isn't it. Anyway, if we get that place sorted properly, you can use it as an escape when I kick you out."

It took us all day to go through the plans several times and I had little to say against them. King had already sent his team in to fix and secure the roof and windows of the property, but it seemed that he and Jean had been in cahoots about the rest whilst I'd been miles away.

"I hope you like it.", she said as we settled in front of the fire with a bottle of red.

"Jean.", I turned and stared as the flames lit up her face, "Of course I like it. I like it because it's as good or better than anything I could come up with. I like it because it gives us something to do and it should be manageable with a little help. And I like it because it works."

"But.", I continued, holding her closer, "I like it most of all because it is you."

We fell asleep in front of the fire that night and were happier than we had ever been.

Chapter Thirty-Three

Christmas at the cottage was like something out of a fairy-tale. I sometimes think that if I'd looked out into the garden on that unusually snowy Christmas Day I might have seen animated birds and woodland animals frolicking around and singing sugary songs. Not that we'd planned it that way. We were too exhausted to add the scheduling of the festive season to our agenda so we'd only put together the basics. Jean and I knew each other well and knew that we weren't great Christmas people. We liked the traditions and we liked the general feeling of goodwill that pervaded even the least religious heart, but our days of getting excited about it were long gone. I'd made the effort when I had the children. It was what you did. When they grew up, if they ever got the chance to, they could make their own choices. Meanwhile, Fran and I had chosen to let them enjoy the magic of the mainstream and believe in Father Christmas.

In the run up to this Christmas we'd not had a single day off as we renovated the cottage. Our present to ourselves was to take a break from the works but the cost of this was a long hard slog to get the cottage up to spec before that break. It was nowhere near finished although we had hit the targets we'd set ourselves. The kitchen was done. It was the heart of our home and the room we spent most of our time in. The style magazines wouldn't have been interested in it, as it was more about function than fashion. Nor could we claim to have done anything revolutionary with it. It was simply a homely, clean and well-equipped room, warmed by the Aga that we never allowed to go out and always with just a hint of the herbs and spices we used pervading the air.

The bedroom was also completed as were the bathroom and the small box-room that I had as my den. In the bedroom, a four-poster bed dominated the scene, onto which I had carved a number of floral motives, much to Jean's surprise and delight. Our en-suite was state-of-the-art, contrasting nicely with the classic theme of the bedroom. We were still working around boxes of items that were waiting to be installed in other rooms and battling to stop the new carpets bubbling with fluff every time we walked on them. But we were happy with the progress that we'd made. There was just one other major work that had been completed, but that was my secret. At least, until Christmas Day.

"Come with me", I said to Jean as we finished our wake-up coffee, "but make sure you've got your wellies."

She followed me out of the backdoor, both of us taking a moment to adjust to the sharp chill of the snow-covered scene. Aside from a small path that we had cleared down to the back of the garden, we'd chosen to leave the work needed here until the weather got better. I had had other plans though and had been working on my little secret whenever I had an opportunity.

"What are we doing, Steve?", Jean asked me, "It's freezing out here. Don't tell me you've hidden my present under the snow."

"Stick with it", I told her, "we're nearly there. Look, just off to this side."

I let her precede me through a patch of ragged brambles, knowing that she had enough room to get through without snagging herself. She stopped just ahead of me and gasped.

"Oh, Steve", she cried, "it's beautiful. How?"

I let her drink in the sight before I replied. What she was looking at was the 'fairy-glen' hideaway that I had copied from one of her sketches. Of course, I'd tweaked her design a little. On first impressions, aside from the thousands of LED lights that sparkled across the area, it looked simply like a place of refuge and peace with a bubbling stream running around its periphery and several stone benches to chill out on. A carefully disguised roof covering, woven from a lattice of interconnecting vines had kept off most of the snow but also allowed the natural light of the morning to flood into the space.

"I hope you don't mind.", I whispered to her, "Happy Christmas."

"Oh Steve", I could see tears welling in her eyes, "it's wonderful. How did you manage it?"

"It wasn't easy", I said, "but every time you went into town to collect supplies, I did a bit of work. And the big stuff, I had installed when we were both out. Apart from that, it's quite simple really. A few lights, a little imagination and of course, your plan to work to."

"You laughed at that picture when I showed it to you.", she protested, "Why the change of heart?"

"Because I love you,", I told her, "as simple as that. And if it's what you want, why not? I'll have my workshop next year, but for now, we have your fantasy den to enjoy. I have enhanced it a bit though. Check this out."

I moved over to the rear of the plot where a huge sheet of slate was currently glistening with a film of flowing water. Reaching around to the side, I pressed a button and the slate rose slowly, diverting the water back and away to the stream whilst revealing a steaming hot-tub dancing with multi-coloured lights.

"No way!", Jean gasped.

"Fancy a dip?", I asked, pressing another button to allow a changing pod to rise up out of the earth, "Costumes are in here, along with the glasses and a nicely chilled bottle of bubbly. Come on, race you."

It didn't take us long to strip out of our dressing gowns and into the swimming costumes and within minutes we were soaking away at thirty-nine degrees, watching the sun shimmering through the foliage above.

"Before you complain and say that this is too much and you haven't got me anything,", I said as I uncorked the champagne and filled the plastic glasses, "you should know two things. One, I'll get as much pleasure out of this as you and two, this part of the glen is a gift to us from Mr King."

"Jason?"

"Do you know another?", I asked before explaining that while I'd been working on this subterfuge, he had helped with supplies and contractors before telling me that he was giving us both a special present as part of the deal. He insisted, mainly because we hadn't asked him to do all the work on the cottage.

"If you must wear yourselves out with manual labour,", he'd said to me, "then you'll need something like this to work your muscles loose again."

We spent long enough in the tub that morning to work through just one bottle of bubbly. We could always come back later. As we dried off in the heated changing pod, we showered, made love and showered again, before wandering slowly back to the cottage. The heat from the hot-tub had permeated deep into our centres and we didn't even feel the chill anymore.

"My turn now.", Jean said as we sat back down in the kitchen.

"Right, you need to close your eyes,", she told me, looking at her watch, "and ignore anything you hear for a minute or two."

I did as I was told and sat with my eyes shut as Jean moved towards the front door as the sound of a tractor drew nearer. I had to confess that at that point I thought Jean had seriously misjudged me. Yes, I was a bloke and I liked my toys, but a piece of farm machinery? It would take some pretending to carry off faux-delight at that one. Then I was reassured by the sound of the door closing and the tractor departing.

"Okay," she said as she came back to the kitchen, "this is your present. I had to keep it out of your sight, so George up the road has been looking after it. Here you are."

She handed me a cardboard box with a simple ribbon tying the lid on. I pulled the bow loose and was just about to lift the lid when it moved on its own and a wet nose pushed its way towards me. Taking the lid off completely, I was soon engulfed in wet kisses and loving whines from a black and white puppy.

"Oh Jean.", I didn't know what to say, "This is fantastic. How did you know?"

"Come on, Steve,", she laughed, "I know that you and I love being together but don't think I haven't seen those times when you're on your own and just yearning to get out and about into the fields with a companion. He's called Fred by the way."

"Fred!", I held the puppy close to me, "Good name. He looks like a Fred. Thanks Jean, you're right, sometimes I like being alone but I've always wanted to share my time with a dog. Guess this forces me to love something else as well as you. That's going to be a new departure for me."

Neither of us approved of giving live animals as Christmas presents and if we'd have heard about this one from somebody else, we'd no doubt have shook our heads and expressed our disgust. But, for that Christmas, our first together, her choice of present was perfect. I still had Gilly, but she was more at home in the marina now and, ultimately, she was still only a robot. Now, with Fred, I had another tether to draw me back into the mainstream and hold me back from my Kingfisher activities. Did I regret that? Not a bit. Give me the two of us and now this new addition and all the time we had together and I had all I needed. I'd paid my dues. In the New Year, I'd think it through a bit more, but maybe now was the time to hang up the suit or hand it over to another.

Aside from a few silly additional presents that we'd hidden under the single branch that we had decided would be our tree for the year, the rest of our time up until the three o'clock deadline was taken up with Jean preparing a full traditional Christmas dinner and me playing with a boisterous puppy, whilst we both sipped at sherry. The three o'clock deadline was important to us. That was when we sat for ten minutes and listened to the Queen. This year, she was presenting her final speech, having decided that, at one-hundred years old, she was probably entitled to retire. It wasn't just the Queen we respected, as much as this tradition of Christmas. It made us proud to be a part of our country and it also marked the turning point in the day.

As we turned off the television, Jean and I sat in the kitchen, pulled the naff crackers that had appeared from somewhere and laughed at the stupid jokes they contained. Starter had to be prawn cocktail. We both liked it but I would have preferred whitebait and she would have gone for camembert, but this was Christmas and the rules of the meal were set in stone. As was the wearing of paper crowns.

"Here's to our first Christmas.", I raised a glass of bottle number one of the wine for that day, "And here's to us."

We clinked glasses and tucked into the starter, chatting about all and sundry and praising our wonderful Queen for making another Christmas special. After that, it was time to lay out a spread that would feed us for several days, whilst I ceremonially carved the turkey. Our plates bulged with the meal that looked like it would never fit into out fairly slight frames, but we worked steadily at it and enjoyed every mouthful.

"I don't want to ruin the moment.", Jean said, "but isn't there something wonderful about this meal, as a way of marking the start of a new future, but also of burying the past?"

I asked her to clarify.

"We don't talk about family.", she said, "Not much anyway. You know a little about mine and I know the bare details of yours, but just here, now, do you not think we should reminisce a bit? I remember family Christmases quite fondly. What about you?"

I had to think hard about my response.

"I agree.", I said after draining my glass and refilling it, "There's a lot we don't know about each other. But, that's not because I want to keep things from you. It's just that I have to ask if they add any value to us?"

"Go on.", she said.

"Well, you know I have a past.", I said, "We all do, of course. But, and this is where people seem to think that I'm hard and unfeeling, for me, that past can sometimes be painful. I'm not unfeeling. You know that, I hope. I just

226

see things differently, I guess. I can't do all the sentimental tosh about things that were never actually how we claim to remember them to be. And, to be frank, the things I do remember are hard to carry."

"What like?", she asked.

"Nice try.", I laughed as I answered, "I told you when we first started seeing each other, that a lot of my past would remain in the past. You have to trust me. There's nothing weirdly enigmatic about this and it's not that I'm trying to make myself out be some sort of mysterious shadowy figure dangling nuggets in front of you. What you see and what you know me as, well, that's what I am. And that's what I want to be. I've seen things that nobody should ever have to see and I've done things that I would never admit to. But you're the same there. You've seen stuff that I don't want to know about, because I couldn't handle it."

"It's true," she sighed, "and you're making sense. I guess I'm just one of those people who prefers to talk about things, but you may be right, why should I burden others with my experiences? I'm out of the journalism thing now, so maybe we should look to the future instead. Boy, have I seen some stuff in my time."

"But I'm not ruling it out.", I insisted as I reached out to hold her hand, "We can talk about anything you want to talk about if you want to. For my part, over time, I'm sure I'll open up to you some more, if it's right for us. Please, don't take any of it personally. No, actually do take it personally. This is a personal thing for you. I want to be with you and I want to enjoy my future with you, and to make that more enjoyable, I believe that my part should be about the here and now and not about the highs and lows of what put me here."

After that, the wine and the food helped the conversation move into a lighter vein and, by the time the pudding was ablaze in front of us, we were chuckling and giggling like school-children, egged on by the silly little incidents that are the heart of life even if they are rarely worth recording. Things like Fred falling asleep on the chair in front of the Aga and running in his sleep; like the reminiscence of the worst joke ever and the inability to stop laughing at it; and like the mispronounced name that sounded funnier for making me look like an idiot.

We finished with a platter of cheese and biscuits. Neither of us was remotely hungry, but we both valiantly pursued that cheddar and stilton as a duty. With the last mouthfuls, we cracked open another bottle of champagne

227

and I proposed a toast to us and to the life we were living. From somewhere and without warning, I burst into tears. I'd never cried in front of Jean, not even when I had a sniffle after a good film, but those tears were unstoppable. My instinct was to try to hold them back, but I stopped myself and just let them roll on. I wasn't ashamed of those tears as they were tears of the purest and deepest joy that I had ever felt. In some ways, they were an extra gift to Jean to show her just how much she meant to me and to thank her for taking a broken man and helping to rebuild him.

That Christmas was the best I would ever have. It was a day of love and of fun and of passion and of companionship. It was, to paraphrase my old friend, Mr Dickens, the best of times. We were just another couple to the outside world, but to each other, we were the opposites that attracted and the sum of all that could be expressed about love.

"This is the best Christmas I've ever had.", I told Jean as we settled to watch some rubbish on the television that evening.

"Mine too.", she told me, "and thanks for everything."

"We don't have to thank each other.", I said, "we just need to let what we are together happen. I'm so glad I found you."

And I'm so glad that we had that Christmas. Within six weeks, Jean would be dead.

Chapter Thirty-Four

In so many ways, I've been there, done that and got both the T-shirt and the scars to prove it. But these are the hardest words I've ever been forced to write.

We woke after a fairly heavy session in the hot-tub, drinking in the New Year and watching the numerous firework displays from the comfort of the bubbling water. Not surprisingly, we both had headaches, but whilst mine cleared in an hour or so, Jean couldn't shake hers off. On top of that, she felt sick for long periods of the day and I have to confess, I half hoped that she was carrying our baby.

When she didn't feel any better the following day, she took herself off to London to see one of Jason King's private physicians. I remember telling her that she was maybe being a bit melodramatic, but she must have had some sort of sixth sense about her condition because, when she returned a few days later, she asked me to join her in the kitchen over a glass of wine.

"Steve," she said, holding my hand and looking deeply into my eyes, "I'm not going to beat about the bush. I'm ill. In fact, I'm very ill."

"Okay," I said, "you've got me to look after you. We can postpone the work on the cottage and I'll nurse you through."

"No, Steve." she struggled to continue but got there in the end, "I'm dying."

"No," I protested, "you can't be, it's only a headache. Jason's guys can do wonders."

She moved to sit next to me and we embraced as she told me what the doctors had discovered. She had a brain tumour. It was large enough to be affecting her quite badly and appeared to be growing rapidly.

"It's a risky operation," she said, "but it is operable."

"So, have the operation." I replied, "I can't lose you Jean."

"It's not as simple as that," she sighed as pulled away from me, "you see, the brain tumour is just the primary. I'm riddled with secondary's and they're too far gone."

"Listen to me.", she continued, "King's doctors have offered the latest and the best treatments but there isn't one of them who's confident that they can stop the spread. Barring a miracle, they're giving me a month at most."

"No.", I couldn't take this in, "No way. We've just got married, we've got so much to do. It can't be. There must be something they can do."

"Believe me, Steve.", she held my hands tightly, "if there was any chance, I'd take it. I'd go through anything to be free of it and to carry on our life together, but it just isn't going to happen. All we can do is make the most of the weeks we have left together. I'm sorry."

We sat in that kitchen all night. One minute we were racked with tears, the next, we found something to smile about. Fred sat with us, knowing that there was something wrong but able only to offer a soft embrace as comfort.

When Jean slipped away into sleep, I eased myself out from her arms and wrapped her in a blanket. I stood in the kitchen doorway looking at the woman I loved and still not believing that she wouldn't be here in the Spring. I called Jason.

"Steve.", his voice said it all, "I knew you'd call. I'm guessing she told you then?"

I told him that she had.

"I can't think of a single thing to say to you.", he whispered, no longer the confident, ex-monarch and mega-businessman that I had once known, "Jean is like a daughter to me. You're both so special in my life and I don't understand how this can happen to you."

I asked if there were any hope at all, even by breaking the rules and bringing untested technologies into play.

"We'll never stop working on it.", he told me, "I've been in touch with ORB and even made contact with other international groups that you're not supposed to know exist. Bless them, even James and Adam have stopped everything and are trying to teach themselves anatomy, microbiology and any other subject that might help. Believe me, if there is a way, we'll do what we have to do, but I don't think I can give you any good news."

I thanked him and hung up. Fred walked into the lounge and sat with me on the settee. I stroked him and he slept in my arms, but I wasn't going to give in to sleep. I wasn't going to accept this. Death had been a constant companion to me in my life. I wasn't prepared to let it attack me again. I'd seen people die and I'd done death's work for him and taken lives myself. But to have to watch the person I loved die slowly, that was too much. How could I cope? And, more importantly, how could Jean cope, knowing that she was ticking her days of life off like an advent calendar?

She woke me at lunchtime the following day as she cleared up the mess that Fred had made while we both slept. I leapt up and tried to take the cleaning things off her, telling her that she shouldn't be doing that, when she pushed me back onto the sofa and stood threateningly over me.

"This is one conversation that we are going to have once, and once only," she shouted at me, "I am not an invalid and you are not going to wrap me up in cotton wool for the little time I have left. When I can't do stuff, of course I'll ask you. But for now, it's business as usual. You understand?"

We'd had rows before but I'd never seen her so fiery. I stopped myself from whispering a lame apology and let her calm down a bit. When she'd cleared up and taken the mess outside, she came back in with coffee for us both and sat next to me.

"You're right, Jean," I told her, "and who am I to say anything when you've got such a burden to carry? I can't think of anything worse than what you're going through. I'll try. I don't know how, but I'll try to help you through this awful time. How can you live with it though?"

"I have to Steve," she said as she sat beside me, "I don't have a choice. It's bizarre and unreal to think that a few days ago we were enjoying our first Christmas and looking forward to so many more, and then, this. But I can't change it. You can't change it. I haven't got the luxury of taking weeks to come to terms with it, so I've got myself through that stage. I've lived. I've played my part, I think, and I've loved. I never believed I was immortal and I've lived in a way that I could accept death when it came. The hardest part though, is the waiting. A quick death would have been brutal but done and dusted with. A longer prognosis would actually be harder, I think. But this, a month, it's tough. We can't change it though. I'll let it run its course and fight as long as I have to but, towards the end, don't keep me hanging on. Until then, let's do the things we've always wanted to do."

Which is what we did. Most of our bucket list involved spending time with ourselves. The great landmarks and the famous places didn't seem as special in the light of our situation. The Taj Mahal was just another building, the Grand Canyon a scar in the rock and Niagara Falls just a waterfall. None of them meant a thing.

We did go into orbit on one of the new commercial space flights that one of King's compatriots arranged for us. And we toured the depths of the

231

oceans courtesy of another of his contacts. Other than that, we travelled around the world in King's private jet, simply because it was something fun to do and it was something that we could do together. Then, as Jean started to slow down, we prepared for the end.

George had looked after Fred whenever we were away and we knew that he would take him off us whenever we needed to be alone. We liked having him around though. Jean particularly wanted him with us as though she were able in some way to leave a permanent impression on him that I could keep with me. He sat with her throughout that final week. As did I.

"Steve," her voice was thin and tired now, "I don't think it will be long now. You don't want me to fight the end, do you? I feel as though I can let it come and it will be just like falling asleep."

I told her I wanted her to fight for every second that she could give me, but that that was just me being selfish.

"You do whatever you have to darling," I told her, "I don't want to see you suffering like this, but I don't want to lose you either. Man, this is just the worst. Where's the justice in this?"

"Steve," she reached out and put her thin and trembling fingers into my palm, "it could have been worse. We've had time to say goodbye, and the pain isn't as bad as they'd said it might be. No one lives for ever. In a way, I feel quite honoured to have been allowed to walk into death like this. It's not injustice. It's just a part of life. I've had a good one overall. And you've been the icing on the cake."

"Jean," I whispered, "it should have been me. Don't you get it. I'm the one who should be suffering like this. I'm the one who's smoked all the carcinogens and drunk all the alcohol. And I'm the one whose hurt people the most."

"No Steve," she sipped water through a straw, "that's not true. I know more than you think I know and I know you're a better person than you think you are. I don't just marry trash you know!"

We managed to laugh together and then she drew me closer.

"I can't thank you enough," she whispered to me, "for the times that we've had together and for everything that you've been to me. I loved you from the first time that we met and I've loved you for the person you are, even though there have been some changes."

She looked into my eyes.

"Zip, I've always loved you," she smiled as she slipped away, "and James was right. It's in the hands. They can't change the hands. But, with you Zip, it was in the eyes as well. I know they changed them but the soul behind them stayed the same. Thank you, Steve, thank you Zip, I love you."

And that was how Jean said goodbye. She slipped into unconsciousness and I held her for most of that night until I woke to find that she had breathed her last. Fred had been with her to the end and was lying facing me with his head across her chest. I picked myself up, called Fred to follow me, then made the necessary calls.

I don't make any excuses for the person I am. If it helps to explain though, picture this. Four months to the day after wedding Jean, I wore my new suit to see her cremated and shared that experience with the same people who'd been with us for the wedding. I left the crematorium on my own and walked into the nearest town. On the high street, bustling with the day to day activity that makes no concession to personal tragedy, I dropped the contents of my wallet into a busker's hat.

"Cheers mate.", he shouted as he continued to play, "Nice suit."

That led me to a charity shop and a change of clothes. I folded the suit neatly into a carrier bag and laid it at the busker's feet, walking off before he had a chance to open it. That was my yesterday life and I didn't need it anymore. From there, I headed to the station and began my journey back to the boat. Only Jason King knew my intentions. He understood why I wouldn't be in attendance at the big memorial service that Jean's journalist colleagues had put together for her. He understood why I'd asked him to give the cottage to Adam and Charlotte and why I'd asked him to liquidate all of my assets and divide my share of Boat Space between the team and Tony and Kate. He understood why I needed to get away and, all credit to him, he let me go.

Chapter Thirty-Five

The keys for my boat were hanging anonymously with all the others on the pegboard at the marina. Each set had the obligatory cork ball hanging off the ring and, for a second, I was reminded that one of my outstanding projects was to develop something a little more suited to the twenty-first century to keep keys afloat. I stopped myself immediately. That was something I no longer did. I was finished with Boat Space, finished with delivering justice and finished with dreaming about a brighter future. Life was life and inevitably ended in nothing more than death. I might have days, weeks or even years, but whatever time span I drifted through, I would remain a vapour and return to dust. Call it an Ecclesiastes moment.

Before retrieving the key fob, I had to let my hand rest on the large K that hung down next to the flotation ball. Only a few people had access to Kingfisher and the keys were designed to protect themselves. Had an unauthorised person held them, they would have melted away to nothing after a few minutes. They recognised me though. They knew my hands. It was always the hands wasn't it? The hands that touched and felt their way through love and labour. The hands that connected people and were first to inflict a blow. And it was the hands that held the new-born, caressed the lover and forged the creative works that flowed from the mind. Jean had known all along. I sort of knew that she knew but she carried it well. I'm glad she shared with me before she left and I'm glad that she accepted me after all that I had done.

Those same hands caressed Fred as I retrieved him from the compound behind the boatyard. His presence would have been too much in the period immediately after Jean's death and so he'd come here for a short while. He'd lived with us long enough to miss us but he was also young enough to accept the hospitality of anyone who fed, watered and cuddled him. He still seemed pleased to see me and the feeling was mutual. I'd only just decided to keep him with me. Everything inside me wanted solitude and escape from all that had been the past, and yet, there was something else, a still, small voice inside me, that said Fred had to be a part of the future. People I could do without. Possessions too, although I was still better off than most. But to have rejected that puppy? No, it didn't seem right.

Taking Fred meant that I also had to take Gilly. She'd been a fixture in the marina for a long while now and it was clear that the few people who knew that she could be switched off rarely chose to do so. She and Fred had bonded in the most bizarre way. Gilly was Fred's new playmate and his surrogate mother. Other dogs had met Gilly before and got on well with her, but they had always been that little bit reticent as they detected that there was something just not right with her. Fred didn't have the life experience to make that judgement. Jean had found him in a rescue centre where he'd been dumped at just eight weeks old. He'd only just arrived when she decided that a dog could be for Christmas and for life, and his time there was brief. I was fine with having the two dogs. One, two, maybe even more, it didn't really matter. One was young enough to grow into a great companion who would allow me space when I needed it, the other could simply be switched off.

I stayed at the marina until I received a parcel from Jason King. It arrived on the 1st March 2026 and I offloaded the contents into the boat. The parcel contained the sum total of the worth that I had asked King to liquidate and was neatly stacked in blocks of mid-value notes. It would be enough to see me through my lifetime. I might pick up casual labour on the way to top it up, or I might choose to deplete it and buy some land somewhere to make a base for myself. It was all I needed to keep me on my journey. I stored it in the hidden lockers that had once been full of the tools of my trade but which now sat empty after I'd deposited most of the Kingfisher items in James' lab. I kept the owl, for old times' sake and I kept a few of the weapons, for reasons I couldn't explain. Even more bizarrely, I chose to keep the lightest and the newest of the suits. I genuinely believed that I would never wear it again, but I wanted it there as a reminder. The pod went and its holding space was filled with more cash, however, the bike remained. That, of all the toys, I might be able to use. In with the cash went the little I'd retained as a memory of Jean. There were a few photographs, her latest notebooks and the letters that she'd written to me as she lay in bed and I worked around the house. They were safe in that waterproof vault and I wasn't sure when, if ever, I would look at them again.

With all my worldly goods, two dogs and a boat that was all I would ever need in a boat, I left the marina in the early hours of the following day and headed out onto the canal. I was off on the Grand Tour that Jean and I had planned, but not because I was going to take over her role in documenting the details of all that I saw. No, I was doing it simply because I had to go somewhere. I had to keep myself busy and at least make the effort to move about. There would be some great experiences, I knew that and looked forward to them. Most of the journey however would be nothing more than a distraction to stop me contemplating all that could hurt me from the past and the harm that the futility of the future might cause me.

Jean had always said that I was heartless. She knew better of course, and it was more of a joke between us as we got to know each other. Numerous other people have said the same about me though, and with good reason. It's not that I don't have feelings. No, I probably have them as much and as deeply as anybody. It's just that they hurt too much, for too much of the time. That's why I switch them off. If it was toothache, I'd be criticised for not blocking the pain with ibuprofen or any other painkiller. Why must heartache be different? Why all this talk about sharing feelings and talking things through? No, that wasn't my way. I had enough agony stored away in me after all that had happened recently that I had to keep the lid on it. That was why the memorial service would have been too much. I was full of pain and hurt and one extra portion would have tipped me over the edge. When I lost Fran and the children, I lost too much time to the anti-depressants that numbed my senses. I wasn't going along that route this time.

As to justice, well, that could look after itself. I didn't put Jean's death down to an injustice and was happy to go with her view that there was actually some sort of perverse justice in being able to prepare for death. From my side, I could argue that it was unjust on me but frankly, did I deserve any better? No, they were the questions that could never be answered and so, like my feelings, thoughts of justice, hope for the future, pride in my achievements and plans for the rest of my days were buried deeply away.

With the boat licensed under the company's name and with King's agreement that it would be kept licensed and insured, I had no need of an address. Thinking this through, I realised that I also had no need for an identity. My bank accounts were closed, I carried only cash and it had been a long time since I'd used any sort of personal e-mail. My first act as I entered the waterway from the marina was to drop the last of any identification documents into the cut. If I was ever free, then it was at that point. Yet, it was a freedom that I would have happily given up.

I cruised like this for six months. I had a routine of sorts but it was one that, as with any canal-based activity, was subject to a high degree of flexibility. Looking after the dogs was my first priority. They were fed and watered at the right times and their walks took place from eleven in the morning until at least one in the afternoon, although we often returned many hours later. Gilly could go on forever and Fred, as a puppy still, was always up for more exercise. Once those two were sorted, I had my time to myself. I never drank until midday. After the twelve bells though, the gloves were off and I kept the booze flowing. I smoked like a chimney because I wasn't worried about clinging onto a life that was so pointless, and I read anything that I could get my hands on because I had to have something to do and books were as good an escape as anything.

The sunny days of Spring and Summer would see me on the towpath, dogs at my feet and, to the unknowing eye of the passer-by, truly living the dream. Pills remained out of the question for me. I'd had them before and vowed never to have them again. Switching off feelings with alcohol is a lot more enjoyable and a lot more effective. Pills would have been a sledgehammer to stun me but the wine and the beer and the gin and the whisky were gentle hands that massaged me into numbness. It's not an approach I advocate. But it worked for me.

I also talked to myself a lot during this period. Never in public, or at least that I'm aware of. I talked to other people as well, but it was the talks with myself that helped me carry on. Every evening, using the recording equipment that I retained on board, and which had an almost infinite storage capacity, I would confess to all that I had done and tell the boat how I felt about anything and everything. It's those recordings that have helped me fill in the details of this blank period that stretched into a year and then some more, during which I was out there in the world, on my own and no longer a part of it.

Early on, I retained a fairly decent standard of appearance. I shaved, as much because I didn't like the feel of stubble after more than a week's growth and I showered as much as the next man. It was the showering that first began to slip. I'd look at the luxury wet-room, think about having to clean it after the shower, then consider the necessity of the wash, usually choosing instead to wipe the worst away with baby wipes. The dogs didn't complain about the smell and my nicotine-numbed nasal passages kept me immune from the worst of it.

The clothes I wore were nondescript and consisted of supermarket jeans, non-branded boots or trainers depending on the season and an eclectic mix of t-shirts, most of which had been promotional items, acquired for nothing. In the main, they were freebies from breweries that I'd picked up along the way, although I was amused to find an old friend in a t-shirt that I'd picked up from the States many, many years ago and which boasted of 'Simpson's Faucets – The Flow to Go With'. Socks, if I bothered with them, were always white tennis socks, and always the same design. That way, they didn't care if they were married with their partner after a wash-cycle. It was all practical and easy living.

I moved to paper plates and disposable cups after about three months. When my bins were full, if there wasn't a nearby facilities block, I simply dug a small pit and burnt away any evidence that I'd passed through. Books came from charity shops or through the mutual exchange that boaters indulged in via those same facilities blocks which were regular stopping points on my travels. Water was always plentiful, thanks to the generous tank installed by ORB, and I never had to think about fuel or electricity as I'd left the marina with new and upgraded batteries.

If I'd ever felt inclined to listen to the recordings that I made, I would have picked up two familiar themes. These were themes that stirred me enough to want to comment on them and were the two themes that fuelled my journey into bitterness and anger. They were other people's problems and the ever-present problem of injustice.

With nothing to lose and even less to live for, I found myself listening a lot more than I spoke myself whenever I was in company with people. I had nothing to say. For all my childhood dreams of growing up to be an influential voice of society, now I was in my late forties, I was at the stage of accepting that I was never going to be famous. Thankfully, I was quite rich. That took some of the edge off the revelation. But if I was not somebody that others would listen to, I found myself, for reasons I still can't understand, being somebody that people felt comfortable to open up to. The pathway was familiar. A trip to the pub and the usual chat about the dogs and the canal. Then a period of silence before the person I was talking to would begin to share things that I would never have shared had they been my issues.

Sometimes, the problems that people told me about left me with the feeling that I was so blessed in so many ways to only have endured the suffering that I had. There was the one-legged mother with the one-armed child who had lost her husband and her two other children in a motor-boat accident. There was the young lad who suffered chronic and unbearable pain every day of his life, having contracted a rare form of malaria on a dream holiday to Africa. And then there was the homeless guy who I treated to a pint and a meal after he'd helped me through some locks. He was just out of prison, having served a short term for theft. Theft that had become a necessity because he was one of the silent minority for whom the welfare state didn't have any immediate answers. He'd tried to do it the right way, but hunger won out and he'd targeted the wrong people to steal from. Believe me, you look hard enough and listen long enough and you'll hear stories that will make you so glad to be in your own position.

For the most part, and I am almost ashamed to say this, the complaints that people raised made me want to grab them and chuck them in the canal. Why did people take themselves so seriously? And why did they get so worked up about the smallest of things? You could usually see the problem-children by the looks on their faces. They seemed to carry the burdens of the world on their shoulders and the strain told in their expressions. Funnily enough, the real sufferers were usually the ones who tried to keep the world out and hide their emotions. No, it was the ones who looked so pained that I dreaded getting into conversation with. These were the people who sat in the churches and judged the rest. They were the takers and never the givers. And they felt so justified in their anger. They were the ones for whom problems, paradoxically, seemed to be a welcome part of their identity.

The worst of these had to be the elderly couple who were at their wits end because the drains in one of their second homes had been damaged by local builders who were dragging their heels in repairing them. Note that this was only drains and only in one of their numerous homes! But these sorts of complaints were far from unique. There were dog owners contemplating the tragedy of having to have their beloved pet put down because it had started chewing their furniture. There were young couples worrying that their little treasure might not get into the school that they preferred. It was always, I noticed, about stuff. All the extra stuff that people seemed to fill their lives with bought them a momentary pleasure which was more than offset by the stress incurred in keeping that stuff up to date. There was a retired vicar who had lost his son over forty years ago but who had shared this fact with me within minutes of our meeting. The loss of his child had, I think, had a devastating effect on his two siblings and the vicar's ex-wife, but I could only deduce this because all he wanted to talk about was the lost life and the great tragedy of it and the burden that he had to bear.

Maybe it will all be published someday. I really don't think it matters whether it is or not because these same conversations are there and all around us to find. I listened to so many, and shocked myself by keeping calm through them all. I had nothing to give in return but so many of those conversations ended with the speaker feeling better. I kept my own counsel until I returned to the boat and then the venom spilled out and the bile raged into that recorder. How could they be so passionate in their indignation about such tiny issues when there were so many others, people like me, who had suffered beyond imagining, seen every dream vaporise into a living nightmare and who carried with them not just a broken heart but a shattered one? Who were they to demand the attention in a world where there were so many more suffering so much more and crying out to be listened to if only these people would leave a void in which their voice could be heard? I know that the drink didn't help me when I was in this sort of mood. It took away the inhibitions of social control that would otherwise be there and it exposed my thoughts and feelings for what they were. Still, it distracted me from having to think about Jean, because thinking about Jean was the time-bomb ticking away in me that I would not recognise.

Then there were the injustices. They were mounting up. Partly because I was letting myself see more of them and partly because the very laws and norms of our nation, the laws that I had sought to uphold in the past, were more and more becoming the source of injustice. Vulnerable kids were being forced into the hands of the drug dealers because one well-placed member of the middle classes had lost their son to a gardening chemical that youngsters were using as a legal high. All the while, the council estates became less habitable and the voice of the inhabitants was reduced to a whisper. Parliament now took time out to discuss the trivial issues that some busybody wanting to be a somebody had stirred up into a petition online and so the white papers that would make a difference to the majority were side-lined until the next session. It had all started off so promisingly. We were an inclusive nation with Christian liberal values and were open to listening to people's grievances. Now the law said that the basis of those human values was in itself an anachronism and the church bells had had to fall silent because the minarets weren't allowed to broadcast their message. Christmas was Winterfest and nativity plays now featured pantomime characters to replace the Holy Family.

And then there was the injustice of the minorities. Not the old-school injustice of persecution which, quite rightly, the law had all but eradicated. No, this was the injustice of the new prejudice against the majority when any minority chose to make its case heard. It was everywhere, from the hijacking of the long-established institution of marriage and its redefinition to include, from what I can gather, any form of legal union between man, woman, sheep, goat or even a piece of household furniture. After that, it had been the injustice of the laws that silenced opposition voices that were deemed to be racist, sexist, homophobic and any other form of prejudice you'd choose to cite or make up. Our majority democracy had been transformed into a minority dictatorship.

I had a portable radio on the boat for a short time. I smashed it against the wall one night whilst listening to Radio Four and being unable to bear the linguistically incompetent work of a continuity announcer that even now, after twenty-five years of support by his Pygmalion-inspired tutors, just could not get the diction right. I'm not racist. I just wonder how many of his supporters would put up with their bistro soup being served to them by somebody suffering from Parkinson's. How many hundreds of people had put the hours in to train themselves to reach the required standard to apply for a radio announcer's position only to find that it wasn't about the quality of their work, since to employ the best would be to discriminate against someone else who really wanted to 'have a go' at the job?

That's another reason why I said so little. I could so easily be accused of every prejudice under the sun, but that would be fundamentally wrong. I may have been bitter and twisted with anger but I still loved even the least lovable people. It was bizarre really. Maybe it simply reflected how much I had given up on looking for righteousness in this world. Humans were to be pitied rather than punished and it was only the fool who let hatred stain his heart.

It was all madness. I sometimes regretted giving so much of myself to the cause of justice, but it was all different now. Whereas, in the past, I'd be raging with fury and plotting a rebalancing which I delivered swiftly, now, I just recorded my thoughts and let others tackle the problems if they wanted to. No, I may have blurred memories of that time, and there may have been the odd article in the press that purported to report the activity of the Righteous Corrector, but I can tell you this for sure. It wasn't me.

Chapter Thirty-Six

The boat that limped into the small yard in Derbyshire in January 2027 was still recognisable as the one that so many brilliant and committed people had put so much work into making look so tidy. Underneath the dirt and the dents that is. The person at the helm was less recognisable. The last vestiges of care and concern about image were well gone and now that the engine on the boat had ceased to work, Steve Barratt just felt fine and dandy about the way the world was treating him.

Having lost the engine, I still had all the power that I needed but there was nobody out there who could even begin to understand how that engine worked, let alone consider fixing it. Because of that, I hooked up a small electric outboard and struggled along to the nearest place that offered long-term moorings. I'd hole up here. I'd done quite a bit of the Grand Tour this time, but they were all places I'd visited before and I'd not been remotely interested in exploring beyond the instantly visible, but now, the future was to be what was left of me living out what was left of my life on what was left of my boat.

So much of living on the water was about knowing the right people and being in the right place at the right time. It was this process that led me to find the mooring that I needed, which was quickly secured after I'd borrowed a phone and arranged everything. I'd resisted the call to go back into any sort of marina for as long as possible but now that the engine had died, I didn't have much choice. Fortunately, this marina was at the basic end of the spectrum. It was an old facility, dug out long before the concept of luxury boating facilities was conceived, and it had the only two things that I needed, which were water and waste disposal. I use that term to include all manner of waste, after all, I was still only human. Aside from that, it had the only other requirement that was essential for me, it had solitude. There were no more than forty boats on site and of these, only a dozen or so were occupied for any length of time. They shimmied the boats around for me on my arrival and this maintained the distance that we, the long-term residents, preferred between us. Not that we were aloof about it. It was just one of those unwritten rules that we all abided by; you passed the time of day with your neighbours but your privacy was paramount.

They were a good bunch and they accepted my presence amongst them without any fuss. Three of them were younger people using the base as an affordable home as they saved for a deposit on a mortgage, four were elderly couples choosing to live out their time in isolation rather than being deposited in a care home. There were five of us who were single males, each scarred in our own way by the ravages of the outside world and all of us hiding in the shadows of alcohol. Then there was Maria. Maria had to be eighty if she was a day. She was the nominal manager of the facility but kept herself to herself. I liked Maria. She would always give you a cheery wave if she saw you and was there to respond to any needs you had, almost before you realised that you had a need.

It was a decade or so since Maria had lost her husband of fifty years. They'd been on the boats for half their lives and had hosted their children, their grandchildren and now their great-grandchildren on board their small and basic boat. Maria changed my life. Not because we shared the pain of losing a loved one, nor because we shared a mutual feeling that we were living out our final days in that place. No, she changed me because she cared for me. She never interfered and she never chastised but there was always a bottle of milk on the deck of the boat when I'd been on an intense bender, and the dogs were always to be found on her boat when their carer had let them down.

If I was ashamed of any of my behaviour during this period, it would have to be that I let those dogs down from time to time. It didn't matter that Gilly was not what she seemed. If Fred suffered, then she suffered as well. I didn't beat them or mistreat them wilfully. It was just that there were times when they were put through a mental distress that they felt intensely and which they simply couldn't understand. My drunken rages into the microphone may not have been understandable by their words, but the dogs knew the feeling behind them and they cowered together. They were the original suffering innocents and I can make no excuses for the hurt I caused them. Aside from the mental anguish they endured, there were the days when they were set aside in favour of my own self-pity, or days when they didn't get out and about for their walk because I was too wrapped up in my own misery and too drunk to take them anywhere safely.

Maria knew about those days. They were the days I barely remembered and the days that were followed by her gently pushing open the stern doors on my boat to let the dogs back in. I'd wake on those mornings and be shaken by regret. And yet, those dogs came back to me with a love and a forgiveness that bought us closer together and which helped me temper, in some small way, the excesses that so distressed them. That unconditional love that seems unique to dogs is something that we humans could learn a lot from. So much of it is about memory, I believe. They remember, but they don't dwell on yesterday. Each day to them is a new day of hope and they truly live in the moment.

On my good days, I tried to repay Maria's kindnesses in whatever way that I could by helping her with some of the things that she struggled with. She was the sort of person who would never ask for help but common sense dictated that she would always appreciate a helping hand. My clothes stayed clean because of Maria. Not because she did my washing, but because she gave me an incentive to make that trip to the launderette that I needed to make, putting both our clothes through the machines. Similarly, I made something of an effort to wash because of Maria. It was all well and good for me to let myself go and no longer care about my appearance but that would have excluded me from the occasional afternoon invites onto her boat for tea and cakes. The dogs looked forward to those times and, I'm happy to say, so did I.

There were probably more good days than bad. Days when I would walk to one of the nearby pubs with the happiest dogs in tow. Days when I would take a folding chair and some cans and sit at the lock that was nearby, chatting to passing boaters and offering a hand if they needed it. I probably looked a bit threatening, almost as if I were panhandling for tips when I helped out. At the time, I didn't think about that. I just wanted to be a part of things for a while. And that was how Maria helped me out the most. She encouraged me to break out of my self-imposed isolation and take the first tentative steps back into the real world.

"It's all right for me," she told me one day, as I sipped Earl Grey in the country-cottage surroundings of her small lounge, "but you Steve, well, you're still so young, aren't you?"

"I don't feel it," I replied.

"Well of course you don't," she laughed, "That's because you've decided to wait for the end. You've let yourself think that there isn't a future and that this is the final chapter. Which means that you have to think yourself older than you are."

"But," I paused as I wondered whether to open up a little to her, "I don't see a future. That's the problem. It's like I've done my bit, paid my dues and now, the days, the weeks, the years that I have left are mine to let slip by."

"Which is where you have a problem," she smiled as she poured out another cup of tea and passed me another slice of cake, "because our lives are not our own to waste away like that. Why haven't you just committed suicide?"

"Because that's wrong," I said, "and no, don't ask me why I think that."

"But that's what you're doing Steve," she reached out a gnarled and calloused hand to hold mine, "don't you see? You're killing yourself every day and letting your life slip away. It's a longer process, but son, it's suicide in my book. What happened to kill your hope like this?"

I began to explain. I held nothing back and, for the first time ever, I told another human being about the man that I was and what had turned me into the man I had become. I told her about seeing Fran and the children lying dead in the road, about the pain and the injuries and the hurt that I had caused in seeking justice, and I told her about Jean and how I had watched the new love of my life slip away before my eyes.

She didn't interrupt me and she didn't throw me out when I confessed to things that clearly shocked her. When I finished, I felt strangely cleansed, but also a little ashamed that I had opened myself up in such a complete way. It wasn't as if I could blame the booze. I was stone cold sober at the time and probably so for the first time in a long time.

"Sorry," I gave a lame smile as I concluded my confession, "but you did ask."

She tidied away the tea things and resumed her seat next to me.

"A younger me," she laughed, "would have used that trip to the kitchen to call the police and arm myself with a knife. As it is, I think I understand a little. And, for what it's worth, I can see that you may have been called in some way to do what you've had to do. As for your suffering, well, I can't say anything. I can see why you've given up, but I think you should maybe rethink. There's a lot of need out there still. I do my little bit but this old body isn't up to much. But you. You could still make a difference. Goodness me, you're not fifty yet. Have a think about it. You have a gift. It's the gift of life. Don't let it be a curse to you. Instead, embrace it."

She paused and wiped her eyes.

"Or put an end to it tomorrow.", she said, "Don't think that you can live waiting for death. Embrace your life or welcome death but please, for the sake of those who don't have the choice, don't sit on the fence anymore. Tomorrow, next year, maybe in a decade's time, something will bring a little light back into your life. Trust me, I've been around long enough to know that's the case."

Feeling cleansed and strangely refreshed, I went back to my home and stayed up late into the night thinking about what Maria had said. Grief was okay I understood, but self-pity stalked it closely and that wasn't productive. And really, who are any of us to think ourselves so important and indispensable? Most salient though, I chewed over everything that she had said about my self-imposed death sentence. Maybe she was right? Maybe, I had a serious decision to make? And, if suicide wasn't an option, how did that decision look?

Having drifted off to sleep with these thoughts nowhere nearer to being resolved, I woke up halfway through the following morning and searched through some of the sketches that I'd done until I came across the one I remembered. Maria wanted no reward for her help, but she had talked passionately about the subject of that drawing and it was the least I could do. The picture was one of my better efforts. It was of the roundhouse at Gailey where, as she'd confessed to me, Maria first met her future husband.

As I slipped it into a plastic sleeve and climbed out of the boat, I saw one of the other boaters leaving with a phone in his hand. He came slowly over to me.

"Sorry, Steve,", he whispered to me as he completed the call to the emergency services, "Maria's dead. She seems at peace. I found her a few minutes ago. She must have passed quietly this morning."

I stepped into the boat and saw Maria seemingly asleep but no longer breathing. Her face radiated peace and, in her hands, she held two photographs. One was a shot of her husband taken when he was in his prime, dressed in black tie and tails and receiving a corporate award. The other was a family portrait taken the previous year and full of the many faces of the generations that had begun in Maria's womb. I let the sketch that I held fall to the floor and left it there, fully aware that it was nothing compared to what those photographs represented.

I'd like to say that I honoured her memory by changing. I didn't. In fact, I toasted her life with one too many whiskies and suffered badly for it when I woke in the middle of the night. Despite the residual alcohol in my system and the headache that wouldn't go away, I couldn't get back to sleep. I'd miss Maria. Since taking myself out of circulation there wasn't anyone else that I could say that of. I used the time I had to tell Maria how much she had meant to me and to apologise that I didn't say those words to her face. If this had been a Hollywood movie, the moon would have suddenly shone much brighter and its beam would have shone into the boat's cabin and told me that she knew all of this. As it was real life instead, I let the silence speak to me. It was more than a silence though. It was peace, like nothing I'd felt for a long time. It was the sort of peace that made you forget yourself and all that the past had touched you with, and it was the sort of peace that hinted at something in the future worth holding out for.

Fred joined me on the sofa and I rubbed his ears and stroked him gently as he nestled against me. He didn't want to lose me. He'd survive of course and probably transfer his affections to another the moment I was six feet under. Or would he? We had a bond between us and it was a bond that seemed to be tightening against my better wishes. With Maria gone, I had to stick around just to look after Fred. He was the sign of the hint of a hope for the future. I smiled as I drifted off. Maria had given me her gift and I saw the light that she had promised in the slowly closing eyes of my canine companion.

Chapter Thirty-Seven

12th May 2027
From the desk of Jason King
Dear Steve,

It's been a long time. Too long. The team here are all well, but we miss you. I trust that you are looking after yourself and finding some peace in your grief.

Forgive me for making contact with you. I respect your privacy as much as any and the decision to make this approach has not been easy. You are, of course, free to ignore the contents of this letter and none of us will think any the less of you for doing so. That's why I chose to write rather than see you face to face. Your response to this missive must be yours and yours alone.

In short, we have a situation. Not an imbalance of justice situation, but one that threatens the lives of many people. I need to tell you that it is a situation that ORB have asked us to assist with. And it is a situation that crosses national boundaries and touches senior organisations at the highest possible level.

I believe that Kingfisher might be able to help us with this situation. Adam, James and Charlotte are on-board and agree with my thoughts. We don't need you. None of us are that indispensable, but we do want you to be a part of this. Your imagination, skills, perception and in-field prowess would be a huge asset to us.

And yes, this is a mission with a high probability of fatalities. We are all accepting the risk knowing that few, if any of us, might live to tell the tale. If you can't find it in yourself to join us, please think of us. Meanwhile, I enclose a single-use phone should you wish to contact me.

With much love and best regards always,
Jason

I found the letter attached to the inside of the boat's cratch cover as I returned from Maria's funeral. Despite the family being spread across the country, they had agreed to bury her in the church nearest to the moorings as so many of her friends were nearby. I stood quietly at the back of the church, packed as it was with hundreds of mourners and I listened to the eulogies that spoke so much of the woman who had come and gone from my life so rapidly.

She was still influencing me from beyond the grave. For one thing, although I knew that there would be no formal dress code for this burial, I felt that I owed it to Maria to spruce myself up. I took a long time in the shower that morning, having first shaved off the straggly attempt at a beard that I had hidden behind for so long. The feel of the smooth skin where once had been a messy mat of greying hair felt strange. The waste shower water, thick with grease and dirt, testified to the poor levels of standard that I had maintained and again, the scrubbed skin that I felt was strange to the touch. I'd walked into the village the previous afternoon and purchased a shirt and a pair of countryman's cords, as well as a pair of brown brogues that pinched with every step. My choice of outfit was limited. Still, if it helped keep that small shop open, then so be it. I looked in the mirror as I dried myself and dressed. I didn't realise quite how much I'd let myself go. With all the beer and wine, I'd been worried about piling on the pounds and had eaten less and less as I drank more and more. This forced starvation was offset by the number of times that I'd eaten out and replenished much needed calories, but still, the body that stared back at me from the mirror was barely recognisable as being the same one that had once bulged with carefully developed muscles. My bones were visible under yellowing and wrinkled skin. The muscles on my upper body had fast faded away, although my legs stayed in shape thanks to the dog walks. It was a revelation to me. Not a pleasant one.

I nodded at many of the people who passed by me at the church, knowing that their responses were less an acknowledgement that they recognised me but more a common courtesy. A couple of people from the marina could see through my new look and they passed positive comments. Generally, though, I was simply an anonymous mourner at the funeral of a very special person.

Maria also managed to reach out to me through the words of the people who stood to share their thanks for her life. Her family were united in grief and yet, they weren't morose or self-pitying about things. They accepted death as a natural part of life and, although upset, were more focused on the many years of joy she'd given them than the years that they would be without her. Then it was time for the multitude of friends and acquaintances to share their memories. Maria had helped them in ordinary ways. As a younger woman she had always been there to talk to, to help with practical concerns like childminding, or to simply be somebody who made you feel worth something. In her older years, she had helped and served boaters and towpath users in all the familiar ways and also in some unheralded but nonetheless heroic circumstances. A sixty-year-old Maria had stepped into the canal to rescue a toddler whilst all the youngsters nearby screamed in panic. A sixty-five-year-old Maria had clambered onto a burning boat and pulled the sleeping owner out seconds before it had exploded. A seventy-year-old Maria had broken her arm when she'd reached out to stop a freewheeling windlass hit a young girl's face. And a seventy-five-year-old Maria had spent a year of her life knitting small items of clothing to be shipped to disaster victims across the world.

I'd known the eighty-year-old Maria and I wished I'd met her sooner. Nobody at that service needed to know how she had helped me, but it was clear that everybody there was there because she had helped them in a similar way at some point in their lives.

And that was Maria's final gift to me. She made me realise that the real superheroes are the ones that nobody hears about. They are the people who do those little things and offer those few words of encouragement that make the big differences to people's lives. I'd got myself so wrapped up in wanting to be able to make the headlines and deliver justice in a dramatic and forceful way, when the reality was that justice came in the simplest disguise. It was the giving of gifts that came anonymously, it was the smile of acceptance to the socially rejected and it was the time given to get to know the person you least wanted to be with. I might talk about righteous corrections but it was Maria and the millions like her who were the true Righteous Correctors. I didn't want to go back to what I had been, but Maria showed me that I didn't have to. I could use my gift of life to make a small difference in the time I had remaining.

I left that service understanding that death creates ripples. Even the death of the most anonymous of people causes a ripple of disturbance on the waterways of life. The great and the famous, the celebrities and the

251

household names, they passed and the ripples they left were more like waves that crashed against the shore. Those waves were big and powerful and made a lot of noise, but they were over with so quickly. The world moved on. For someone like Maria though, her death created a longer-lasting ripple. It was a ripple that went deep and long in many directions and would gently stir the waters for years to come.

The letter was a bit of a shock. It wasn't that King had tracked me down. That would never be too difficult as long as Boat Space continued to pay the licence for my boat. A quick call to the authorities and the transponder that was compulsory on all vessels using the canal network would pinpoint my location. I could read between the lines and, even on that day that I had resolved not to go back to where I had been, I knew that it was calling me to a finale. I had a choice. We always have choices. This was either a temptation back into a world I no longer wanted to inhabit or it was a genuine request for a last swan song that would end in closure or death. I've always been a reluctant crusader. Even when I was at the height of my success and popularity in ORB, I retained an element of uncertainty about what I was doing. Now, I had the biggest choice to make. Was I guilty over the work I'd done in the past? Was I being asked to atone for the lives I'd taken? Of all the redeeming choices that I'd made, this one was the most important.

The suit still hung in the wardrobe of the boat. I took it out and felt the mysterious fabric against my fingers again. The helmet's visor reflected my face back to me and I searched that image for any form of guidance I could find. Maria had said that I had a calling. Whether that was true or not, it was always my heart that led to my final decisions. It was my heart that had drawn me away from the world and hidden me in an alcohol-numbed isolation that I was happy to be my existence. Now it was my heart that told me to go back. To play the game once more and go out with a bang and not a whimper. I switched on the phone that had been in the envelope with the letter and pressed the speed-dial button.

"Hi Steve.", a familiar and unmistakeable voice answered.

"Hi Jason.", I smiled to myself as I greeted him.

"Well?", he asked.

"Mr King, Sir,", I replied, "the Steve Barratt that you once knew is not the man I am now. I'm a physical wreck, completely out of shape and probably as messed up emotionally as well. I can barely get out of bed some days and, on those that I can, I find it increasingly difficult to connect with the outside world. I'm dependent on alcohol and nicotine to keep me going, and that self-medication is destroying me. The boat that I was once so proud of is now a shadow of what it was and it doesn't even have a working engine. I've got two dogs who are my only companions and who deserve to be given a lot more attention than I give them. I'm a nobody and I am content to have dropped off the face of the Earth as far as official channels go."

I paused and was again impressed by the knack that King had of being able to simply listen.

"But," I continued, "if you can accept all of that, then I guess, you can count me in."

PART THREE:

PART THREE

Chapter Thirty-Eight

After being collected by one of King's chauffeurs, I spent a night at his house being given a full health check and mini-makeover by his medical team. They weren't impressed by the way that I'd let myself go, but they had the equipment and skills to patch me up. They cleaned out my lungs, flushed my system with unknown solutions and pumped me with new muscle mass. It was the sort of treatment that, if commercially available, would revolutionise the way we lived. But it would be a long time before the techniques were released or revealed. The incentive had to be for people to look after themselves and not expect to be fixed every time they messed up.

I was glad they made the exception for me, and I felt better than I had for a long time when I clambered into King's helicopter to join him for the journey to London.

The dogs were in the care of Mrs Quinn. Fred took to her straightaway, whilst Gilly was more concerned that I was leaving. Bizarre when you thought about it, but I no longer questioned the things that Adam and James were able to come up with. I didn't go for the long farewell. They would be fine without me and Mrs Quinn was more than happy to have them as company. If I returned, I might kid myself that their enthusiastic welcome was a reflection of how much they had pined for me, but that was mere sentimentality on my part. If I had seen them for the last time, they would be perfectly happy where they were.

The flight to London was brief. The helicopter swooped smoothly over the English countryside and was soon moving past the outskirts of the big city. It had the type of clearance reserved for very few people. And the pilot was worthy of that level of trust.

As one of King's newest toys, the cabin of the helicopter was no less luxurious than a First-Class suite on the best aircraft. We used the time to talk a little and catch up on what we had been up to. The marine businesses were going very well and both the overt and the covert team were expanding. Tony and Kate were having another baby, and Adam and Charlotte had finally decided to tie the knot. Meanwhile, James was transforming into a leader capable of taking over when necessary.

I thought of the changes that had come about over the years. How I, The Kingfisher, had risen and descended into nothing, whilst the humblest and the least socially able had grown into the new heroes of the future. Charlotte was already turning down offers to lecture on criminology, having seen her first text-book hit the mainstream bestsellers lists. I had no regrets. I missed them, but they were the new generation. Maybe I'd helped sow a seed or two but they were blossoming now and the future looked safe in their hands.

"Coming in to land now gentlemen.", the neatly suited steward advised us.

I looked out of the window and watched as we followed the Thames before banking slightly at London Bridge. We slowed and hovered over the roof of a hospital, then the pilot set her down directly in the centre of the target.

"It just looks a bit less suspicious.", King said as we departed the craft, "landing at a hospital. Doubt anyone will question that."

From the hospital we took a taxi to Oxford Street. Aside from the fact that it had finally been pedestrianised, it was as familiar to me as ever. Some of the shops had changed but the old landmarks were the same. It was so much quieter now though. The whole of London was operated on electric vehicles and it had been the first city in the world to introduce moving pavements. The underground still rattled below the surface and never failed to cope even as the population of the city kept growing, reaching levels that nobody would have predicted after the European experiment was terminated. It was early evening now and London was in its daily period of change from being a destination employment and shopping location into the entertainment hot-spot of the country. A few shutters were descending but I knew that most of the shops would stay open until the last penny had been squeezed from the last bulging wallet.

We stopped at a building I recognised. It had been a boutique for one of the major fashion houses in my day, but they had all moved away now, believing that there was a certain amount of cache in being off the beaten track. It was now a mixed retailer, albeit one that aspired to serve the wealthiest of customers. One glance in the windows showed me that it was a smaller version of the premium department stores that were Oxford Street's staples. When I say smaller though, it was still big enough to take up half

258

a block of shops and clearly extended quite a way back into what had once been a car park that I'd last used on the one occasion I decided to drive into the centre to visit some clients a long, long time ago.

We entered the department store and King led me past the high-tech perfumery and make-up counters, until we were at the rear of the ground floor where a sign pointed to a 'Platinum Lounge'. After a few words with the keepers of the gates of this exclusive domain, we were ushered in and invited to help ourselves to drinks and snacks. I chose a plain tonic water. It had been a couple of days since my last drink and I wanted to keep it up. King poured himself a whisky and we settled down to wait. Others joined us. I thought that I recognised the odd face, but couldn't actually place those people. It was all very refined and all very quiet. By the time we heard the voice announcing that the shop was now closed, there were fifteen of us in the lounge, each of us wondering whether or not we should heed the warning and leave.

"Ladies and gentlemen," a short, bespectacled man addressed us, having entered the lounge from what must have been a second doorway, "please bear with us for a moment. We will be closing down shortly and we can talk more then. Meanwhile, you may be interested to see our little show."

We left the room just as the shop's speakers came back to life and announced:

"Security checks complete. All visitors have departed. Prepare for transition."

For a few minutes, nothing happened, then we began to hear the slightest rumblings and the gentlest sounds of mechanical movement. We watched in awe as the shop began to change before our eyes. Gleaming display cabinets folded in on themselves and transformed into banks of monitors, communication consoles and computer workstations. Some of the units rose up into the ceiling as multiple banks of desks and chairs began to fill the floor. Within ten minutes we were no longer standing in a department store but were now in heart of an operation that looked capable of launching a flight to Mars.

"Welcome to The Order for Restoring Balance," the bespectacled man said proudly, "The heart of justice in the heart of the nation. Please, follow me."

He led us back through the lounge and towards the steel door that was now revealed at its rear. The door opened as he approached and we followed him into a large, thickly carpeted lift. He pressed his hand against the wall and the doors closed, opening again within seconds although none of us had felt any movement. Before us, across a short, covered walkway, was another door, this one policed by two armed guards. They stood to attention as we passed them and entered into a very plush meeting room, then they closed the doors and we heard locks engage.

"Please, take a seat.", our escort said to us, "And please relax. We are now in a totally secure environment. This chamber is completely impervious to any influence from the outside world. We could be on the moon and be more visible than in here."

He smiled at his little joke and watched us as we settled down. Then he moved to the head of the large conference table and his demeanour changed. He removed the glasses he was wearing and picked up two pills that he swallowed and washed down with a glass of water. His face tensed as the tablets took effect and his hunched and slight frame seemed to unfurl before us.

"That's better.", he said as stood fully before us, to all intents and purposes, a different man, "just an extra precaution. Pills that scrunch me up and tickle the old nerves to make me look different. Not the usual for me but then, I don't go up there much. Anyway, let me introduce myself. I am Giles Housman, current President of the Order for Restoring Balance. That's ORB to our friends."

I looked across at King who simply raised his eyebrows and gave me a look that seemed to say, well, who did you think we'd be meeting?

"Thank you all for coming today.", Housman continued, "and at such short notice. I don't need to tell you that your presence here is appreciated by us all, your various employers included."

He paused and scanned the faces in the room.

"As some of you will know each other.", he said, "I think it unnecessary for me to point out that, aside from royalty, presidents and prime-ministers, you are representatives of the very highest levels of your respected nations. Your heads of state are fully aware of your being here and would have attended had such a gathering been something we could pull off without alerting the world's media."

He paused again and took a drink of water.

"Similarly.", he continued, "you have been provided with nothing in writing, nor any electronic communications about your reason for being here. There is a reason for that. This meeting is deniable to the utmost and is of the highest degree of confidentiality. You are welcome to take notes if they help you, but I must advise that you will not be able to take any of those notes away with you. At the risk of causing insult, I believe it prudent to state the obvious and tell you that your own loyalty and candour is beyond reproach. You are the select of the select and I shall pull no punches in the information that I give you. However, a betrayal of that trust would be a fatal mistake. The door is there should any of you wish to leave now."

There was silence in the room and a few brief glances were exchanged between participants. Nobody took up his offer though.

"Good.", he smiled as he resumed his address to us, "Now, I know that you are a group not used to being talked at in what may seem to be a patriarchal way. However, and unfortunately, I must ask that you bear with me as I will need to have a fair amount of your time before we can move onto more open discussions. Please, make yourselves comfortable."

There was a shuffling of backsides in seats and the clink of glasses as drinks were poured. Whilst we settled, a large screen descended behind Housman on which were the three letters that had meant so much to me in the past.

"Those of you to whom ORB is a new concept,", Housman resumed his lecture, "have already been briefed about what we do by your respective employers, that much I understand to be true. We are an ancient and secret order with a mission to correct imbalances in justice. A few years ago, we experienced a crisis in our organisation that I am pleased to tell you left us in a position to rebuild for the next generations to come. We remain eternally grateful to the man who set that change in motion."

I tried to avoid his gaze.

"Since our little wobble,", he continued, "we have grown from strength to strength and are now a much more inclusive and democratic movement, no longer hiding away in an underground bunker but instead, here, in the heart of it all, with a team that are free to come and go as they wish. Generally speaking, that is. A few of us remain off the radar, but for the most part, our operations are planned and conducted at night in the control room that you saw appear just now."

The screen turned blank behind him as he talked.

"So, to our current situation. And apologies for the long build-up that has been necessary. You see, we are and have always been a scientific order.

261

We have tapped the best minds and explored the most complex areas of all the scientific disciplines to perform our duties. Some of those innovations have slipped through into making life better for all. Most, remain with us. And as scientists, there are certain Holy Grails of discovery that we have always aspired to find answers to. Time travel eludes us, and I believe that may always be the case. A cure for cancer is close, but still not within our grasp and, despite all our progress in the social sciences, we still fail to understand fully so many challenging traits in humanity. However, I can tell you that we have discovered perhaps the Grail of all Grails. That is, we have perfected nuclear fusion."

He paused to let this sink in.

"Yes," he continued, "after many long and difficult years, ORB has cracked the problem of nuclear fusion and you are currently sitting several thousand feet above the world's first and only fusion reactor. But that is not why we are here today. Your governments are all aware of our progress and there is unanimous agreement around the world that this is a secret that must remain a secret. You see, the world is not yet ready for nuclear fusion and until it is a free gift to all and a safe gift, we must keep the wraps on. Any nation having a head start in this would become a truly dominant nation and would control the world's power supplies. On top of that, when I mention safety, I do not allude to the reactor. It is safer than anything, I can assure you. However, until we are certain that this process cannot be used for harmful purposes, we must keep the technology to ourselves. I need not explain that a power source akin to a miniature sun could be the most destructive weapon known to mankind."

The atmosphere grew tenser with every sentence that Housman dropped into our laps. I looked around the table and could see the great minds before me trying to comprehend where this was leading to.

"We did, however," the speakers voice snapped me out of my daydreaming, "agree to share this technology with certain global powers. As some of you may be aware, ORB is a British operation that works solely within its national confines. It is not alone though. There are, and have always been, several other similar bodies, scattered across the globe, each one anonymous and autonomous within its national boundaries. With us today we have my opposite numbers from the American, the Japanese and the Australian versions of ORB. They were to be the first to receive this technology. The Japanese and the American groups for research purposes, the Australians as a solution to the drought that has ravaged their country for the last decade. With unlimited power, fusion can both desalinise the oceans and simultaneously seed clouds to break the cycle. But I digress. You need first to know a little about how the system works. Please may I introduce our Chief Scientist, William."

We turned to watch as one of our colleagues rose to take Housman's place. He reminded me of James. A little older perhaps, but he had that distracted look of the savant and was clearly not too comfortable in being asked to make a presentation.

"Thank you.", he laid out papers before him and tweaked the monitors until they displayed his first slide, "I will try and keep this as simple as possible. I hope that I don't offend anyone by doing that, but it really is a most complex technology that could keep us here for days."

The image on the monitors changed to show two spheres. One dominating the centre whilst another much smaller one was attached to its outer edge.

"The fusion process that we have developed," he explained, "is a two-stage process. The first process is to generate the fusion reaction, and the second, by far the hardest, is to find a way to contain and control that reaction. This image represents the fusion reactor as the larger sphere. Needless to say, it doesn't look anything like this but please allow the image to represent the containment and control unit that is, even as I speak, generating billions of watts of power right below our feet. The second, smaller sphere is what we call the Seed Sphere. It is within this sphere that the initial fusion reaction is generated. Once the smaller sphere is active, it can be used to seed the reaction in a larger unit. Hence the name."

He paused to see if we were with him and seemed happy so far.

"Good," he continued, "now, let me show you what a Seed Sphere looks like."

He reached under the desk and withdrew a grey metal ball, roughly the size of a grapefruit, perfectly round but with two small protrusions extending from it.

"This," he told us, "is one of only six active fusion spheres. This one alone has enough power to generate electricity for the whole of the UK. It's a powerful beast but…"

We looked on in horror as he dropped the ball onto the floor, none of us quick enough to duck for cover but all of us believing that this was the end.

"I'm sorry;", he laughed as he picked up the sphere, "I needed to demonstrate that this is a powerful beast but perfectly safe. Apologies for the dramatic illustration."

We watched as he dusted the ball off and polished it in his hands.

"So then;", he continued, "in order to get working fusion, you need this sphere and a safe fusion reactor. Once the reactor is ready, the sphere is activated and the process begins. Now, let me show you how that activation occurs."

We watched as he lifted the ball and signalled for the lights to be dimmed. He switched on an ultraviolet tube that lit everything up with a sharp blue tinge. As he did this, we saw four small dots appear on the surface of the sphere, then another single one underneath.

"Under UV light;", he explained, "these small marks appear and indicate where the sphere is to be held. If you observe, as I place my fingers and thumb onto the dots, a control panel will illuminate."

We watched as he did this and saw a small panel revealed on the surface of the sphere.

"To activate the sphere;", he informed us, "you need two things. Firstly, a living human hand to hold the unit and secondly, a six-digit code which is entered on this pad here. The code is there for obvious reasons but the need for a living human to be present is a second line of defence since we know that self-preservation will ensure that all safety measures are adhered to. And that, is pretty much fusion 101 as we have developed it."

"But let me show you a little more;", he continued, "in order that you might understand the sheer power that one of these spheres contains. The following is a recording of a test that we conducted using our previous underground headquarters as a testing ground. Please note that the sphere being used then was approximately one hundred thousand times less potent than this one here."

He moved to one side and we watched as the screen displayed a video of a much smaller sphere being mounted into a vice on a workbench that I recognised as being Adam's old laboratory in ORB's underground city. The camera panned back and a countdown marker dropped from ten to zero. At zero, there was a blinding flash, the sound of a tremendous explosion and then silence as the film showed the dust settling. When the image cleared we gasped as one to see that not only had the laboratory been destroyed, but the whole surrounding area had been reduced to the original rock and dust that the complex had been carved from.

"What you see here", William explained, "is an unexpected by-product of the fusion process. We conducted this experiment purely as a matter of routine, expecting only to see the fusion energy dispersed and a nominal amount of damage to the surrounding area. We were, as you can imagine, shocked at what happened."

"After much research into this experiment", he told us after taking a quick drink, "we discovered something unexpected and incredible. Remember, there was no explosive charge attached to that device. No, what we concluded to have happened is that the fusion sphere, on releasing what we must assume to be the primal energy of creation, converts whatever it is in contact with into its sub-atomic particles and then utilises those particles to continue its destructive reaction. In short, it converts anything and everything into explosive material."

He left the sphere on the table and returned to his seat.

"I feel I must add one rider to William's otherwise excellent presentation", Housman resumed, "and explain that thankfully, the fusion sphere's reaction is not a perpetual process. although highly destructive and parasitic to the utmost, it eventually loses energy when not contained. Mind you, I do not underestimate the damage that was done by that one small device."

"So, I trust that that gives you all an overview", he continued, "but now we must move on to the purpose of our meeting today. I have already advised you that we are ready to share this technology with some of our compatriots. That's why there are six spheres in existence. The one that is seeding the fusion below us, the one that you see here, two for our US colleagues and one each for Japan and Australia. Remember, these are a larger version of the sphere that you just saw on that film. They each possess the capacity to both power the world's great cities, or destroy the same."

He struggled for words and looked around as he prepared to continue.

"It is with great regret", he said, his voice sombre and humbled, "that I have to inform you that the four Seed Spheres being shipped to our compatriots have been stolen."

Chapter Thirty-Nine

"Please.", Housman tried to hush the angry voices that were demanding answers from him, "Please can we save the retribution for later. If it is any consolation to you, I can tell you all that I have tendered my resignation and that I take full responsibility for what has happened. I will see this crisis through and then step down. Meanwhile, I understand your anger and frustration but we must address this situation head-on and with total focus on damage limitation. Our time is short and I acknowledge that you will not want to hear from me again, so I will now hand you over to the Commander-in-Chief of NATO, General Isaac Gordon, to continue this briefing."

We watched Housman take his seat, angry at him to varying degrees, but strangely sympathetic to him in his unenviable position. I was seething. ORB had failed again. This was AMY and the virus all over. This was mopping up incompetence and putting our lives at risk to clean things up. But then again, this was bigger. Our lives were already in the balance. Not only ours but those of thousands, no, millions of innocent people. I'd done it before for different reasons, now I had to switch off my emotions in order to stay objective. The damage was done and all we could hope for was to work together to find a solution.

"Before I begin,", Gordon's voice was deep and resonant, "I feel that I need to explain a little about how this situation has occurred. Mr Housman has, graciously, accepted responsibility, however, I believe that every precaution possible was taken to protect these units. Let me explain that first, before we move on to our plan of action."

He detailed the complicated security measures that had surrounded the spheres since their shipment from the ORB Headquarters in London. Everything possible had been done to ensure that they were tracked at all times and in such a discrete way that no chancer might think they were worth a second-glance. Their transit was faultless and managed with military precision. At every hour of every day, ORB knew where they were and that they were under the highest degree of scrutiny. We listened with some confusion until Gordon explained:

"The problem that we have identified.", he told us, "And the root-cause of the theft of these spheres is, sadly, very simple. They were never shipped in the first place. They were substituted by an individual at this centre, replaced by perfect replicas and somehow removed from here at a later date. In Mr Housman's defence, the shipment process was perfect, however, these spheres were swapped on his watch and that is, as he agrees, indefensible."

"So, how and when was the swap identified?", King's voice echoed loudly through the room.

"Thank-you.", Gordon replied, keen to move on, "and a good question. You are all aware, I'm sure, of the National Defence Network. Developed by our own incarnation of ORB in the States, this was installed in the UK in 2022. In case you have not been briefed, it is a covert electronic shield that surrounds the nation and which is used for a variety of purposes, not least of which is the tracking of suspicious persons and packages. Mr Housman wisely installed NDN chips in all of these spheres. In order to facilitate their smooth transition out of the country, he advised the NDN control centre to look out for these chips and allow the carriers safe passage. By chance, the day after their anticipated transfer date, an NDN controller contacted Housman to double-check the reference numbers. Since they should already have departed, Housman confirmed both their movement out of the country and their not having been identified by the defence shield. The upshot is that the parcels were opened, the spheres checked and the exchange identified. The only positive note on this is that, since their movements have not registered with the NDN, we at least know that the real spheres are still in the UK."

"And the person who exchanged the spheres?", I asked.

"Currently being sought.", Gordon advised, "and I assure you that there will be no trial by jury for him when he is detained. We have CCTV image of the swap taking place. The individual has not been seen for a couple of days but we are very close to finding him. Again, thanks to Housman's additional security processes, all ORB staff are covertly fitted with National Defence Network chips and in places that they cannot be easily removed. We hope that the individual's ignorance of this will lead us to him, in the same way that it led us to identify the exchange a lot earlier than he would have expected."

He looked around to see if there were any more questions. We remained silent.

"I want to try and keep this brief and straightforward.", he said, "So let me tell you our standard approach to this sort of issue. We need to look at the usual set of questions. Who? What? Why? How? When? And where? But before we look at these, I think we have to make some assumptions. First off, we can safely assume that these spheres were stolen for nefarious reasons. At best, for a ransom, at worst, to use them as bombs. They are useless for anything else as the technology is in the reactor much more than the sphere. Whoever has them can't simply build a fusion reactor around them. Secondly, I believe that we have some time. I may be wrong on this but, for one thing, the six-digit code will be a challenge to crack. Also, since we have let the dummies continue in transit, the thieves will not know that we know that they have the true spheres. Of course, there is also the element of planning any attacks and that will take time as well. Finally, I am fairly certain that the culprit within ORB did so for financial reasons. On this assumption, we should be able to track money flows and that might lead us closer to their current location. Aside from that, all bets are off and we need to address this with an open mind."

He let this sink in and waited in anticipation of our challenging his assumptions. None of us were quite ready to. Not yet.

"In our standard analysis.", he continued, "we can pair up the questions. The who and the why are one and the same. If it's for a ransom, they will contact us, if for terrorism, we can start to search for known activists. The what and the how are also linked. If it's not ransom, then it will be bombs and that video we saw showed how that works. We should note though that as a bomb these spheres need be held by a living person therefore the bomber will be a suicide attacker. The when and where can go together. In short, we don't know where specifically, but the only threat is to the UK as they cannot leave without us knowing. The likelihood then, is one of the UK's major cities. As to the time, we simply do not know."

"And do we have any answers to any of these questions?", a laconic Australian voice cut the silence.

"No.", the General was frank in his reply, "But we have a number of suspects that we can rule out. Initial speculation would ordinarily be around the usual suspects. I can tell you, our intelligence shows no activity in these areas. North Korea is out and I can tell you all why in confidence. Their illustrious leader has a soft spot for miniature dogs and we have been supplying these to him for years. They are not dogs. They are in fact animatronic creations that give us a deep insight into the thinking of that man. He is no threat. The Saudis or any of the other ex-oil producers might be potential suspects, now that their economies are crumbling since we all moved to electric vehicles. But, they have major investments in the UK and we can't see them destroying the assets that they have. Then we have the religious activists. They're a real possibility, as too are the African nations who still seem unable to exploit their natural resources and who still seem to bear a grudge against colonialism."

"You could have stuck with the no.", the questioner replied before turning to the rest of us, "Any of you guys got any thoughts?"

The General was about to resume speaking when I spoke up for the first time.

"It's a conglomerate.", I said, unsure as to where that had come from, "It stands to reason. This is too big for any one organisation to pull off and if it's terror, we're talking about the death of millions of people. There isn't an ideology out there that would support that. This has to be a new grouping with a wider agenda."

"Thank you, Sir.", Gordon looked at me, "and you are?"

"Steve Barratt.", I replied, "Ex-ORB, currently freelance."

Heads turned to me. Heads that carried eyes that looked at me with a new respect. I heard a whispered comment pass from one delegate to another. Something about Kingfisher.

"Okay, Mr Barratt.", Gordon said, "you may have something there. At least, we've looked at all the usual suspects and not seen anything, therefore there seems to be some logic in looking out for something that we have never seen before."

He paused and I could see him trying desperately to dig out a nugget of information that lay deep in his mind.

"The Alliance.", he said, staring at us, "You guys heard of that one?"

"Only rumours.", King answered, "and never anything positive to go on."

"We have some data.", a tall Asian lady who had remained silent so far spoke up, "Again, most of it based on rumour and speculation, but we will share what we have with you. Mr Barratt may be right in this. It is their sort of thing I would suggest."

"So, can you enlighten us a little please, General.", Housman asked, "Or maybe yourself, Lucy?"

Gordon asked Lucy up to the front.

"From what we know," she began, "The Alliance is an organisation somewhat like ORB and its counterparts, but with directly opposite intentions. Whereas our Orders seek to work for the cause of justice, they seek to work for the cause of self. They are the rich and the powerful and influential people who unite under a banner of self-promotion and what they call Neo-Darwinism. In their view, if we are all just animals and our purpose in life is to survive as the fittest, then we have a moral duty to eradicate weakness and so advance the human race. It is, I hope, a corruption of the values we share around this table, however, it is in many ways a logical corruption. Because their values absolve them of any moral responsibility, the ends will always justify the means."

"And why does the current situation point to them?", I asked.

"For two reasons.", she replied, "One is that your suggestion of a conglomerate fits into their profile. They will use multiple means to achieve their aims. They will play on radicalisation, patriotism, political aims, academic theories and even the promise of a place in history to recruit the people they need to carry out the attacks. They will have no problem finding people willing to die for their cause. And secondly, they are passionately anti-UK. Even though many are UK citizens, their vision of a world without morals and where individual utility is the only measure of worth, flies in the face of the parliamentary democracy that the United Kingdom has spawned, the Christian movements that have spread out across the globe from here, and the general values of Great Britain that colonialism passed on. On top of that, they despise English becoming the new lingua-franca. No, they hate this little island nation."

She finished speaking and retook her seat. Housman addressed us again.

"We have multi-agency operatives in every town and city in this country," he said, "but we believe that one of the major cities, Birmingham, Glasgow, Leeds, Manchester or London will be the target. Every possible resource that this nation and its allies have to spare is out there now seeking more information. When you leave this meeting, we leave your response with you. Whatever your organisation and whatever your capabilities, please throw all you have at this. Believe me, this is a situation that none of us wanted, but now that it has come about, I believe that we can turn it to our favour and defeat this unknown enemy. We must work together this one time, and if we fail, then millions will die."

He wiped a tear away from his eyes, not at all ashamed at the emotion in his response.

270

"And finally," he looked us in the eye one by one, "I need to share one last aspect of our work on fusion with you. That work has turned an awful lot of the conventional wisdom of science on its head. It has discounted the accuracy of carbon dating and other assumptions based on how we thought that atoms behaved. In fact, it has pointed us more to the concept of intelligent design than to the notion of accidental evolution. Therefore, I ask you, whoever you are and whoever and whatever you perceive your God to be, you may be advised to pray to them in this hour of darkness."

As he headed to the exit door, we rose to follow him, taking his departure as a sign that the meeting was over. I couldn't help myself smiling as I rose to follow, thinking how its only when he's in trouble that man wants to find God to turn to. For how long had man been trying to disprove the existence of a Deity? But everything was different now that the chips were down.

I paired up with Jason King and we left the room together. From there, we were escorted to an alternative exit and found ourselves on a London underground station platform. The others were nowhere to be seen.

Chapter Forty

"Well?", King asked me as we slipped into the stream of travellers leaving the station.

"Well, indeed.", I replied, struggling to think of anything to say, "I'd like to say that it's good to be back, but you'll not mind if I don't lie to you?"

He laughed and led me onto the street, then towards a little used alleyway that took us away from the crowds.

"We'll go to my club.", he said, "It's just around the corner. A little refreshment seems in order."

As we navigated the streets, we watched the multitudes of people as they scurried past us on a typical London Friday night. There were the massed ranks of office workers, suited and booted and getting ready to wash away the city before heading to their distant homes. There were the theatre-goers and the party people, dressed to kill and bright with the thrill of the pleasures to come. And then, there were the hordes of tourists who represented every nation under the sun. We said nothing but I knew that we were both thinking the same thing. London couldn't stop growing. The rest of the nation endured the mad obsession with which this city was feted and glorified, watching as new buildings rose and new grants were cashed in to fatten up this leviathan. In the past five years, its population had passed the ten million mark. And that didn't include the visitors. A small bomb would cause devastation and massive loss of life. The effect of a fusion bomb was beyond imagining.

Once at our destination and past the bowing and scraping porter who welcomed us as long-lost friends, we found a table in one of the lounges and ordered large whiskies. They arrived within minutes and we sat in silence as we let the liquor caress our throats. It had been a few days since my last drink. I never kidded myself that I was on the wagon and, tasting that Scottish delight again, I knew that I would always be partial to a drop. Perhaps in more moderation in future though.

"So, what are your thoughts?", King asked me.

I took my time to compose my answer, conscious that a way was opening up in my mind but one that needed careful coaxing.

"You remember," I answered cryptically, "the old country and western song with the line in it, 'freedom's just another word for nothing left to lose', at least, that's what I think it was?"

He nodded.

"That's my initial feeling on this.", I said, "I've got nothing left to lose now. This is the make or break one. I'm up for it. What other choice do I have? If we come out victorious, then I'll consider it my swan-song. I'm too old and too weary to carry on with this. And if it goes the other way, then that's fine. I've lived enough."

"And any practical thoughts on where we go?", he asked.

"Only instinct.", I replied, "Only instinct. And you?"

"There's a part of me", he sat back and made a temple of his hands, "that wants to believe that this is a money thing. We'll get a ransom demand, pay up if we have to, and that will be that."

I waited.

"But,", he continued, "there's a greater part of me that says this is about the power that those spheres give to the holder. The truth is, I think we're on the countdown to a major attack. What's more, we've got so little to go on and, despite what Gordon might say, I don't think we have much time either."

"I agree,", I said, "on both counts. I don't think we have the luxury of time to sit on the fence speculating, nor do we have the right to dreamily hope that this is a threat we can buy off. I've made my decision about where I want to go with it. You see, what was said about this 'Alliance'. Something in me says that that is where the answer is. And because of that, I also believe that we are not talking about ransoms, but about bombings. I could spend my time hedging all bets, but my heart tells me not to. There are huge resources tackling this and we know that beyond the conventional forces of law and order, the likes of ORB are putting resources in that your average man would consider to be the stuff of sci-fi. If we all try and reach a conclusion and act in one direction, then I think we'll run out of time. I think the way ahead is for us all to follow different lines, co-ordinate as necessary, but use the depth of resource we have to pursue every angle."

He sat passively as I explained, giving nothing away in his facial expression.

"Keep going.", he urged me on.

"I'm saying that I think I should go it alone on this.", I told him, "Not as some renegade loner, but as a free agent following my heart. Of course, if you get leads then you can call on me and I'll drop everything to help. It's just that, I don't know, I just feel that with so much resource we may miss things. Teamwork's great but it requires a consensus, and that consensus necessarily narrows the options being considered. It's counter-intuitive, sure, but does it make sense to you?"

"Steve.", he leaned closer to me, "I have never had a problem with your instinct. You're right, we need to cover as many angles on this as we can and if it works for you, then fine, go it alone. I presume you are convinced of The Alliance's involvement in this?"

"If not them, then another conglomerate.", I answered, "It's the only thing that makes sense. Who else would threaten this sort of death toll if not a group who thought nothing of human life. Any other organisation would protect its own and its own interests. You take out a UK city and the collateral damage is huge. Our cities are not, and have never been the preserve of the white, Anglo-Saxon. They are hubs of diversity and integration and they don't stand isolated in the world. Take London, how much of this city is in the hands of foreign nationals? No, it has to be something new and something bigger. I'll go after The Alliance or whoever it turns out to be."

"And the location?", King asked.

"We need to cover all bases.", I told him, "But I want to be where the greatest risk and the highest casualty rate will be. I'm staying in London. I'm sure that I won't be alone, but you need to make sure that the other cities are covered as well. ORB has the manpower. If we miss it and it's not a city, then so be it. We can't cover everywhere and we may have to accept the decimation of smaller towns and villages. I just don't see it though."

"I'll make sure that you have all the resources you need.", he finished his drink and we rose together, "And I can't object to anything you've said. I've heard rumours of The Alliance but never more than that. I move in circles where there are always whispers of plots and plans against the existing order, but nobody thinks it will happen. With The Alliance though, there's a real feeling that they are more than just talk. Now, where are you planning on staying?"

I hadn't thought about such practicalities and realised as I stood there that I was ill-prepared for a long stay. Then I looked at King and saw the gleam in his eye.

"Paddington Basin.", he said as he passed me the key to my boat, "I think you'll find it all in order."

I took the key and saw the familiar logo hanging from the ring.

"And Steve,", King drew me close to him and put his arm around me, "you be careful. I know you think you've got nothing to lose, but we'd rather have you in one piece."

"I'll try.", I answered, "But if it doesn't end well, then no regrets, eh? We've played our part and there will always be others to take over."

I left before he had a chance to say any more. As I walked the streets of the capital, I was at peace. I could only do my best and if we weren't successful then the world would carry on regardless. This was a time of potential death and devastation, but we weren't ready for Armageddon yet. At least, I didn't think we were.

Back on the boat, I took myself straight off to bed, giving my mind time to assimilate the jumble of complex facts that it had been bombarded with and also a little time to shake off the fatigue of the last few days. If it happened tonight, then so be it. There was only so much one man could do.

******

After a few dead-ends, I decided to try the lock-up in the hope that I could at least start making some progress. It was one of only a handful left in use after the whole London Bridge area had become gentrified, staying open only because it held a long lease that the owners refused to surrender. I walked in as a regular customer. This wasn't one of those occasions where a disguise was necessary, nor did I feel particularly concerned that my face would be registered. I no longer wanted to hide behind a mask. Not when it wasn't called for.

"I need a filter for a DT-306 diesel engine,", I told the man behind what passed for a customer counter, "but with a left-hand screw. Somebody told me that you were the place to come to."

The man looked me over. I probably didn't look like an enthusiast but then, nor did he look like a shop-keeper. A stub of hand-rolled cigarette drooped from his mouth and his work uniform was a greasy, stained vest, complimenting a pair of shorts that were once beige but now told tales that you didn't want to think about.

"Not much call for them these days," he muttered, opening a worn ledger and running a greasy finger down the pages, "but yeah, we should have one. Let me go and check."

As he disappeared into the darkened area at the rear of the unit, I looked around. Nothing unusual. Not at first glance anyway. The few shelving units that stood on my side of the counter were piled high with stock that clearly didn't move very quickly, and the dust on the vinyl bench-seat where I assumed customers were invited to wait, told me that I was one of only a few people to visit this shop.

"There you go, mate.", a grubby hand dropped the worn and tattered box containing my filter onto the counter, "Thirty-five quid. Bit steep I know, but rare as hen's teeth these now. Cash is it?"

Guessing that they would decline my offer to pay by other means, I opened my wallet and took out some notes. I left the wallet open on the counter, making sure it was in the line of sight of the owner. He didn't disappoint me.

"Sorry boss.", he said, "I didn't realise. Just a tenner to you."

As he said this he nodded towards the plastic screen in my wallet that displayed a single letter A, elaborately scrolled and illuminated with multiple colours.

"Oh.", I smiled as I passed the money over, "that was careless of me. I'm guessing you are with us?"

"Too right.", he leaned closer to me, "We can't carry on like this can we? Only so much space in the country and our blood's getting thinner every day."

I made the right noises and was just about to leave when he looked about him and beckoned me closer.

"Listen.", he said, "things are starting to move. I'm about to close up here, you want a quick snifter?"

"That sounds good.", I replied, letting him lock the door and lead me through the warehouse and into his office. It was as grim and dirty as I expected. As was the glass that he passed me before cracking open a bottle of rum and pouring me a hefty shot.

"Cheers!", he said, tapping my glass and downing the drink.

Three rums later I was beginning to feel a little queasy. Not because of the drink. No, I could handle all that he sent my way. It was his conversation that made me sick. He started with the tamer comments that were a part of

276

free speech and which you heard many times in the pubs and factories that sported the Union Jack. But once he started, he couldn't seem to stop himself and all I heard was vile and venomous hatred towards every nationality that he could think of and the simplistic and misguided anger of the died-in-the-wool bigot. I tried to block him out as much as possible by concentrating on what little there was in that office. The walls were adorned with hard-core images of women which did little to improve my opinion of Rob, as he wanted me to call him. The floor had once been carpeted but was now a sticky mess of cigarette burns and spilt liquids. Behind his desk there was a bookcase, full to overflowing with old western novels. The desk itself offered no relief either. Not unless I felt that seeing statuettes of slaves being beaten was more pleasant than hearing his ranting.

"You're a bit quiet, mate.", he said, eyeing me suspiciously, "You are one of us, aren't you?"

"Rob, mate,", I hated myself for what I was about to do, but needs must, "I'm quiet because I've got nothing to add. You've hit the nail on the head and I couldn't have put it better myself."

I let the praise sink in.

"You know,", I told him, "I've studied our cause a great deal. Read the great writers on the subject and been to the lectures. You have said, in just a few words, what writers like Gibbs, Sutton and Watkins have made into whole books."

"Well, I wouldn't know about that,", he seemed almost lost for words, "as I've never read a book in my life and I can't be doing with some of these academic blokes. But, cheers, mate, you've made my day."

"Look,", I said, "I'd better be going now. Things to do."

He escorted me back into the shop and I made my way to the door. I wanted to get out of there as soon as possible and before he called on any of his mates to join us. I'd taken a punt and been lucky, but Rob wasn't somebody I wanted to cross. I was just at the door when I heard him shout.

"Oy!", his voice seemed to echo with menace.

I turned, wondering what I would face.

"You forgot your filter!", he laughed as he threw it across to me, "See you when it happens. I'll look out for you."

I waved goodbye and hurried away, dropping the filter into the nearest waste bin that I could find. I wanted to get back to the boat and wash the stench of that place off me, and I certainly had no intention of taking a memento with me. The worst of it was, it seemed to have been a wasted journey. It only confirmed some of what I already knew, but it didn't take me any further forward. Still, it was a line of investigation that I could tick off my list. A list that seemed impossibly long and which waited for me on my return to the boat.

Chapter Forty-One

'The Aberdeen Star', 26th May, 2027

'Fisherman Arrested After Boat Hits Seawall'

Police in Peterhead have confirmed that the Captain of a local trawler has been arrested and detained in custody following an incident yesterday when his boat struck the seawall as it returned from a night cruise.

It is understood that the vessel refused to respond to calls from the coastguard after being seen by other fishermen to be returning to port in an erratic fashion. As emergency services waited for it to dock, they watched as it slewed to starboard on passing the harbour entrance, then, with a whine of its engines that indicated a last-minute effort to reverse, it failed to stop until it was firmly embedded in the newly completed sea defence.

One witness says that the Captain and crew who were offloaded at the scene appeared to be in a highly drunken state. Today's action by police would seem to indicate that this was the case. Another witness has also described the Captain's garbled shouts to bystanders that there were pirates at large and a man overboard in the North Sea and that rescue ships were needed immediately.

Further investigation by the coastguard has failed to identify any missing persons or any evidence of unregistered ships having been in the area.

++++++

'Manchester Evening Express', 4th June, 2027

'Airport Operator in Massive Recruitment Drive'

The operators of Manchester and Birmingham Airports, UK Aviation PLC., have begun an unprecedented recruitment drive following a massive spike in the number of travellers booked for the coming months. This is excellent news for both regions and should help to revitalise the economies of both the North-West and the Midlands, both of which have suffered recently after central government cutbacks.

A spokesperson for UK Aviation told this paper, "We have never seen such activity before and can only assume that it is the coming of age for our regional airports after many years of preparation. We are fortunate enough to be in a position to charter enough aircraft to meet demand, but we urgently need to recruit cabin-crew, baggage handlers and all manner of additional support staff."

The reason for the increase in bookings remains a little unclear. The major London airlines are not reporting a decline in numbers, which would seem to indicate that UK Aviation's assertions are incorrect. Our own investigations have been unable to pinpoint any particular reason for the additional demand which is to destinations all over the globe.

Anybody interested in applying for positions with UK Aviation is asked to visit their website and follow the links to their standard job application form.

++++++

The news reports were just another line of information to join the thousands that were backing up on my desktop. Along with the reports there were additional notes filed by the various organisations involved in looking to find that elusive breakthrough.

The incident with the trawler was old news to me. I'd been kept up to speed on the situation that was unfolding as it happened and had listened to the crews of the pursuit boats as they targeted the ship. On board, according to the operators at the National Defence Network, was the rogue member of ORB who had swapped the shipment. As they approached the vessel, surrounding it and ordering it to stop, they watched as he appeared on deck, saw what was happening and decided to jump into the icy waters of the North Sea.

It was a blustery night and by the time that the body had been recovered it was blue with the pallor of death. Whilst Rod Ford could bring nothing new to the party in terms of evidence, his possessions yielded one important clue. His wallet had the familiar A symbol of The Alliance boldly fixed inside. That at least gave us the confirmation of who we were up against and what Ford's motivations had been. The crew had heard him talking as they made the crossing towards Scandinavia, where Ford believed he was going to be collected. Interviewed by the boarding party, they were able to give us some idea of why he had done what he had.

"All the time," the captain said, "he kept saying that the existing order was a waste of time and that if you didn't believe in it then you had to be against it. I think he thought that we were a part of his group, but the truth is that we were simply paid a huge amount to transport him. We couldn't really understand a lot of what he said and were looking forward to disembarking him as soon as we could. No, it was just a constant ramble about the order and ORB, whoever they are."

The Captain and crew would be allowed to keep their fare as some form of compensation, if we came through, but for now they would need to work off the drugs that we had given them and endure the sentences that they were given, if any.

The report about the increased traveller numbers intrigued me. It had come out of the system via one of Charlotte's search engines. She figured that if large scale destruction of cities was afoot then it seemed logical to assume that those who knew would seek to leave. The logic was correct. But, in my view, a little too correct. Either the elusive powers we were battling against had underestimated the impact that mass migration would have on the regional airports, or they were directing us away from where the action was.

ORB and the official forces for law and order, increased their activity in these two cities, General Gordon being vociferous in his belief that what we were seeing was to be accepted at face value. They asked King to persuade me to join them in this thinking and in the work they were doing outside London.

"Why not?", he asked on my final refusal.

"Because,", I repeated, "and for the last time, I don't feel that it is the right place to be. If it's all kicking off there, then fine, I missed the action. But you have massive resources in place that I can't really add a lot to. But if, as I suspect, it's a red herring, then I need to be here. It's too obvious. And do we really think that The Alliance cares that much about individuals? You and I know that the leaders of this group don't even use the mainstream travel channels. No, I can't see it, but, I think we can use their subterfuge for our own advantage."

I explained to him how and we finished the conversation with him telling me he'd get James straight on to it.

Whilst all this had been going on, I'd carried on doing my own thing and exploring my own angles for over a week. As snippets of information came my way, I made personal visits to numerous places around the capital and let myself be drawn to the smallest things that might give hints as to the nature of the leviathan we faced. It was the strategy that I had chosen to adopt. It was the only strategy that I could think of. And it fitted in with the information gathering that we were all involved in.

When I was much younger, travelling around as a representative of a vendor of sanitary products, I had been asked to fly to Ireland to meet with a hotel owner there who was interested in installing our latest line of silent-flush lavatories. The flight was brief, less than an hour, but it was a flight that taught me a lesson I never forgot. Whilst we were taxiing, the two guys in the seats in front of me looked out of the window and began a conversation, not about the engines, but about the upper section of the central turbine cowl, which, I understood, their company had designed and manufactured. They were so excited that the conversation continued until we landed again. And I had listened to every word they said.

As we came to a halt at the terminal, I let the experience teach me what it needed to. Now I realised that this complex world that we live in is a product of millions of similar people, passionately designing, making, retailing and developing the minutiae of everything that surrounds us. Each of us has a place in the world because the world has so many places to fill, and so many small pieces to fit together. It was the memory of that revelation that was driving me on in my search for the people behind The Alliance. They would be impossible to find if I looked for them. But if I looked for the lowest common denominator, then that would lead me in a steady upward climb to the higher echelons. At least, that was my thinking. I couldn't offer anything else, but it seemed like the right thing to do.

And I had the skills to do it. I'd met everybody and anybody on the waterways and I could chat with them all. Some of it, like with the owner of the filter shop, was about playing up to a role, but for the most part it was about being open and honest and willing to listen. People liked to talk about themselves. People needed someone to affirm their identity and not create conflict. I could do that. I'd learnt to listen and I'd long ago stopped judging. I knew that if I pointed the finger at anyone, there would be three pointing back at me. No, I had no claim. Not after some of the things I'd done.

So it was that I tramped the streets, visiting mosques, malls and meeting rooms. I used the tube network and must have travelled the length of every line numerous times. But still, I got nothing concrete. The breakthrough I needed just wouldn't come. I left behind a calling card at every location. Adam had re-equipped the boat with all the toys I'd ever need and I was leaving behind robotic beetles at every destination. They were self-directing towards any human activity and could broadcast audio, cleared of background distortion, from a source up to twenty-five feet away. They were also programmed to remain unseen and, if found, to self-destruct. But even they failed to provide the information I needed.

Not only was the boat equipped with a range of the latest gadgets. The engines had also been repaired and the interior communications equipment stripped out and replaced with the newest versions. The biggest change though was the pod. I opened the hatch on my first day back on board and was surprised to see that the pod was no longer there. I called Adam.

"Oh yeah, man," he laughed, "I forgot to tell you. You see, pods are so last year!"

"Meaning?", I asked.

"Meaning man," he replied, "that you don't need the pod anymore. Not now that you've got the new suit."

He talked me through the changes and told me that my personal files and money were in safe storage. When we'd finished, I opened the boat's wardrobe and pressed the button to reveal my replenished store of suits. Sure enough, there was a new one there. It was a little bulkier than the others, but weighed less than any of them. I put it on and slid into the empty space where the pod had been. As the hatch closed above me, the helmet came to life and I saw the familiar electronic display screen in front of my eyes. I waited. Nothing happened and I racked my brain to think of my next step. Then the screen changed before me and faded away into a single, central point of light.

"Welcome, Steve Barratt", a soft, female voice whispered in my ear, "how can I be of service today?"

"I'd like a demonstration please", I replied, "of what you can do. Should we leave?"

"Exit checks completed", the voice said, "please relax and enjoy my short demonstration."

I heard and felt the side of the boat slide away as the suit swelled around me to form into its own version of the pod that I had been so used to. We slipped into the canal and I lay back as the suit sank to the bottom and began to move through the water. It was a strange feeling. Although I was lying on my back, I was watching a screen that showed my forward motion in perfect clarity. We picked up speed and I flinched and cringed every time we seemed to be about to hit an obstacle, only to find that the suit had worked its way around and was continuing on ahead.

"Exit the water now", I told the suit.

"Certainly, Mr Barratt", I heard, "exit will commence once a suitable departure point is identified."

A minute or so later, I was on the towpath underneath a deserted bridge and free from the spying eye of any CCTV cameras.

"What else can you do?", I asked.

"I am a multi-purpose, self-propelling suit designed for the protection and defence of Kingfisher", it told me, "in which capacity I have a range of weapons that can detain or destroy according to your instructions. I have also been designed to allow you access to any location that you desire to reach. Fitted with the latest anti-gravity control systems and the highest capacity ion-drive propulsion system, coupled with a first-generation neural computer, I can do whatever you want me to. Within reason."

I felt certain that I heard the hint of a flirty smile in that last remark, but I let it pass. It was time to test the suit.

"Take me to the top of The Shard", I challenged her.

284

"Computing trajectory.", she whispered, "Prepare for launch."

I held my breath as I let the suit lift me gently off the towpath and put me back into the water. We cruised at a speed I couldn't bear to think about and were soon out into the waters of the Thames, after cresting a series of lock gates. Deep under the Thames for a couple of minutes and then we were travelling up. The water disappeared and I felt myself rise higher and higher until the movement stopped and I was able to lift the visor of the helmet.

"You have arrived at your destination.", the suit told me with more than a hint of mischief in her voice.

She hadn't needed to. I could see where I was. The whole of London was stretched out before me as I stood against the vanity fins that topped this monolith and had made it, briefly, the tallest building in Europe.

"Amazing.", I said to myself, settling down with my feet over the edge and wondering at the possibilities that opened up before me.

It was that sight of London that snatched me back to reality and to the urgency of the current mission. The toys and the tools were great, but seeing the vast expanse of the metropolis laid out in my vision, like an intricate and near-impossible jigsaw puzzle, only reminded me that it might soon be a desolate wasteland. It didn't seem possible that just one of those innocuous spheres could reduce all I now saw to nothing, but I knew that when ORB told you a fact, you took it as a proven fact. I shuddered at the responsibility that was on all of our shoulders. The suit instantly warmed up and pressed closer to me, reading my shudder as a response to the cold.

"I could get to like you.", I told her as I closed the helmet again, "Please take me home."

Chapter Forty-Two

The information just kept coming. James came up trumps on the project that King had given him and the source of the finance for all that train travel was beginning to become clear. The rest of the team saw it and changed tactics.

"Thanks to new information," Gordon was patched into a conference call that reached out all of us, "we are scaling down the Birmingham and Manchester activity. We revert back to an open view on the target city as before, but additional resources will be moved to London."

"From what we can tell," he continued, "the increase in air travel stems from an elaborate system of prize draws, employee discount schemes and loyalty programmes. It is a scheme that cannot be financially viable for any of the interested parties and yet it continues. Flights are booked using pre-paid debit cards, which means that they cannot be flagged up against other legitimate flights. Somewhere, deep behind the scenes, is the source of that finance. I am confident that we will be able to establish it soon."

We watched as he adjusted his webcam and moved a small object from out of view into the centre of the screen.

"I am looking at this project," he resumed speaking, "with a glass half-full approach, rather than a glass half-empty one. We are not making the progress that I feel we need to make, but we are moving forward. This small, seemingly innocuous item here, is a sign of that progress. It is a shield that can contain the power of the fusion sphere for a few hours. Let me demonstrate."

He placed the remaining fusion sphere on his desk and attached the small, disc-like object which clamped onto the surface with a tinny clunk. Once there, it began to glow and a luminous sphere of energy wrapped itself around the object it was attached to.

"If we can get close enough," he explained, "we can fix this to the active sphere and it will hold the fusion reaction. It won't hold it forever, but it should be long enough to get the bomb out to sea. And that's another breakthrough that we have made. It appears that the all-consuming appetite of these spheres ends with water. They don't seem to be able to convert it to useable energy. Any questions?"

"How soon will those attachments be available to us?", a distant voice that I didn't recognise, asked.

"We are manufacturing them now,", the General replied, "and will distribute them to everybody in the field from later on today."

He waited for any more responses.

"Okay,", he continued after a minute of silence, "now to some of the half-empty sides of the project. Firstly, we need to be more careful in our public presence. I am hearing too many rumours of the so-called Flying Ghost of London and similar stories and we need that to stop."

I couldn't believe what I was hearing. Was that really his main concern?

"Secondly,", he continued before I had a chance to react, "there are some of you out there who are concentrating too much on the smaller details. Let me remind you that this is not the sort of attack that will be masterminded by a handful of common labourers. Set your sights higher. We need quality of information, not quantity."

"Hang on a minute,", I couldn't stay silent, "you're getting a little personal here, if you don't mind me saying."

"We don't have time for this,", he replied, "this is not about one person."

"We don't not have time for this.", I answered back, "Setting aside your petty concerns about a mystery figure being seen around London, I think that your dismissal of the little things is a bit premature. Do you really think that the people who are behind all this are going to be the ones who turn themselves into a fusion fireball? No, it's going to be the grassroots workers, the 'common labourers' as you like to call them, who are spurred into giving their lives for the cause. And they are going to be the ones who are less careful in what they say and do. Don't forget, it was the carelessness of a few people low down the food chain that gave us the symbol that The Alliance works under."

"I agree.", another unknown voice spoke up for me, "I'm an ORB field operative and I can't tell you how many times I've been successful because I've let the smallest hints lead me to the biggest catches. By all means, look to the source, but please, do not despise the day of small things, to paraphrase the good book."

The Preacher, I thought to myself. I'd never met him but had heard rumours of his work. Good to have him on my side.

"Let me just say a few more things," I started again, "and then that's it, I'll have said my piece. Regarding my little forays into the world, let me tell you why I do it. It's not because I want people to look up and see me, and I'm sorry that that has happened. No, the reason I need to get out there is because this project is draining me. There are times when I sit with pages and pages of documents in front of me and I just want to walk away from it all. There are times when I give up hope that we'll ever make a breakthrough. At those times, I get out there and I find a place to sit and remind myself of what we are working for. Believe me, you look out over London, see it's streaming lights and the tiny figures scurrying and hurrying about and it gives you a sense of purpose again. I need that. I'm sorry. I'll try to be more discrete. As to the smaller things, all I can say is that I have no intention of changing my approach. If you don't want me to be a part of this anymore, fine, but that doesn't mean I'll give up."

I paused to take a breath.

"And finally," I continued, "and a little more constructively, maybe. I think I can narrow down the target areas for you. What you said about water makes sense. So please, give me a moment to load up a map."

I played with the keyboard on my desk and managed to find the file I needed which I dragged into the conference area.

"If you look at this map," I explained, "and work on the two facts that we know, one, that there are four bombs and two, that they don't like water, then I believe you can draw a cross centred on Hyde Park. From that centre, you then have four quarters to London, each the size of the anticipated explosion. This is London remember, it's a river city so you'll never avoid water, but if you use this map as a guide, the centres of each quadrant are Wembley, Stoke Newington, Bow and Richmond. There's water there, yes, but whoever's behind this will be factoring in that they must accept that weakness in the spheres. They will want maximum impact within the unchangeable constraint of existing waterways, therefore, I suggest that we work on these being the detonation points."

There was a contracted pause and I wondered if they'd cut me off. Then the General's voice came across the speakers.

"Regarding your other comments," he said, "I remain unchanged. However, I think you may have something with this map. Can everybody else please note this and integrate it into their work. Now, if that is all, we need to get to work and start making inroads."

288

"Wait a minute", I recognised Jason King's voice immediately, "can I ask if we have any plans for evacuation?"

"No.", the General answered straightaway, "We are not going to evacuate. That is an order that is being passed to me from the highest authorities."

"But that's obscene", King replied, "and, if I may say, a tad arrogant. We know the threat and we are fairly certain of the locations. Are you saying that we make no move at all to alert people?"

"I repeat what I said", Gordon's voice was harder than ever, "we have no plans to evacuate nor will we make any public safety announcements. The decision has been made on the grounds that the panic would be uncontrollable."

"In that case", King said softly, "you can count my team out. I can't stand by and see millions die when we could at least give them a fighting chance to get away. I'm sorry, we will continue to work on what we are working on, but I have a duty. Do with me as you will."

We all heard the click as his line was terminated. It was followed by another series of clicks which I knew signified the departure of James, Adam and Charlotte, but there were several more as well. I remained on the line.

"We are not the masters here.", Gordon moderated his voice, "We must keep discipline or we will not survive this challenge to the country. Now, back to work and let's keep the flow of information going."

We all disconnected and I sat staring at the blank screen. This wasn't the time for disharmony but I couldn't disagree with King's approach. I knew I could trust him and that I would still have the full support of his team. But for all the talk and for all the planning, we still didn't seem to be getting anywhere.

I sorted the hundreds of scraps of paper that were scattered on my desk, poured a cup of coffee and started to work my way through them again.

After several hours, the pile was halved. After another hour it was halved again. I scrapped any notes that referred to a location that did not specifically have a tie to The Alliance. They were still being monitored remotely and the information that the beetles sent back was automatically sorted by the computer to alert to any use of certain key trigger words. Only those locations that I had visited, where there had been some sort of a reaction to the symbol in my wallet, remained on my desk. There were still twenty of them, but that was more manageable than the original two hundred or so.

Frank's Filters still nagged at me, so he took up the first position on the sheet of board I had set up in the boat's saloon. Next to him, after careful filtering, I selected two of the religious groups that I'd encountered to join him. There was 'The Holy Tabernacle of Christ the Victorious' and the 'Hounslow Islamic Centre'. I'd worked my way through too many mosques, churches and temples to remember them all, but only these two gave me cause for concern. The Tabernacle was a mainly black congregation of radical Christians who welcomed me to join them after the service when I'd opened my wallet at the first offering. It wasn't the money I dropped into the plate that gave me access, but the glint of the symbol I displayed.

"Welcome, Brother,", the Pastor greeted me, "and thank you for your generous gift."

"That's nothing,", I replied, "and thank you for a moving service."

He took me to one side and asked me how things were progressing. I had to wing this one.

"All fine,", I said, "you have the date?"

"Oh, praise the Lord!", he could barely contain his excitement, "We have a date? Please, we haven't been supplied with it yet. When is it?"

"I'll see what the delay is.", I told him, "And will make sure that you have it as soon as, if there's no problem. Perhaps there's a reason that the information had been withheld from this group. Is there maybe, some hidden dissent here?"

He assured me that there wasn't and that the day of The Rapture was being anticipated by all.

"The Lord works in mysterious ways,", I told him, "so hold fast. It won't be long."

After these words, I was passed around the crowded room and plied with numerous cups of tea and rich, sugary cakes that explained the size of some of the members of this flock. All the time I was taking in the surroundings and making mental notes of the little comments that were passed.

The notes that I had pinned to the board now read:

Frank Howell – Frank's Filters – Racism/Nationalism
– Office? What's missing?
    Rev. George Smith – Tabernacle – Religious extremism
– List members? (James)

In Hounslow, my reception was less courteous. I was escorted to a small office, high in the mosque's upper floors, and asked to wait for the Iman.

"Can I ask who you represent?", he asked as he entered the room, "I did not recognise the symbol that you carried in your wallet."

That was a great start for me. If he genuinely hadn't recognised it, then I wouldn't be sitting there with him.

"Metropolitan Police", I told him, showing him an up to date warrant card, "we are following up on rumours of radicalisation. Please, they are only rumours and I am only here to ask a few questions."

"We have nothing to hide here.", he assured me, "And we, like all good and right-minded citizens of this country, dislike Islam being used as a form of weapon. Ours is a peaceful religion. We seek to co-exist with all our brothers and sisters of whatever faith or none."

We talked for well over an hour, at the end of which we parted on good terms. My parting plea to him was to ask him to keep an open mind and to contact me if any of his younger members displayed signs of nervousness or pending activity. I had a feeling about this place but not as a driving force. I just felt that other visitors had been there enough times for The Alliance symbol to be recognised. I believed the Iman, but I also believed my gut. Another note was added to the board read:

Ibrahim Ahmed – Hounslow Mosque – Religious extremism – Rebel? Awaiting contact?

And so it went on, late into the night. Everything on that board meant something, but as I looked at it, it seemed like it all meant nothing. The list was whittled down. I dismissed the individuals who, for all their rhetoric and enthusiasm, I just couldn't see making a stand when it came to the final accounting. I also dismissed the most obvious attempts to mislead. There were at least a dozen visits that yielded the date of June 26th to me. I could have worked to that, but it didn't seem right. Would an organisation as elusive and secretive as The Alliance allow such information out? Only if they intended it to be grasped mistakenly. The positive side of this was that it thinned out my targets, as I could exclude the ones that gave the dummy date. The negative was that, knowing the false date, confirmed to me that the actual date would have to be before that for the misdirection to be useful. I looked at my clock and saw that the calendar had flicked over to the 19th June. Hating to admit it, I had to reconcile myself to knowing that we had less than a week.

By the end of the night I had nine locations that I felt could lead me where I needed to be. The objective was simple. I had to know who would detonate the bombs and when. That was the priority. We also needed to know who was behind the planned attacks and the only way to find that out would be to get information from the source before it was eradicated. Bringing them to justice could wait until later. The final priority was minimising casualties. I could do nothing to aid that cause. King was more than capable.

In addition to the filter shop, the mosque and the church, I added the following to the board, which now read:

> *Frank Howell – Frank's Filters – Racism/Nationalism – Office? What was wrong?*
>
> *Rev. George Smith – Tabernacle – Religious extremism – List members? (James)*
>
> *Ibrahim Ahmed – Hounslow Mosque – Religious extremism – Awaiting contact?*
>
> *Dr James Theakston – Harley Street – Fertility clinic/ Cloning? No clients mid-June on.*
>
> *Graham Johnston – Greys Theatre – LGBT Activist – Performance artist? 'See you in Goa?'*
>
> *Sean Burns – Man-Up Gents Club – Male rights activist – Printed leaflet?*
>
> *Carly Wilkinson – 'F Empower' – Female rights activist – 'Strike at football? – Danger?*
>
> *Ruth Goldsmith – Fashion distribution – Zionism – Office clock? Relocation of business.*
>
> *Bill the Fruit – Covent Garden – Homophobia – 'Boasted of shipments' – Courier?*

I typed this all into my computer, sent James some cursory requests and fell asleep with my head on the desk.

Chapter Forty-Three

It was Charlotte who woke me at just after eleven.

"Hey, Steve,", her voice was strained in an effort to sound cheery, "hope you don't mind me calling. James is working on your stuff, but you and I need to talk."

I put her onto speaker and poured out a mug of the last of the coffee that had stewed away gently in my galley.

"You talk,", I said, hoping the caffeine would hit home soon, "I'll listen. Had a long night."

"So we gathered,", she said, "that's why I left it until now. Okay, so here's the deal. Jason wants you to know that we're there for you but that we are pulling out all the stops to work on evacuation. Any thoughts?"

"I'm with you all the way.", I said, "I know where our supposed leaders are coming from but if you guys can minimise casualties, you go for it. If there's a way, you'll make it happen. For me, I'm committed to the end. We all have to do what we feel compelled to do. I can't leave now. If I come through, all well and good. If not, I'll have died trying."

"We don't want to lose you.", she resisted the tears that I could feel were threatening to break out, "But we respect your decision. If you need anything, just ask."

"I could do with some of those disarming things.", I said.

"Already with you.", she told me, "We called out Kirsty last night and she's been fitted with as many as we felt she could safely carry."

"Kirsty?", I asked.

"Sorry, that's how we've come to know your new suit.", she laughed, "Kingfisher Intelligent Response Suit, Trial 1. I know it's a bit laboured, but, be honest, 'pod' wasn't the most inspired name ever. Mind you, I'm surprised she hasn't told you herself. Anyhow, using remote access, we asked her here while you were asleep and fitted her up. She's back with you now."

"Okay,", I replied, "any more surprises?"

"No.", she laughed again, "Mind you, she's full of surprises. Anyway, to business. I'm calling because I think I can help with the list. I've been through all the other data and I agree that the nine targets you have are the best we can hope for. However, I have a reverse search engine working in the background that continues to crunch every bit of data that comes in."

"I know you haven't had time to check the feeds yet.", she continued, "but every one of your proposed targets is ticking the right boxes. The conversations we're recording are peppered with references to The Alliance, the event, India and assorted other leads. We've sent the tidied-up data to you in order for you to have a heads-up. But you need to get cracking. It is all about illusion."

"What do you mean?", I asked.

"Nothing is what it seems.", she answered, "but that's not necessarily a negative. I ran your info through a very simple correlation matrix and it threw up the anticipated data. Every target is identified as extremist in some way, therefore a high risk. They all represent a threat. Some allude to a certain date. Some hint at locations. For example, we have the Tabernacle in Hyde Park and the racists around Neasden way."

"But?", I asked.

"But it's all a smoke-screen.", she said, "I ran my own reverse search, starting with the proposition that The Alliance are the instigators. It all looks very different then. Every group you are looking at is simply being used. They will not lead us to the location. In fact, wherever they are choosing to rally, we can exclude that point. This isn't about the actors in the drama, it's about the script-writers."

"So why the correlation?", I asked.

"Simple.", she replied, "They need groups who will go to the farthest extremes to further a cause they are passionate about. None of them would destroy London. It doesn't make sense. Think how long that city has ticked over smoothly as a multi-cultural, inclusive mix of every personality type under the sun. Yes, there's tension in radical groupings, but not enough to warrant what we're looking at. And the number of participants is too small. They'd never have the resources as small, breakaway factions. No, these groups are being used as a distraction and as a means of putting the whole event together. Each of them can yield the clues that we need to confirm date, time and location. It's up to you to see if you can put it together."

"In just a few days?", I whispered the question to myself.

"But you're not alone," she said, "because you've got us and you've got the ORB team on your side. They have two operatives working in the same way you are. We're exchanging information as necessary, but we're leaving the three of you alone as much as possible."

"They've only got two?"

"No, their others are covering the cities that we've discounted," she explained, "I can't see them getting targeted but we can't be sure. Not until we know where the four devices are. The General seems to be quite set in his ways and I don't think he loves you as much as we do. He's still focused on using volume of resources across a wider geography. Maybe because you are so set on London. Typical of The Alliance. They can even create division amongst their pursuers."

"They've played us all very well, particularly the groups we're chasing," she continued after a pause, "tapping into their bigotry, passion, phobias and self-interest to put up a smokescreen but also to lay the foundations for what they are really doing. If you stay that one step detached from their public face, you should be able to see behind."

"Any evidence of this yet?"

"Only one example I can give you," she seemed pleased to be able to offer even that, "Looking at the leaflet you picked up at the gentleman's club. Seems that they are distributing materials. The mad thing is, they're so wrapped up in their passion for male supremacy that they don't realise they've printed the feminist's literature!"

"I guess that's something," I said, smiling to myself, "and it gives me a starting point."

"One last thing," she continued, "about the Tabernacle. You wanted a list of members?"

"Yes," I replied, "have you got it?"

"It wasn't difficult," she told me, "not when you think of the money these places must bring in. They're not going to throw away the Gift Aid on donations, so we have a full list from HMRC. But it doesn't tell us much."

I thought for a moment, trying hard to remember what exactly it was that I'd wanted from James.

"No, not just a list," I said, "I'm sorry, I was tired when I requested that. Can you send it to me filtered to include regular hospital attendees below retirement age, then, filtered by registration with providers of domiciliary social care? That should thin it out a bit. And while you're at it, look at Bill the Fruit's shipping system. I think that's how the spheres are travelling."

"We're on it.", she told me confidently, "Now, get out there and do your stuff. Look after Kirsty and look after yourself. Oh, and don't be surprised at the next J for Justice stunt."

We finished the conversation and I downloaded the files they'd sent me. I ate whilst I read the information, keying locations and actions into the mini-tablet that I would take with me.

By mid-afternoon, I was airborne again. And I didn't care who saw me.

My first stop was at the 'Man-Up Club'. It didn't open for business until later in the afternoon, staying open until three a.m. to purvey its filth. The same applied to Saturdays. Seemed they had enough business without needing to pander to the weekenders. And from what I saw when I last visited, they were raking the money in. When price is not an issue, you can have what you want. The Man-Up club played to this. Each of its 'theatres' exploited a different expression of sexual dominance. I hadn't seen them all, thankfully. The ones that I had seen had been more than enough. I'd watched a young girl, no more than eighteen, being passed from one person to the other and having to let them do with her what they wanted. I'd had to keep quiet when I saw the fresh tracks of blood that poured down the back of a leather-clad 'slave' doing all she could for her masters. And so it had gone on. The open agenda of the place was that men could come along and use the girls and the women there as they wanted to. The darker side was in the persona of Sean Burns. The club was a means to an end for him. He wanted action against the decades of female liberation that, in his words, had "...cut the manhood off every red-blooded bloke in this country and turned us into passive servants.". I'd nodded in fake agreement.

I'd been invited to a private audience with Burns on the strength of my supposed Alliance connection. What had actually happened is that, on arriving at the club, I'd seen the leaflets that they had scattered about the place and had managed to pocket one before being noticed. When I asked for Burns, the bouncer eyed me up and down and asked what it was about. I'd taken the leaflet out of my pocket, unfolded it and told the guard that we were concerned about the print quality. He knew who 'we' were and I was in with Burns within five minutes.

The upshot of that meeting was that I saw their print room. Burns himself was obnoxious. The club was disgusting. And the whisky they tried to force on me was some sort of imported fake. Still, the sacrifice was worth it. Now that I was back in the club, alone and suited up, I made straight for the print room. Kirsty had sent out an army of spiders to open doors and cover any cameras, alongside which, the beetles kept their ears open for any sound of activity. I hadn't even considered being discrete about my movements. The Oxford Street shoppers could gawp and stare at me all they wanted as I flew past them, high over their heads. Let them have something to excite them. They might set the wittering world of social media gossip alight with their observations but I would be long gone by the time they'd all shared their theories on who and what I was. I couldn't travel incognito anymore. The attacks might start at any second and I needed the support of Kirsty and my electronic friends.

After searching the print room for ten minutes, during which time James was trying to gain access to the club's network through the connection I'd made into the phone line, I was still no further ahead.

"Anything?", I asked James.

"Give me a few more minutes,", he said, "I'm going to try something new."

I left him to it as I searched the room some more. The breakthrough came in the simplest way. I pulled out the huge full-colour printer and rummaged around in the dusty space behind it. It was the same old story. The room itself was immaculate and, no doubt, cleaned meticulously after every print run, but whoever did it chose not to get into the unseen areas. Their weakness was my gain. I found a handful of discarded scraps of paper. They were the sort of bits that got chewed up in an overheated feed-roller. I opened them one by one and let the helmet of my suit scan them in and tidy up the image.

The first couple of pieces of paper were fragments of the leaflet that I already had a copy of. It was a call to arms to all right-thinking men across the nation to take back the control of their lives and be the head of the household again. I smiled at the memory of reading this full leaflet. Who honestly believed that men had ever been the masters of the universe at any time in history? All that had changed now was that women were able to express their independence openly. They'd always been at least equal in their relations with men. They'd never been the submissive doormats that they were prone to be portrayed as. Check out the history. Even in ancient times you might read the rules that demand female subjugation, but the reality was that they gave as good as they got. Why had the rules had to be written? Then of course, you had the Dickensian world of the Victorian era. A time of female enslavement? I don't think so. Pickwick felt the wrath of the silent sex, and young Nancy fought back when it mattered. In short, Burns was chasing shadows. But that didn't make him harmless. The Alliance was helping him with his cause in return for his printing their other leaflets.

I saw half of a torn flyer that advertised a National Front meeting in Hackney. When did they resurface? I caught the top of a Pride flyer which had been crumpled up with a page of a booklet that described some of the evils of homosexuality. And I saw an almost intact A6 handout that detailed the contact number for the 'F Empower' movement. The irony was sweet. The documents confirmed that Burns was ignorant of what the machine was spewing out and they confirmed a link between opposing groups. I felt vindicated.

"Okay, Steve.", I heard James in my headset, "I've got access and I think we're getting somewhere. Nothing to help you I'm afraid but I've managed to get a robot into the line and it's working its way to the source. I'll monitor it. You get onto the next location. Did you find anything?"

I told him the little I'd discovered.

"It all helps.", he said, "You got anything there about 'Students Against Capitalism'?"

"No.", I answered, a little confused.

"I'm picking it up from residual memory in the printer.", he explained.

"Thanks a million!", I couldn't help laughing as I replied, "That's all we need, more leads when we aren't even making progress on the ones we've got."

"But isn't that the point?", he reassured me, "The Alliance know that we'll be sniffing out data, they can't stop that. Their only hope is to bombard us with so much data that we can't see the wood for the trees."

"You're right.", I replied, "Of course. Just make sure that the other ORB guys are being fed all of the info as well. I know we can trust them at least. And keep crunching the numbers, I'm lost without you."

"No problem.", he said, "And don't worry. They may want to throw us off the scent, but they're not reckoning with us, are they? We'll beat them Steve, hang in there. And yes, I'll pass it all around and see where it leads. Where next for you?"

I told him as I pocketed the evidence that I had and made my way out of the building.

"When do you want the info on the Tabernacle members?", he asked as I reached the roof of the building.

"How many names have you got?", I asked.

"Just three that tick the boxes you gave me,", he replied, "although we've got the rest if you need them."

"Can you feed me the pastor's voice track?", I asked.

"Sending it now.", he said, and I knew he was, "I'll patch the numbers to Kirsty. See you later."

I heard the connection break with a small click. Ten minutes later, I was back on the line to him to tell him that I'd got the date.

"June 22nd,", I said, "and make sure everyone out there knows it. I'll try to get a time and some locations but it's a start."

"But that's a Tuesday?", James said, "Why choose that over a weekend?"

"Because we wouldn't expect it.", I replied without hesitation, "Think about it. An anonymous day and an anonymous date. More of their diversionary tactics. Believe me though, I know it for a fact. Trust me."

And, to me, it was certainly a concrete fact. I'd heard it from all three of the contacts that I'd made with the less mentally sound members of the Pastor George Smith's flock. They were all so excited to hear from their leader. The first one, an early-onset dementia victim who needed a lot of home support, was a little confused when I got the date wrong twice. At the third attempt she confirmed my proffered suggestion, referring to a note that she had in a pouch tied to her wrist.

"If I didn't know your voice,", she'd said, laughing, "I'd think you were one of Beelzebub's demons trying to test me."

"Oh, Mary,", I reassured her, "how could you say that. The Lord is with us both. You know that don't you? And you'll be ready when we come to pick you up?"

"Yes, Pastor,", she replied, "I don't know what I'm saying sometimes.".

I waited a moment.

"Now Mary,", I said, "can you tell me what we were talking about?"

"Oh, hello Reverend,", she answered, "how are you?"

I didn't feel good about it, but needs must.

At least we had a date now. I would have preferred it to be more than three days away.

Chapter Forty-Four

Bill the Fruit closed his stall early on a Saturday afternoon. He had to drive quite a long way down south to his home and had always considered his Saturday nights with the pub's darts team as his well-earned reward for his weekly labours. I followed him until we were clear of the city and heading towards the Kent coastline. At the first opportunity, I fired a small shot to take out his rear tyre and watched as the van skidded and braked to a halt just after turning off the dual carriageway. There were other people around, but there always would be on a sunny June weekend day like this. I didn't have the luxury of subtlety with Bill.

I watched as he jacked the van up, removed the old wheel and then positioned the spare ready to be fitted. Unseen by anyone on the briefly deserted road, I swooped down, attached a harness to his waist and carried him the short distance to the nearest patch of undergrowth. I dropped him from my grasp a little earlier than I should have and heard his leg crunch as it broke on impact with the earth.

"Oops.", I said as I let myself down gently beside him.

"What the...", he began.

"Now Bill.", I said, "I really don't want to hear your potty-mouth again and I sincerely hope that you will simply shut up and listen. But first, is your leg sore?"

"Course it is.", he hissed back.

"Good.", I sneered back at him, "it's supposed to be. Now, I'm going to give you a painkiller. It's against my better judgement as I really am enjoying seeing you in pain, but it's necessary if we are to move quickly."

I let the dart hit his leg and watched as he settled back in a semi-comatose state. I let him watch me break the other leg.

"Just testing that it's working.", I told him as I withdrew my boot.

"So far.", I continued, "that's two legs. I can carry on and, because I prefer to be honest with people, I probably will. Think yourself lucky if it's just bones though, because if you mess me about I will start to play with your

300

blood. How would you like to be HIV positive? That would be one to explain to your queer-bashing friends wouldn't it?"

I let him stew for a minute before sliding him up against a tree, having to turn my gaze away from the bones that stuck out through his trouser legs. I asked Kirsty to scan the wounds and do what was necessary.

"Left leg, simple fracture," she told me, "right leg, open veins, will cauterise."

The smell of burning flesh stung my nostrils and seemed to bring tears to Bill's eyes. Or was that fear?

"You've been shipping goods for The Alliance.", I told him, "And I need to know where the last consignment went."

"I don't know what you're talking about.", he replied, the drug causing a stream of spittle to drop down his chin.

Having broken his arm cleanly at the elbow and twisted his hand in order for him to see its bizarre positioning, I tried again.

"Four items, possibly in one crate. Each one the size of grapefruit. Tell me when and tell me where."

"I can't tell,", he tried again, "they said they'd kill me. And my family."

"It happens.", I shrugged as I reached out to take hold of his other arm, "You play with fire, you get burnt. Ready?"

I was just about to snap another bone when he started to cry and pleaded with me to stop.

"Alright,", he sniffled, "I'll tell you what you need to know."

It was less than I wanted but more than I had previously. I patched the information to James and asked Bill for more.

"That's all I can tell you.", his eyes told me he was telling the truth, "Honestly."

I told him what would happen next. We couldn't risk him contacting The Alliance so he'd have to stay where he was.

"We'll shoot you up with enough to knock you out for a day or so, after which, if it hasn't been nicked, you can shuffle to the van and try and get help. Meanwhile, your family will be looked after. If your bosses do too much damage, we will be looking for an eye for an eye though. Your daughter's the most likely candidate."

"Wait,", he said, "I can tell you more. But please, spare my family."

"Don't tell me you're having a crisis of conscience,", I said, "not after all you've done. Still, try me. I might be convinced."

301

"The only other thing I can tell you", he said, "is that when they picked them up, I heard them saying something about transplants. I thought that was what they were going to use them for. Illegal organs, you see? I never saw in the boxes. Please, that's all I know and all I can tell you."

This time I knew that we had exhausted the source. I covered him with loose foliage and administered a tranquiliser. We could pick up the garbage later.

Before heading back to the city, I slipped into the van and checked it out. There was nothing in there. So little in fact that I knew it had been cleaned out after the spheres had been shipped. Having got airborne again, I heard James calling me.

"The route he gave checks out", he told me, "I've got tracking numbers and collection points and have passed them all to Gordon. But that's all. Seems that they were carried by hand once Bill had passed them on. We're running through all the CCTV now. Might take a day."

"Okay", I said as I soared past the Dartford Crossing, remembering that I hadn't paid my toll on the way over, "so what do you make of the word 'transplant' in this context?"

"I don't", he replied after a pause, "it doesn't make sense. Maybe just a reference to them moving the spheres. I'll get Charlotte to have a think about it."

I finished the conversation and flew high to minimise the time it would take me to return to Oxford Street. Ten minutes later, I was on the roof of a famous department store and taking some time out to think. We were making progress. Bill's information confirmed the presence of all of the spheres in the capital, but even with that, I doubted Gordon would throw every person he had at the city. True, they might have moved out to the regions again, but there were limits to even The Alliance's subterfuge.

The evening was warm and sunny. I wasn't sure when I'd sleep next. Thankfully, we had longer days to work but there still seemed too much to do. Of the nine leads I was pursuing, six remained. I'd wait until later to visit theatre-land. Always a place that yielded more after a high-spirited and successful performance. Alcohol and vanity opened the darling actors and producers up. Somewhere else first then. I dropped down towards Harley Street.

Theakston's name was all over the internet. Some sites praised him as a revolutionary saviour of mankind, whilst others likened him to a modern-day Frankenstein. In between these extremes, there were numerous citations, references and press releases that filled the middle ground. At thirty-two, he had pioneered a fertility treatment that promised to end the agony endured by childless couples. At thirty-four, he was struck off for allegedly paying volunteers to create what he called 'body shells' and which were rumoured to be the starting point for his work on cloning humans. Now forty, he practiced in Harley Street under the umbrella of a corporate body that bypassed the powers of the GMC. He still called himself Doctor, as did his patients. He was able to do this on the basis of the PhD he'd been awarded from a little-known American university.

The clinic was in a discrete location, sharing space with a dental practice. Those who used the good doctor's services were also those who had diamond-white smiles that they could afford to keep in perfect condition. His patients were carefully selected. Detailed searches through numerous databases weeded out any who might suffer a crisis of conscience as the treatment programme progressed. It was a simple solution to a complex problem. Provided the ethics didn't worry you. From the vast amounts of rumour and speculation that abounded on the web, I was able to get the gist of why this treatment wasn't widely available on the NHS. Those who benefitted would swear that they had simply followed a regime of artificial insemination, followed by daily interventions to prevent the foetus aborting. The reality was that they were allowing Theakston to implant the shell of a human baby, artificially formed in the laboratory. Once in situ, the new parent's genes were fed into the shell and the baby grew in their likeness.

Whatever my own stance on what he did, my interest in Theakston was more immediate. His links with The Alliance had been easy to establish and, on my first visit, I had been given five minutes of his precious time, posing as I had as a representative of one of the major drug companies. That wouldn't have been enough to grant me access. I'd only achieved that by letting his nurse see the emblem in my wallet.

"I was asked to drop by," I'd told him, "to assure you of the company's continued support. And to invite you to a seminar later in the month."

He'd thanked me for the reassurance but declined the invitation.

"I'm sorry," he'd said, "but, for reasons I'm sure you will understand, I'm going to be out of the country for a few months. Off to India to conduct more research and look at a new facility there. You should come and meet me when we're settled."

I'd given him my card, trusting that he wouldn't seek clarification of my identity, and we'd parted with a firm handshake.

Now I was alone in the abandoned clinic. This was more than a simple weekend closedown. Filing cabinets had been emptied, computers removed or wiped clean, and the racks that had once held vial upon vial of samples were now empty. The doctor's diary lay open on his desk. The pages prior to last Friday were full of scribbled notes, appointments and doodles. The pages after were blank. In the small ward that had seen the nurse attending to a lady in the early stages of labour on my previous visit, the bed was stripped clean and the smell of antiseptic was strong. Next door to this room, all that remained of the operating theatre was the huge light that was now suspended over an empty space. As I walked the rest of the clinic, I tipped James off about the doctor's departure. He began the process of searching through travel records to locate him. I'd leave it with them to follow up, meanwhile, I needed to find out what Theakston had left behind. There had to be something.

After an hour in the building and having used all the means that I could think of to search the place, I still hadn't found anything. Maybe all I'd get was the link to India. Useful in the long-term but no real help to me now. I decided to give up the search. Walking back through the abandoned rooms, I looked left to right but all that he had left behind was emptiness.

"Stop.", the voice was firm and clear as it echoed around my helmet.

I looked around and took up a defensive stance.

"It's me, Steve.", the voice sought to calm me, "Kirsty."

"You gave me a fright.", I told her, "what's up?".

"You're missing something.", she said, "I don't like to interfere but I am programmed to help you at all times. Let me show you."

As I looked up, I scanned the room again. I couldn't see it. Then a small dot appeared on the visor of the helmet and moved to centre on an object in the corner of the room. It was barely visible behind the reception desk and I'd not given it a second glance. I walked over to where Kirsty guided me.

"I'm not seeing it.", I told her.

"Let me help.", she replied.

I moved the helmet to face a stack of empty boxes. I'd searched them all. They were a mixed assortment of cardboard, polystyrene and thin plastic, but they shared one characteristic in that they contained no information. Then I felt the helmet nudge my head a little to the left. Dead centre in my vision the spot rested on one of the boxes. The image changed as my visor screen dimmed. Then I saw what Kirsty wanted me to see. The faintest outline of script revealed itself on one of the plastic boxes. I read the words, 'Fragile: Human Transplant Organs'.

"I'm impressed,", I told her.

"Everything leaves residue,", she explained, "it's just a matter of having the ability to see it. I keep records of everything that you hear and see. That box should mean more to you than it does."

I understood straightaway what she was alluding to.

"Charlotte,", I made the connection, "narrow down the CCTV search to identify the image you can see before you."

"The box?", she asked.

Kirsty enhanced the image and filled in lettering. At the other end of the line, Charlotte fed what was being sent into the main computer and soon had a complete picture of the target item.

"We'll get straight onto it, Steve.", she said, "I assume you're thinking that this is how the spheres were transported. Makes sense."

I left her to it, thanked Kirsty and set off for the West End. I was beginning to think we might still be able to pull this one off. We had at least fifty hours in the bank, maybe another twenty or so. There was hope yet.

Chapter Forty-Five

'J for Justice Seaside Extravaganza':

Dance for Dave

Dave Williams died today. He took his own life after being
worked so hard he didn't feel able to carry on.
J for Justice are calling for an end to the culture of work,
work, work that is plaguing this country. Too many people
are being put under too much pressure and we need to tell
all employers out there that a sensible work/life balance is vital.
So, come join the party!
On **Monday 21st June,** J for Justice will be hosting the beach-
party to end all beach-parties. Stretch your weekend out and
show your bosses that none of us are essential and we can all
give up a day for FUN!
FREE Travel by coach or train. Just follow the signs.
FREE MONEY: Yes, as a passionate supporter of our cause,
Jason King has chosen this event to give away his personal
fortune of SIX BILLION POUNDS. How's that for an incentive?

Come to Brighton and let's rock this nation for Dave.

The guys at the marina never ceased to surprise me. The flyer appeared on my
screen just after I'd woken up in the early hours of Sunday morning. By that
time, it was the main headline on the news channels and would be the only
topic of conversation all that day. By the time I was up and about in the city
again, I could already see the logistical operation in full flow. Coaches were
being assembled all over the capital and the roads to Brighton were filling up
with early starters. It was a masterstroke, and the sun shone on the enterprise.

"Why Monday?", I asked Adam, who was the only one I could get through to.

"Man, Tuesday would be too obvious,", he explained, "but don't worry, we're on top of it."

"Do you not think London's making it obvious though?", I'd noted that the other cities weren't included.

"Good point,", he said, "but we talked about it and the logic is that Dave worked in London and it's the whole London work ethic that we're making a play on. We're fully aware of the chance of the other cities being hit, but we can get this one through unnoticed we think."

"Mind you,", he continued, "James is putting out the feelers in the other places. If they decide to make the same stand, man, well, it doesn't come back to us, does it? I know I'd make the journey from Birmingham for a slice of the cash and a day off."

"So, it's true about King's fortune?", I asked.

"That's proving to be the trickiest thing man,", he replied, "but yeah, he's giving it all away. We're all flat out on it now and I tell you, it isn't easy getting hold of cash and gold on a Sunday. Mind you, there are enough dealers out there prepared to give up their rest day. Ironic or what, man?"

I left them to their project. I had places to go.

The previous night, after a painful few hours with Graham Johnston at the after-show party, I'd gained a little more information that might or might not be useful. I spurned his advances, promising that one day we might get together, and I'd been accepted as one of the gang even though the best outfit I could get together was a hideous cream suit that I borrowed from a small boutique.

"You simply must let me introduce you to my tailor,", Johnston had said to me as he led me through the throng, "he could work wonders with your style."

I'd thanked him and downed another large gin and tonic, waving the glass to a passing waiter who replenished its contents. I would drink Johnston into oblivion if I had to. At least I'd appear to. Adam had helped me out with a refinement of my home-made drink diverter and nobody noticed that every mouthful I drank disappeared into the hand that I wiped my mouth with.

"You were telling me about Alfonso?", I probed the theatre owner, "Please, you must tell me more. He sounds so very interesting."

"Oh, darling,", he laughed as he tapped my shoulder, "you will not believe what we have in store for this week. Alfonso is going to stage the most unforgettable piece of performance art on Tuesday."

He explained that the work would begin at ten a.m. and reach a climax at noon, with Alfonso's draping one of the nation's most popular landmarks with the rainbow colours of the LGBT cause.

"I can't thank The Alliance enough,", he whispered in my ear, "you've been so helpful and so affirming."

"And you got the props?", I ventured.

"Oh, yes, of course,", he looked at me questioningly, "but you know that. I personally signed for them."

"What I meant,", I had to draw him closer and let him feel my hand in his, "was that you got them in top condition. We have had problems with transit sometimes."

"Oh, I see.", he replied, "Yes, all in perfect condition. I do know what you mean though, these delivery people can be so careless. They must love you though, what with all that tape. I nearly broke a nail."

He continued rambling on about some of the experiences that he'd had with couriers and lost packages, blaming them for breaking a dozen crystal champagne flutes that he had spent years collecting.

"Mind you,", he chuckled, "they all seem to be coloureds these days don't they? They aren't as careful as we are, I find. Probably something they put in the curry."

He laughed at his own joke and I tried to smile as I weighed his passion for his own cause against his passionate prejudice against others.

"Now I really must be off,", I told him a little later, "as I really do need to get my beauty sleep. Until Tuesday then?"

We embraced and left the party. Kirsty was waiting for me a few streets away, tucked behind an abandoned car. Having changed, I asked her to take me to a new location but she was reticent.

"You need sleep.", she told me, "My scans suggest that you are not working at a satisfactory capacity and I would suggest that we choose to work after you have rested."

She was right. I could have pushed myself harder and stayed physically active, but my mind was wandering. I agreed with her and returned to the boat where Kirsty administered a draught to grant me a couple of hours of sleep and a boost to my energy when I woke. I was soon back in the field.

With the bells of the numerous churches that dotted the city playing a background theme, I went back to Ruth Goldsmith's warehouse in Bethnal Green. The feeds that we'd had from this location had made numerous references to Zionism and the return of the true faith. That had been all though. It was enough to mark her as one of the radicals who The Alliance could use, but I felt there was more to it than that.

There were a lot of shipments waiting to be collected tomorrow. So many in fact, that the racks of clothing were mostly empty. It spoke to me of another departure and this was confirmed by the notes that I found on her desk. She was heading away on Tuesday morning, flying to Israel with her family. The office hadn't been cleared out like the clinic, but then again, its contents were a lot less valuable and were all easily replaceable. That said, she hadn't left much behind that I could go on. In fact, the only thing that seemed out of place was a Bible. I'd searched the place several times before the significance of this struck me. I opened it to where the thin strip of ribbon showed it had last been referred to. The pages opened at Mark's Gospel, Chapter Fifteen. A faint pencil line ran under verse thirty-three, "At the sixth hour darkness came over the whole land until the ninth hour". Had I not spoken to Johnston only a few hours ago and convinced myself that the bombs would be detonated by his performance artist at noon, I would have been happy to find this piece of information. It didn't make sense. If this was the time of the event, then did that mean that they would be staggered? I scanned the image of the page and moved on. Above the desk was a sign in Hebrew. I asked Kirsty to translate it.

"It's a quotation from Joshua," she told me, "which translates to 'at twelve noon, the sun stopped in the middle of the sky."

"Great.", I whispered to myself.

"But the quotation is wrong," Kirsty told me, "I have cross-referenced it to other translations and to the Torah and, in the original, there is no reference to twelve noon."

"Okay," I told her, "keep it all for the record, but let's go. I'm guessing you're not seeing anything else in here?"

"Sorry Steve," she said, "it looks like we've got all we can from here.".

I left the place disappointed. I thought we were on to something with the timing but every step forwards seemed to be hampered by another in the opposite direction. I was running out of leads now and the clock was ticking.

By mid-afternoon, I was still no further ahead. That was when the Iman rang me.

"I apologise that I was a little sceptical and annoyed when we last met," he said, "but now I want to make atonement. I believe that one of our brothers is planning an action that might cause harm."

He gave me all the details. The young man, formerly John Holdcroft, now Ibrahim Islam, had been a model student after converting several years ago.

"Believe me," the Iman continued, "I saw no signs of the changes in Ibrahim. When his family contacted me to raise their concerns, I realised that I had missed things that seem obvious now. But please, if you can do anything to stop him, then do it. This is not the way of our faith."

I assured him that I had no doubts about his good intentions and gave him a brief overview of some of the other extremists I'd encountered.

"I know it's not about Islam," I told him, "in the same way that all those others hide under a banner of a cause. Doesn't matter how they choose to package it, it's all the same. People want to feel that they make a difference. The strong carry on regardless through days of doubt and by doing little things that contribute to the greater good. The weak want it all at once."

"But," I continued, "we can leave the post-mortems and the recriminations for another time. Holdcroft can't have made the transformation alone. Do you have mentors in your mosque? Could one of them have encouraged him?"

"We have a team of five," he explained, "And you may be right. I have so many demands on my time that I defer to those colleagues. I can't believe that it has been going on right under my nose. Let me give you're their details."

He gave me the names and addresses of his group leaders and we ended the call.

At least this was a concrete lead. Here was evidence of somebody who ticked all the right boxes and might be the first that we could target as one of the bombers. Given the right motivation, any of us could be manipulated to die for what we believe is a higher cause. Sadly, the Muslim faith opens the door to those who are tempted by a reward for their self-destruction. Not that Christians and Jews and all other variants of religion haven't found similar motivations. But I had a more pressing challenge. I had five people to visit and there was only one of me. I couldn't do this on my own. Then I realised, I didn't have to.

It was in the early hours of the following morning that the group of us got together to discuss our findings. We were all aware that it was now Monday. Even if we'd missed the transition, the sight below us on the streets of London was a reminder. Convoys of coaches, twenty-four-hour trains and streams of private vehicles crawled slowly out of the capital towards Brighton. King's party looked like it would be a great success. There were even flocks of twinkling lights where bicycles travelled in convoy through the night, weaving through the jams and making good progress.

There were some downsides to what King had chosen to do. For one thing, huge resources had had to be thrown at the exodus. Police and army personnel had been drafted from all forces, but still, the numbers involved in the search for the spheres were diminished. This in turn had upset General Gordon. We'd been present at the teleconference earlier and, despite the poor quality of the feed, we'd seen the anger and vitriol on his face. It wasn't all about King and my independence though. Few of the ORB team had any respect for Gordon's leadership and even his officially assigned team were getting frustrated at the lack of progress they were making. All of which made it more important that we form a new team. That's why I'd made contact with the other operatives who were working this case with me.

It felt odd to be sitting with Charlie Burrows again. He was kitted out as The Indigent and loaded with all the latest tech that ORB could throw at him, but I'd still beaten him to the top of the Shard. It was a petty bit of payback for his having moved faster last time. Neither of us made an issue of it. Alongside The Indigent, The Preacher stood in his cassock. He didn't like to be known by his real name and never revealed it. Next to him were two colleagues from the international orders that were working with us. 'Whisperer' was something of a distraction to us all. She was from the States and her outfit seemed to be made from an impossibly thin material that showed every curve of her body. She described herself as a cypher. Her weapon was invisibility, achieved through silence and stealth. Finally, there was D.

"You can call me danger, disaster, disease or even Dave," he'd said as he introduced himself, speaking with a thick Australian accent, "but I go by D. It started off as The Dingo but I kicked that into touch when they came up with the suit for me. No way, I said, and I designed my own one."

It wasn't a subtle suit. It was solid, like a suit of armour, with an exoskeleton of fine wires that facilitated its movement. Of all of us, he looked the most formidable and the most well protected.

311

"Light as a feather this.", he continued, proudly tapping the metal chest-plate, "But she's as solid as rock. Mind you, she's not great for making a discrete entrance. That's why I leave that sort of stuff to my buddies."

After the exchange of a few more pleasantries and the odd battle story, we got down to business. There was more than enough room for us all up there in the heights although it might have been a little less melodramatic if we'd chosen a hotel suite instead.

"First of all.", I said as I tried to bring about a little order, "let's talk about our Muslim friend. From my side, I drew a blank with my lead, although one of my team has tracked the delivery of one of what we think is the spheres to the suspects workplace. With that in mind, the only concrete evidence I can offer is that he is one of the bombers, equipped with the device but sadly, currently missing."

It was Whisperer who had struck lucky with her contact.

"Okay.", she began in a voice that seemed to roll like a mountain stream, "so this is what I have. Our guy was radicalised by the teacher I met, but even he was scared by the things that Holdcroft was talking about at the end. It took me a little while to get into his mind, but once he was under my influence I fast-tracked through all the memories he had stored and can offer a few facts. I've since been to his home, as I think we all have, and they match up. One, the location. Why would he have maps of Richmond Park on his computer? I think that this is part of the deception. We put him down as working away from his Hounslow base, but I think he is so far gone he doesn't mind taking the mosque with him. It's the closest we have to a location."

"I agree.", D interrupted, "Did anyone else read the notes on the pad? My suit told me that Teddington had been written and scribbled out."

"Good.", Whisperer continued, "and no, I missed that. So, secondly, the teacher I had under, kept referring to Holdcroft's obsession with noon. Apparently, he'd fiddle with his watch and his phone and set them to 12:00 whenever he was nervous.".

"But we're still not sure of the time.", I said, "and I've got an earlier one from the Zionist link."

I explained what I'd discovered the previous day.

"Kingfisher.", The Preacher spoke to me in that properly affected vicar-voice that we're all so familiar with, "your Bible knowledge isn't the best. The sixth hour in Joshua is generally accepted to be noon by most scholars. I think that we have the date and time now. Agreed?"

We all accepted his assertion.

"I think that exhausts that line of enquiry.", Burrows spoke up, "Let's make sure that our teams have the latest images of Holdcroft and put him aside for now. I need to tell you about a line that I've been following."

He told us about a visit that he had made to a Student Union bar just off the Edgware Road. He'd sat outside and pan-handled, had been successful in his efforts and had even been invited into the meeting.

"They had me down as a great example of the failure of the capitalist machine.", he smiled as he recalled the incident, "but when they asked me to say a few words, I played the drunken silence thing. That went down a treat. I was a victim through and through and, even though I pretended to sleep for the rest of the meeting, I gained some great info.".

"Just a moment.", I held my hands up in apology for interrupting, "let me send you across an image. Kirsty, transmit leaflet, students, Man-Up club."

"Yep, that's them.", Burrows agreed, "Planning a rally in Oxford Street. I gather they intend to use a device to take out the front of one of the boutiques in Bond Street. I've only been able to get a list of all members of that University, but I have the name of Sarah as the main speaker."

"I can fill the blanks in there for you.", D offered, "Our guys found one of the packages being delivered to an address in Hertfordshire. Big old mansion. Didn't make sense to them so they searched a little more and it's the home of a banker, his wife and two children. The kids are both students. One of them is called Sarah. Coincidence?"

We agreed it wasn't. That identified our second bomber. Oxford Street didn't make sense from our quartering of the city, but it would certainly have the most impact. And what better way to dupe the bomber than to tell them it would only break a pane of glass or two?

"Add to that, the Tabernacle.", I said, "and their talk of rapture and I think we have three. My only concern, is that my suspicion for the fourth explosion seems to be way off. I've got a performance artist pulling a stunt in central London and his mentor has had a package delivered. The geography doesn't make sense on that. Any thoughts?"

"They may be making sure.", the Preacher said, "covering their bases in case one gets stopped. You've got to admit that the centre of London is the high-impact zone. And let's be honest, they don't know how powerful these things are."

"But," Whisperer whispered, "if they do know about the water stopping the explosion, the Thames will minimise the impact. There's something not right there. Any other thoughts on the fourth?"

Nobody had any more to offer. The sun was up now and the exodus away from the city was visible to us all. We also began to see the first of the dedicated workers battling their way through to shops and offices. Without being explicit, King and the gang had done all they could, but there would always be those who didn't take the bait. Short of an official evacuation, it was always a certainty that more people would be lured by the workplace than by King's generosity.

"Okay," I said, "we've got some good leads here. Can I suggest that we each take a target and pursue that as a priority? Preacher, the Tabernacle? Charlie, the students? D, Ibrahim Islam? And Whisperer, the performance artist? I know the city better than any of you and can make myself available to support as you need me. Meanwhile, I need some time to review what we've discussed. I'm not convinced we're there yet. Does that work?"

They agreed and we went our separate ways. Despite losing the troops on the ground, I felt sure that we had enough time now and enough information to act together and stop the bombings. There was still the possibility that we were caught in the snares of an Alliance diversion, but we could only go with what we had.

Back at the boat, I sorted through every file and all the data that we had accumulated. It wasn't over until it was over and until that moment I would keep looking for evidence.

Chapter Forty-Six

Just when I thought that the marina team couldn't surprise me anymore, they sent me a visitor. She appeared behind me in the saloon of the boat, her reflection in my computer screen causing me to turn around in shock.

"Relax, Steve," she said, "Jason sent me."

I looked at the apparition before me. I was in jeans and t-shirt, otherwise I'd have thought I was looking in a mirror. Whoever was behind the mask was hidden. I was looking at Kingfisher. I was confused.

"The name's Zara," she told me, removing the helmet to reveal the face of a girl who couldn't have been any older than twenty, "and before you get too worried, the guys were too busy to tell you and left me to make my own plans. I guess you'd call me their latest trainee. They only had these suits though. Still, I can understand why you like them."

She explained that she had been sent as a support and that we had a job to do that required more than one Kingfisher.

"And if you have any doubts," she said, "think about this. I've gained unopposed access to your highly secure boat, I know you are Kingfisher despite your current outfit and I haven't come empty handed."

She drew back the blind over the window and I saw a pair of kayaks tied to the side of my boat.

"First of all," she said, "that is, after you've offered me a cup of tea, which I decline and then choose the beer that you offer instead, I need to tell you about Ireland."

We opened the beers and she told me about her findings.

"When you tipped off James from the club," she explained, "he found a trail that led across to Dublin. We couldn't spare you to make the journey and they were heads-down on the Brighton project. So, I offered to go. That's when Adam produced Kirsty Two and introduced me to her skills."

"I flew her to Ireland," she continued, "and landed at the offices of Eire Finance. The long and short of it is that this is where The Alliance moves its money from. Their systems are very secure. It took me longer than I'd hoped and I lost a lot of data as I worked, but that's my real skill. You think James knows computers? You want to see me in action!"

I didn't doubt her. She finished the beer and waved the bottle for another. Why not, I thought.

Over the next hour we shared information and she filled me in on what she'd found. All the links that I'd already established were confirmed by her. Johnston, Theakston, Goldsmith and Bill the Fruit had been wired money from The Alliance. As had Frank at the filter shop and Burns at the club. No links were established with the student activists, the F Empower group or the Mosque. That concerned me but Zara was less worried.

"I told you I lost a lot of data," she explained, "and that's probably that stuff. Anyway, with the data I've got, we've alerted international authorities and they are pursuing our leads. Seems like most of the top people are in India just now. But Gordon won't allow any action until after the event. I can sort of understand this on two counts. First, the guy is a complete idiot who cares more about his career than about saving lives, but secondly, it does sort of make sense. We alert them, they pull the plug, we don't retrieve the spheres."

I agreed. We had to see this through to the end, but at least we had a handle on the real guilty parties.

"Now to my other reason for visiting," she said, "and I hope you can bring yourself to help in this. It's about the beach party. Just about now, King is in the process of handing out vast sums of money to all who are attending. From the feeds I've seen, there must be a million or more there and the place is awash with happy faces. Food and drink are free, wherever you choose to eat. Jason's line of credit seems good enough for all the pubs and the finest of restaurants."

"Shame we're missing it," I said, remembering that I hadn't eaten since early that morning, "I could do with a break."

"Well," she replied, "you may not have to."

I looked at her quizzically.

"You see," she continued, "the next step is up to us. They arranged the party for Monday to stop the Alliance being tipped off. In theory, people could shortly start making their way back home soon. We have to stop that happening."

"Not too easy?", I asked.

"Not too difficult either,", she replied, "but you may not like the plan. Remember the virus that you used in the AMY case? The one that killed King's daughters?"

Like I needed asking if I remembered that situation.

"Well,", she said, "that's what we have to do in Brighton. You and I need to go down there and strafe the place with a new version of the virus which will knock everyone out for twenty-four hours. If you can't bring yourself to do it, I can go alone, but I can only carry enough for half the people. You in?"

Last time, the death toll had been less than a hundred. The potential this time was for a much higher count. My being the cause of the ending of so many innocent lives still caused me shame and regret. I kidded myself it wasn't my fault but it had been my actions that had killed them.

"When do you need to know?", I asked.

"Like, now.", she shrugged her shoulders, "We need to be there in the next hour."

I don't know why I even went to the trouble of debating the issue. It was inevitable that I would go. That's why we were airborne fifteen minutes later and why we separated halfway along the A30 and spent the next hour spraying a steady stream of microscopic virus-carrying nanobots into the atmosphere. I convinced Zara that we needed more than this. On our return journey we buckled the rail lines, took down several strategic road bridges and generally rendered the return route to London impassable.

By the time we returned, the virus was catching and the television news was changing its coverage of the event from one of joy and goodwill, to one of shock and horror that the airborne terrorist recently spotted in London should have chosen to strike at such a peaceful event. I could live with that. I long ago ceased caring what people thought about me. We'd done what we had to do and, however tomorrow panned out, we knew that a lot of people were now out of danger.

Zara slept on the couch. We'd set alarms for four a.m. but were already up and breakfasted by that time. I sent her out into the city to have a scan about and to orientate herself with the general layout of the place.

"Be careful,", I told her, "because they're after you. The police and the army won't touch you, they know Kingfisher is on their side, but after yesterday's stunt, you'll be running from every vigilante and do-gooder who sees you. And you know how destructive vigilantes can be!"

317

When she'd gone, I suited up myself and spoke to Kirsty.

"What am I missing?", I asked her.

"If I knew, Steve,", she replied, "I would tell you. However, the fact that you know you are missing something is a positive. That's half the battle."

I reviewed the notes I'd made again and again. Two attacks so close together didn't make sense. There was something wrong with the students or the performance artist. Both were confirmed as activists, both working at noon and both had received a sphere. No, that was wrong, both had received a parcel. Then it struck me. Johnston had complained about the state of the parcel he had received and how the tape that covered the packaging had damaged his nails. The transplant boxes were sealed with locked clasps. They didn't have any tape on them. The performance artist was a decoy. I transmitted the data to the teams.

"You see,", Kirsty said, "it's all in there. Keep searching."

It was like something from a Hollywood movie where I was expected to look inside myself and find the answers. Sadly, the real world didn't work like that. I was all spent for now. Maybe something would come up later.

I joined Zara on the roof of that famous department store. We checked our kit and divided out the weapons we had.

"Is it enough?", she asked.

"It's what we've got.", I said, "So yes, it is enough. It will have to be."

"Let me introduce you to some friends.", I told her, "Follow me"

We caught up with The Preacher first. He was headed to Hyde Park but we rendezvoused just off Kensington High Street.

"Hyde Park doesn't make sense,", he told us after I'd made the introductions, "and I've already been able to scan the Pastor and he is clean. I think that he is using somebody else to carry the device. All I can do is be a part of this and follow my heart."

We left him and moved on to meet with D.

"Looks like the demo is off,", he said, "because of this Brighton thing. Most of the students seem to be down there. So much for rejecting the trappings of capitalism. But the girl is on the move somewhere. I've got the parents locked up in their very nice house and I've left behind a search unit that will scour every inch of the place and feed me any details. I've told the parents to call me through that, if they suddenly decide they know something, or if they hear from her."

"If you need us.", I said, "just give us a shout. We're one more on the team now and I think we'll need as much help as we can. Good luck with it."

After D, we tracked down Burrows.

"Hey, Zara.", he greeted my companion with a hug.

"Charlie.", she replied, a bit ashamed at the connection.

"Zara used to be with ORB.", Burrows explained, "Highest performer in all her categories and a new agent in the making. Then she heard about your lot and jumped ship. Hope they're treating her right."

He updated us on his own progress.

"We've got just about the best identification software there is.", he told me, "Way beyond what you can imagine. Not just the usual facial recognition etc., but able to match identities through anomalies. It scans vast areas and picks out the incongruous. The person that doesn't fit. Then we can target the dust mites to check it out."

"You're using the mites?", Zara asked.

"Of course.", he answered, "and they work as well as your demonstration ones did. I've pulled Holdcroft's DNA from his home, now all I need are some suspects to test it on. I'm confident we'll get him. He doesn't seem the brightest of the bunch and we've got a fairly limited space to scan. Look, I better get on."

We left him and caught up with Whisperer. She was on the roof of the services at the end of the M1 and didn't seem to notice as we arrived.

"Hey, Whisperer...", I began before being hushed by her upheld hand.

We watched as she sat still for another five minutes before slowly returning to a conscious state.

"I'm beginning to see it now.", she said, "I just needed time to let the data compile in my mind. You should try it."

I introduced Zara and the two embraced.

"You're too young for all this.", Whisperer sighed, "I just hope you get a chance to bank some more years of life before they suck you in completely. It's not all it's cracked up to be."

She updated us on her progress since dropping the pursuit of the performance artist. She was homing in on the F Empower group. That was what she'd been doing when we caught up. By drifting into a deep, meditative state, she was able to subconsciously assimilate masses of data, sorting out irrelevancies and picking up patterns.

"There seem to be four key players.", she told us, "One of whom is in a relationship with a junior member of the group. The girl took in the parcel.

That much we know. After that, the trail grows colder. I'm having to make some assumptions, which I don't like doing. Mind you, stereotypes don't happen without good cause. Look at the map. So far, we think we have the perps for the two southern sectors. That leaves me working in the north and I can't find any links with the eastern quarter. That puts me in the north-west and I have a hunch. Look over there."

We scanned in the direction that she was pointing and saw the uppermost tip of the huge arch that spanned Wembley Stadium.

"They seem to refer to football quite a lot.", she said, "The last bastion of male supremacy or some such rubbish. It's a bit obvious, but it's a start."

Having agreed that she was probably on the right track we headed back towards the city. As we crested over the Thames aiming for our high vantage point again, I waved Zara to follow me and we landed at London Bridge.

"This place still bugs me.", I told her as we stood outside Frank's Filters which was closed, "And more so now that you tell me that Frank was being paid. What for?"

The shutters opened as I commanded the beetles inside to make them, then we closed them again and stood in the still and dusty air of the lock-up. We moved through the unit until we were at the office where we stood and looked for what we were missing.

"Too many phones.", Zara whispered, pointing to the desk.

"Check them out.", I told her, thinking she might be onto something.

Then I realised what was wrong. It was so stupid of me. The evidence was there right in front of my eyes and I'd missed it. For a man who, by his own admission, had never read a book, he had an awful lot of paperbacks on that bookcase.

"Kirsty,", I spoke to the suit, "scan the books for dust levels. You see anything?"

I saw the lights flashing on the visor and waited.

"Every third book.", she said, "All the others haven't been moved for a long time, but every third one had been referred to recently.".

I took the third book in and flicked it open. I think I hoped that something would fall out, but that would have been too easy. I took the book to the desk and studied every page. Still nothing.

"Give me ultraviolet please.", I asked Kirsty.

At first, I thought that I'd gone down another blind alley, but then I caught the glimpse of a faint mark on the chapter heading. A fine line was drawn under the second 1 of chapter 11. I scanned the bookcase and saw there were four shelves. The third book along in each row yielded numbers 1 to 4 respectively.

"Kirsty," I said, "if I flick through these pages can you read any UV highlights?"

"Certainly Steve," she said and we began.

Having finished all the third books on the top shelf she told me what I needed to know.

"If you ignore the missing 07," she said, "then the rest of the pages show me what appear to be mobile phone numbers highlighted in the page numbers. Let's complete the rest."

I let her take control of the suit and within two minutes she had extracted, scanned and replaced all the relevant books.

"Yes," she confirmed, "all phone numbers. I have them stored, currently awaiting results of searches on the user identities."

"Steve," Zara said, "the lines don't make sense. Two are normal telephone lines but the third is the latest generation of scrambled high-security lines. The only other place I know that has these is Downing Street. Why would he have them?"

I told her about the phone numbers and we raised our hands in a joint high-five.

"Looks like a decent lead at last.", I said, "Now, if I can just get them to James he can triangulate them."

I watched as Zara looked away.

"I'm sorry, Steve.", she said, "we can't use the marina guys. It was Jason's choice. He said that they had to go down with the virus along with the rest. Part of it was to keep up the pretence but I think he wanted to make sure that if it didn't work, like last time, then they all paid the price. Sorry."

I was tempted to utter a profanity. I chose not to.

"The Met's Anti-Terrorism Squad.", I said, "It's our only chance. They must have the gear we need."

"Zara," I turned and held her arms, "it'll have to be you. Kirsty will bring up the building plans and get you in but you'll need to hack in and get the data we need. Sorry, but I can't think of another way."

She left immediately. With the eerily quiet office all to myself I made contact with the others and asked them to be ready to receive directions. I looked at the clock. If Frank kept it up to date, then we had a little over two hours. I was beginning to think it wasn't enough.

Chapter Forty-Seven

Beside the phone numbers, we had one secret weapon that The Alliance hadn't counted on. Despite the vast resources they'd thrown at this project, their meticulous planning and they're pernicious exploitation of the petty prejudices of misguided individuals, they hadn't banked on the weakness of human emotions. Sarah made the call to her parents at 11.40, just moments after emerging from the tube to walk the short distance to New Bond Street. D kept us up to speed as he tracked her. She walked slowly, looking around furtively all the while, her face a picture of confusion and sadness. The mass protest that she had planned was a washout and the crowd of a dozen or so people that she joined were hardly going to rock the foundations of capitalism.

Our visors displayed a live link to D's movements. We watched as he scanned Sarah's body language and then as he read the moment correctly and saw her withdraw the fusion sphere from her bag. D fired a handful of the neutralisers and we held our breath as the ball was dropped to the floor. Its glow flared up in our vision and we heard D's voice telling the activists to lie down on the floor. He called in for a helicopter and we breathed a sigh of relief when we heard it swoop in overhead then fly out to the sea to drop the sphere deep into the water.

"Mission accomplished.", D told us, "What do you want me to do with the kids?"

"Leave them for now.", I told him, "and see if you can help Whisperer. Head north and she'll guide you in."

It should have been a moment of celebration, but it was a bit of an anti-climax. With all the weeks of preparation, investigation and planning, it seemed a little too easy. We'd all been geared up for battle and for moments of heart-stopping tension, but D had simply taken the bomb away from the youngsters. Was it all going to be so straightforward?

We'd lost track of the F Empower group when their phone went underground at Watford. Whisperer was certain that they were headed for

Wembley which was now surrounded by massed ranks of armed forces and as many of the emergency services as could be spared. The last contact that we'd had was at about the same time as Sarah was being stopped.

"She said something about a Vicar?", Whisperer told us, "Maybe that the Vicar had a load? Does that make any sense?"

It didn't. Not at that moment anyway.

Meanwhile, Charlie Burrows was homing in on Holdcroft. We agreed not to give him the respect of his Muslim name as he was no more a representative of Islam than the worst televangelist was a representative of Christianity.

"I've got him in my sights now.", The Indigent informed us, "Standing on his own towards the top end of Richmond Park. I make it 11.50. I'll set down and make my way to him. There's quite a number of civilians about though. Early lunches I guess, and a few school parties. I need to try and draw him away if I can."

"Good work.", I said, "I'll come over your way in case you need help. Preacher, you making any progress?"

"Something's not right.", The Preacher replied, "They're just singing hymns and the Pastor is clean. I thought he'd be moving by now. I'll go over and check their minibuses again. It's got to be here somewhere."

It was then that I realised how stupid we'd been. The Tabernacle was in Dulwich. That was near enough to Bow to take out the south-eastern sector. The gathering was a decoy. It was obvious, now that we knew that Holdcroft was in the same sector. And why had we thought for one moment that the good Reverend Smith was going to give his life in service?

"It's at the Tabernacle. Repeat, it's at the Tabernacle.", I told them, "Preacher, either head to Charlie or get out of the sector. Check the buses but, if they're clean, I think we read this as another set-up."

"Zara.", I waited until she answered, "get together everything you can and send it to the Tabernacle. But don't follow me. That's an order."

"Come on Kirsty.", I told the suit, "let's see what you're made of.".

We covered the couple of miles in minutes. I landed on the roof of the church and scanned the area. I looked at my watch. It was 11.57. Burrows called in.

"Approaching Holdcroft.", he said, "Preparing to deploy…"

The silence was followed by a distant boom. Then the blast wave hit me. I couldn't hold myself against the roaring wind and was smashed

323

against the numerous chimney stacks on the roof before being lifted up and sent tumbling to the ground. Kirsty stopped my fall and I landed on my feet.

"Injury assessment.", I requested, through gritted teeth.

"Multiple fractures to right arm, collarbone and ribs. High likelihood of internal bleeding. Advise termination of mission.".

"That ain't going to happen.", I told her, "Seal the injured area. Monitor for loss of blood. Then take me into the building."

My visor said 11.58. I didn't want to think about what had happened because I knew there was nothing I could do for Charlie. Time was running out and our initial success was fading. I looked out from the street and saw the black cloud appear. Despite the pain of Kirsty's first-aid, I continued to watch as the cloud approached. The first wave descended a few seconds later. They swarmed past me and through the shattered windows of the church, homing in on what they'd been programmed to find. I didn't have the luxury of searching for the weapon and my only hope lay in these creatures that were now descending.

"Kirsty.", I said, "forget the repairs, put everything into these bots. I want full infiltration, total penetration. Lock them on to whatever they touch."

I could hear nothing over the drone of the plague of insects now consuming the Tabernacle, but I could see that they were not alone. They were followed by wave after wave of more of the same, which in turn were followed by the first of the birds. Kingfishers covered the building, as incongruous in the setting as they were essential to its survival. Then came the owls. It was all we had left and Zara had done exactly as I'd asked. We had nothing more to give but at least we could say that we had gone down fighting.

As I rose to follow them into the building I saw a billboard on the opposite side of the road. It was advertising a football match. I stopped and could have screamed.

"Vicarage Road.", I called across the network, "not Wembley. Repeat Vicarage Road, Watford FC. Not Wembley."

Deep down, I knew it was too late. We had one-minute left. It was out of my hands now and all I could do was wait. The Tabernacle was large and sprawling. If the creatures stopped the bomb, I'd know soon enough. If not, I wouldn't have to worry about it.

The second blast was a softer breeze coming in from the north. I waited. The streets were beginning to fill with those who hadn't left the city and who were now curious about the sounds they'd heard and the rumours that were beginning to circulate. I stumbled into the Tabernacle building, wincing with the pain, and called the creatures to stop. I waited. Then the blue-green vision came closer, it's progress slowed by the glowing sphere that it held. The kingfisher deposited its offering at my feet. The hands of the bomber were still attached to it, caught up in the force-field that had disarmed it. I didn't want to, but I smiled. At least I was safe.

With the second sphere on its way to the North Sea and the police searching through the building for the remains of the team whose bodies had been stripped clean by the army of creatures I had unleashed, I called the team. Only Zara and D replied. The Indigent and the Preacher had gone together when the foul and incompetent form of Holdcroft had detonated his device two minutes early, having fiddled just too many times with his watch. Whisperer had died in sight of the F Empower activists who were making a stand for feminism in Watford. She had been so close.

"Steve," Zara said, "I've never seen anything like it. It's just an empty space. And it's so silent."

She tracked my location as Kirsty lifted me gently towards the outer reaches of the bombed-out zone and we met on top of what remained of the new apartments built from Battersea power station. D joined us shortly afterwards. We stood for what seemed like an age and looked out over the vast, empty space.

The fusion bombs weren't like the bombs that had been dropped to end the Second World War. They were hugely more powerful, but they left behind no traces. They burned, they destroyed and then they simply died away. There was no nuclear winter with a fusion bomb. There were no crumbling pieces of the buildings that had stood in its path. There was only silence in the empty space where so much had stood before.

"Kirsty," I said, "is there any sign of life?"

I watched as she deployed every available scanner that she had.

"Sorry, Steve," she told me what I already knew, "Nothing."

There was no consolation in the fact that we'd stopped two of the devices exploding. There should have been. We should have been able to look at the devastation and understand how much less it was because of what we'd done.

325

We should have been able to find a shred of hope in the lives of the people who now wandered around in a daze through what remained of London. It had been bisected. Everything west of Paddington was gone.

But there was nothing to celebrate here. The numbers of dead were incalculable. There was only silence. And it had all been over so quickly. Even the water had failed to stop the devastation. Against such a powerful enemy, the thinning upper reaches of the Thames and the narrow stretches of the Grand Union canal could provide no protection. The fusion reaction had simply jumped across the water and continued to consume the substance of everything that lay in its path. We'd thought Watford too far north, but the perpetrators had understood better than us just how much force those spheres could drain from vast stores of fuel in this heavily built-up part of England.

"Steve," a groggy voice that I partly recognised came over my helmet, "you alright?"

"Jason," I whispered, "you're back with us."

"Tell me it's not as bad as they say.", he pleaded.

"I wish I could,", I told him, trying to keep the tears from my eyes, "but believe me, it's worse. I can't tell you. It's so much worse."

"Jason?", Zara asked, "Did the virus work?"

He confirmed that it had and that there had been no adverse indications amongst the visitors now waking up.

"How many do you estimate you saved?", I asked.

"Last count, we had just shy of one and a half million here.", he replied, "More than we could have hoped for and not all out of London, but still, it's something."

"It's more than something,", I told him, "it's a miracle, that's what it is."

We talked a little more but the time for planning wasn't now. It was in the hands of the authorities and now was about volume of helpers rather than any special skills. Other than the very special skills of humanity that I knew would be our victory in this time of despair. I confirmed that James, Adam and Charlotte were all fine, then we left them to it. They had a lot of people to care for.

"What now?", D asked.

"I don't know,", I replied, "I really don't know. There's nothing we can do here."

"India?", he asked.

I looked around me. I ran a tentative hand over my shattered right side and felt the satisfying sting of agonising pain. I thought about the lives lost, the families, the children, the friends who would never know what had happened. Then I thought about Charlie and the other colleagues we'd lost.

"You got enough information, Zara?", I asked her.

She confirmed that she had.

"India sounds good then.", I said, "It's time for justice."

Chapter Forty-Eight

I woke up in a hospital bed a week after the bombings. It took me some time to get my bearings but the presence of Mrs Quinn bustling around beside me helped me to understand.

"So, you're back with us then.", her voice was welcoming and friendly as always, "Sure, now, you need to take it easy. But Mr King will be so pleased."

I lay there and tried to recall the events that had led up to this second visit to King's most private of wards. I wasn't that far out of it that I couldn't remember. The memories were bitter-sweet as they filled my mind.

D had been a pilot prior to joining his underground organisation and it had been a lot easier than we'd anticipated for us to commandeer a private jet and take her to India. Zara had set up the electronic smokescreens that kept us from being stopped by Air Traffic Control. D had done the flying. My part in it was to close down any human challenges that might have prevented our flight. That had meant the unpleasant hiding away of the existing crew and passengers, drugged up for a few days and deposited in a redundant hangar on the outskirts of the airport. They might thank me some day. The country was in deep shock and mourning and there was little to cheer the soul in the patchy media that was trying to make sense of what had happened.

In London, deep in the ORB centre on Oxford Street, Housman offered us what support he could. I had to admire his courage. He had stayed with the fusion reactor all through the danger period and had thought nothing of his own safety. He needed to be there to pull the plug if the surrounding area were to be destroyed. As it was, the reactor continued to function as normal and its output proved to be a huge benefit to the emergency services in the aftermath. Its future had already been decided though. Housman told us that it would be dismantled and all records destroyed.

"One day,", he'd said, "mankind's desperate need for limitless energy might be a stronger force than his need for ultimate power. The science would come again. Perhaps, when it does, we will be ready for it."

By the time we touched down at Dabolim Airport we had been accepted as a legitimate party, consisting of a pilot, an air-hostess and a reclusive businessman recovering from surgery. The clothes we wore fitted the part. Our work suits were stored in the little luggage we carried and our pictures matched the passports that Zara had created mid-flight. The other two seemed relieved to be free of their other uniforms. I would have been had Kirsty not been such a comfort in easing the pain of my injuries. D had put the craft into auto-pilot and removed a piece of his own suit which he crafted into a metal plate that kept my shoulder and upper arm fixed in position. Everything else was bandaged. It hurt like hell, but I wasn't going to let my injuries stop this particular mission.

The preparations and the flight took only eight hours. D wasn't one for borrowing anything but the latest and fastest jet. With the time difference, that put us out on the streets of Goa in the early hours of Wednesday morning. We would dearly have loved to crash at the nearest hotel but we had to endure another taxi ride out to the Hanson Resort before we finished. Once there though, we booked into the best suite available and set our alarms for an early breakfast. The Resort wasn't a considered choice. It was where we knew The Alliance members were holed up. Hanson himself was a shadowy figure, rumoured to be building up stakes in some of the world's poorest nations. Tourism provided him with a legitimate cover, after all, the visitors he attracted weren't too concerned about conditions beyond the high-security walls. They wanted luxury and sunshine and beautiful beaches. Hanson gave them what they wanted.

I'd slept better than I had for a long time. I suppose I should have been kept awake by the thought of the desolation we'd witnessed and the scale of the tragedy we'd left behind. But that had been yesterday. We couldn't turn the clock back. And I was so tired. The others grabbed enough rest to be perky when they woke me at seven. I could tell by the look on their faces that they'd been awake for hours and had been working all that time. We ordered breakfast to the room and I let the coffee surge through my weary body before settling down with them to hear the update.

"Thanks to information we've received from King and Housman," Zara explained, "we know that Goldsmith, Theakston and Johnston are here as well as the elusive Mr Hanson. We also know that Hanson has a private island a few kilometres from here, which we assume has other guests just now. Fortunately, King sold a number of his assets to Housman, at crazy prices I might add, but that gives us the data that the transactions came from this location."

"Another interesting thing," D spoke for the first time, "is that the HQ of Eire Finance was mysteriously destroyed by a bomb just after Zara's visit. The press and the police are putting this down to a pre-emptive strike prior to the big ones, but I think we can safely say that we know better. The information we have already extracted from those computers is priceless."

We continued to discuss the state of play as we loaded up on much needed calories. We hadn't had time to come fully prepared but we had enough resources for what we needed to do.

"Your Kirsty has repaired herself," Zara told me, "and my Kirsty is fine. D's suit has replaced the part that's currently holding you together, so all told, we have the minimum of what we need. That said, D's suit is too heavy to travel underwater so I'm in the process of securing a mini-sub for us on the pretext of us going sightseeing over the corals. That should be all we need."

"And is Housman geared up at ORB?", I asked.

"Completely," D said, "and he's also patched into my guys back home and Whisperer's team in the US. Man, are they upset about their loss."

There was a moment of sadness that we all shared, remembering the colleagues we'd lost.

"Let's not forget," I said, "that we're doing this for them as much as for the millions who died. We can't fail. We owe it to them."

The timing of The Alliance's celebratory party was as nasty as they were. The first toast would be raised at twelve noon, Goa time. They wanted to mark the hour of the day before, but clearly didn't want to quaff champagne for breakfast. We knew this because Zara had been able to access the funding for the caterers, which in turn led her to their own database. James had taken over at that point and there was now nothing we didn't know about the menus or the waiting-on staff. We also knew how tight and extensive the security was going to be. Still, forewarned is, as they say, forearmed.

The sun was already high and hot by the time that we boarded the small motorboat that we had hired along with the mini-sub. We looked like all the other groups of party people taking a picnic out onto the water. The small outfit that we'd hired the vessels from warned us to stay clear of the area around Hanson's island and provided us with an alternative route instead. Once loaded up, they waved us off and watched as we headed to where they had sent us. As they did so, we scanned the beaches and identified the numerous bodies there, trying to look inconspicuous but simply too heavily dressed to fit in. They all carried cameras with telephoto lenses that could both scan the horizon for miles and transmit the image to a mainframe. Fortunately, ORB's influence was not as limited to only Britain as we had been led to believe. At the same time as we were departing, three locals were diving into the water in a nearby bay.

We met up as we laid anchor at the spot we'd been advised to stop at. The beach was still visible, as were the guards. Making a meal of preparing for our dive and covering ourselves with very British modesty, we were able to swap places with the locals and were soon suited up and in the water, helping D into the sub.

"Just a minute," one of the new crew said, "I need to just sort something out on that machine. It's not something you're supposed to know about."

He slipped into the water and resurfaced a few minutes later carrying a small, white box.

"It's a tracking device. They fit these to all their vessels." he explained, "partly to aid in any rescue, mainly to stop the gear being stolen, but also as a nice little side-line as they sell the data to interested parties. We'll take it in turn to move around with it. As far as anyone knows, you're still here and having a lovely time."

With all the preparations in place, we dived under the water and let Kirsty and Kirsty Two take us to our destination. We had the sub locked between us and spent the journey staring at the metal mask that clung to D's face, convinced that it's expression had changed to one of determined anger. It was a short journey and one that still presented challenges. There were very few sectors of Hanson's island where we could safely land and these changed continuously as the guards moved about. It was easy enough for Zara and myself, but bringing a six-foot tall, metal clad superhero to the shore was a tad more exacting. Fortunately, the cave that the locals had told us about was still accessible. It was less a cave than a worn indent in the rock, but it provided enough cover for what we needed. I surfaced first, secured myself at the rear of the opening and guided the sub in backwards. As the rear end touched my legs, I released the roof bolts and D slithered and clambered to stand beside me. We left the sub there, slowly taking on water.

Once on the island, we flew in short bursts through small forested areas and across newly-cleared open spaces. From the mainland or from the air, the place looked uninhabited and indeed, almost uninhabitable. The image betrayed the truth however. This was a modern playground for the very richest, equipped with a golf-course, a leisure complex and numerous beautifully crafted lodges. The centrepiece was a dome. It's covering was of reinforced glass but that only became clear as we approached it. The glass was active and projected the image of the surrounding area on its surface.

This was our biggest challenge. We knew that whoever was in the dome could see us, but we could see nothing of what was happening inside. Not too much of a problem for me though. I released some insects from the backpack attached to my suit and let Kirsty reshape them into an image of indigenous species. Wherever you were in the world and however hard you tried to keep them out, it was a universal truth that insects would find a way in. They slipped into the dome without any trouble and we let them lead us through the inside as we watched on our monitors. I let them rest after a while and looked at the others.

"Any thoughts?", I asked them.

"Man,", D sighed, "that place is buttoned up tighter than a widow's smile."

"I'm not seeing anything either.", Zara said, "Looks like the only way in is through the main entrance. I guess they put the caterers and the rest of the staff in place before the guests arrived. I was hoping for a tradesman's entrance at least."

"Kirsty?", I asked, becoming increasingly dependent on her advice.

"I've computed all options for entry,", she replied after a pause, "and the maximum chance of success that I can offer you is thirty-six percent.".

That was enough for me. There were three of us. Even if only one of us made it, it was worth it to exact revenge on The Alliance. The others looked at me expectantly. I could see that they didn't share my optimism.

"Kirsty,", I said, "do the same calculation for our getting this far onto the island and for our having stopped two of the fusion bombs."

"Thirty-one percent and twelve percent respectively.", she replied, waiting a moment before adding, "Which means that I should congratulate you."

"We're looking at this the wrong way.", D suddenly sat up and faced us, "It's not about us having to get in without being noticed. We've already done that with the insects. Why do we need to be there?"

"This isn't about us. None of it is.", he continued, "It's about justice. That's what we do. We've just got to reinterpret what justice means."

"Go on.", I said.

"We're here to make sure these people come to justice.", he said, "I know we want to hurt them and punish them and, for my part, tear them slowly apart limb from limb. But maybe that's not what we're here for. Justice can wait. We just need to observe."

He was right. We'd become so engrossed in revenging the deaths of our friends that we'd failed to stay detached. We were worrying about a problem that wasn't actually a problem at all. I looked at my watch. It was ten to twelve. The insects showed us the last of the guests arriving and the door to the dome being sealed. We only had to watch now, and make sure that we weren't the only ones to see and hear what happened inside.

"Mind you,", D removed his mask as we sat and completed preparations for the first stage of our attack, "I'd hate to see them walk out of there, and I think I might have an idea."

Chapter Forty-Nine

The footage that we shot and transmitted that lunchtime remains, to this day, the most frequently viewed file ever uploaded to the internet. It begins with a close-up image of every attendee to that lunch, each with their name and address superimposed on top. It was how it was transmitted by us from the island, with Kirsty pulling up the data that she could and Housman filling in the blanks as he routed it into every media server around the world. The final still is of Hanson as he stands at the podium waiting to address the room.

"Ladies and gentlemen," his speech began a little quietly until we upped the energy output of the insects, "welcome to this most wonderful occasion and to the meal that marks the beginning of a new era for The Alliance."

The audience stops him with their enthusiastic response to this opening statement.

"Yesterday," he held his hands up for silence, "yesterday, in that most feted of cities, London, we showed the world what we are capable of."

Another pause for applause.

"Now," he continued, "I think of myself as a half-full glass person, rather than a half-empty one. I am not as upset about only taking out half of the city, as I am proud that we took out the other half. Nor will I linger on the tactics deployed by certain people to diminish the death toll. One million or so who remain alive means nothing against the four million who died."

This time the assembled guests rose to give him a standing ovation which lasted for two minutes.

"In every nation," he continued, "and from the lips of every tongue, the name of The Alliance is being passed around. People are hearing about our stand for humanity and I believe that they will not reject us, but join us. The days of a fool's morality are over. The days of false doctrines and subjugating lies are over. The day of the strong is here. The day has arrived when true survival of the fittest is the doctrine we not only accept, but by which we live. This is not about freedom for all. What has that done to the world? It's only brought us a world of dependence, waste and inefficiency. Now, we embrace a future of utility. Let me demonstrate."

This is where the video is edited for mass viewing in some principalities. It was the hardest part for us to sit through.

"This gentleman is seventy years old.", Hanson pointed to the elderly, Indian man that was led onto the stage to stand beside him, "and is past his usefulness. He has used up his savings and has no assets left. He is, in short, dependent on others to keep him alive. And I have to ask myself, why? Why, when the world is short of resources, do we waste them on him?"

The man is seen to struggle as the guards hold him firmly. Hanson approaches and slits his throat, stepping back quickly to avoid the jet of blood that pours from his neck.

"And now.", he continues as he returns to the podium, "the problem is solved. Utility, utility, utility, must be the new mantra. The call for a new age when we, the strong, the haves, the powerful, no longer find ourselves dragged down by the weak, the broken and the expendable. We are man, we are animals and we are flesh. Let's celebrate true humanity and be the people that nature intended us to be. Now, party on, you've earned it."

We chose to cut the recording at that stage. It was partly a necessity as the creatures were running out of power, but it was also a moral choice on our part as we simply didn't want the world to see the orgy that followed. Nor our response to it.

Once we'd checked that the feed had uploaded okay, we moved onto the second stage of the plan. This was D's baby. We let him take the lead.

With the dome closed and the lunch underway, the guards were more relaxed. They weren't complacent, not by any measure, and were clearly being paid as the best of the best when it came to hired mercenaries. They weren't a match for D though. He simply walked up to them and gave them all he had. His armoury made our suits seem like fancy dress. When he'd told us that his approach was a lot less sophisticated than ours, we'd humoured him and even joked about it. When we saw him in action though, we stopped smiling and went to help out.

One by one the guards fell as D's suit opened out to reveal rocket launchers, machine guns and grenades, all of which sent bodies flying in all directions. Zara and I cleaned up the wounded with terminal shots of laser light that simply decapitated them, but we struggled to keep up with D's onslaught.

We were outflanked and outnumbered but we had a weapon that ignored such statistics. We had the lives of our fallen comrades to atone for and those guards were worth nothing compared to the people we'd lost. Within five minutes, just as we heard the party music starting deep inside the dome, we'd felled the last. D was on his knees, blood seeping out of the gaps in his armour plating. Zara and I were exhausted but generally wound free. I'd taken a couple of bullets but Kirsty had sealed the wounds and injected painkiller once she'd confirmed they weren't life threatening. Zara had a broken leg. Kirsty Two compensated for this and took the weight.

"You ready to finish this?", D snarled.

We didn't have a chance to answer because he was already back on his feet and setting the explosives around the doorway. It blew out easily and we unleashed the last of the virus robots that we'd remembered were in our suits. The music continued to thump away, but soon it was the only sound in the dome. D shot out the amplifiers and we stood in the silence remembering how still it had been after the last of the bombs.

"You sure about this?", I looked at the other two.

"Never more certain in my life.", D replied.

"I'm sorry,", Zara said, "but can I pass?"

We let her. This was something that both D and I could do without the memory haunting us for life, but Zara was still only a baby. She left the room as we walked through the sleeping masses and removed their hands one by one. We made sure the wounds were cauterised and we gathered up the pieces into one heap. These were the hands that had taken millions of lives. The hands that were the instruments of minds that would soon have their twisted and corrupted philosophies weighed and judged by the world. They were hands that wielded power, but which lay powerless now forever.

And that had been India. I don't remember the journey back or at what point I arrived at King's house and was treated in his clinic. Now that I was awake I could see that we were already well into July and that I'd lost a couple of weeks somewhere. I chose not to turn the television on as I knew it would only show me things that I didn't want to see. I only wanted to eat now, and to get better, and to get back onto the canal and away from all this madness. Mrs Quinn must have read my thoughts. She bought me a very unhealthy cheese-burger with chips. It didn't touch the sides.

"You get yourself ready now,", she'd said as she left me with the food, "because you've got some visitors here who can't wait to see you."

336

"Am I okay to get up?", I asked.

"Of course you are.", she laughed, "You're under my care now and when I tell you you're healed, you're healed. You may be a bit stiff though, so take your time."

With the burger gone, I followed her advice and eased myself gingerly out of the bed. I could tell straightaway that she was right in saying I'd healed, but that didn't ease the pains that coursed through muscles that hadn't been used for weeks. I felt my shoulder and my arm, checking out the new scars that had been added to this battle-weary body. There were a couple more where the bullets had been. Other than that, I could have been a lot worse off.

I opened the door and got into the lift to take me into the main house. I was wondering who my guests were. The answer came as soon as the lift doors opened. I was knocked over by two dogs.

"Fred, Gilly!", I knelt down to receive their hugs and wet kisses. They whined and ran around my feet, returning to kiss me again and vying for attention. It was so good to see them again. They reminded me that not everything had changed.

"They've been waiting for you.", I recognised Jason's voice straightaway, "Seems like even Mrs Quinn is no substitute for you. They're beautiful dogs. You'd never guess the little one was an Adam creation."

The dogs held me close and prevented me from getting up to greet King. He joined me as we tumbled around on the floor. I managed to grab his hand when the dogs were distracted by a sound from the kitchen.

"Good to see you, Jason.", I said, barely able to hold back the tears, "And thanks for whatever you did to me down there. Seems it did the trick."

"We patched you all up.", he explained, "and then I had you bought here. D is back home. He was the worst off of the three of you. How he stayed upright with all that metal inside him, I don't know. Still, he's well on the road to recovery now."

"And Zara?", I asked.

"She's a tough one, that's for sure.", he laughed as told me where she was, "Tells me not to worry, that it's only a broken leg and she'll be fine. She's at the marina with the rest of the guys now. And yes, before you ask, they're all fine. That is, as fine as you can be these days."

"Is it still as bad?", I asked, dreading the answer.

"Yes, look, let's have a drink.", he ushered me into the sunlit conservatory, "I'll update you."

With a large whisky fast disappearing in his glass, and over several refills, he gave me the latest news.

"Estimates now,", he sighed, "are somewhere between the four and the four and a quarter million mark. Some of the houses were so densely packed, it's unlikely we'll ever get a true figure. And yes, it's the only news on the news just now. It's been a couple of weeks, but nobody quite accepts it yet. Talk about a nation in grieving. This is a world in grieving. Everyone lost someone and some lost everyone. It's horrific."

He told me how the area had been cordoned off whilst scientific experts checked the radiation levels and maintenance experts sealed off any live cables and leaking pipes. ORB had been right in their assessment of the expected damage and also in the fusion bomb's absorption of everything in its path.

"You remember the image of the demo bomb and how it took everything back to soil?", he asked rhetorically, "Well, that's how it was. It's like half of London had been pulled up by its roots and spirited away. Not a nice sight. And not confined to London only. North of Watford took a huge hit. It went as far as Milton Keynes. The only thing we got wrong was our confidence in water being able to stem the expansion. It worked fine when we dropped them in the sea, but the inland waterways were just too small to make a difference. And with so many bridges across the Thames, the reaction just used them to continue its advance."

I held my hand up to indicate that I'd heard enough. I needed to know, of course, but one could only take so much at once.

"And The Alliance?", I asked.

"Well, now,", he came over to me and put his hand on my shoulder, "thanks to you, they are all being held in a very secure camp, just outside of The Hague. Their trials will be accelerated and look to be a done deal already as they can't find any lawyers willing to defend them. Even court appointed ones have been exempted in this case."

"The compound,", he continued to explain, "is no more than a series of cages with the most basic of amenities. And it's open to the public to view. They only let them in a few at a time, but the queues beat Disneyland. Oh, and their wounds have all healed up now. They try and hide the stumps but aren't always successful. It was brilliant work you did. I reserve judgement on the hands but you moved before they had a time to disperse. Superb."

I thanked him but also told him that I didn't feel particularly proud of what we'd done. Nor was I ecstatic about the bombs we'd missed.

"Steve," he held me closer, "you did all you could. Gordon should have thrown more resources in the right direction but he chose to do it his way. He was still trying to figure the big picture when the first explosion happened. He's retired now, thank goodness. Mind you, I think it best if you two never cross each other's paths again. Boy, is he gunning for you."

"I appreciate your support," I walked away and stared out of the window over the vast acreage of King's garden, still lovingly tended by Mr Quinn and son, "but you did your bit as well. How many do you estimate?"

"Somebody gave me a number near one and a half million," he told me, brushing the figure aside, "so it did some good. I don't regret it one bit and I know that the money that we dished out will help people rebuild."

"This," he opened his arms to indicate the house, "and the marine businesses, are all I have left. It's great. So much simpler and I still want for nothing. They're trying to paint me as some kind of hero, but I tell them it was a coincidence. I'm just glad I was in a position to act."

"You okay if I go for a walk with the dogs?", I asked him, not wanting to ruin the time together but as full of the situation as I wanted to be for now.

"Go for it," he said, opening the door to let the dogs in, "and take as long as you want. There is just one other thing though."

He reached into his pocket and withdrew a small box. I opened it.

"It is," he said, "the highest order that this country can award. They insisted I accept it on your behalf."

"Thanks," I replied, "but still, little consolation."

As I headed to the garden he called to me.

"They wanted to offer you a knighthood as well. But I declined that for you. I'm guessing that was the right move."

"Absolutely," I told him, "and thank you. You did right. After all, who do they award it to? I change names so often I don't even know who I am most of the time. And anyway, what's in a name?"

With that, I picked up a couple of tennis balls that were lying on the grass and threw them for the dogs to fetch. They seemed happy enough for me to be back. I guess, in a strange sort of way, so was I.

Chapter Fifty

'Cheshire Tonight', 25th September, 2027

'Charges Dropped in Offensive T-Shirt Case'

Cheshire Constabulary confirmed today that it would not be pursuing any further action against a man arrested after members of a local church complained about an offensive t-shirt that he was seen wearing. The t-shirt, depicting Jesus on the Cross, calling down to his friends, 'Hey, I can see your house from here', caused outrage when it was seen by a group of Methodists when they relaxed after a day's walking in a local pub beer-garden.

At the time, one of the church elders, Ray Wilson, explained to this newspaper that his church would prosecute this offence to the full and ensure that the wearer face the highest penalties of the law.

Although giving no reason for his change of heart, it was this same Ray Wilson who asked police to drop the case last week. An inside source has told this paper that the church seems to have reconsidered its approach to this affair and would simply like to forgive and forget.

++++++

'Stoke Courier', 12nd October, 2027

'Pottery Saved at Last Minute'

Workers at the Royal Standard pottery were relieved to be told earlier today that the factory would not be closing down and that their jobs were safe for a good few years. It had been rumoured that the business was to be moth-balled by its current owner, local entrepreneur R. J. Singh, despite it having increased profits year on year for the past decade.

Speaking at a meeting to address his workforce, Mr Singh apologised for any uncertainty there may have been over recent weeks, during which time, the canal-side factory was rumoured to be being prepared for sale to a house-builder.

"Your contribution to the local economy,", he told the team, "and the skills that you have, coupled with the passion that you put into the work you do, has made me decide that there is more to this business than I could ever know.".

One of only six potteries remaining in the local area, Royal Standard are one of the oldest and continue to export their uniquely styled 'Waterways Ware' across the globe. Mr Singh purchased the pottery only six months ago from one of the consortiums in the former billionaire Jason King's portfolio.

++++++

'BBC Radio News', 15:00, 22nd October, 2027

"And finally, on the lighter side. Staff at a Birmingham animal sanctuary arrived at work this morning to find that the premises had been completely rebuilt after fire destroyed the property only three days before.

Over one hundred rescued cats and dogs perished when the family-run rescue centre was set alight by vandals earlier in the week and it was thought that the charity might have to shut up shop.

Jane Gills, who is the founder of the shelter, doesn't

know quite how the building was transformed back to its former glory, which appears to have happened within an eight-hour time frame.

'It just doesn't make sense, but I can't complain. We left the building after tidying up about nine o'clock yesterday evening, then, this morning, we came back to carry on at six and it looked like this. The only thing that we have to be careful of is that some of the paint is a bit tacky, but other than that, it's better than it ever has been. I don't know what happened, but in my view, it's some sort of miracle.'.

Insurers have already re-visited the premises and signed off the works completed, offering to replace the charity's computers and other electronic and veterinary equipment immediately.

In a country still reeling from the London Event, it's nice to be able to report that the milk of human kindness doesn't yet seem to have run dry.

++++++

It took them until mid-August to extract my boat from the thick layers of mud that now filled what had once been Paddington basin. The two dinghies that had carried my insect saviours were long gone, but the boat that Adam built had survived intact. At the first sign of it taking in water, it hermetically sealed itself and allowed just enough water into the bilge to drop it safely to the canal bed. There it lay, silently waiting as the world above was transformed. It resisted the ingress of the Thames as it flowed in to fill the vast voids that had once been teeming with cosmopolitan life, and it continued to emit its faint homing signal.

They took her away at night. Hoisted onto a low-loader, she made the slow journey North overnight and I was there to greet her as they relaunched her into the upper reaches of the Leeds Liverpool Canal. Skipton had been as good a place as any for me to start again. I'd always been a fan of the place and it carried memories of both Fran and Jean. It was also far enough away from the madness of the chaos of city life and the seemingly endless talk about what was now known as the 'London Event'. I climbed aboard and began the two-day process of tidying and freshening her up after her stint under the water. She'd survived remarkably well. All I had to concentrate on was stripping out the perishables that had filled her with a stale odour of decay and then scrubbing and cleaning every surface until it shone like new. They'd offered me a replacement, but I was fond of this craft. She was all I needed. More than I needed for the most part. And she was home.

Whilst I set off to cruise again, the team at the marina laid plans for their own future. James continued to work on J for Justice, now more popular than ever, and was in the process of training the next generation of his apprentices. I sometimes heard talk of them, but they operated in the background and were, like him, happier in their own world of microchips and sub-atomic particles than they were in the wider world of people. You couldn't blame them really, not when you considered what people were capable of doing.

Adam and Charlotte were preparing to get married. It had already been planned, but Charlotte's pregnancy accelerated the timing. They'd invited me and I'd accepted, happy to have something to aim for in September. Tony and Kate were onto baby number three now, whilst their family expansion was matched by the expansion of the work of the yard. An unexpected consequence of the London Event was that housing was in very short supply. The yard worked day and night to produce the simple liveaboard boats that they were famous for but even then, they still couldn't keep up with demand.

Meanwhile, Jason King reviewed his finances and capitalised on opportunities that he had laid down years back. The Lichfield and Hatherton Canals were now both fully in water, thanks to his investments and he was enjoying a good return from the businesses that he had placed along the route. He would never be a billionaire again, but he wasn't short of money. He kept his previous house, bequeathing it to the Quinn's in the event of his death, but he spent most of his time at a new property that he'd constructed backing onto the newly refurbished waterways. He moored a small boat at the end of his garden, spent a lot of time sitting on its deck with a fishing rod in his hand and looked, to any passer-by, to be the image of a happily retired man. Of course, that wasn't strictly true. Beneath that same property there beat a futuristic heart. James had all he needed in the old marina and Adam and Charlotte would continue to use the base there for their work. J for Justice accepted donations quite willingly and had more than enough capital to work with. But King had more to offer still.

Zara was the first of his new generation of field operatives. She lived in a fully-equipped motorhome and travelled the country busking on street corners and looking out for opportunities to help the cause of justice. She was still young, but the relatively few years that she had under her belt were weighted with experience. I'd offered to yield Kingfisher to her but she wanted her own identity.

"I'm not really a bird person.", she chuckled as she thought about the costume she'd worn so recently, "But, Kirsty Two almost convinced me. No, I'm more of a traveller. I want the open road and not the water. I think it'll be something like The Minstrel. I quite like that. And think of what I could do with a fully armed lute!"

So, King was helping her to find her own level. ORB remained a force to be reckoned with but they needed new operatives as well. Housman left the Order and worked with King for a few months, helping him to set up his new laboratories. The fusion reactor had been dismantled and the Oxford Street premises left abandoned. ORB would find its own new home elsewhere, but Housman no longer felt that he could be a part of it.

As for me, I got back into my old lifestyle with a very grateful heart and with the suits and the weapons locked away for good. Like they had been before. Although, this time I told myself it was properly for good. King wouldn't let me return the kit. He told me that he didn't have the space for it, but I knew that he was giving me the opportunity to decide for myself. It wasn't that I didn't want to help to advance the cause of justice. No, after the Event, I wanted to contribute more than ever. Not on the front line, but doing those little things that I could to help. I wasn't unique in this. I never had been. After the Event, people changed. Their petty worries and niggling prejudices were put aside in favour of embracing life. The Alliance had never understood that elusive quality of humanity that transcended the animal in us. We were more than the flesh and bone that they believed us to be, and we would never give way to their thinking.

The t-shirt incident was a great illustration of how things had changed. I'd done that one as Steve Barratt, Righteous Corrector, although I was a little reluctant even to resurrect that identity. It was more that I'd found a disc on the same day that I'd met the family of Colin North. They were lovely. I saw them as they sat having sandwiches on a bench just beyond where my boat was moored. Fred saw them as well, and their sandwiches.

"Fred!", I shouted as he jumped off the boat and headed towards them.

344

"I'm sorry.", I apologised to the family when I'd finally got Fred on his lead.

"Don't worry.", the mother had said, "the kids love dogs. Can they play with them?"

So it was that we'd sat and watched them play with Gilly and Fred whilst Carol North told me of the situation they were in. It was as simple as the press had reported it. Colin North, thinking it witty, had worn the t-shirt to the pub. The Methodists had protested and he had been arrested.

"I mean.", Carol said, "I hate that t-shirt as much as anyone, but to arrest him. It's madness."

When we parted, I checked out Ray Wilson. I found his address and put a tracker on his car. I asked James to reach into the depths of his computer. And I visited him at home a few times, usually after dark.

He changed his mind about the prosecution after my last visit to his house. I watched him enter the living room, saw the expression on his face as he saw me sitting there and heard him begin to call out.

"Shush.", I said, rising to greet him and extending a hand that he instinctively took in his own.

As I removed my hand, he looked down at his own palm and saw the RC disc there. He'd obviously heard of me before as his eyes narrowed in fear.

"What do you want?", he asked.

"The same as I've always wanted.", I replied, my voice muffled through the bandana I wore across my face, "justice."

Then I played him the tapes. The numerous times that he'd been speeding along built-up roads, slowing only as he approached speed cameras; the websites that he'd visited that were borderline legal; the copyrighted material he had stolen for his sermons; and the times when he was stumbling around the house after a few too many red wines.

"I think.", I said to him, "that the expression is something like, judge not lest you be judged. Drop the case. That's all I'm asking."

"But…"

"No.", I interrupted him, "no buts. This is about freedom. I agree with you that the t-shirt is offensive but then, some might be offended by your theft of music and your speeding. If you're doing it in God's name, then you're wrong. Don't you think God has bigger things to concern Himself with these days? If you're doing it in your own name, then you have to accept the balance. Just drop the case."

I'd left the area before hearing about the outcome. I'd like to think that North and his family were enjoying a picnic together at the same spot, and that he had on a slightly less controversial article of clothing.

Singh happened a few weeks later. I was heading down from Cheshire and into the potteries when King asked if there was anything I could do. It was actually very easy. I met with Singh at home and, as he opened his front door, I handed him the surveyors report on the ground radiation being emitted from underneath the factory. I let him read it as I waited, then I showed him another report that showed the levels of radiation under his family home.

"It's very simple," I told him, "and all you have to do is forget the plans you have for selling off the pottery and its land. The radiation isn't what it seems, but there is no way that you could convince any surveyor of that. You persist and I do the same with all your properties and your family's properties too. Goodnight."

It was Adam who had developed the faux-radiation. It was harmless in itself but it worked by reverse-engineering the equipment that was available to surveyors. A simple solution that deceived the scanning equipment and could make the safest of locations look more dangerous than a burnt-out nuclear reactor core. It did the job. And still I hadn't had to don the ubiquitous outfit.

I did use it for the animal shelter. I needed its speed and manoeuvrability as I commanded the army of robots that Adam sent me to rebuild, repair and repaint the burnt-out shell. It wasn't just an act of unprovoked charity. I'd been in the area anyway, and when I heard about the arson attack, I remembered the name of the place. It was the shelter that had rescued Fred and from which Jean had bought him to me. I owed them and it was a joy to help them out in some small way. It also gave me a chance to share the workload with a new-found friend.

Chapter Fifty-One

It was still the people that made living on a boat so enjoyable. Not just the passers-by who you knew looked at these little tin cans and wondered about the people who lived in them. There were more of us around now, and it was becoming a more respectable thing to do, but we remained strangers to those who dwelt in bricks and mortar. We were the different. We were the other. To them, we were poor, struggling, loners and, possibly, dangerous. It was only when you met them on the towpath and engaged in conversation that they understood that we were the same as them. The mystery of what went on behind those tatty curtains was nothing more than the mystery of what happened behind the nets of suburbia. They discovered that we read books, watched television, listened to the radio and even, that we had internet access. They also discovered that some of us were doctors, teachers, middle-managers and even writers. It never ceased to give me pleasure to be a part of one of those conversations when the veil of mystery was torn in two.

Then there were the other boaters. Jean had been right. There were more stories here to tell than could ever be written down. There was the couple who had given up good jobs to try their hand at selling books off a boat. I moored next to them somewhere near Sandbach and was able to restock my library, although they couldn't help me out with the third book in a brilliant Ken Follett trilogy that I had been immersed in for the last couple of weeks. The weather was disappointing and it presented them with a huge challenge as they tried to trade. Not only was rain the biggest enemy of books, but it also kept people away from the towpaths. They were stoical about it nonetheless, happy to have escaped the rat-race and still able to survive on the savings they had. I forget their names, but I can't forget their dedication. As I was leaving the following day, they approached me with a package in their hands.

"Got it for you.", the man said.

"What's that?", I asked, letting the dogs run up to them to say goodbye.

"Your book.", he told me, "the one you wanted. Got hold of a copy for you."

I took the book and paid him, wondering how they'd pulled that one off. I didn't ask but I knew that, despite the humble beginnings of their new business, they were passionate about service and would make it through.

Then there were the other trading boats that I passed along the way. I waited outside Chester whilst a self-trained artist painted a portrait of the dogs for me. She was just starting in this line but already had a number of orders. It had all happened by accident. Having found herself retired, she tried her hand at painting a few of the traditional forms of canal art and progressed from there. The painting was beautiful and will be a permanent reminder to me not only of those canine companions, but also of the hidden talents that hide away in so many people. I was sure that despite what the nation had been through, the bombings, for all their harm and heartache, would bring about more of this discovery of skills as people chose to explore the potential inside themselves. That was the new zeitgeist of the age, as the lost promise of security and the belief in a guarantee of tomorrow freed up those who would otherwise have planned their lives more rigorously. It wasn't a carefree, hedonistic foolishness, but instead, the expression of a new-found freedom and a desire to make things that little bit better.

I found my level with the trading boat that offered everything needed for home brewing. It was always a challenge on a boat, due to limited water supplies, but it started me on a passion that continues to this day in a slightly different form. I don't go for the fancy recipes, although I did experiment with some lethal combinations of hedgerow plants. No, I was happy to let the brewers and the vintners do the hard work and let me feel that I'd earned the beer and wine that I drank. I was a little more controlled than I had been, but I was never going to be a fully-paid up member of the temperance movement.

Aside from the traders, there were the day-trippers, the hire-boaters and, of course the liveaboard residents. Some I'd met before. Most were new faces. Some boats I recognised but they'd changed hands as their previous owners had moved on, or passed away. All were a happy bunch, although to listen to a few of them, you'd think they were never happier than when they were putting the world to rights or telling you what the problem with the canals was. Even with these people, time passed with them wasn't as draining as with those who I often met in the pubs and who clearly had real worries weighing them down. It was another characteristic of canal people. They might fuss and moan and complain, but they didn't carry those complaints around with them every day, dragging them down and twisting their faces with anger and bitterness. No, they just told it like it is and from the perspective that their own situation was as good as it gets and they were comfortable with life's imperfections.

Bernie helped me to paint out some of the scratches that I'd accrued since moving back on board. That must have been around about October, just as the last of the Indian Summer was passing over and we were all preparing for the colder weather. We were moored together just past Etruria. I was merrily sanding and scraping away when he approached and we had the usual rambling conversation about anything and everything and the shared contacts that we had. He grabbed a piece of sandpaper as we talked and we worked together until the first coat of paint was due to go on. I bought out my box of brushes and he rummaged through until he found one he was happy with. By the end of the day, that side was done and we agreed to turn the boat tomorrow and do the other side.

"Been a while since I've done this.", he told me, "But she looks good, doesn't she? You've got a nice boat there. Reminds me a little of my first one. I had that boat for thirty years. She was my part of the divorce. Still, best move I made. My daughter's talking about getting one as well, when she retires next year."

That led to the inevitable question about his age and I nearly fell over when he told me.

"I'll be eighty-six next month.", he said as if it was just another fact, "I was a war baby. My Dad never returned from the fighting but he left me behind to help me Mum. Mind you, that all seems such a long time ago."

"You must have seen a lot?", I asked him.

"Oh, yes.", he smiled as he replied, putting his hand on my shoulder, "I think I can safely say that I've seen the best of it and the worst. You're still young. You've got a long life ahead of you, but I'm happy to be where I am now and not to have to face what you might have to. That London thing was wicked. I thought I'd never see man do that to man for such a stupid reason, but you never can tell, can you? No, I've served my time. I'd like to hit the hundred, but I take it as it comes now."

He was right. I was still young. I felt like my life was over and that I'd had the best of it, but I was still only mid-forties. I'd suffered a little along the way but the war-wounds didn't really trouble me. And, like Bernie, I'd seen the best of people and the worst. Perhaps now I had paid my dues and could relax a bit. That said, it wasn't as if I was under a huge amount of pressure.

I'd been in the Stoke area because of its travel links which I needed as I prepared for the event that was the highlight of the year for me and which still fills me with a deep and satisfying joy. At the end of September, Adam married Charlotte in the same village church where Jean and I had tied the knot only a couple of years before. I won't say that it didn't hurt a little to be in that same building and to see the new life being forged in front of me against a backdrop of the lost future that Jean and I had looked forward to. If there was any blessing in the type of death that Jean endured, it was that we had time to talk about moving on. She would have hated to see the drunken, broken wreck that I became. She wanted me to live life to the full and not to make her death my own as well. It would have been. Bizarrely, it had been The Event that gave me my life back.

At the reception, I was introduced to the sister that I didn't know that Philip Rivers had. He made a bee-line for me as soon as the party started. If his voice hadn't been so distinctive, I might have wondered who he was. He looked so different. Gone was the timid young lad who thought he had no future and, in his place, stood a young man who carried himself with confidence and who had earned his place as Manager of the boat-builders.

"This is Dana.", he told me as he dragged his sister to meet me, "Dana, this is Steve. You know. The one that I told you about?".

"It's an honour.", she said to me, "and I can't thank you enough for how you've helped Philip. We thought we'd lost him, but now, well, look at him. Hard to think that this is my little brother."

Dana was a Doctor. Five years older than Philip, she'd been in general practice for a couple of years. The family resemblance was only slight. She was slim, whilst Philip liked his beer and didn't worry about it showing on him. She was a fiery red-head, whereas he had the blackest hair imaginable.

"I'm not really his sister.", she whispered to me as we stood together later and after he had gone to dance with his gang, "at least, not his natural one. I was adopted. But I love him to bits anyway. You saved his life, you know?"

I brushed her compliments away.

"No, please.", she made me look in her eyes, "You need to know that. Philip was broken-hearted when he heard about Jean and how it affected you. He's so pleased to see you. And so am I."

350

"Ah, but you don't know me.", I tried lamely to steer the conversation to safer ground.

"I know of you.", she replied, drawing us to the side of the room, "But, I don't know as much as I'd like. The fact is, I was wondering if it might be possible…"

She stopped mid-sentence, uncertain whether to carry on.

"Go on.", I encouraged her, "You may as well spit it out. What's on your mind?"

"I want to be a part of it.", she said, turning her head away as she spoke.

"Of what?", I hid my question behind a laugh.

"Of what you do.", she said more determinedly now, "I want to be a part of this team. Righteous Correction, J for Justice, secret agents."

"I don't think you do.", I told her, "It's a lot to ask. And maybe now isn't the right time and place. Why don't we meet another time? You can come for a cruise on the boat, see what Philip gets so excited about."

We agreed and set a date. I didn't really have any other commitments. Her diary was a bit less flexible. We arranged to meet in Birmingham in October.

Chapter Fifty-Two

Dana was naturally beautiful in that way that needed no make-up. She had a perfectly proportioned body and was armed with a cheeky flirtatiousness that I don't think she was even aware of. Despite all that, I never for one moment thought of her in a sexual way. Besides which, even if a new relationship had been my desire or intention, the age difference was uncomfortably wide. That said, I found myself thinking about Dana a lot and looking forward to our spending some time together. There was something about her that I liked. She seemed to have a uniquely hungry spirit inside her and a passion to serve. On top of all that, something inside me told me that she might help me to move ahead in the way that I wanted to. Prior to her visit, I made contact with Jason King and was in full possession of all the facts about her. Facts that were encouraging.

I met her at New Street Station. She only had one small case, which I offered to carry for her, not being surprised when she said that she'd be fine. We walked through the madness and chaos of the city centre, now busier than ever since becoming the new London. I showed her the new Parliament building that was being hastily constructed on semi-derelict land that had once housed the factories that were the work-engine of this nation. Shortly after that, we were walking down through Gas Street Basin and I helped her onto the boat.

"Apologies for the security measures.", I told her as I made her wait in the entrance to the boat whilst the computer scanned her and her luggage, "but I'm sure you understand why."

The machines passed her as being safe and I gave her the five-minute tour of the boat, placing her bag on the pull-out bed that I'd converted earlier from the dining table. That was after she'd been introduced to the two dogs. They liked her. Fred in particular, never one to make me feel he needed me, made a new friend and gave me that look he was so good at when she let him follow her around.

"It's all pretty much as you'd have in a house.", I explained, "Everything's normal, except of course, the dreaded toilet. Don't worry, it won't bite. I'm sure as a Doctor though, you're not that squeamish."

She settled in and we walked the canal in the chill of the October evening, eating out at a very nice restaurant that I'd used many times before. We talked small talk and I picked up an evening paper on the way. It was that paper that told me the news about the rescue centre.

"Could you just excuse me for one minute, please?", I asked her as we returned to the boat, "I need to do a little bit of, shall we say, private, work. I'll just have to shut the door across."

I made contact with Adam and told him how he could help me. He promised delivery within a day or so. The items would be dropped near the boat and home in on me.

"Thanks,", I said, "and thinking about it, could you do me one other favour?"

I told him what it was.

"Probably the same size as me,", I answered his last question, "although, adjust it for the gender difference as you think appropriate."

I returned to Dana, apologised for leaving her, then offered her a drink.

"Just a mineral water.", she said, "I don't actually drink alcohol."

I was surprised. She didn't seem to be that sort.

"It's not what you think,", she said, "and please, go ahead and have one yourself. It's a medical thing. I tried one drink once and something happened. Apparently, I am hyper-sensitive to alcohol. That's why I leave it. It could be worse, and it saves me a fortune."

"Could do with a dose of that myself,", I said as I poured a smallish whisky, "but I think I'm in control of it now."

"So,", I continued, "what do you really want to talk about?"

She was totally open with me. It was as she'd said at the wedding. She'd heard how Philip had been helped by a mystery man, armed with various gadgets. She'd delved into things as much as she could and made the link with King and the marina. And me. But that was all she knew, apart from the copious amounts of information that had made their way into the public domain after London, about the unnamed heroes and heroines who averted a bigger catastrophe. Some of it was accurate, some dangerously perceptive, but a lot of it was fantasist's speculation.

"Then, when Philip introduced us at the wedding,", she concluded, "I thought I'd take the chance and stick my neck out. Now, here we are."

"Here we are indeed.", I sighed, "But the question is, where do we go from here?"

"I want to know, Steve, that's all.", she implored me to talk, "You can trust me. I won't tell anyone and I have my reasons. Genuine ones. I'll tell you more if you give me a hint of what I'm dealing with."

"You know,", I turned and looked her full in the face, "that expression, the one that goes something like, if I tell you, I will have to kill you? Well, before I say anything, let me be very, very clear. I think we can trust you. The truth is, I've had every data file pulled on you and you come up clean. But if you share what I tell you with anyone unauthorised, you will be killed. So, do you still want to know?"

She settled in to listen after agreeing to the conditions without hesitation. I told her about ORB, about how I'd got involved with them, and I gave her a flavour of some the things that I'd done. I confirmed Jason King's role in it all, and the reasons he had split with the Order. Finally, I filled her in on London.

"Boy, that's some story.", she said as I finished up, "And it explains a lot. You hide it well but the scars are there aren't they?"

I shrugged her concerns away.

"Never mind.", she moved on, "I don't need to know. But you must be aware of what I'm going to ask you next."

I nodded.

"And?", she asked.

"It's not for me to say.", I told her, "It's as simple as that. You've approached me, I've spoken to you and you've made your request clear. What I need to know though, is why?"

"And please,", I stopped her before she had a chance to say anything, "remember that it is that single word and your response to it that will decide whether things progress or not. So, why?"

"You're going to tell me that its corny,", she began, "but I'll say it anyway. I want to make a difference. A positive difference. More of a difference than a GP alone could ever make."

"You're right,", I replied, "it's corny."

"But, that's not all,", she continued, "you see, I think that I have gifts that can be used. Special gifts. And that's not me being arrogant or vain, it's just the way it is."

"We know all about your gifts,", I told her, "and yes, we're impressed. Starred First, Oxford, top of every group you've ever been in and, more importantly, feted by every pharmaceutical company around the world, but choosing instead to practice as a GP."

"Although," I continued, waiting to see the shock on her face, "your work as a GP isn't the only work you do, is it? Let's see now, rumours of a breakthrough contribution to the company who finally developed the total cure for HIV, more rumours of support to businesses developing a reversal cure for MS and then, the biggest rumour of them all. Let me see, patent number: XF/11/RG567/089. Single dose cure for childhood leukaemia. Filed by The Young Person's Cancer Trust. Making them a fortune by all accounts. Anything to say?"

"I knew somebody would find out one day," she sighed as she spoke, "and I'm only glad that it's you. But, it's not exactly what it seems. You see, I told you one of the reasons that I want to join up is to use my gifts. Let me show you what my gift is."

She asked me to take my shirt off. I obliged and registered the look on her face as she saw the multiple scars that now criss-crossed my torso.

"Hmm," she said, "bullet wounds, knives and even the odd burn. You earn your reputation."

She put her hand on my shoulder, the one that had only recently been repaired and which still gave me trouble, especially on cold mornings.

"You have a guy called James," she said as she moved her fingers gently over my shoulder, "who works with you. Phil's told me about him. He has a talent. When it comes to computers and the invisible world of the atomic, it's like he can see deeper than anyone else."

I nodded, feeling my shoulder starting to warm up.

"Well, that's similar to my gift," she explained, "But in biology, not physics. I can feel the individual cells in bodies and I can sense the pulse of life at its most basic level. They did a good job on this shoulder. King must have access to some of the best surgeons there are. But they didn't quite put it right. Still, it's an easy fix."

It almost felt like her fingers had penetrated beneath my skin, but there was no pain. My shoulder relaxed and seemed to yield to her touch. Then the heat built up some more before subsiding as she removed her hand.

"It won't trouble you again," she told me, "in fact, it's better than ever now. Can I do a couple of the ribs as well please. They won't take a second."

As she slept that night, I thought about our next steps. I'd never seen anything like what she could do and I knew that her assessment was right. She was to medicine what James was to computer science. Her motivation was there. I'd known it from the start, but I'd needed to know more than simply her

355

passion to make a difference. I liked the anonymous way she was already doing more good than most of us and that spoke volumes to me. The only missing link, as far as I was concerned, was to understand how exactly she wanted to contribute. Did she understand the dangers that we faced in the field? Did she even begin to comprehend just how difficult it was to look someone in the eye and then calmly remove that same organ? Could she accept that she would disappear and her name would never be spoken again? I thought maybe she could. When Adam's delivery came, I'd be able to find out for sure.

Before the package arrived, I had lots to work through with Dana. I wanted to test her and compare her reactions to my own. I began at the beginning and we spent the whole of the next day running through the casebook of my past missions. In general, she responded well. Her proposals for action were tamer than my actual response had been, but that wasn't necessarily a bad thing. In some cases, I listened to her ideas and then blew them apart. She hated it when that happened. In other cases, she suggested a game plan that would have been a lot easier and a lot more effective than what I'd actually done. I brushed over those ones.

"Steve," she said as she settled that evening with Gilly and Fred either side of her, "I didn't realise just what you'd had to do. Let me ask you now. Why?"

I'd already told her about Fran and the children and what had started me out in this. I'd explained the choice I had made to become another person, in order to pursue justice. And I'd told her how I had tried to quit, but just kept getting drawn back in.

"I'm not like you," I told her, "and I don't see that I have a gift. Everything I do is helped along by machines and numerous technologies. That's why you're that bit special. ORB operatives and King's team in general, we don't have supernatural talents. We're not like the comic book superheroes of old. We play a part but, underneath the uniform, we're just ordinary people. If we have a gift, it can only be a passion for what we do, and maybe an active imagination."

"You do have a gift, Steve," she said, "believe me. If I had to define it in medical terms, I couldn't. If you asked me to explain it in simple terms, I couldn't. But it's there. It's that willingness to serve however you are called to serve, to do what needs to be done and to defy convention. It's that power to rise above the norm and challenge conventional wisdom. And what makes it special is that you have to do it anonymously and humbly."

356

"Maybe," I answered, "but I feel like a fraud sometimes. And it's harder to justify things now that the technology pretty much does everything we need it to."

That's when I told her why I had wanted to see her so much. Why I had decided to pursue her request and let her in on the secrets I knew. I told her that I wanted to move on. My luck would run out and I was less passionate about things now. In short, I wanted to retire from this bizarre second-life and hand over to someone else.

"We're going to have some fun tomorrow," I told her, "but if it works out and you still want to be a part of this, then I'll recommend you. I'll tell Jason that I've found a replacement."

Chapter Fifty-Three

"Don't worry,", I told Dana, as we shuffled around in the confined space of the boat preparing for the day, "they won't expect you to have to live like this. It's my choice, and not to everyone's taste."

"I like it.", she replied, then paused and added a rider, "But no, I don't think I could do it all the time. I need a bit more space and I like the security of staying in one location."

"Whatever happens,", I assured her, "nobody will expect you to be someone you're not. They'll help you build an identity around the person that you are. That's what happened with me. I'm a boater first, a solitary soul that struggles with the sound and fury of that space beyond the water. Kingfisher is a reflection, not the source."

My plan for the day was two-fold. Firstly, I wanted to cruise with Dana and show off the lifestyle that I so enjoyed. We'd leave Gas Street and head out through numerous locks until we were on our way back towards the heart of the Staffordshire waterways. That would be my Winter home. I wanted to relive the past and visit the old places, and I needed to convince myself that I could let go of yesterday and being to live for a new future.

Once out of Birmingham, we would return that evening by other means. That was stage two of the day's activities. I had some work to do and Dana was going to help me.

We took the easier route out of the city centre, travelling East along the network of arms and junctions that took us to the bottom of the Walsall Canal. Not the most picturesque of our options but certainly a smoother introduction to boating than having to work the lock-flights at Farmer's Bridge and Aston. I got my first taste of Dana's fallibility at Smethwick. This was her introductory set of locks and, at the first one, despite my detailed and enthusiastic coaching, she still got it all wrong. As is the tradition on the canals, I was at the helm while she worked the paddles and swung the gates. At least, that was how we'd planned it. When the lock wasn't filling after a lengthy wait, I grabbed the centre-rope and clambered up the weed-stained ladder to see what the problem was.

"Okay", I told Dana, "now, you've emptied the lock fine. And you did the gates okay."

"But it won't fill up?", she was genuinely puzzled.

"Maybe", I said as I took the windlass from her, "we should drop the lower paddles first. That might help."

She watched as I closed the paddles on the lower gates, stopping the outflow of all the incoming water and allowing the lock to fill. It was the same mistake that I'd made on numerous occasions when I'd been a novice. I tried to be encouraging but Dana was clearly annoyed with herself.

"So stupid of me", she said, "and so embarrassing. You must think me an idiot."

She got it right at the next lock, but at the third lock, she forgot to check that I was ready and sent the boat flying first, backwards into the rear gates, then fast-forward into the front gates.

"Sorry!", she shouted, "I forgot."

The boat had had to put up with a lot more than that before. And I'd been in worse situations. It didn't really bother me too much and it was a standard error made by those new to the system. It was worse when you had another boat's crew do it to you. They were trying to help so you didn't want to have too much of a go at them, but sometimes it made for some scary moments.

"It's a slow world down here", I explained to Dana as we continued on our way, "and the usual rules about speed and motion don't apply. We live on canal time here. That's the time when what happens does so at its own pace and will reward impatience with an even longer delay. And it's the natural chronology that says that we have to fit into the situation and not try to make the situation fit our notion of time. Lock queues are a chance to make new friends and guiding another boat up or down a lock is an opportunity to show that you are a part of this slower world. Next time, a thumbs-up to the skipper to confirm he's ready, with a little less enthusiasm on the paddles and it'll be fine."

What I didn't tell Dana was how happy I was that she had made these errors. The reports that I'd read and the list of her achievements, not to mention the power she demonstrated last night, had all made me think that she was a little too good to be true. James would never have made those

359

mistakes at locks. He was able to see the maths behind them. Dana was a brilliant biologist and Doctor, yes, but she was not so hot on mechanics. That was good to know. We all need our weaknesses.

We moored up that afternoon in a spot that offered a little bit of countryside hidden away in the shadows of a very functional urban space. It was the sort of place that they told you to avoid if possible, but also the type of place where I had met some great people. If you take the boats off the canal, make some areas a no-go zone, then boats become the intruder. I preferred to face the less-used spaces head on and show the locals that we wanted to keep their part of the network moving. Aside from a few late-night revellers knocking on the windows, my approach had paid off. Young and old, cyclists and under-bridge drinkers, they all liked to see the boats and they paid back your respect for them by respecting you. Healthy concern was always a sensible precaution, but fear only ever nurtures fear. So much of it was about ignoring the conventional wisdom and trying an imaginative approach: I remembered Manchester and the warnings I'd been given about a certain lock flight. That flight presented no problem to me as I simply welcomed the groups of youths who were hanging around and enlisted them to help me for the price of a few cans of beer. They saw me through and we parted as friends.

I was vindicated in my choice of location when we chose to eat at the local pub. It was a proper spit and sawdust place, once the haunt of weary boaters and a building that hid its heritage well under years of poor renovations. It was also a pub that did what pubs do and it had a great choice of proper beer at sensible prices. I was glad that Dana didn't drink because I knew that if she did, she would be a wine drinker, and that place didn't have a bottle on show. Having the dogs with us helped. Fred had some sort of in-built homing ability that meant we would never have to worry about finding a drinking hole. Once inside, he would tart around with anyone and everyone and he was impossible to dislike. Gilly was a little more reserved and tended to sit on my knee, although we had to keep her on a lead as she could bolt without warning if another dog arrived.

The only problem we found though, was they didn't serve food. It was a problem quickly solved.

"You'll be alright.", the landlady told us, rolling out the words in a thick, Black Country accent that I wouldn't attempt to emulate, "I've got all the take-away menus here and you just go ahead and order whatever you want. I'll sort you out with plates and cutlery. You just make yourselves at home."

It didn't happen like that in many places. Dana was stunned. We were the least likely people to be sat in that place and yet, far from being looked on as strangers, we were welcomed as family. When the food arrived, we passed around some of the extra starters that we'd ordered for the other pub-goers and, by the time we'd cleared our plates, we already knew a little too much about some of the things that were going on locally. The hot topic of the night was the daughter of the local Vicar who had just been arrested on a drugs charge. When they exhausted that, we discovered that Geoff had run over his own dog last week, but that it was making a full recovery, Margaret was seeing a lad young enough to be her grandson, and Terry had just moved in with Jim. That's Terry, a male, and Jim, a male. Things like that, apparently, didn't go on around here.

We left at closing time. Or at least, we left at the official closing time. There were quite a few still in the pub when we departed giving us the sense that closing time was a very loosely defined term. We still had work to do, and I was glad to have Dana with me, or I might have been persuaded to stay a little longer.

"You sure you'll be alright?", Dana asked me as we walked the short distance back to the boat.

"I'll be fine.", I told her, "My metabolism is the opposite of yours. Give me half an hour and I'll be sober again. Mind you, I don't often operate at a zero blood-alcohol level. I find a little juice in the system helps me do a better job."

Back at the boat, we unpacked the gifts that Adam had sent us. They were assorted animals, scraped together from prototypes that he had around and included squirrels, rats and various birds. Dana looked confused.

"My friends.", I told her, "This is how it all started. They blend in with the surroundings, usually. Tonight's a bit different. I just want to show you what we can achieve with a little help."

"I'll miss them all.", I told her, "but they are becoming less necessary. Remember the old days when you got your music on a vinyl disc and had to load it into elaborate machinery? Well now, it's all invisible and played through the air. That's the way of these beasties. We don't really need them anymore. You'll be working in a much more modern way, I'm sure."

I demonstrated the abilities of some of the animals, and then opened up the inner-heart of the boat for Dana to see the vast array of electronics that supported us in our work. I took her through the tracking system and the locator controls, explaining that tonight, we would let the computer do the work. We zoomed in on the piles of building materials that had been delivered to a discrete location earlier in the days, and I let the computer put together the image of what we would be building.

"Which just leaves one thing.", I smiled as I went to my wardrobe, "Your suit."

I closed the door to my room and emerged minutes later in my work outfit.

"You have a slightly different version,", I told her, "although Adam asked me to tell you it's only a prototype. You get to choose the final look."

I unwrapped the last of the packages we'd received and handed Dana the box containing her suit. Her hands trembled as she opened it, at which point, I excused myself and let her try it on. When she called me back, I liked what I saw. It was plain, dark grey and with a squarer helmet than mine.

"How do I use it?", she asked.

"Don't ask me,", I laughed, "ask her. Adam tells me that she's called Patsy. Prototype, androgynous, test suit one. PATS1. Mine's Kirsty. Similar logic."

And so it was that Dana was introduced to the joys of underwater travel, anti-gravity flight and increased powers of sight and sound. She took to it straightaway. That was no surprise to me as Adam had explained that this suit was different to mine in that it had organic sensors. It was more of a second skin than an exoskeleton. It was perfect for Dana.

The work on the animal shelter was over too quickly. It had needed an army of helpers but with the two of us assisting, the refurbishment was completed before sunrise. We had to leave before we could get all of the paint to dry, but it had come together well. Dana loved the suit. It helped her stretch beyond the confines of her own human limits and perform actions that she'd only ever dreamt of. To me, this was fairly normal. Okay, it was a departure in terms of the type of work I was doing, but I was used to being in a suit that made me superhuman. It would be a while before Dana truly understood that, with the kit we were provided with, the only limits were those we set ourselves.

We slept late the following morning, letting our bodies recover from the exertion of the night before. I woke before Dana. I'd set an alarm to make sure that I did. I had a small job to do that had to be done without her knowledge. Using the smaller of my keyboards, I lay in bed and typed out a message to Jason King. It was a long and detailed report, rambling in parts and over-technical in others, but the core message was simple: Dana was something special and somebody that King really ought to meet with, and soon.

Chapter Fifty-Four

Come December, Dana Rivers was no more. She continued to practice medicine, but was now doing so under a new identity and away from the public gaze. This was a new departure for Jason King. He was no longer striving simply for justice. Now he sought justice and healing. In a nation still reeling from The Event, desperate for the opportunity to overcome its collective grief and to believe again in the goodness of humanity, King sought to make his contribution. All I knew was that she had taken on the identity of The Medic. She was working with James as a part of the J for Justice campaign and they were thriving together. That order was now the one that was synonymous with correcting imbalances in the judicial system. Righteous Correction appeared to be so yesterday.

For my part, I was happy with that. The red button still remained unpressed, although it seemed to call to me every day. That button had always been there. It was the button that I was to press if the security of the boat and its secrets was under threat. And it was the button I was to press if I ever chose to permanently distance myself from my alter ego. It was the button that turned the boat into any other boat on the water and which removed, destroyed or disabled any of the additional trimmings that it was fitted with. I'd hung up the suit for the last time. That much I was sure of. And yet, there remained a part of me that was reluctant to completely surrender that part of my past. I guess that was all a part of the transition. Losing an identity is never easy and only possible when a new one takes its place.

That new identity for me was to be as a cataloguer of the waterways. The idea had come to me when I'd met Bernie and realised the number of potential years that lay ahead of me. In that time, I could cruise the network multiple times and pursue the dream that Jean had had. I would spend my days exploring every mile of the canal network and record the minutiae of what I saw. The record would be available to all who wanted to access it and would detail the hidden wonders of this secretive part of England. It would map out the best dog-walking routes, the quirky pubs that allowed you to order take-away, and it would explore the history of the most fragmented remains of buildings along the way. I was looking forward to those years of freedom. They would be years of a true freedom, released from the past and embracing every day as if it were my last. And I would leave behind a legacy. It might be read by millions, or it might only help a handful of curious individuals. It didn't matter to me. I wasn't in search of fame and glory, nor did I need to earn the riches that tempted others. I had enough and that was enough for me.

It was the beginnings of this project that saw me Wintering in familiar territory. I'd planned to trawl the old haunts to bury the past, but now I had a secondary purpose and one which would make the process one not just of burial, but of resurrection. The same places where yesterday would be put away, were those where I would put on the future. For that reason, I was moored up opposite to the house that Fran and I had shared when the first snows of the year fell. The house had changed little over the years and I was pleased to see one of our Boat Space boats moored up at the end of the garden. The owners could never know the links that vessel had with that house, nor could they begin to comprehend the previous owner. Ten years ago, I was ten-foot away, playing around with a ratty old Springer. Now I was on the opposite bank and in a different boat. Who could comprehend the huge experiences that spanned that narrow gap?

With the waterways quiet and the temperature still above freezing, I made an initial pass of the area and took the boat first, to Gailey and Penkridge, then returned back on myself to Wolseley Bridge, Rugeley and Fradley. The towers of the power station were long gone, replaced by a new housing estate, but the monolith that is the Armitage Shanks' works remained. It would be my first entry in the journal I had chosen to write. The world had used their products for years, their name was familiar to all who'd ever passed water, and yet, the factory was no historic landmark. I proposed to change that. I wanted people to stop here and wonder that such a hidden gem could have changed the world in its own way so much. If you were passing by road through the town of Armitage, you'd likely miss it. But from the canal, it was all different. You could see how the building had been constructed to work with the waterway and you could watch the transfer of their wares from the building and onto the lorries that would take them out to the houses, hotels, palaces and prisons the world over. And it was all so English. You won't see any of your Japanese scrubbed-clean, gleaming façade here. No, the windows were still broken and covered in a fine white dust, whilst the rejects were still smashed by sledgehammer in the yard, for all the world to see.

I couldn't think of a better start to my new work and spent several days in the area mapping out the walking routes nearby and the various 'must see' parts of this tiny enclave. This was the town that was home to the chip shop that served food beyond compare. The best fish and chips served alongside the finest kebabs and all from an almost invisible building. This was also the town that had pubs worth visiting in their own right. The Crown was finally maximising its potential as a canal side haunt, returning to its former glory and standing as an illustration of what the water was all about. Here was the canal, traversed by an original bridge, upon which the ancient road continued and beside which stood the original building built to serve the bargees who moved the wealth of the nation about.

I was quite excited as I began to record the smallest details of what I saw. Of course, over time, things would change. They always did. Sometimes for the better and sometimes for the worse. All I could do was provide my own snapshot of places as I saw them in my small portion of time.

Beyond Armitage, Fradley offered the same boating facilities that it always had and remained a popular destination for boaters and walkers alike. The pub, so full of memories already, guaranteed to offer more at every visit and I even considered making mention of the piggery worker who I met again on this visit. There were numerous characters on the cut and Jean had wanted to record them all. I was tempted, but chose to forego this aspect as they would always be there. I would try and encourage people to the places, hope that they understood the culture of friendliness to strangers that was so much a part of boating culture, and then trust fate to lead them to the types of encounters that had been the richest part of my own life on the canals. That said, I recorded the piggery as a point of interest. It was on a nice walk for the dogs and one which the walker could vary according to whether they wanted to escape from it all, or divert to a local supermarket instead.

Choosing not to take the Coventry Canal this time, I dropped down to Alrewas, checked out the pubs that remained and called on the owners of the house that I had always wanted to buy. I wasn't in the market, but I did want to check that they were okay with me putting it in the book. They were fine with it. And why not? This was quintessential England and had to be recorded for posterity. Aside from the thatched roof, it embraced its adjacency to the canal and had a little boat moored up outside. The owners too were always ready with a wave to passers-by and that made a difference. Too many people hid away in their homes. You couldn't do that. Not if you wanted to connect with humanity.

Coming back on myself and up towards Great Haywood again, Christmas was nearly upon me. That was how I'd planned it. I wanted to spend my Christmas in Weston, moored at The Saracen's Head and closing the year with a final farewell at the church. There was plenty to fill a chapter of a book here and I spent the first few days retracing old walks and cataloguing what I saw. The Saracen's had been transformed. It had been a good pub before, always happy to see new dogs. Now it was a small hotel and had been comprehensively modernised. I thought that I'd be disappointed at the death of one of my favourite places, instead, I was impressed that they had taken the best and somehow made it better. They still welcomed the dogs and were there with free treats for them straightaway. I was so impressed I chose to have my Christmas Lunch there. And yes, I could bring the dogs.

The owners of Weston Hall also gave me free reign to snout about the place and write them up in my book. The Hall had been a regular for Fran and I when we had something to celebrate. The décor had changed a little but the ambience remained in the casual restaurant built into the old cellar. I enjoyed a few pints there with the owners giving me the potted history of this five-hundred-year-old building. They gave me the full tour and all the information that I needed about the various ghosts that were supposed to inhabit the place. I can't say I believed in all that but it went in the book anyway. It wasn't for me to judge. My new role was as a chronicler and not a critic. Let people make their own minds up.

And so, it went on; the festive season came and went and the New Year appeared. This was 2028. It was more than just another change of date as it was the first new year since the bombings. Across the nation, everybody used that time to embrace the opportunity ahead and try to make a clean start. Millions mourned as the new bell installed in what was left of the old Houses of Parliament rang in its first new year. Millions mourned but also offered their thanks that they were not among the millions who had been denied their time. It was a time of great sadness, but also a time of genuine togetherness for those who remained.

I walked back from the pub and headed to the church as their own midnight service was ending. Tonight, I would say goodbye to Fran and the children for the last time, touching the plaque that had been installed in their memory before walking into the future. As I held my hand against it, a familiar voice spoke to me.

"I remember you," the Vicar said, "from a number of years ago. Is that right?"

"You've got a good memory," I told him, "yes, it was me. Five years ago, I think. I've been by a few other times though. They were very dear to me."

"That's right," he held out his hand to me, "you were a close friend of the family. Well, good to see you again and a Happy New Year."

"And to you," I replied, letting his handshake turn into an embrace.

"Yes," he looked closely into my eyes, "I do remember now. We talked about justice, I think. Gosh, how much I remember of that day. Are you staying nearby?"

I told him about the boat and about my plans. I would be leaving in a day or two but wanted to use the space at the Saracen's to work on the first chapters of my book. I was also able to access the web using their free and fast service rather than the shaky connection that I had on-board.

"Perhaps I'll see you there," he said as he turned to return to the Vicarage.

"Maybe," I answered, "or if not, in another five years."

We parted and I returned home. Within a few days I would be heading away again, hoping not to be constrained too much by ice, but willing to accept whatever happened. Remembering that Vicar reminded me of the struggles I'd continued to have in knowing what was right or wrong and in understanding my role as a killer for justice. I don't think I ever squared the circle and yet, now I didn't have to. That was all yesterday and I was free to be me now. At least, that's what I thought. It didn't quite work out as I'd planned.

,

Chapter Fifty-Five

'National Daily News', 2nd January, 2028

'Police Arrest Vigilante Suspect'

West Midlands Police have confirmed that they have arrested a suspect in relation to the so-called 'Righteous Correction' case, recently reopened by its new Chief Constable. The arrests took place in a late-night raid on a canal side pub in the Staffordshire area.

The unnamed suspect, a male in his late forties, who is believed to live on a boat moored nearby, was detained after a tip-off from a local Vicar. Armed police surrounded the pub where the suspect was drinking but were able to affect an arrest without any apparent resistance, despite his being protected by two dogs.

In a statement to the press, Chief Constable Victor Donovan, said that, although these were early days in the investigation, he is confident that charges will soon be bought and that multiple unsolved crimes will finally be cleared up.

It has been a number of years since 'The Righteous Corrector' was last reported to have struck and it was generally believed that this self-styled vigilante had died in a boat fire. Occasional offences occurring since and using his distinctive RC motto, have been put down to copycat offenders who are either hiding behind that persona or who seek to emulate the Righteous Corrector's search for perceived justice.

(See Also: The End of an Era? Editorial, P.17)

Seems we can never truly distance ourselves from our past. I was relaxing in the pub and making plans for the new year, the dogs sleeping peacefully at my feet, when the Vicar appeared next to me.

"Thought I'd find you in here.", he smiled as he approached me, "can I get you a drink?"

I accepted the offer and waited until he returned with the two pints and sat beside me.

"Cheers.", he said as he lifted his pint.

"Cheers.", I replied, "And thank you."

"Not at all.", he settled in next to me, "I'm glad that I didn't miss you. You see, when you left last night I got to thinking about what we had talked about the last time. The whole search for justice thing and the right of man to revenge injustice. I think that was it, wasn't it?"

"Something like that.", I said, "all to do with the Righteous Corrector. Remember, how they attribute those acts to the late husband of Fran?"

"Oh, yes.", he replied, "I think about that one a lot. I didn't really see the connection when we first met, but in a way, it's a bit of a landmark for the church. That plaque draws me every time I pass it."

"And do you understand better for it?", I asked, curious now about where this was going.

"Who can truly understand.", he said, "when the mysteries of the universe are so deep. And after all that happened last year. Where was God when those attacks happened? I don't know."

"It's beyond me.", I told him, "And I don't have your training or knowledge. I guess we all have to make our own choices."

"Your right.", he said, "That's exactly the point that I've reached. We each have our own choices to make and we can't sit on the fence. It's probably better to make a wrong decision than no decision at all, although we never really know do we?"

"And sometimes decisions are so hard to make.", he continued, "in the face of pressures. Some put pressure on you to take one path, but your head or your heart tells you to take a different route. I've had such a decision to make very recently. One you might relate to. You see, I was asked by my Bishop to keep an eye out around the church. To look for one thing in particular."

I waited as he took a deep draught of his beer. My senses were coming alive and I was checking out the building as he paused.

"Yes," he resumed where he'd left off, "you see that plaque that you were looking at, well, it's a sort of homing beacon isn't it? Numerous people have come to see it, acknowledging its connection with a certain person. I suspected of course. Even on that first night, I had my doubts. But I wasn't being pressured then, you see. I could choose to leave it in the hands of God. But this time, once I knew, I had to act."

"Knew what?", I asked.

"They gave me this device," he showed me a small black box as he leaned closer to me, "that I was to run over the plaque every time I suspected it had been touched. I did the same yesterday, after you'd left. This time it gave me a green light. And that's when I had to make my choice. I just hope I made the right one."

He rose to leave and leant over to me, drawing me to him before he planted a kiss on my cheek. Then I saw the blue lights and heard the vehicle doors slamming.

"A kiss?", I said as I waited.

"Please," the Vicar hurried away, "don't think that I am a Judas. It wasn't an easy decision, but I have to go with my conscience. Good luck."

"You're no more Judas," I smiled as I replied, "than I am Jesus."

Then it took all my effort to hold the dogs back as the waves of armed police entered the building. I wasn't going to resist. I had always known that this might happen. I just had to sort a couple of things out first.

"Jim," I shouted at the barman, "will you look after these two for a while."

He nodded. He got on well with the dogs.

"And," I asked the most senior officer now standing before me and putting me in loose manacles, "Is there any way that I can go back and make the boat secure. Maybe get a few essentials?"

They let me. That was when I pressed the red button. I was accompanied, of course, but they didn't see me press it. As I moved about the cabin and loaded up on clean clothes, vape stuff and other bits and pieces, I knew that underneath me, the Kingfisher and all that that identity had entailed was disappearing. Some would make its way back to the marina, most would simply disintegrate. Pressing the red button would alert King. That was a consequence I'd have preferred to avoid, but I had no choice. He'd be there for me, but I would do this alone.

371

When he visited me the following day, he told me what he suspected had happened. He had to be brief as we were both aware that the room might be recording our words. That said, the watch that Adam had given him to wear would provide nothing to an eavesdropper but a very poor rendition of a Beethoven symphony.

"It all goes back to General Gordon," he told me, "and his dismissal. I knew that he might pursue you but none of us thought he'd get a link with you and Zipoly Hardacre. Seems we underestimated him. He lifted your prints from the meeting room, before you were suited up and had gloves on. They ran them back to Hardacre. He was confused, but knew there was a connection with you and Weston. Along with many others, he asked the Bishop to help out, I think you know the rest."

"They gave him a fingerprint ID kit," I said, resigned now to what had happened, "and I brushed the plaque. Stupid. I should have known. It's the hands. It's always the hands."

It had been those hands that had done so many things. They'd held my children and they'd reconnected me to Jean. They'd nursed her through her illness and they'd buried her. Now, they were to finish me.

"We've got the best defence lawyers available," King told me, "and we will throw everything at this. We're here for you, all of us."

"Not this time," I told him, "and I mean this, so please listen carefully. You and the new team, you're too precious to be threatened by my presence. This meeting, yes, we get away with it because I'm known to be an ex business colleague of yours, but beyond that, no. There can be no connection. You are the future and nothing can jeopardise that."

He looked at me for what seemed like an age. We respected each other well enough to allow a difference of opinion.

"That's your final stance?", he asked me.

"Yes," I told him, "It has to be. Thanks anyway."

"Just to fill you in on the rest then," he said as he rose to leave, "as you can imagine, the various people involved considered Gordon's actions a breach of the highest level of protocol. He died last night. Suspected heart attack. Seems he was influential in getting the new Chief Constable in place. We're onto that one and will act if necessary. I'm only sorry it's too little, and too late."

We shook hands and he wished me luck. Then we parted. To some it might have seemed like a cold and heartless way of saying goodbye, but we both knew that if we let it linger we'd fall apart. I might shed some tears later but I knew that I would not be alone.

And that was how 2028 started for me. Not what I had been expecting. Not the new future that I was looking forward to. But there it was, and here I was, and the rest was uncertain, to say the least.

"There are a lot of anomalies here.", the interviewing officer told me as we settled in for the first of many sessions, "More than I'm happy with, but please, don't be under any preconceptions about where I'm coming from. I realise there are things here that might be perceived as political. I'm not interested in all that. I'm a copper, plain and simple. You came along without any hassle and we appreciate that. If we can keep this simple, that would be a great help. Agreed."

"Fine with me.", I told him, "and I'll try to cooperate as much as I can. So, where do you want to begin?"

"Let's start with who you are.", he wrote notes even though the interviews were recorded, "Can you tell me you name and address."

"Steve Barratt.", I replied, "narrowboat Kingfisher, various locations.".

"Okay.", the officer sighed as he wrote that down, "so, Steve Barratt. Definitely?"

I smiled and nodded.

"My name is Roman.", he told me, "Detective Inspector Stuart Roman. Always had the name, but the titles have changed over time. Have you always been Steve Barratt?"

"I am Steve Barratt.", I told him.

"Now, here's the problem that I have.", he said, "in that you are Steve Barratt, of that I have no doubt. You check out better than most and there are some very highly placed people who vouch for you. But your fingerprints match a Mr Zipoly Hardacre."

"Deceased.", I said, "Whereas I am very much alive. And the DNA?"

"Express results have come through.", he said, "no match to Zipoly Hardacre. They're doing a more detailed match but seem adamant it won't change. Who are you?"

It carried on like that for pretty much all of our first session. The issue was that they had a set of matching fingerprints but nothing else on me. No two sets of fingerprints had ever been found to be the same. It just didn't happen. And yet, in this case, it seemed to have happened. I liked Roman. He seemed straightforward enough and I didn't envy him his job. But he wasn't making it easy for himself.

"What are the charges?", I asked as we sat down to begin the second interview.

"None as yet.", he said as he fiddled with the recording equipment, "You're still being held on suspicion but no charges yet, however, I'm glad you mentioned that."

"Before you,", he began as he started the official process, "you have a list of three hundred and twenty-seven offences linked to the person of the Righteous Corrector, a title that he, or she, bestows on themselves. Can you please tell me anything about that list?"

"Yes,", I replied, looking straight at him, "it is a list of three hundred and twenty-seven offences linked to the person of the Righteous Corrector, a title that he, or she, bestows on themselves."

I smiled as Roman sighed.

"Sir,", I continued, "I quite like you and I think that you are as straight as you come across. I'm sure that you are very good at your job and that you have done this many times before, but you're making it too complicated. Ask me the right questions. I won't lie to you. I may not answer, but I promise you, I won't lie to you."

"Okay,", he started again, returning the list to the folder that lay in front of him, "are you Zipoly Hardacre?"

"My name is Steve Barratt.", I replied.

"Not Zipoly Hardacre?"

"My name is Steve Barratt.".

There was a pause and I looked at him, urging him to carry on.

"Have you ever been known by the name of Zipoly Hardacre?", he asked.

"Better.", I replied, "And in answer to your question, yes, I used to be known by the name of Zipoly Hardacre."

"The Righteous Corrector?", he asked.

"I was Zipoly Hardacre,", I replied, "then became Steve Barratt. To help you with the questions that I know you still have, my DNA was adjusted to read differently and my appearance was changed to what you see now. I have never been known as the Righteous Corrector."

"No?", he seemed to plead now.

"How can I have been.", I said, "Nobody knows who the Righteous Corrector is. Ergo, neither you nor I nor anybody else could be known as the Righteous Corrector."

I paused and waited until he was about to change tack.

"Try the list again.", I whispered as I leaned across to him, "see where that gets you."

And so, with a little bit of encouragement, he recorded my confessing to the first of the crimes on the list. I was never going to avoid justice. How would that fit with who I was. But I wanted to sound out Roman and make sure that he kept us both as safe as possible through this process. There were people out there, both for us and against us, who would jump at the first opportunity to direct our lives along paths that we didn't want to take.

He let me take the list back to my cell and when we met for the third session I handed it back to him with a small dot next to sixty-two of the incidents. I was amazed just how many faux actions had been taken under the RC banner. Before I did that, I asked him to keep the recorder off and I told him a little about the life I had been leading. With some of the facts explained very explicitly and with his own suspicions about the powers that were surrounding this case, it was easy enough to make him understand that this was my gift to him, and not for public consumption. He could have Zipoly Hardacre, the Righteous Corrector, but in return, the identity of Kingfisher remained a secret. Fair play to him. Unlike the late General Gordon, he was a man of his word who, even to this day, has never breathed a word of what I told him.

Chapter Fifty-Six

The court case was scheduled for March. Prior to that I was held in a remand centre, in solitary confinement but with enough in the cell to keep me from going insane. Charlotte and I had often had the discussions, as she bandied notions of criminal justice around and I tried to recall the little I had studied all those years ago. Prison was the punishment. Prison wasn't for punishment. Now I understood better than ever. I thought I'd be able to cope. This was one of the two outcomes that were inevitable. Either I would die in service, or would be held like this. Of the two, this was probably the better option, although the first few weeks were hard.

For the past however many years, I had been free to roam the waterways and enjoy the space surrounding them. I was free to go to the pub when I wanted, take the dogs out where I chose and to fill up my days with a rack of activity, or let them pass by with nothing done. Now, I was in a space no bigger than my boat's lounge, which wasn't so bad, except that I couldn't leave that space. The four walls were an impenetrable barrier that bound my freedom. That was the hardest part of it.

I did all I could do keep my mind active and to learn to live with the confinement. I read and listened to the radio. I watched television, and took my time cleaning out vape sticks and rationing their use. They gave me a lot more than other prisoners in similar circumstances. It was their way of compensating for keeping me isolated prior to my trial. They were worried about the reception I might receive if forced to share a cell. Some of those in the same building might well have been affected in some way by my actions or by those of J for Justice. Others might hold me up as some sort of hero and be inspired to revolt. So, as with all things, swings and roundabouts. Solitude and isolation, but distractions as well.

Within a month, I felt myself going native. It had happened more quickly than I'd anticipated and despite my every endeavour to remain a free-spirited individual. It was just so much easier to sink into the routine and become nothing more than a caged pet. Not that it was all plain sailing.

Oh, no. There were days when I felt the walls closing in on me and I scraped and clawed at them until my fingers were red raw. I'd had nightmares like this before, but they had been just that, nightmares from which I awoke. Here, alone and unable to act for myself, the nightmare was a reality. They helped me through these times as well. They gave me the drugs that I'd always rejected. The drugs that I'd refused as I suffered the pain of bereavement despite how agonising that pain was. Then though, I'd had my reasons. I'd wanted to feel the pain and let it destroy me. Here, it was different. The drugs provided a form of time-travel. When I took them, I switched off, waking up a day closer to the trial. Not that that promised any relief. I already knew the outcome.

King continued to work on the case, despite my asking him not to. He procured the details of the deeds that I'd confessed to and had a team of lawyers and barristers anaesthetising the acts with legal argument. He didn't tell me any of this on the occasions that he visited me. When he came, we just talked about generalities. He did most of the talking because he had a lot more to tell me than I had to tell him. The marina was doing well and he was settled now along the Lichfield Canal and doing all he could to make it a destination that represented the future of canals. I smiled as he told me that he had been able to ban the old work-boats that plagued the other canals. Neither of us liked them. Yes, the history was great, but history could be seen in a museum. The canals were crowded enough without these cumbersome boy's toys demanding special privileges.

"It took a bit of craftiness on our part," he told me, "and we had to lower the draft in a few selected spots and narrow the passing points, but we got there."

Other than that, Adam and Charlotte were working harder than ever and supporting Zara and Dana as they grew into their roles. Marriage seemed to be good for them and the baby was due any day soon. James was James. He was lost for most of the time inside the invisible world of the sub-atomic, although, when he did surface, he and Dana spent a lot of time together.

"Are you running a justice programme or a marriage bureau?", I asked him.

"You wouldn't believe it would you?", he replied, "First Adam, now James. You remember what they were like not so long ago. And Phil Rivers, some of his apprentices and the others we've encouraged. If it helps to think of the good we've done, then do it. It wasn't all about the missions and the violence."

I asked that King be the only visitor that I received. They would have let me meet many more of my friends and acquaintances but one was enough. I didn't want the obligation to fall on others. Nor did I want to burden others with my situation. Jason was different. He bought me a taste of the outside world that helped me forget my lack of freedom for a while.

Towards the end of this period of my confinement, they moved me to a single cell that was within the main wing of the prison. That room had a window and that window meant a lot to me. The view was nothing more than average, revealing as it did, no more than a few trees poking up out of an isolated landscape, but the breeze came through the slight opening that they allowed in that window, and that was like a breath of life to me. This move meant that I also heard the clamour and cries of human voices for the first time in a long time. The shouts and laughter of the other prisoners, the words of encouragement and the threats of punishment from the warders, and, more importantly to me, the songs of the protestors camped outside the prison. Nobody had told me that they were there. Apparently, they'd been demonstrating since the place of my imprisonment had been made public.

I'd not been aware. The personal vow that I'd made when I'd allowed myself to use television and radio was that I would switch off or switch over whenever the news was on. It was too present for me. It was too much a reminder of the world that was rolling along outside those walls and in which I was no longer allowed to play. Jason King had kept it quiet as well. He'd even tried to stop them and explain that it wasn't something that I would have wanted. They didn't listen and remained in place, their numbers swelling at the weekend but a presence always there. For once, Jason had been wrong. They lifted me with their shouts and I was only sorry that I would disappoint them in the end.

"Justice for the just!", they shouted, "Free Steve Barratt! Release the Righteous Corrector!"

I wondered how many of them would remain if they truly understood the depths that I'd stooped to. How many would stand by me as I revealed the weaknesses in me that had made my delivery of justice questionable? And, for all that I enjoyed the attention and the support, I couldn't be on their side. For justice to be upheld then I had to face justice head on.

That was why my opening words to the court both surprised and upset the spectators crammed into the room. The Judge asked me to state my name.

378

"Zipoly Hardacre.", I said without hesitation.

That was followed by a tortuous and protracted debate about the legality of trying a 'legally dead' man, which, in turn, was followed by a long and tedious period of listing the crimes I was being tried for and that took several hours, not helped by regular interruptions from the public benches. When he'd finished the Judge asked me that all important question:

"Do you plead guilty, or not guilty?"

I had to wait to speak as the officers of the court removed some of the protestors and called for silence from the ranks of people crying out, 'Not guilty!'. I appreciated their understanding and optimism, but had no choice about my response.

"Guilty.", I replied.

As soon as I had said the words, a barrister rose and asked the judge for a dismissal of the case. I hadn't expected that. Nor had I expected the reason for his request.

"As you will be aware,", the barrister began after gaining the judge's permission, "this prosecution process was begun on the instructions of the Chief Constable of West Midlands Police, a certain Mister Victor Donovan. Since the time of my client's arrest, certain facts have come to light about Mr Donovan that I believe we are all aware of and which have forced him to not only resign his position but also to be confined to prison awaiting trial. Can we proceed with a case that is known to have been pursued under the instructions of a highly ranked, but now deceased U.S. Army General, who is alleged to have paid large sums of money to Mr Donovan in order that that action be taken?"

The judge considered the argument for a short while and seemed inclined to meet with the two sides to discuss it further. He looked across at me.

"Mr Hardacre,", he asked, "you have heard what my colleague has said, and you understand his point?"

"I do.", I replied.

"And do you,", he continued, "feel that this trial is unfair or that we should pursue his points further. In short, are you happy to continue with this trial as it is?"

The barrister looked urgently at me and I could see him begging me to support him. I was only partially aware of the justice meted out to Donovan and of the connections that had been discovered between him and Gordon.

They might have a point. This could be my get out of jail free card. But I wasn't going to play it.

"Your Honour," I replied, "I am happy to continue. Let the games begin!"

The judge thanked me although I could tell by his tone that I might have gone a bit too far with my reply. Given the rest of what he was to see though, my words were nothing. It was all so bizarre. I had a legal team defending me when I didn't want defending and a crowd of people behind me who I had just let down badly. I let it play out as is was going to, knowing that even the most clear-cut and simplest case can be tied in knots and bound in chains by the legal profession. This wouldn't be a Jarndyce and Jarndyce, but it could well end up going on for a lot longer than it needed to.

King looked over apologetically at me and shrugged his shoulders. I smiled to let him know that I didn't mind. I'd been through a lot with him and I owed him the courtesy of allowing him to take his own path. There was also a part of me that looked forward to hearing the approach his team would take. It would be like watching a lengthy play, carefully crafted and with twists and turns in the plotline all the way. And it was certainly better than sitting and staring at four walls all day.

Despite my confession, the defence's argument centred around my actions being in self-defence. At first, that was a bizarre notion and I almost thought I should have let them go for the insanity option that I'd been offered. As the case progressed however, I could see where they were coming from. The prosecution case dragged on as they worked their way through the thirty or so charges that had been selected from my original confession. There was more than enough there for them to start with and they were the more serious offences. Several of them involved my murdering others. Several were of mutilation. Others were simpler grievous bodily harm, false imprisonment, theft, unlawful entry and the like. Although I drifted away for a lot of the time, I did enjoy seeing the newly-promoted Roman giving his evidence. He would benefit from my openness and from Donovan's demise. And why not? I'd also asked King to do what he could to help smooth the guy's career. He was no saint, I'm sure, but I really had seen something in him. Honesty perhaps? Or maybe that much rarer combination of honesty mixed with humility?

Facts and dates and photographs and all manner of other evidence were shown to the jury. This trial was, seemingly, going to be made a tad more arduous for them, but in return, they had the privilege of an experience they could dine out on for life. This was a case that was still talked about and would be for a long time.

My unrequested team's opening gambit laid out the path that they would take for the whole case. They selected the crime that had first set me in the road to where I was now and detailed their take on it. I wiped away tears as they talked about how Slater had been responsible for killing my family through his reckless driving and how he had escaped any meaningful penalty.

"Your Honour," my barrister explained, "Mr Hardacre endured suffering beyond anything that we can understand. He watched his family die and cradled his daughter's lifeless body."

He paused and looked directly at the jury.

"But," he continued, "he accepted the court's verdict in the case and made no retaliation. It was only later when a journalist advised him that Slater had possibly caused the death of another elderly couple, that he felt compelled to act. He chose not to take a life for a life. No, instead he chose to disarm a loose cannon that could go off again and again and cause even more deaths."

He paused again, keeping his focus fully on the twelve jurors.

"Which is why," he resumed in a softer voice, "we contend that far from being the evil criminal the prosecution would paint Mr Hardacre as, he is, in fact, a hero. A hero who acted to defend himself as a road user and, simultaneously, every citizen of this nation against the threat that Slater posed. In removing the victim's eyes, he left Slater with the life he had denied others, and yet, he protected us all by preventing Slater ever driving again. In defending the nation, it therefore stands to reason that he was defending himself. Self-defence, your honour, self-defence."

As he sat down, the public gallery erupted in cheers and the sound of applause filled the room. That was all that the judge could take and he ordered the public to be removed for the rest of the trial. They missed quite a bit more, but truthfully, it was all in the same vein. For every charge that had been raised, the defence argued eloquently and confidently that my acts were ones of self-protection. There was a slight variation in some instances. If the physical defence of self didn't quite cut the mustard, they took a more oblique approach. They argued that justice is a force for protection for all and that by defending and protecting justice, I was in turn defending the nation and myself. That explained to me why they were the best in the field, and for a time, they almost had me convinced.

After two solid days of my defence team's case, I held up my hand to seek the judge's attention. He looked at me and then at the barrister who nodded his willingness to yield.

"Your Honour," I stood and spoke slowly but clearly, "and members of the jury, please forgive me for interrupting proceedings. I don't know how this court thing really works, but I felt that I had to speak out."

I took a long drink of water.

"The arguments that you are hearing," I continued, "are very interesting. For that reason, I have let the defence team continue so far. However, I feel that I must now call a halt to proceedings. I have entered a plea of guilty. I chose not to make a defence, but a very good friend of mine intervened and I have respected his concern by allowing the team to get this far. Sadly, I must now dismiss that team and simply repeat my initial plea. I am guilty. We must let justice be done."

There were murmurs around the room and the judge had no choice but to adjourn the sitting for the day, instructing everyone to return tomorrow. The rest of the day was spent with numerous people who concluded that I remained sane and that I had the right to make the choice I'd made. It was all a bit tiring, but the outcome was the one I wanted. The following day, I was alone in court, the defence benches being empty.

Chapter Fifty-Seven

Once I was free of a legal team, the case was bought to a fairly swift conclusion. I regretted allowing them to try and argue for me, but I owed it to Jason. He wanted to see me walk free. No one at the marina, within ORB or amongst the protestors and demonstrators could quite understand my decision. They thought that I had slipped back into self-destruct mode, but that had been Steve Barratt, not Zipoly Hardacre. To me, it was simple. I could not seek to extoll the virtues of the criminal justice system if I expected to be exempt from its scope. I didn't want to go to prison. I would have loved to have let them carry on with their arguments and get me off on a technicality, but that would have been against my principles.

It would all have been over a lot more quickly but for two things. Firstly, there were numerous attempts by various interested parties to call for a mistrial on the grounds of my suffering mental health issues. The facts spoke for themselves. I was somebody who had endured an amount of suffering beyond the sanity of man to survive, and yet, every time they tested me, I kept my cool and they could find no sympathetic psychologist prepared to section me.

The second thing was the hardest for me. Jason King asked to appear as a character witness even after the defence team had been disbanded. I tried to prevent it happening but the judge allowed him to speak. It threatened the whole case for me.

"Ladies and gentlemen of the jury," King began, "it is my honour to address you today to speak in defence of my friend Zipoly Hardacre. After much soul-searching, I have chosen to appear before you today to tell you about the life that Mr Hardacre has lived since his supposed death."

I couldn't believe what was happening. King told them about his secret life in the service of an underground organisation and of the activities of ORB and the field operatives that worked for them. He introduced them to the clandestine world that I had inhabited, along with all its dangers. He detailed the injuries I'd suffered, the pain I'd endured and mental challenges that had been a day to day part of that life. The judge didn't allow me to stop him. I tried several times but was silenced as soon as I tried to speak. I had to listen to the whole of King's speech and was powerless to stop him.

"You see," he concluded, "the man before you, is more than Zipoly Hardacre. He is also Steve Barratt, Kingfisher. That man is a hero. He has risked his life on numerous occasions, performed duties that would break most of us, and, he has saved millions of lives. Yes, Steve Barratt was active in London on the day of The Event. He alerted another operative to the location of one bomb which was safely destroyed, and he disarmed another on his own. In doing so, he received serious injuries, the scars of which still cover his body today. I ask you to take these things into consideration when you reach your verdict. Steve Barratt holds the highest commendation that this nation can bestow on any public servant, but he would never tell you that. He is not somebody who deserves to be locked away for the rest of his life."

There was a stunned silence as he resumed his seat. The judge frantically scribbled notes on his pad, then looked across at me.

"Mr Hardacre," he asked, "would you like to respond?"

I couldn't believe that King would do that for me. He had laid open not only himself but all of the team to save me. It was too high a price to pay. I was only one man and I wasn't prepared to save my own life at the expense of stopping Adam and James and Charlotte and all of those who needed to be kept anonymous in their work.

"Your Honour," I said, "ladies and gentlemen of the jury, Steve Barratt certainly sounds like some sort of superhero. Mr King speaks eloquently about him and the list of his achievements is certainly a source of inspiration. However, this trial is not about Steve Barratt. It is about me, Zipoly Hardacre. And I am guilty."

And that was that. The judge ordered the testimony of King to be struck from the record and imposed a serious penalty on anybody who made reference to what had been said at any time in the future. Once that had been made clear, and I knew that King and all the other operatives were safe, he asked the jury to retire to consider their verdict. Somehow, it took them two full days, but I really had given them no choice in the matter.

They found me guilty.

Epilogue

And so, I write these words now, sitting in a small but comfortable cell that will be my home until I die. The sentence was fair, given the number of crimes I'd committed, but the number of years doesn't really mean anything since it is more than the span of life I could ever hope to achieve.

I could tell you that I'm languishing in a darkened cell and rotting away in self-pity, but that wouldn't quite be true. The authorities are sympathetic to me. I live in a low-security prison, with multiple privileges and could ask for nothing more. I long ago chose to forsake the comforts of modern living and all the trappings of wealth, which means that I now have at least as much as I had before, if not more. All I lack, in theory, is my freedom.

In theory, at least. The truth of it is, I feel that now, I have found a freedom beyond any that I've ever experienced. I am free to be me. I am free to think my own thoughts, to read, to write, to sing, to dance. And I am free of the doubts.

I have so much music around me as well. The whole world of symphonies and popular songs comes flying in to me in a stream of data and there's more there than I'll ever have time to listen to. I never learned to play an instrument. Maybe now will be the time? Meanwhile, I'll continue to let the professionals move my soul with every note.

I think that Jason has forgiven me. He tells me he has and I can only hope that he really means that from the bottom of his heart. He came to visit earlier today. We looked at the photos of Adam and Charlotte's baby, and he told me the date of James and Dana's wedding. I asked him to apologise that I wouldn't be able to attend.

"Bit tied up elsewhere.", I told him.

Adam and Charlotte had adopted Fred and Gilly. At first, Adam had suggested that having a baby and two dogs might be too much, therefore it would make sense to switch Gilly off. The suggestion was badly received by Charlotte, although she could understand the logic. Either way, it didn't matter in the end. The decision was Fred's. No sooner had he been parted from his best friend, he'd started to whimper and give that downcast look that I remember so well. The absence lasted less than twenty-four hours. They were reunited and live happily together now, Gilly as much a part of the family as anyone.

It's nice for me to be able to use my talents a little. They let me work in the carpentry shop and I've been passing on my skills to a younger generation. I'm allowed a free rein in what we make, although the obviously illegal or dangerous are barred. As are the small RC discs that all my trainees want to have a go at. It's become something of an icon now. I see pictures of the celebrities who wear them as a fashion statement, and I see young and old sporting them as a lapel badge. There's a certain amount of solidarity that comes from justice. Though I don't want to be held up as a hero, I'm certainly not intending to stop the production of these items on copyright grounds.

So, this is the future that was waiting for me. Had I been pre-warned, I might have tried every trick under the sun to avoid it, but now that I'm in it, I feel quite alright. The world will continue to roll on outside the steel gates that bind me, and forces for justice, both those that are public knowledge and the various clandestine ones, will continue to do their best to make the world a more just place. We'll never get it right. After all, we're only human. But that doesn't mean we shouldn't try. I'd like to help out if I could. It's just that I'm not allowed to play anymore. You can't begin to understand how free that makes me feel.